Running Wild Novella Anthology

Volume 1

Editors Jade Blackwater and
Lisa Diane Kastner

Text copyright © 2017 Running Wild Press

Cover image copyright © 2017

Creative Director, Dan Fernandez.

Published in North America and Europe by Running Wild Press. Visit Running Wild Press at www.runningwildpress.com Educators, librarians, book clubs (as well as the eternally curious), go to www.runningwildpress.com for teaching tools.

ISBN 978-1-947041-03-5 (pbk)
ISBN 978-1-947041-02-8 (ebook)

Library of Congress Control Number 2017954459
Printed in the United States of America.

Contents

Let Me Go

By Sara Marchant

She rode the bus. She carried no luggage and got off long before the bus stop at the town square. She disembarked near the state mental hospital; the reason for the little town's continued existence. It was summer, full blown. She wore a long denim skirt and blue plaid blouse snapped closed over a demure petticoat. On her feet were battered western boots, the leather soft with age. She had a shapeless denim bag over one shoulder and a large silver bangle on her left wrist. The turquoise in the middle was discomfortingly large and real.

She looked tired and dusty, like people get after stepping onto a bus, let alone those traveling the width of two quite large states. It was difficult to tell her age until she reached up and pushed the dirty black hair from her forehead and rubbed her dark eyes in a sleepy little girl gesture. Then one was able to see that she was young.

She cut across the highway and skirted the edge of the rolling green lawns that began the territory of what the local kids called the loonies. Around the west side, about half a mile in, there used to be a hole snipped in the bottom of the chain link. There wasn't a hole now, but times were tough and she could see where it was neatly repaired with wire.

With the hole re-opened, she slipped through and spied in window after window. When the mid-day heat beat down she relented and made her way back to the fence, through the hole to the highway. She did not hitch a ride. She retreated into the ditch when cars passed. She was not hiding, just avoiding detection.

On the outskirts of town she cut through alleys and down dirt roads, constantly heading east until the lanes were paved and wide enough for two cars. She cut north and walked until she hit her target. This town was built around a central square set with a garden gazebo. The city hall stood ornately at one end with the fire station facing it across the ridiculously green grass. On opposite sides were the downtown stores: the pharmacy, a bookstore, a grocery, the fabric emporium and a diner that refused to believe the 1950's ever ended. Where the movie theater still proclaimed Ava Gardner and Richard Burto...an art gallery existed and it was this building's alley from which she emerged. With stealth she skirted the sidewalk shadows and peered around the corner. She froze in place as a beige-uniformed man wearing a Sheriff's badge moved from the doorway.

"You'll let me know, now." He spoke to someone inside.

He strode to a waiting Bronco, jumped in, and drove a full circuit of the square before parking it in a reserved space in front of city hall. Not until he had entered the thick doors did she move from concealment. She did not go into the art gallery, but turned right, crossing the street to walk in the small green gloaming skirting the gazebo, and into the fabric store.

A grandmother with two children and blue hair struggled to tip bolts of fabric onto the measuring table and a middle-aged woman with a wig of improbable red curls assisted her. They looked up as the girl passed them to the empty cutting table. The children, too young to be in school, followed her as natural as the tide with the moon. She had picked up a tape measure and marked an area above her knees on her denim skirt before one of the women found her voice.

"Why, Sylvie Sullivan," the auburn wigged woman, Mrs. Henley, said. "You haven't changed a bit!"

Sylvie smiled and unbuttoned her skirt to remove it. She laid it across the cutting table. With the tape measure in place she looked around for scissors. The small girl grabbed a pair of pinking shears and handed them to Sylvie right as the other child, from his seated position on the floor, informed the room at large, "She hasn't any pants on."

Sylvie leveled the shears at him. "Mind your own beeswax, buster. I've got a slip covering what's important."

The kids giggled and the blue-haired lady scowled as Mrs. Henley stared at the telephone. She was debating whether the joy of gossiping was worth interacting with the Sheriff. Sylvie stopped cutting the denim to look up and give the saleslady the big eyes. Mrs. Henley relaxed, and with as much interest as the little ones waited to see what Sylvie would do next. Sylvie finished hacking off the skirt before putting on the remainder. She handed the shears back to the little girl, patting her on the head before ducking out the door. Her head popped back in and she asked, "Please Mrs. Henley, just give me a head start. Five minutes." Then she was gone again.

The two ladies began a furiously whispered conversation over the merits of discretion versus human decency, which ended with Blue saying, "That poor man." Auburn answered in turn, "Poor man, my eye."

Nevertheless, Mrs. Henley made the call; the joy of telling the Sheriff that Sylvie Sullivan was back outweighed her reluctance to talk to him. It was more like a seven minute head start than five, but it still wasn't enough time for Sylvie to avoid hearing the Bronco's tires squealing around the town green.

The gloaming deepen and Sylvie's stomach growled. She crept around the back alleys outlying the town center until she reached the Village Diner's back door. A chair propped it open and a thin, but exceptionally pretty black youth looked up from the dishes he washed. He grinned at the sight of her.

"I thought things seemed more exciting all ready." They slapped palms and then knuckles wetly.

"I need to stay until dark," she said and he nodded. "Where is he?"

By the gentle tone of her voice he knew she didn't mean the angry Sheriff. "At his day job helping the new vet. Drives the guy around 'cause he's a dwarf. Can't reach the pedals and the wheel together, isn't that something?"

He chuckled at her and continued. "By the time it's safe for you to leave and get home, he'll be at his night job. You know about that one?"

She nodded, face averted, one hand at her rumbling belly.

"Here." He gestured her to the sink. "You take over and I'll get you a plate."

Sylvie took up the dish washing and he moved into the kitchen. When he returned, many more buckets of dishes had been pushed through the hatch and she was in the process of sorting, scraping, and washing. Her technique had improved with the years.

"I've been similarly employed." She admitted with a funny little bow.

He brought plates for both of them and they ate burgers and French Fries and coleslaw, he with the hunger of the naturally thin, and she like someone who hadn't seen a meal in a while. Afterward she looked a bit green.

"What's been going on, Maxie?" She asked.

"Not a damn thing, girl, since you left."

"Aside from the dwarf vet, of course."

"Yeah, aside from him. Cute little guy, every time I see him I picture a pointy red hat." Sylvie smiled. Max smiled back.

"Then 'bout five days ago, today's Friday, so it was Monday, right? Yeah, suddenly that crazy man started acting like the old days, when we was kids." Max raised his sketchy eyebrows and she nodded in acknowledgment. "I guess I should mention that while you were gone he was pretty normal. Well, normal for a white man, that is."

"Then Monday the Bronco starts tearing around the square again, he's over at your Auntie's shop every day- and it's not like those two have ever been friendly- and he's handing out tickets for jaywalking. Jaywalking! This town ain't even got crosswalks, how're we supposed to jaywalk?" He waited for a response but Sylvie laughed too hard to

5

answer. He handed her a clean dishtowel to wipe her eyes before continuing.

"Plus, he's eating practically every meal in here, eying me if I put in an appearance and being Mr. Nosy again. That man hasn't remembered my existence in four years, which my mama is thankful for, but since Monday, seems we're good friends. What's new with me, my family, my friends? I got any mail lately, postcards? Still spend time with them hooligans from school?"

"No, I do not." He said softly, and she nodded in understanding. "And girl, you can imagine what he is making your brother's life like right now."

"He is not my brother," she whispered and the anger was back in her tone.

"What he is, is set upon." Max leaned back, his tale finished. "Are you staying at your Auntie's?"

Startled, she looked him in the eye. "Where else?"

"Just asking. You've never been close."

"But as long as he is here, there, I mean…"

"Oh yes, you know that mama's boy."

"Mama's boy, yourself." She literally pointed and got to her feet.

"Maybe I'll see you both tomorrow?" Max asked, hands once more sudsy.

Sylvie smiled. Nothing here changed. "I'm positive we can work something out." She melted into the dark of the alley.

On the other side of town, not toward the west, behind the City Hall where the modest mansions sat, but east, toward the looney bin, but not yet that far, were humble family homes. These houses contained three bedrooms, one small and two smaller, a living room, an eat-in kitchen and a glassed in back porch where the washing machine sat. Every town in the United States has neighborhoods like these. One little bungalow a bit better maintained than the others, located in the middle of the block, was where Sylvie let herself in.

She'd come the back way of course, across the railroad tracks. Never in her memory had trains ever used those tracks. No one alive could remember a train coming through town, but on really still nights of her childhood Sylvie heard whistles- loud and lonesome, from a great distance. Sylvie slid through the loose section in the low chain link fence. The glassed-in porch door was held closed with a latch that popped open if you jimmied it right.

The dark house smelled like the swamp cooler. She walked from room to room, avoiding the closed door of his bedroom, until she reached the kitchen. From years of ingrained behavior she opened the fridge door, and in its light glimpsed the feet under the table. Sharply indrawn breath made a hiss as she slammed the door closed. The feet crossed at the ankles. They were bare.

"We were expecting you earlier." Annie's creepy habit of waiting in the dark to catch those breaking curfew hadn't abated.

Sylvie flicked on the light to regard her coolly. "Hello, Annie. Miss me?"

The other woman had not flinched at the light. She hadn't in the past either, Sylvie reflected.

"Unless you want certain company, dearie, I'd turn that light off." Annie's hair had gone gray. It was actually gray in color, not white. The color of the wicked step-mother's hair in Cinderella, gray. Sylvie turned the light off.

"Your hair," she started but stopped, unsure of Annie's reaction.

"I got tired of coloring it." Annie sounded surprised at the subject.

"The color is so apropos, Stepmother." Sylvie opened the fridge again and removed a can of soda. The pull top was loud in the quiet house.

"You're making a Cinderella joke, aren't you?" Annie asked. "I thought maybe you'd have changed. Four years is a long time when you're a teenager, but obviously no such luck. Nicky already made the wicked stepmother line. You two still think with one mind."

Annie sounded so incredibly tired and fed up, Sylvie felt at home and ashamed of herself; which amounted to the same thing. She slumped against the counter and waited for more, sipping the overly sweet drink.

"You stink, Sylvie" Annie almost sounded kind. "And you've cut your hair. It makes you look like your mother."

Sylvie stopped sipping. No one ever mentioned Polly. That was the biggest no-no in the Sullivan family. You could: come in late, truant, drunk, high, dressed inappropriately, escorted by the Sheriff, pee your pants, or set fire to the backyard 'accidentally;' but no punishment ever matched what was meted out when Sylvie mentioned her real mother. When the weather was humid Sylvie's ear ached on the side that had hit the coffee table when she flew backward from the force of the blow she'd received from daddy. In his defense, he'd looked as shocked as everyone else.

"Maybe you should have a shower and go to bed. You must be tired, walking all over hell and back today." Annie paused. "I know you've eaten, I can smell the diner on you."

Without another word, Annie removed herself from the room and presently Sylvie heard her bedroom door close.

"Damn Indian," Sylvie muttered, but very quietly.

In the dark just before the dawn, the house shifted as the front door opened and a large man entered. He was not fat, he was tall, broad-shouldered and so big one expected to hear a thump with each footfall, but didn't. He slid through the dark as quietly as his mother had earlier.

He made his way to his bedroom, but didn't turn on the light. He saw Sylvie's open eyes as she sprawled out in his bed. He waited by the bureau for her to speak.

"Won't you ever stop growing?" She sounded impressed and sleepy.

"I have. I'm sure. You'll get used to it." Every time he opened his mouth, people listened for a rumble, gravel, boulders crashing. Instead they got black velvet. Sylvie wanted him to tell her a bedtime story.

"I've loved you all my life."

"And I you."

The words were rote. Max wouldn't have blinked to hear them, nor would any of their peers in town. Annie, down the hall, one bedroom between them and her, put in her earplugs and turned her face away from their wall.

In his bedroom the soft conversation went on. There were letters spread across his bed, crinkling as the two moved and he began straightening the mess she had made. Sylvie didn't move, but let him work around her supine form.

"My room is full of boxes. I can't see the bed."

"She gave it away. You never slept in it anyway."

"My clothes are gone, too."

"I noticed."

"The clothes in the closet, baby. I've nothing to wear."

He stopped moving. "She sent them to you, the first year."

"I never got them."

"She doesn't lie about things like that," he said, moving one of her hips to release a letter imprisoned beneath.

"I didn't say she did. I meant they were never given to me. Those people made me dress like the Amish."

"With the bonnets?" He chuckled, while sorting the letters back into some order. She'd always believed he could see in the dark.

"Long skirts, long sleeves, hot and boring. Come to bed," she said.

He did. For the first time since Annie had sent her away to her daddy's family, Sylvie felt safe, she felt right. This was where she belonged, no matter what anyone said. Daddy had forbidden it, but daddy was dead. Annie hadn't approved, but she had gotten old and tired and had given up. The people in town could gossip all they liked, it was none of their concern, and she'd never given a damn. Even their friends, sweet Max excepted, had judged. Ronny Lanier had christened them the Incestuously Creepy duo the summer Sylvie turned fifteen, but Nick wrote that last year Ronny had been sent to Korea, so that shut him up.

Soon enough, they'd be out of this town. Nick was accepted to a college far north. North enough so it snowed and together they could live somewhere no one had known them since they'd been born and then made brother and sister through no will of their own.

Dawn came and Nick was asleep and Sylvie kept very still so as to not wake him. She must have dozed, for she heard voices from the kitchen and one of them she'd recognize even in her dreams. She left the bed and the mountain of sleeping man in it.

Her clothes were gone from the hamper- no, the whole hamper was gone. It was nice to be back with something like a mother, Sylvie reflected as she donned an undershirt of Nick's and a pair of clean underwear Annie had thoughtfully left folded on the bureau.

In the kitchen Annie shared space with the Bronco driving Sheriff. She sat at the table, drinking coffee and eating a grapefruit. He stood leaning against the counter much as Sylvie had the night before. He looked older, more lined, but sullen and overly heated, so some things hadn't changed. For the moment they didn't see her. Annie whistled through her teeth, a habit daddy always detested.

The Sheriff muttered angrily at Annie. She was supposed to have called him; they had an agreement, present a united front to the little delinquent. Sylvie shifted in annoyance and they both looked up.

Annie grimaced in relief and prepared to leave, still whistling.

"You have a guest." Annie spoke a little too loudly as she departed. When she turned her head Sylvie saw she wore her earplugs.

Sylvie faced the angry Sheriff. His eyes were bloodshot as he stared at her in the life-long peculiar manner. He straightened from his slouch and she skirted the other side of the table. That move looked preparatory to a pounce. Sylvie eyed his posture as he forced himself to relax, or pretend to, and then she nonchalantly sat down in Annie's vacated chair.

He took in her outfit and swallowed. "I'm here to put you on warning." She raised her feet to the other seat and crossed her bare ankles. Nick's undershirt was big, but it had ridden up.

"Warning you about your behavior…"

"Pour me a cup of that coffee, there, behind you, okay?" She pointed just left of his crotch and he stopped talking.

Amazingly, he did it. Jerking a cup from the mug tree, he slopped some liquid into it and set it down in front of her. She added cream and sugar before looking around for a spoon. Without thinking he handed her one from the cup of extras kept on the windowsill. Realizing what he had done, he flushed red with fury.

"What are you warning me about?" She stirred her coffee and listened to his teeth grinding.

"Your behavior," he said. "Do you know how calm it's been these four years? No drag racing on High Mack Road. No laundry disappearing from lines, reappearing on the village green arranged like crime scenes. No crop circles ruining fields, no graffiti. No shoplifting of the entire town's supply of condoms and subsequent water ballooning of my Bronco. The crime wave ended."

She stretched her arms above her head, before knotting her fingers together on top of her messy hair. Sylvie noted smugly where his eyes were drawn as he flushed again with anger.

"So you've missed me?" And she smiled a vicious smile.

He took a step forward, then a step back, sideways toward the door. Sylvie remembered the blue haired grandma saying: 'Poor man.'

"Back one day." He shook his finger at her. "One day and one night and those gravestones of your mama and grandma are pushed over again."

"I think those loonies make lousy gravediggers." Sylvie shrugged. "Why would I do that? And how?"

"Oh, you got some muscle at your beck and call, I don't doubt." He crossed his arms, satisfied at having her on the defensive.

It was Sylvie's turn to uncurl menacingly from her studied nonchalance to face him. She moved closer, step by step as she spoke. "Subsidence makes those gravestones fall. Everyone knows the cemetery is old landfill. And don't you ever try to implicate him."

By the time she finished issuing this threat her voice was hoarse and husky and soft. He knew from experience that when she got this close and this quiet she was at her most dangerous. There was a scar in the meat of his hand to prove it.

"You need to watch it, missy," he said as he backed to the front door. "You're of age now and you'll get more than a night in detention and a lecture from the judge."

She followed him out the door onto the scrap of porch, seemingly blind to the people going to work, the children waiting for the summer school bus across the street under the silk oak tree. The air smelled of cut grass and dew in these hours before the heat of the day had a chance to burn it away, and a breeze blew her thin T-shirt against her, revealing the underpants beneath. She raised one hand to his shoulder, somehow suggesting that she resisted his attempts to embrace her. A hurt frown of confusion was on her face as she leaned in, tilted her head back to convey that she pulled away from him.

"That's right. I am over eighteen now. All sorts of things are legal."

She was too close. He couldn't move without touching her and she leaned in as she finished speaking, before her words registered in his mind. She moved even closer while jerking her face to the left and he knew that to anyone watching it would look exactly like he'd attempted to kiss this under-dressed teen and she had repulsed his inappropriate advances. He leaped away as a burned man from the fire, and he didn't raise his flaming face until in his vehicle speeding off. But his headache throbbed all day.

Inside the house, Annie threw the laundry into the dryer and commented to the shuttered back windows: "That poor man."

"She couldn't twist him around if there wasn't something to twist." Nick responded from his door.

"Since I was fourteen, Annie," Sylvie said from under Nick's arm. "The old perv." And they closed the bedroom door behind them.

They emerged sooner than Annie expected, dressed to go out. Nicky wore the chinos and white polo he used as a uniform when driving the veterinarian. They were headed to the diner to meet the old gang for breakfast. Did she want to come?

If Annie was astounded at the invitation, the first of its kind, she didn't let them see it. With no trace of emotion, she declined, but pointed out it was after ten o'clock and breakfast long over. As they headed out the door, she called a reminder to Nicky not to be late for work and to Sylvie to 'don't get caught.'

Sylvie popped her head back in and blew a kiss, recognizing this as a sign of forgiveness on Annie's part. After the biting incident, when her parents realized Sylvie was incapable of behaving herself or that they were incapable of making her behave, instead of exhorting her to 'be good'; they'd merely asked that she be so good at being bad that she not get caught.

They walked to the diner, Sylvie disjointedly chatted the way people do when they haven't seen their loved one in years. Nick was mostly silent, listening, but ventured a comment about acquiring new clothes for her when she stopped briefly to adjust her overlarge oxford shirt.

"The only stores now with clothing is the hoity-toity shop you hate and the variety store." He admitted.

"I saw a pretty dress at the fabric store. One of those samples Mrs. Henley makes up to illustrate how even an idiot citizen of this town can sew." Sylvie kicked an empty can of chew into the gutter.

"Are those for sale?"

"Oh sweetie," she said. "Everything is for sale."

As they approached the town square Nick elbowed Sylvie gently to draw attention to the figure waiting on the corner. The young man casually tossed his head in the direction of the Sheriff's Bronco parked behind the building. They conscientiously crossed the street precisely where crosswalks would be if the town had crosswalks.

The young man entered into the diner and, in order not to brand him with their company, Sylvie pulled Nick further down the block into Mrs. Henley's store. She was delighted to see them both. She thought it a great compliment that Sylvie wished to purchase her ready-made items. In fact, it was about time to display new things and Sylvie was doing her a favor by prodding her into action. Sylvie ended up with the striped shirtwaist dress, two peasant blouses; one short-sleeved, one long, a tartan skirt that Nick thought awful, and an outfit from Halloween that turned Sylvie into a Communist Chinese peasant.

This costume she insisted upon wearing immediately. Her ragged western boots added the perfect "je ne sais quoi," declared Mrs. Henley in all sincerity. Nick paid her the ridiculously low sum and after impulsively hugging them both, she waved them out the door before running to the phone.

Mrs. Henley's family were enemies of the Sheriff's family going back so many generations that no one could remember the exact genesis of the mutual antipathy. Therefore, Mrs. Henley and her mother had always been big fans of Sylvie and her trouble-making ways— as long as that trouble was directed at the Sheriff. They hadn't enjoyed their laundry being stolen off the line any more than the mayor's wife had. Today Mrs. Henley's mother, Maud, had a few suggestions for future outfits for Sylvie

"Is that orange sateen still plentiful?" Maud wondered. "You could whip up a harem girl outfit from Butterick's A-rab collection. She can wear that to the July 4th celebration and that man's eyes will pop out of his head in front of the whole town."

At the diner, practically empty in the off hours, Max and the young man ate cheeseburgers with Nick and Communist Sylvie. Max had to keep a napkin in his non-burger-holding hand because every time he looked at Sylvie, with her hair tucked into her little Commie cap, he leaked tears of laughter.

"Whoo-boy, you have a God given talent for pissing people off," he declared. When she'd made her entrance; the town's mayor and pharmacist took one look and departed in a righteous capitalist fury.

"It's actually very comfortable." Sylvie tucked back the wide sleeves to grasp her burger. "I can see why three billion Chinese wear it."

The young man, Jamie Lanier, the younger brother of the Korean exiled Ronny, patted Max on the back when he choked on his giggles. "You'll have to get used to life with Sylvie again, man. Or you're gonna choke to death."

Max took him seriously and calmed down. "So what's the plan for tonight?"

Nick frowned around his bite of cherry pie. Sylvie stroked his thigh. "I don't have any."

The two other boys frowned. Sylvie innocently smiled and reached for the fries on Jamie's plate. He smacked her hand, but Nick slid his fry-laden plate to her elbow. "I have to work," Nick said. "And I'm sure Sylvie needs to catch up on her sleep."

Three pairs of eyes widened in surprise and then avoided meeting. Sylvie turned to Nick, or rather his shoulder. He obliged by dropping his gaze to meet hers. She tightened her lips and squeezed her eyes half-shut at him; it was the face of a flirting cat. It was her displeased face and historically, it had always worked.

"Please Sylvie," he said. "It's only one month and we'll be outta here. Just stay under the radar until we can escape."

Sylvie's eyes popped open, shocked her displeased face hadn't worked, and she returned to her burger. Everyone silently finished the meal and Max's mama plunked more pie on the table, prepared to glare at Sylvie if the opportunity presented itself. It didn't because Sylvie's attention was elsewhere.

Out the window, the Sheriff's Bronco pulled into a parking spot. He saw the quartet through the glass and pointedly ignored them. Striding into the diner, he took a seat at the counter, his back to them. They were the only customers left and Max's uncle behind the counter moved to take his order.

"Is that drive-in still open?" Sylvie asked Jamie around a mouthful of pie.

She had caught him gawking at her, studying what exactly made the Sheriff lose his mind. Everyone knew the Sheriff and Sylvie's mama had been childhood sweethearts. Back when they were just Buddy and Polly, they had been as inseparable as Sylvie and Nick, aside from the incestuously creepy aspects of course. But the Knapp family had always been touched and eventually Polly went to the looney bin and Buddy went to learn to be a sheriff and they only let Polly out because Sylvie's daddy took over the asylum and found

Polly awfully attractive. It was also not secret that Sylvie was a seven months child and that her birth caused Polly to get even crazier, and Polly's death to send the Sheriff off his rocker as well. None of these facts were secret but no one talked about them, either.

It was a purely Sylvie-inflicted phenomenon, the Sheriff's nuttiness, Jamie theorized. The Sheriff was normal while she was gone, but the town had been bor-ring.

"It's still there. It's like watching a film through plastic wrap though, and the sound isn't so good because most of the speakers don't work."

"No one goes to watch the movie, kid." Nick pointed out.

"You're going to the movies without me?" Nick said to Sylvie.

"Well, can I go to work with you?"

"No."

"Then I'll go to the movies with them." And she thrust her chin at the two grinners across the booth.

They were all very careful to ignore the man at the counter.

"Where are we really going?" Max asked as she climbed into Jamie's car that evening.

"The car, with you in it, is going to the movies. You're gonna drop me at the looney bin." She waited for one of them to make the requisite joke, but neither of them was that insensitive, so she went on. "I had an idea about breaking into the record room and seeing about my mama."

Jamie stopped the car in the middle of an admittedly deserted intersection to turn around and stare at her. "Are you nuts?" He said, all sensitivity forgotten.

Sylvie laughed. Max kept an eye out for traffic and nervously pulled at Jamie's arm. "Let's go, man. You know he's out there somewhere."

Jamie stepped on the gas, but didn't turn around. Max's anxiety increased and Sylvie stopped grinning. "Watch the road!" She pointed out the windshield at distant headlights. "I'm not crazy. I just want some answers and the grownups aren't talking."

Jamie finally relented and turned around. Max released the elbow he tugged and faced Sylvie. "What do we do? Just go to the drive-in while you're doing your 007 act?"

"You are my beard, my cover," Sylvie said. "Don't you remember the drill? Go to the movie, mingle, be seen and say I'm around somewhere. Come on, guys! I've been gone so long you've lost your nerve?"

Both boys glared briefly at, and then ignored, her until she pressed Jamie's shoulder silently asking him to stop. They were close enough to walk. She still wore the Communist outfit, but her boots had been replaced with cheap rubber flip-flops. She slipped into some bushes without a word and the car drove on.

The drive-in was pretty busy for a poorly maintained movie house, but then the citizens of the county had few entertainment options. The boys were successful in acting like it was any normal summer evening at the movies. They parked where the speaker didn't work, in fact only frayed cords remained of what had been the speaker; so they bought some popcorn and wandered until they found speakers that did work. When asked eagerly for the whereabouts of Sylvie, they gave indifferent shrugs and muttered, 'around somewhere,' indicating with vague gestures of head and hands the general vicinity.

They made it through the double feature with only sweaty palms and slight headaches from the murky picture on the big screen and joined the exodus from the lot. It wasn't until a quarter mile from the drop off point that they spotted the Bronco behind them, it's headlights off. Jamie began a string of profanity that only ended when they passed the area where Sylvie had waited. He braked.

"Don't stop! Keep going," Max tried to work the gas pedal by shoving on Jamie's knee. "We're leading him right to her."

Under the general anxiety of the moment both males felt a surge of excitement that had been missing. The Bronco's engine gunned into roaring life and pulled up behind them. The high beam headlights flashed on, illuminating not only their waggling heads in the car, but the two figures on the side of the road.

Sylvie and Nick didn't bother to end their embrace nor the kiss. Sylvie merely moved one hand from around Nick's neck and used it to block the light from their glued-together faces. Her legs were twined about his waist and he supported under her bottom with one hand, while his other snaked around her waist, up her back, to hold her head steady in his large, brown hand. The kiss seemed to last a year.

"Never fails to give me the willies," Max said conversationally.

"Hmm." Jamie honked the horn of his dad's old Buick 8 impatiently. In the background the Bronco's motor gunned again and then was quiet. The car door slamming finally broke up the love scene and the Sheriff reached them as Sylvie's feet hit dirt.

"Is there a problem, officer?" Sylvie asked.

"Shouldn't you be at work?" The Sheriff glared at Nick in his white orderly's uniform.

"I'm on a break," the bigger man said. He checked his wristwatch. "Just about over. There's your ride, honey."

He pushed Sylvie gently toward the waiting Buick and prepared to turn.

"Someday ..." The Sheriff was too angry to continue. Nick smiled kindly and nodded in agreement, still pushing Sylvie toward the car.

"Maybe the Sheriff would like to drive me home?" Sylvie said and everyone faced her as if she were Satan himself.

The Sheriff stomped back to the Bronco and it roared off. When the dust of his departure had cleared, Nick was gone and Sylvie sat in the backseat. "Home James," she intoned and he was quick to oblige. He would be glad to be rid of her.

When Nick came in at dawn, he threw a thick folder on the bed next to her. A photograph of a young woman, a much frailer version of Sylvie, spilled out. "You could have just asked," he said.

It was hot. It was the hottest part of the afternoon that made one's mouth dry like licking a bone. The blood pounded in Sylvie's head with the rhythmic singing of the cicadas. She'd ripped her cheap plastic shoes on the walk through the bush around the asylum and so returned to her faithful boots. One of the soles was loose and each time it clunked against the paved road, sticky from the heat, it sent a wave of pain through Sylvie's left sinus. She felt very cranky.

She spent a day and a night in Annie's cool, dark house pouring over Polly's purloined file and thus forgot about the sinister heat that awaited her outside. Halfway through her journey across town she wondered if everyone was right and she was crazy for undertaking this hellish trip on the surface of the sun. Then she recalled Annie patiently explaining things Sylvie didn't understand when all Annie wanted was not to be reminded of her dead husband's dead first wife. Sylvie wiped the sweat from under the rims of the sunglasses stolen from the asylum's lost and found, and trudged on.

She planned on hitching, should the opportunity present itself, but it was an exceptionally hot afternoon and most people were home watching the Sunday matinee on TV with the air conditioner set to Arctic, and the opportunity did not. It was a sweaty, cranky and very tired girl who walked into the Sheriff's space in the Town Hall, pushed through the swinging wooden door and into the cubicle that passed for his office. She gave him a resentful stare, for at this point it was fully his fault she'd started the journey, and collapsed into the chair across from his desk. He was on the phone and made no sudden movements beyond a slight raising of the eyebrows.

He spoke an occasional yes, no, or I'm sorry to hear that. His mind was not fully occupied by the conversation and so he had time to ponder his visitor and her appearance. Her short, dark hair was black around the edges with sweat. She removed the sunglasses to wipe her wet face with the edge of a hideous plaid skirt, before repeatedly pulling on the front of an embroidered blouse to create a bit of a breeze. There was a box of Kleenex on his desk and she pulled a handful of tissues to rub over and through her damp hair. It was left sticking up like an angry badger and the Sheriff almost found this visit funny.

He gave a last, "I'm sorry to hear that," before hanging up the phone and telling her: "You look like you've been shot out of a cannon."

She glowered at him and swiped the bottle of grape soda off his blotter. Only after chugging it down did she reply. "I want to see the report on my mother's suicide."

Any amusement he felt fled. "What report?"

"Suicide is a crime, right? Therefore there should be a report on my mother's."

He relaxed a little and she got suspicious in response. "You're assuming there's a report, it's conjecture."

"My, such big words for a small town law man."

He slammed his hand on the desk and she burst out, "Got any more soda?" before his anger could materialize further.

The Sheriff wanted to draw his weapon and shoot her for her mere existence, but she did look pathetic in her broken boots, messy hair, and with sweat pooled in the hollows of her collarbones. He swiveled around to open a mini-fridge and hand her a Ne-Hi Orange before pulling out a Corona for himself. She rolled her eyes in scorn, but was too busy rubbing the cold bottle on her red face to make any scathing comments about drinking on the job. Besides, it was Sunday.

He waited until her soda was half gone before admitting: "Any reports on Polly are long gone. There was an electrical fire a few years ago and many files were destroyed."

She stared into his eyes. He tried to determine what form her retaliation would take, but his imagination had never been equal to hers. Admitting this, even to himself, felt like surrender. He was starting to fidget when she finally spoke.

"What about this then?" Sylvie removed the note, soft with sweat, from her bra and threw it on the desk. "How did it escape?"

He opened it tentatively and she saw recognition burn across his now clammy white face. He drank deeply from his beer, smoothed the paper open on his desk.

"Where did you…" He saw her lips seal shut and sighed. "Never mind, you'll just lie for him, won't you? This is mine; she left it for me. I guess I should thank you for giving it back."

He couldn't bring himself to thank her and she was too angry to listen, anyway. "What are you talking about? The note was on the bedside table, Annie told me. I was in my crib in that room and she was in the bathtub. Annie told me." She turned red again as she repeated with emphasis what Annie said and the Sheriff eyed her with satisfaction.

Then he was ashamed as he remembered her as a newly motherless baby. "Yeah, you were in your crib. Been crying for hours, I imagine, 'cause she was long dead when I found her. There was nothing I could do but cause more scandal, for her, for me, even for you and your father; that bastard. But you won't believe me."

Sylvie did. She believed him. The sick look of anguish on his face was entirely real and she was having a hard time hating him.

"I called and told him to come home, there was a family emergency. You finally stopped crying and fell sleep, so I left."

"Why were you there?" Sylvie asked.

He raised his eyebrows chidingly. "The good doctor worked long hours then."

He felt a nasty triumph at the disappointment that visibly suffused her and then was surprised when she merely got up and walked out again, clutching her unfinished soda by the bottleneck. Her walk was uneven, no doubt from the broken boot heel, and she looked like she'd been the one with the beer. He waited for a while, expecting any moment to hear a crash of glass breaking, some sort of violent reprisal, but only the soft swinging of the door could be heard after she left the building.

It wasn't until he went outside an hour later that he found her empty soda bottle balanced on the hood of his Bronco. He didn't know if she was showing him what a restrained adult she was now, or if it was a threat. Knowing Sylvie, as he thought he did, he chose the latter.

During her hot walk home, Nick and his dwarf passenger picked up Sylvie. Normally, she would have been delighted to meet the new vet and would have asked many inappropriate questions, but right now she was too tired. She merely thanked him for the ride and declared herself happy to meet him. He was a well-mannered man and Nick was sensitive to her every mood and so they politely talked around her.

Sylvie shocked herself with her calm acceptance of the Sheriff's triumph. He won another battle in their life-long war (well, her life-long anyway) and she merely walked away. Oh, she had wanted to bash in his windshield with the bottle or throw it half-full against his office door or shake it violently and spray it in his face. But then she thought about Annie, patiently reading her mother's medical file with her although everyone knew Annie had been sick of Polly and her after-death presence six weeks after her marriage to Dr. Sullivan. Then Sylvie thought of Nick, working two jobs, averaging five hours of sleep a day to get the two of them out of this hateful town and she could not bring herself to cause either of them any more grief.

She left the bottle to show old Sheriff Buddy that she wasn't what he thought her. She could be restrained, mindful, and considerate of others; whether she wanted to be or not. She had also opened the door and peed on the driver's seat, but she wasn't going to mention that to anyone.

Annie had laid it all out on her living room floor the way she'd set up a showing in her gallery. Together she and Sylvie crawled around the exhibit of Polly's life, learning and explaining until Annie quizzed Sylvie.

"Let's start at the beginning ..." She pointed to a black and white snapshot.

"That's Polly and her mama right before Grandma died." The lady held the baby at arm's length. It looked more like she shoved the infant off the edge of her knees than tried to cuddle her.

"She didn't die right away after she drank the drain cleaner. She sort of hung around and rotted until the viciousness drained away. My own mother swore that was all that was keeping her alive, viciousness and meanness and when the rot got too bad, it drained away and she died." Annie flipped the photo face down before wiping her hands on her jeans. "They called it a Blessed Relief and I know it was for my mama. With that woman gone and Polly's daddy out of town more often than not, it was just the housework and the two of us girls and Polly was so easy to love then."

"Was she?" Sylvie asked, knowing full well that she herself was not.

"Hmm." Annie wanted to avoid the topic of Sylvie's loveable-ness.

"She was a sweet, easy baby and such a needy little girl, always wanting everyone to like her that my own mama devoted much of her time to reassuring her. I guess I was jealous, but I loved Polly, too."

"This photo is Polly and you and the boy-next-door." Sylvie wasn't ready to talk about when Annie stopped loving Polly.

"Buddy discovered Polly when she was five years old and he hardly left her side for years."

"Weirdo," Sylvie muttered, reaching for another photograph.

"No." Annie slapped her hand and lined up some photos of her choosing. "You have to understand this."

The photographs she dealt out were cheap strip prints, the kind machines at carnivals make, a couple of primordial Polaroid's, and a posed, studio portrait of Polly and Buddy at a school dance, a glimpse of young Annie and a hulking figure caught forever in the corner.

"Polly craved love and attention, always, every moment. It was as much an addiction as Nicky's father's alcoholism. It wasn't normal or healthy the way Polly demanded love, but the only person who ever satisfied her craving was Buddy. It was just as unhealthy, I think, the way he would do anything for her."

Sylvie looked sullenly at the laughing Buddy and her ghostly mother. "I would have loved her. I was her baby."

Annie patted her shoulder tentatively. Sylvie had never permitted affection from her step-mother and Annie touched her the way one would a dog one wasn't sure might not bite. "Of course you loved her and I'm sure she loved you, but she was very ill by then…Your parent's relationship; it was wrong and your daddy knew it. But your mama thought he was rejecting her and that made her even crazier. Plus, as soon as she was out Buddy was right back at her door, sniffing around."

"It's his fault," Sylvie said bitterly, but sticking to her guns about his guilt was getting harder.

"It's all our faults." Annie said, but softened at Sylvie's stricken look.

"Not yours, missy," Annie reassured her. "You were a baby. You didn't ask to be born. It was the rest of us, the adults that should have been watching for the signs; but I had troubles of my own by then. My own baby and my own pain-in-the-ass husband, I was distracted."

"When did you marry Daddy?" Sylvie asked over-brightly.

Annie thought a moment, more about the odd brightness in Sylvie's tone than about the past. "After Nicky's father got killed. I had been taking care of you for your daddy and it just seemed easier to move in and after a few months we thought to get married to shut up the townsfolk."

"Damn gossips," Sylvie said.

"Took me a while to realize your daddy was a drunk too." Annie decided to ignore her outburst. "He was more subtle with it than Nicky's daddy."

Sylvie remembered daddy slumped in his chair, the television on, the newspaper opened in his lap, but paying no mind to either. A bottle of something amber-colored stood nearby and daddy sipped at a constantly full glass. Nick's daddy must have been a ferocious drunk.

Annie flicked through the purloined medical file now, stopped occasionally to read something that caused her eyebrows to knit, as good as a shout in others. A folded piece of paper slipped to the floor and Sylvie palmed it more from habit than need. Annie seemed beyond caring what crimes Sylvie committed now. Sylvie flicked the note open, read it once, twice, then closed it and slid it into her bra.

"Do you think I'll go crazy too?" She abruptly questioned Annie.

Annie paused in her reading to answer seriously and slowly. "No," she said. "I don't. You're strong-willed, like your grandmother, but you're not vicious and cold like that woman. You look like Polly, but there's nothing of her in you. Actually, I wish there was...It'd be nice if you sought someone's approval. Would've made my life easier if you'd ever cared about pleasing people or even being liked. You get that from your father."

"No, Sylvie," Annie continued, reading the chart again. "I never worried about you going to the asylum, just jail. I don't know why you can't behave yourself, but it's not because you're insane."

Sylvie, as surprised as Annie, found herself hugging her stepmother. To make up for this egregious lapse, she showed Annie the note in her bra.

"Oh that," Annie said. "I wonder how that got in there."

Sylvie waited, chewing on her lower lip.

"Your father found this on the bedside table. You were asleep in your crib, wet and dirty and all snotty from crying the whole day. She was in the bathtub."

"Who was it for? Whose name was on it?" Sylvie wondered. Her crib was next to her parent's bed. She knew that much because daddy always said he was the one who got up in the night so it needed to be close. Was the note meant for Polly's baby daughter?

"It wasn't addressed to anyone." Annie shrugged and moved to put it back in the file. Sylvie stopped her and replaced it in her bra. "I've always thought Polly meant it for the world in general, but she was never much of a writer."

"Okay, okay." Sylvie held up her hands in surrender. Obviously Annie couldn't shake off old reticent habits and was about to balk. "Let me just ask one more thing, okay? And then I'll shut up."

Annie gave a grudging nod. The girl was being good for a change, maybe her stepmother should reward that.

"I know daddy loved Polly, but did Polly love daddy...or was he just a way out?"

Annie looked at her with real pity. "Daddy didn't love Polly,

Sylvie. Your daddy loved his idea of Polly."

Sylvie's mouth gaped open with another question, but Annie had had enough and she walked into the kitchen. She threw over her shoulder a brusque: "Clean that up and give the file back to Nicky. He doesn't need any trouble."

Sylvie sat still, a little subdued, a little head-achy. She would've liked a nap, but felt a compulsion to hear more about her mother. Annie wasn't going to spill anymore; it was amazing Sylvie had got that much out of her. There was only one source Sylvie could think of and there was something fitting in the irony of it. How would he like to be stalked for a change?

Annie heard the front door slam and came out to find the mess still on the floor and Sylvie gone. She blew out a lungful of held breath, thinking that Sylvie might not be crazy but she was bound to drive Annie into the asylum. As usual, Annie picked up the mess others had left behind.

When Sylvie returned, she was so obviously sick with her headache that Annie couldn't bring herself to scold her for running off. She merely gave Sylvie aspirin and cooked broth and later, when the Sheriff called to rant about a urine soaked car seat, she listened politely until he was done and then never mentioned it again. Sylvie was subdued for too long. Annie and Nick consulted in a quiet way and decided the best course of action was no action. Leave her be, Mama, was all Nick said. Let her figure this out on her own.

Nick returned the medical file, but Annie left the box of photos out on the table and when they packed their bags at the end of the month, Sylvie packed it in her suitcase with her motley collection of clothing. Sylvie became very quiet, her last month in Annie's house. She studied the photos of her mother and father and Buddy and finally, she brought her conclusion to Nicky.

"I've decided what we've been fighting over all this time, what

I've been fighting over is this: who did she belong to?"

"To whom did she belong." Nick corrected her automatically and then could have kicked himself, but she did it for him before going on.

"I thought it was all about who loved her the most or needed her the most or missed her the most, but it's not. It's not." Sylvie looked at him to judge his reaction and he braced for another kick.

"And what did you decide that it is?" He moved his legs out of her way. This quiet version of Sylvie scared him a little. Her boundaries had moved and left him wondering when he would cross her new lines. He had to relearn the map of Sylvie; where were the monsters?

"I've decided it doesn't matter. I can only handle how I loved her or needed her or miss her. But I also know that her memory carries more weight for me than she ever did living and that's not true for Annie and the idiot."

Nick grinned in relief. "Thank god, I was worried there. Your maturity was weirding me out until you mentioned the idiot. I don't think I could handle you becoming all forgiving and forgetting."

Sylvie grinned back and then kicked him, too fast for him to pull away. "No need to fret. I forgive nothing. But they're all such a bunch of jerks...not you Annie!" She yelled into the kitchen, from whence dinner smells were emerging. "Daddy and that Sheriff and Polly, too, really. I can't worry about them anymore, I'm only going to worry about the way I feel about her. How's that for maturity?"

"About all I can handle," Nick muttered and moved toward the scent of food. "So you're gonna leave old Buddy well enough alone?"

"Oh, I guess," she said as she followed him to the dinner table. "I mean, sure, eventually; but I have to do something before we go. I wouldn't want to hurt his feelings by not saying goodbye."

Annie caught Nick's eye as she served mashed potatoes and shook her head gently. There was no point in arguing with Sylvie, it only made her more determined and she had done enough maturing for one day. Let the children eat their meal in peace. They would leave soon and, once gone, most likely not return to this home ever again. To Annie, this was both a comfort and an ache; but most of her life had been this way. There was seldom any sweetness that wasn't followed by an accompanying bitter. Why would her children's lives be any different?

'Let me go' was all that was written in Polly's suicide note. Annie assumed it was meant for the entire world. Daddy, as both doctor and husband, felt it pertained only to him and therefore held an especial guilt. When Sylvie realized that the Sheriff also thought Polly's final plea was directed at him, as her childhood sweetheart and erstwhile lover, she felt some sort of unholy rage that no amount of newfound maturity could tamp down.

She waited in his Bronco late one night, outside the honky-tonk where he went to drink when he wanted to seriously drink. Away in this corner of the county none of his constituents were liable to run into him. He didn't know how she did this. He'd never known when to expect her to invade his privacy, his house, his truck. How did she even get out here in the middle of nowhere, deserted highway, wee hours of the dark and all?

"You'd better not be hitchhiking." He put the key in the ignition, but didn't turn it. She was dressed as usual in what he had once heard described as 'vagabond slut' by her English teacher. He was too drunk to take in tonight's components, but her battered boots and silver bangle were the usual constants.

"I gave that to your mama," he told her for the first time. Why had he never told her this? Why was he telling her now? "She was seventeen and I gave her my grandma's bracelet as a sort of engagement present 'cause I was just a kid and didn't have a ring.

Then she hurt herself and they put her in the asylum and she only got out to marry Mr. Big Shot Doctor and have you. Now every day I have to see my grandmother's bracelet on the arm of a juvenile delinquent who hates me."

During this speech she took it off and examined it. Then while she spoke she turned it over and over in her hands. "I'm not a juvenile delinquent anymore. I'm not my mother. I am not Daddy. I am not the sum total of their parts. I don't know what you expect from me. You seem to need some big confrontation or dramatic speech in the rain or for me to attack somebody or to try and kill myself. But you have to stop."

"I am not Polly. I am not crazy. I don't want to hurt myself or others. So let this be it. Let this be our dramatic confrontation in the rain, but please, I'm asking you politely: Let me go."

He faced out the windshield, both hands on the wheel. But she never took her eyes off him as she backed out of the door. It was only when the door clicked shut that he saw that she had left the silver bracelet on the seat next to him.

Bio
Sara Marchant

Sara Marchant received her Masters of Fine Arts in Creative Writing and Writing for the Performing Arts from the University of California, Riverside/ Palm Desert. Her work has been published by The Manifest-Station, Every Writer's Resource, Full Grown People, Brilliant Flash Fiction, The Coachella Review and East Jasmine Review. Her non-fiction work is forthcoming in the anthology *All the Women in my Family Sing.* She is the prose editor for the literary magazine Writers Resist. She lives in the high desert of Southern California with her husband, two dogs, a goat, and five chickens.

Well Fed

By Miranda Manzano

1.

Henry looks down at his outfit, a crisp pair of black slacks and a white button up shirt. Though it is obvious the clothes didn't cost very much money, he looks nice. He can't remember the last time he looked so nice. He holds a half-filled duffel bag in his left hand and his right arm is bent with his coat in the crook. He rarely wears a coat even in the winter but he brings one with him whenever he leaves the house. A habit taught to him by his mother and reinforced using repetition and guilt. He looks at his right arm, the one holding the coat, and wonders if anyone can tell something's happened to it. It's considerably smaller now than his left arm because of the months of disuse, but maybe you can't tell when he wears long sleeves. He stretches it out straight and bends it again sending shooting pain from his fingertips to his collar bone. He reveals nothing of the pain, another parental gift this one given by his father. He is an even mix of each. Henry has thought about this often. He got his mother's almond shaped eyes, her athleticism, and her natural sociability. He got his father's thick, light brown hair, his tricky knees, and his passive nature. He also got a few things of his own. He is not ashamed of the similarities between him and his parents as some people are. He accepts it. Henry used to reflect on these similarities and think he had to be just like them, that his life was going to be the same as theirs, but he learned over time that one's life is purely situational.

Who your friends are, who you love, and what you do all day, it's all simply chance.

At this moment, however Henry isn't thinking about his parents or chance. He's thinking about the coming day.

The sun rises and reveals itself behind the trees by shooting off absurdly bright colors across the sky. The emerging day feels like it is full of opportunities. As though it has the potential to be long, productive, and meaningful. This is a false feeling and the precise reason Henry hates this time of day. The day will slip away and fall short of expectations. Despite any attempt at making plans the hours will be eaten up by obligation. This day will be like all the rest. Henry, from experience, can be sure of this.

He looks around the train platform out of boredom rather than interest and observes about twenty other people waiting for the train. Like him they all stand on their own, and stare blankly in any direction. Just waiting and standing. Scattered across the platform each person keeps a respectable and normal distance from each other.

Henry takes notice of a woman down by the gate that blocks the track. She is birdlike and petite and wears a shapeless grey jacket. Her luggage leans against her leg and she stares across the tracks giving Henry a profile view of her. She has thin brown hair that disappears into her jacket. She uses a bone thin finger to push her hair behind her ear and glances around. She must feel she is being observed. She looks at Henry and he is caught looking at her. Her face is simple and unemotional, but there is something that makes him look away quickly.

"You don't want to mess with a woman like that," says a man who has appeared at Henry's side.

Henry is not sure if this man has been standing next to him long, or if he has just walked up.

"I wasn't planning on it," replies Henry as he turns to look at the man. He is built like a tree stump, short and round, but extraordinarily muscular. He is dressed similarly to Henry but looks uncomfortable in the outfit. He yanks on the collar of his shirt. The top two buttons are undone but it still looks too tight. He has tattoos that stick out from his shirt sleeves and another one on his stub of a neck that is a thick black bar.

"Yeah, you can just tell. She's a real pain in the ass," says the man.

Henry is surprised at the stranger's crudeness. He doesn't say so, but social cues would indicate to most people that Henry is not looking for a pal or a conversation.

Henry is not a particularly chatty or outgoing man. Though he is no hermit either. He can hold his own in a multitude of social situations from co-workers in the break room at lunch to the barista at the neighborhood coffee shop. But today, waiting for the train, for reasons he is not aware of, and does not think to reflect on, he neither has the energy, nor is he in the mood to humor the man.

Henry decides to reply with a polite "Mhhmm," and hopes he can take the hint.

Instead the man reaches out his hand and says, "I'm Mick."

"Hi." Henry painfully reaches out his right hand to meet Mick's.

"What, you don't have a name?" says Mick. He does not let go of Henry's hand.

"Henry."

Mick shakes Henry's hand vigorously. "Good to meet you Henry."

Henry's arm ignites and he can't hide the pain. He grimaces and Mick finally lets go.

"Hope I didn't hurt you?" says Mick before laughing loudly from his belly like some kind of cruel tattooed Santa.

"No. I'm fine," says Henry plainly.

Miles down the track the single headlight of the train can be seen pushing its way to the station. Everyone turns to watch it arrive.

"So where are you sitting, Henry?" Mick looks at his ticket.

Henry plucks his ticket from his bag. He didn't know where he was sitting. It hadn't occurred to him to check. "Let's see, looks like seat twelve in car four."

"I'm in car two. Maybe I'll see you around the snack car, huh?" He laughs his loud self-congratulatory laugh and walks away to be closer to where the train will board. He passes the woman and gives her a look that is a combination hatred and possessiveness. The woman takes no notice.

The door between the last car and the second to last opens. No one disembarks. This strikes Henry as odd. This is only Greenville. Certainly, no tourist destination, but it's still strange. Henry has never had the opportunity to be an extensive traveler, but he made some trips as a child and then as an adult with his own family. During his travel Henry learned that regardless of the location every trip has certain things in common such as crying and screaming children, crowds, excess noise of no particular origin, groups of people hugging and waving while standing in the middle of walkways. This train platform has not a single one of those things. Henry has a moment to reflect on this while he waits to board. He remembers an article he saw once about the struggling train industry and how they are trying to come up with new ways of keeping it profitable. He thinks it might be interesting to get the perspective of an employee on this train but he can't remember any details. So, he stops thinking about it and boards the train. He is the last to do so.

Henry hands his ticket to a jittery man who does everything in short quick movements. He is dressed in a uniform of khakis and a black polo shirt, he has a clip-on name tag that reads Bauman. He takes Henry's ticket, points to the left, and hands him back the ticket without looking at him. Henry stays in the vestibule and looks into the car. It is sparsely filled; some people have whole aisles to themselves. The woman Henry noticed on the platform sits in the front row. Henry turns back around to the door and watches Bauman as he locks it.

"You didn't yell all aboard," says Henry to Bauman.

Bauman turns around sharply. "We don't do that for this train," he swallows hard. "I could see there was no one else."

"I was just kidding. I guess I've only seen that in movies." As Henry says this he begins to remember. His brain moves slowly like walking through water. Finally, he reaches the memory and he is so grateful to have it. He doesn't worry about how hard it was to find.

Henry has been an employee of the Greenville City Zoo for the last fourteen years. Like many zoos, Greenville has a small train that circles making two stops, one at either end. One stop is right by where Henry spends most of his time, the commissary. Henry spends all day preparing food for the large cats and African animals where he hears the words, "All aboard," shouted every twenty minutes. A purely ceremonial act, as every single person is seated and their doors secured before the woman who runs the train even yells. He's always thought of that woman as a bit of a joke, as if she was built by the same people who built that miniature train. Also, as an occupational habit he tends to look at certain people as animals and in his subconscious mind he goes over the best way to chop her up and split her between the two lions and the caracal who all get a bone-in treat on Tuesdays.

Leaving the train in his memories and returning to the train he is on, Henry realizes that Bauman is staring at him. "I'm sorry, did you say something?" says Henry.

Bauman looks slightly confused and offended. There is a sudden sharp noise of electrical feedback. Bauman flinches and puts his hand to his ear. He wears a small flesh toned ear piece.

Once Bauman has recovered from the sound he says, "your seat is this way, Sir."

"Thank you," says Henry, though he is more annoyed with the man than thankful to him. He knows where his seat is, he is just trying to be friendly. They shouldn't hire such nervous people for this line of work, he thinks. He hopes the other workers are more courteous.

2.

"Stop eight is complete, ready to continue," says Lewis into his headset.

David Lewis Jr. is bored shitless. This is his fifth time taking this trip, so not only is it routine but he has grown tired of the sights. All two of them. In the first leg, there is a small man-made lake where sometimes a few cranes hang out or a gaggle of geese, but most of the time there is nothing. They've passed it already, and he thinks he saw a duck. They are about to pass the second and final noteworthy sight. It's a tree. It is remarkable because it is the only tree in the area and because it stands nearly parallel to the ground. It starts off right, sprouting from the ground like any other tree then it takes a sharp and drastic turn. A permanent backbend. This tree has adapted to its environment. A dry and windy desert forced the tree to either die or grow wrong. The tree made certain sacrifices to survive. This thought makes Lewis laugh. So, melodramatic. He is so bored he assigned character to a tree. Today the tree looks like it has each time he has seen it. With eight hours left in the trip, he has seen the last interesting thing there is to see.

They'll pass through one more town on their last stop, but all you can see of it from the tracks is an abandoned factory that once produced most of the country's yogurt. Evidently the yogurt tides turned and they went under, now the factory's rusting carcass blends into the bland desert. This desert will see them to their destination. A parade of different shades of brown. A collection of dust and brittle bushes. Lewis is not above enjoying the simplicity of nature but the desert is dead. The desert has nothing to offer. The flat colorless scenery leaves him uninspired.

This job has a lot of down time so he's always trying to find ways to entertain himself. He has been unable to convince his superiors that the train needs Wi-Fi, so that's out. His co-workers Franny the Director of Well Being and Craig, Director of Train Security, are friendly and capable but Lewis shares few interests with them. This leaves him on his own. He goes over his safety check lists. He imagines worst case scenarios and what he would do. Then he usually goes in standby mode and lets his mind wander. He thinks about his dog, wonders if he could get a better deal on cell service, and tries to come up with something good to make for dinner next time he's home.

"Hey boss man," says Franny.

Lewis was promoted to Train Director only a few months ago. Franny and Lewis had been peers for many years prior to that. She has only recently started calling him boss man. He isn't sure if it is meant to be a jab.

"What's up Franny?" Lewis swivels in his chair to face her.

In the train's front section are three work stations. Lewis's faces the front. Behind him on his left is Franny's station and to his right is Craig's. Franny's workstation includes three wall mounted monitors to track what is going on in different parts of the train. She has pulled up one of the security cameras.

"It's car four, we've got a lingerer."

Lewis gets up and goes over to the screen.

"New guy?" says Craig from his work station. His desk is more low tech. He has a laptop which has only been used to send emails and play solitaire.

"Yeah, new guy," says Franny.

Lewis speaks into the headset. "Waiting on you Bauman." But all anyone hears is the feedback as the sound ricochets off of Franny's headset. Bauman flinches and touches his ear piece.

Craig and Franny laugh.

"Good job boss. Smooth," says Franny.

"Yeah, yeah, just make sure that one takes his seat," says Lewis.

3.

Henry enters the car and walks down the aisle lifting his bag awkwardly to keep from hitting the chairs on either side. This is difficult as the train moves fast. The train shimmies on the tracks and Henry loses his balance. He is forced to use his injured arm to brace himself on a nearby chair. He drops his coat and it falls on the feet of a passenger. Henry clenches his jaw and breathes deeply for a few seconds to let the pain in his arm fade. Then he reaches down to pick up his jacket. "Excuse me," he says to the man. He gets nothing back in response. He almost looks like he is sleeping, but his eyes are open. His shirt is buttoned wrong and his earlobes hang loose and low missing the disc shaped piece of jewelry that made the gaping hole. Henry thinks the man must be on drugs.

Henry comes to his seat and tosses his bag into the overhead space. He sees the other luggage, one black duffel bag per person. Very neat and organized and confusing for some reason. He feels disoriented, as if a fog moves in on his mind. He feels disconnected from what is happening, dopey and kind of sick. Then he hears a man speak to him.

"Have you found your seat sir?" says Bauman from the front. His hands shake, and he wipes the sweat from his palms onto his pant leg. "Sir? Have you found your seat?"

Henry looks down at the empty seat in front of him and the sight of it comforts him. That's what he was doing, he was going to sit. He feels much better. "Yes, thank you." He sits.

His is the aisle seat; the middle is empty. At the window seat is a slim man with shoulder length slicked back hair. He wears a grey button up shirt untucked and black slacks which are about two inches too short for him leaving his ankles exposed obscenely between the cuff of his pants and the top of his socks. Already Henry pities the man.

He looks over towards Henry and nods as a greeting. The first thing Henry notices is the man's eyes. They are small and beady and perfectly round, giving him an extremely earnest and reptilian look. The second thing Henry notices is the man has no lips.

Henry nods hello back, making no outward reaction to the man's physical appearance. Internally Henry is slightly disgusted. He looks as if he is perpetually snarling like a dog or grinning like an ape, and it's hard not to look directly into his dry hard teeth or the puffy scar tissue that rests on his gums. Logically, Henry can see he is neither smiling nor snarling but a first and sudden reaction is hard to hide. However, Henry does it so well, the lipless man smiles. With his eyes.

Henry looks around. He cranes his neck to see a man with a deep leathery tan and sun-bleached hair. Henry can't help staring at him. He is at the edge of his seat with a straight back. He holds his head still while his eyes dance What a strange person. Henry wonders if he could be dangerous, but decides it's not his place to do anything about it.

Henry turns back around and takes inventory of the pouch in front of him. He finds a complimentary bottle of water, a motion sickness bag, and a safety pamphlet. Nothing very interesting. Henry relaxes and leans back in his chair, rests his injured arm on the arm rest, and looks out of the window. A morning fog lurks where the sun doesn't reach yet. He watches the train's long shadow drag across the terrain.

A whimper comes from behind. It's just a soft cry, a noise a puppy would make, but it shocks Henry's system. Like being stuck with a needle, it pierces him.

Henry clears his throat and blinks his eyes, both of which feel dry. His neck is stiff and he stretches it side to side. He realizes the train's shadow is gone. The sun is directly above them now. He must have been asleep for hours.

Henry hears the noise again, louder this time.

He turns around and sees the same anxious man he noticed before. His anxiety has deepened. He frantically looks around, while he picks the skin around his finger nails. Periodically he lets out little noises. Sweat drenches his shirt collar and it sticks to him.

Henry resolves to ignore it but wishes the man would be quiet. Henry's stomach growls and he feels a bit out of it. He remembers he hasn't eaten yet. Without thinking he turns to the man next to him. "Do you know . . ." then he remembers. The lips.

The beady eyes widen in response to Henry's attention.

Henry is forced to continue or come off as rude. ". . . what the food situation is?"

The man shakes his head no.

He reminds Henry of so many animals that he can hardly get himself to mentally chop him up and feed him to his beloved wild cats. Besides, he is too thin and boney to provide a good meal.

"Hi, I'm Henry," he says.

They shake hands then the man reaches inside his back pocket. He pulls out his train ticket and unfolds it. He turns the front side towards Henry and points to the upper left corner where it has his name.

"Nice to meet you, Benedict Croft," says Henry.

Benedict Croft takes his finger and covers up part of his name leaving only Ben.

"Ben, are you hungry or is it just me?"

Ben nods and says, "yes hungry," with surprising accuracy.

"I don't think I brought any snacks with me. Should we go see about some food?"

Ben nods and they both get up and head towards the front.

"I heard something about a snack car, but I don't remember from whom," says Henry. The woman watches them as they pass.

They reach the front and stop at a sliding door with a two-foot square window made of frosted glass. It does not have a handle on their side and does not open automatically. Henry pushes with no result. He looks over at Ben who shrugs and points to an unmarked button on the wall next to the door.

"Maybe that's it?" Henry looks back and sees he has the attention of several passengers. "This is kind of silly." He presses the button. It buzzes and through the glass they can see movement.

The door opens and it's the ticket taker, Bauman.

"Is everything okay in here?" he says with urgency.

The woman stands up. "Are we not allowed to move around the train?"

"We prefer it if you stay in your own cars. The train is very full and it's much easier if everyone stays in their own cars," says Bauman. He swallows hard.

"We were just looking to get some food." Henry gestures to Ben.

The man looks at Ben and makes an odd sound, a squeak like a frightened mouse then stares at the floor. "There will be an announcement shortly regarding meal time." He hits a button and the door slides shut so fast Henry and Ben jump back.

4.

Peter Bauman has had no sleep. The train was scheduled to leave at 4:30 in the morning so he tried to go to bed early, but didn't fall asleep until late. It wasn't just the nerves that kept him up, but also his mother's elderly cat which he inherited upon her death two years ago. The cat is intent on dying. She eats garbage, chews on electrical wires and crawls in small dangerous places. Peter is sure the cat is suicidal. We all handle loss differently, that's what they say, so Peter decided long ago he won't let this cat throw in the towel. He has thwarted her attempts. Last night the cat's suicidal tendencies manifested when she ate an off brand, men's blue bar soap and woke Peter up puking blue foam. He locked her in the bathroom with a bowl of water and went back to bed. He had nervous dreams about his first day at his new job.

A man who has spent all fifty-one years of his life trying to find a place to fit in, or maybe even a subject to excel in, is good at recognizing when he doesn't. Everything about this job makes him uncomfortable, but they have invested so much time in training and he doesn't have many other options. He decides to give it a real chance. A decision he regrets.

Sitting in the vestibule he feels terrible, and it isn't just because of the lack of sleep. He knows the logistics of what he is supposed to do, it's not hard, but when it comes to interacting with these people and being authoritative, he struggles.

"Approaching stop eight," says Lewis in his ear piece.

Peter flinches every time someone speaks into his ear, he can't help it. Stop eight is more or less his stop. All the passengers boarding, with a few exceptions, will sit in his train car. He will be responsible for them. He takes a series of deep breathes and reminds himself why he is doing this. He reminds himself that he has decided to see this day through even if he quits at the end.

He opens the door. He keeps his head down and checks tickets. He is aware of his shaking hands but there isn't anything he can do about it.

"Stop eight is complete, ready to continue," says Lewis.

The worst part is over. He closes the door and locks it.

"You didn't yell all aboard," says a voice behind him. A voice that should be seated but isn't. His first oversight on the job.

"We don't do that on this train." He shouldn't say that. "I could see there was no one there." He doesn't need to explain himself to these people.

The man has a faraway look. Peter thinks he looks dumb and harmless, like a dog. This thought upsets Peter. Many of his co-workers refer to the passengers as various kinds of animals. He has heard Lewis refer to them as pigs and vultures. Another feature of the job that makes Peter uncomfortable.

The man in front of him looks relatively normal. The kind of guy who takes his family shopping at the mall on weekends. His features are pleasingly average and unmemorable. His one distinctive feature is his right arm which he keeps bent and holds close to his body. It doesn't look right and you can see it causes him pain.

A siren goes off in his ear piece, electrical feedback. He reaches for it instinctively. Another mistake. "Your seat is this way, sir."

Things settle down and he calms himself. He sits in his chair and counts the minutes passing. It's his only comfort.

Two hours pass in peace then the door buzzes. The passengers shouldn't be up.

"Bauman that's you. You know what to do," says Lewis.

He opens the door and says what he knows he's supposed to say. "The train is full . . ." only he lingers too long. He can't muster an authoritative tone or even lift his eyes off the ground. They question him. One has a scar covered face he can't bear to look at.

Peter says quickly, "there will be an announcement shortly regarding meal time." He closes the door.

5.

"The train doesn't seem full," says Henry.

"It's not, he's lying," says the woman.

Ben points up at the luggage rack and says, "same," the best he can.

Henry understands. He's talking about the luggage. He isn't sure why it is worth discussing. He steps down the aisle, back to his seat to wait for the meal time. He notices passengers look up at the luggage. Perhaps Ben meant something else, something that went right over Henry's head. He turns around to Ben. "What about it?" Henry and Ben exchange confused looks. Henry feels embarrassed. He has missed something or Ben has. Whatever it was, Ben doesn't seem concerned any longer.

Again, Henry makes a move to go back to his seat but stops when he sees the anxious man. Henry last observed him a few minutes ago but he looks significantly worse now. His eyes have stopped darting and are focused on the luggage rack. His hands are bloody and the skin that surrounds each fingernail is picked off. He shakes his head back and forth saying no to a question that was never asked. He grabs his shirt at the collar and yanks it, popping off a button. He screams. A short high-pitched scream that gets everyone's attention.

"This doesn't—" says the man.

Everyone is still a moment. They wait for him to finish his

sentence, but instead he screams again. A different kind of scream, a sustained noise, one of terror and utter confusion that makes the room vibrate. His eyes circle wildly and he flails hitting the chairs. Every single second that passes only heightens his pain.

Everyone stares while he fills the car with his fears. All but one. The man whose feet Henry dropped his coat on. The man with the drooping earlobes. He sits in his chair looking straight ahead as if he can't hear a thing. With the foggy unfocused eyes of a dead man he looks peacefully straight ahead. Henry wouldn't feed this man to any animals at his zoo. Even the California condors who would immediately be attracted to the dangling fragile flesh on his ears. Something's wrong with him. He's tainted meat. Diseased or drugged in a way that could be transmitted.

The screaming man quickly sucks in a fresh batch of air and goes on screaming.

The front door opens. Henry turns to look. Two men dressed in the same uniform as Bauman enter. They shove Ben out of their way. Henry jumps out of their way just in time. They pass him and go directly to the screaming man. They pick him up by the arms and usher him out. He flails out of their grasp. Together they restrain him and drag him out of the car. Bauman stands in the vestibule. He holds a small handgun which Henry notices seconds before the door closes.

6.

"I'm telling you, I saw it." Lewis laughs.

"No way are they serving meatloaf again," says Craig.

"When are you guys going to start packing your own lunch like me?" says Franny with her back to them. She stares at her computer screen.

"Hey, this job has exactly one perk, free food. Therefore, on principle I will not bring my own lunch," says Craig.

"I'm afraid I agree," says Lewis.

"Well, then I hope you enjoy your dried out microwaved meatloaf cube prepared and served by disgruntled workers."

"What did you bring?" says Lewis.

"Don't worry about it," says Franny.

"Come on. Maybe I'll buy it off of you."

A beeping noise comes from Franny's workstation. She pulls up a camera. "It's one of the doors. Car four."

"New guy." Craig absent mindedly spins in his chair.

"There are two of them," says Franny.

Lewis presses a button on his headset, "Bauman, that's you. You know what to do."

They watch the camera as Bauman opens the door. They exchange a few words and a third passenger speaks up. Bauman says something else and shuts the door.

"That's it?" says Lewis.

"Maybe it's enough, although Craig you might need to keep an eye on this guy here," says Franny.

Craig rolls his chair over to Franny's work station. He puts his finger on the screen. "That's the same guy who took so long to sit when he boarded."

Franny smacks his hand away from the screen, "I was talking about this guy," Franny zooms in, "he's a little on edge."

"To put it mildly," says Craig. "Is he bleeding?"

"Yeah, it looks like he's going to lose it."

"Lewis, if you can get the rest of the car under control I can get him out of there before he swan dives off the deep end," says Craig.

"Let me talk to Bauman." Lewis presses the button on his head set, but before he can speak—

"You have to go now, he's snapped," says Franny.

Craig opens the door and steps into the service car. It's full of train staff, equipment, and supplies.

"Take Gene with you," yells Lewis.

Craig and Gene leave the car.

"Get the doors," says Lewis to Franny.

"I've got it," Franny types commands and closes the doors from her workstation.

They watch while Craig and Gene grab the man and remove him from the car. In the vestibule Craig sticks a needle in his arm and the man stops screaming. His whole body relaxes and they calmly walk him through the cars.

Lewis walks into the service car as Craig enters from the other side.

"Park him there." Lewis points to one of the seats.

"Secure him," says Craig. He opens a desk drawer and takes out two pairs of plastic handcuffs and tosses them to Gene who restrains the man's arms and legs.

Craig and Lewis go back to their car.

"That was well done," says Lewis.

"If the new guy could keep those rats under control we wouldn't have had to do it like that." He looks at the monitor, "look at them, they're still walking around, doing whatever they want."

"Bauman, get them in their seats," says Lewis into the headset.

"You should get him out of there," says Franny.

"We don't have anyone else. There is only one more stop anyway," says Lewis.

"Yeah, the big one," says Craig. He takes his seat.

"It isn't any different than the rest," says Lewis.

"We'll have a big audience," says Franny.

"The next stop won't be any different than the rest of them. It's just media hype." Lewis can't stand this kind of mundanity. These repetitive work conversations. Meaningless time fillers. Crowds, protesters, media and incidents like the man screaming in car four are not rare or particularly interesting but they insist on having the same conversations every time.

"Car four is back in their seats," says Franny, "and we're about thirty minutes from the final stop."

"Good, they'll be settled by the time we get there. Let's start the report now. I don't want to end up with a backlog like some of the other trips."

"Boss man Lewis runs a tight ship," says Franny. "Except for the new guy."

"His job is so easy. He just has to stand there and try not to spook 'em," says Craig.

"Yeah well all you do is drug 'em, and drag 'em" says Franny, imitating him.

"We're just a bunch of cattle farmers, aren't we?" says Craig. "We haul them, try to keep them from killing themselves or each other, keep them fed and clean. We're just herding cattle."

"I think we're paid better," says Franny.

"I wouldn't be so sure," says Craig.

"There's more to it than that," says Lewis. "As pretentious as it may sound, I'd say we are making the world a better place."

Craig and Franny exchange glances.

"You're right," says Franny. "It does sound pretentious."

Craig laughs, "we're herding cattle man."

"Let's get to work on the report," says Lewis. "Franny what do you figure?"

Craig and Franny turn around to their respective work stations. Craig pulls out a piece of paper and a pen and starts writing his report out.

"Let's see. Showed signs of increased anxiety leading to an outburst and disruptive behavior."

"Slow down," says Craig.

"Expressed through self-harm and, well, screaming."

"Shrieking. It's more descriptive," says Craig.

"Whatever," says Franny.

"Was it a straw moment?" says Craig.

"No. This was different," says Franny.

"How?" says Craig.

"Craig, are you serious? Is this your first day or something?" says Franny.

"This is my first report, usually I just copy yours when we get back to The Vault."

"Do you really not know the difference between what just happened and a straw moment?" says Franny.

"Like I said. Herding. Cattle." yells Craig.

Lewis turns around in his seat. "Keep it down. Geez. And Craig, you should know this shit."

"What the hell do I put down on this form?" says Craig.

Franny takes a deep breath. "The passenger is having a paradoxical reaction to the compound, a known issue experienced by about three percent of those dosed."

"I have to write all that?" says Craig.

"You're hopeless," says Franny.

"Hey, do you think if we ordered a pizza they would deliver it to us at the train station?" says Craig.

"Approaching the final stop," says Lewis into his headset.

7.

With the exception of Henry and Ben, everyone is seated. Now that the screaming man has been removed they have settled back in. Henry considers taking his seat, when the woman at the front stands up. She looks pale and malnourished. Her eyes glow with the intensity that had made Henry look away from her on the platform. They reveal her thoughts and flicker between childlike helplessness and feral hatred. Though to whom these feelings are directed is unclear.

She yanks her jacket down from the overhead storage. She forcefully reaches into the deep pockets and comes up empty.

"They're not here," she says. She pulls her duffel bag to the edge, unzips it and starts pulling things out.

"What are you looking for?" Henry returns to the front of the car.

"Scissors." She rifles through the bag.

"Why?" Henry is completely confused. "These aren't my things," she says.

Henry looks at the contents. It's piles of wrinkled white fabric. "Why do you need scissors?"

"I never go anywhere without them." She pushes the bag away.

"Would you have left them somewhere?" says Henry.

She thinks a moment. Her face is tight and strained. "No. I wouldn't." She quickly looks around the train. "I wouldn't leave them anywhere. What's happening here?"

"Shh." Ben points to a security camera on the ceiling.

"Yes of course. I'm sure train security can help you find your missing things." Henry instantly feels more relaxed and sociable now the crisis is over. "What's your name?"

"Caroline."

"I'm Henry. This is Ben."

"You guys friends?"

"We just met on the train."

"I need my scissors," says Caroline.

Ben puts his hand on her shoulder. He pulls his mouth back at the edges in what Henry believes must be a smile. Caroline smiles back.

The door opens abruptly, as this particular door seems to do. Bauman stands in the doorway.

"I'm sorry for all the disturbances, but I need to ask you to take your seats please. Your assigned seats."

Caroline grabs Ben's arm and she holds on tight. "What's going on here?"

"Everything will be just fine. Please. If you would just take your seats."

The car is silent and nobody moves.

"Please take your seats. Please."

"Or what?" says Caroline.

Bauman says nothing. For a moment, he looks at them. Then, "all your concerns will be addressed shortly."

"I guess we don't have a choice," says Caroline.

Henry silently walks back to his seat.

Ben takes Caroline's hand and presses it against his scarred face before walking to his seat.

When they are seated Bauman closes the door without saying another word.

Henry is annoyed at Caroline. She is being rude to the staff and Henry feels it might have looked like he is associated with her. She should have sat right away. Her missing property will surely be tracked down and for all they know the bizarre man who was dragged out had something to do with it.

Henry is happy to be back in his seat.

He doesn't fully understand what's been happening. He's never been on a train like this. He tries to think about it but before he knows it his minds on to other things. He wonders if it's time to take his car for an oil change and what his childhood dog's favorite toy was. He can't keep his mind off these boring unimportant details. He tires and abandons the effort. He immediately feels better. He remembers another time when he felt like this, unable to focus.

He was on the ground. He had thrown himself against the wall and fallen to the ground. He lay there and lost blood from his arm at a rate he knew was dangerous, yet he could not do anything about it. As blood poured out of his arm like a syrup bottle turned on its side he wondered if he would live. Each second that passed he became less and less able to care.

This feeling of losing grasp on what is happening, the fogginess and the inability to concentrate, that's the same feeling he has now. Soon the memory passes and again his mind wanders.

He looks out the far window. A series of nearly dilapidated and rusty looking houses have backyards bordering the train tracks. The yards are just large enough to fit a few piles of scrap metal and broken children's toys. He thinks about an article he once read about poverty and its relation to crime, but he can't remember any details.

The train slows down. He looks past the lipless man whose name he can't remember and out of the window. The train passes an intersection with bells and flashing lights to keep cars from crossing. There are people everywhere, clogging the streets almost two blocks deep. They wear warm clothing and some hold large signs with writing or pictures on them. They look at the train, some point and yell.

After seeing all this Henry concludes that it must be very cold out. After the train speeds by, he stops thinking about the weather, and the people, and it is all extinguished from his mind.

His stomach growls and his mind is on food. He remembers he hasn't brought any snacks. Then he remembers thinking about this already and for the single moment Henry's mind allows the thought to remain, he is concerned for himself. By the next moment the thought evaporates.

The train is at a crawl now. Henry leans to look out of the window. He doesn't recognize anything. They pull up to a small train station, even smaller than Greenville. The platform is on the right side so Henry has a clear view. Exactly three men are on the platform, all hold duffel bags and are dressed in black slacks and button up shirts. At this distance, the men are practically interchangeable.

They board. One of them enters car four.

He slowly walks down the aisle with his bag in one hand and his ticket in the other. He looks down at the ticket, then up at the seat numbers, and then down at his ticket, and back and forth. He stops in front of Henry. He uncaringly throws his duffel bag in the overhead storage.

"Excuse me," he says to Henry as he slides in sideways to the middle seat.

Now that he is closer, Henry sees he is quite an old man. He has silver hair and shallow lines all over his face. Henry estimates he is in his eighties. He smells like old dusty books and he even looks dusty, as if he's been left on a shelf and ignored. Color has abandoned his hair and skin.

He reaches in his pocket, pulls out nothing and looks confused.

He reaches in another pocket and accidently elbows Henry.

"Excuse me, I apologize. I'm looking for my phone," says the old man. "I need to make an important call you see; my children need me. So, odd I can't find it."

Henry looks at the man again. His face is familiar in a vague way that makes Henry squirm. He recognizes him from something. He can't get a grip on it. He stares at him.

The old man gives up looking for his phone and stares straight ahead.

"Did you give up?" says Henry.

The man turns and looks at Henry, but he seems confused. "Excuse me?" he says.

"Your phone?"

"Oh, thank you for reminding me, I'm expecting a very important call." He repeats the process of looking in his pockets. "You know, the children are dear to me. I just want them to be happy."

He says it like a sales pitch he's said many times before.

On hearing the word, child, Henry thinks of his son, Timothy. Though he is now six years old Henry sees him as a baby. Impractically small and defenseless squirming around and whining. This memory does not dissipate. His thoughts focus and become his own. Something inside him that was off is on again and he's filled with questions, the loudest being, where is my son?

This is not right. That's what the screaming man wanted to say and he would have been right.

8.

Peter Bauman closes the door to car four once again. Getting them all back in their seats after that ordeal feels like a small victory. Very small. During training, he learned that some passengers may make a disturbance such as that one. The job of the vestibule attendant is to keep the rest of the car calm, and seated, while the front of the train handles it. He shouldn't have taken out the gun. He hopes no one saw. It's meant for only the most extreme situations. The problem is that to Peter it all feels extreme. He wonders how the rest of the train is doing. If any of the other vestibule attendants feel as he does. He wonders what the other passengers are like. Are they all so, disturbing? He takes his seat.

They're getting farther and farther away from civilization. A small road is in the distance and Peter sees a pickup truck driving along the same direction as the train. The sun reflects off it and Peter squints. It's so far away he can't tell the color. He imagines he is driving it. He's heading to town to pick something up, a piece of furniture maybe. He listens to the radio, something local.

He owned a truck once. He bought it used and put his company's name on the side. "Bauman's Greenhouse and Nursery". He sold anything you could want, at any time of year you could want it. He loved to take cuttings and root them off season in his greenhouse. He considered it a great display of his natural skill. Though his biggest sellers were lavender plants and peace lilies which people wanted for gifts. Plants have always been his hobby and he should have left it that way. He ran it like a hospital and the plants were his patients. He mourned each death, celebrated each birth. When the English ivy failed to sell he couldn't bring himself to toss it. He fed and watered them, repotted them when needed. No one came for them. They outlived his business which didn't last the year.

When it went under he loaded the plants he couldn't sell into his truck and took them back to his home. All except for a single knobby bundle of bamboo which he planted behind a shed on the empty lot. An act of vandalism unlike him. The plant is incredibly invasive and practically impossible to get rid of. By the following year the whole field was tightly packed straws of bamboo hindering anyone else from easily using that land again.

Two years have passed since his business failed. His debt has grown and he can't keep a job. This one was supposed to be different. Now that he's here on the train, surrounded by people so out of it that they break down and hurt themselves, he can no longer pretend that he can work for this company. He shouldn't have taken this job. He's bad at it and he's happy to be bad at it.

Without anything to look forward to, life can drag on. That's how Peter has felt for many years, but in this moment, he looks forward to quitting this job the second the train pulls in.

They pass a small gas station. They must be getting close to the next town. The last town until they arrive.

"Approaching the final stop," says Lewis, confirming Peter's suspicion.

At every stop there have been a handful of protesters and observers, sometimes even the passengers' families, but this stop is different. The streets are full of people. More than could possibly live in a town this size. They are only picking up three passengers, but one of them is well known. The people hold up signs that contradict each other.

'Burn in hell'

'Save their souls'

'An eye for an eye'

'Tell the truth'

Peter doesn't know exactly what the signs mean, he has purposely avoided learning about the passengers knowing it would not be productive for his work here. One thing he does know is that all these people are wasting their time. No one on the train, or running the train, will care what they say and the passengers won't understand. Though he respects them for trying.

The train stops and Peter opens the door. He sends two of them to car three and one to car four. Despite his attempts to stay out of the loop Peter recognizes the old man he sends to car four. Everyone knows about him.

The old man looks at Peter right in the eyes and says, "thank you sir."

Peter closes the door the very second the old man passes through. He sits back in his seat. Only a handful of hours now.

9.

His whole life Henry never wanted anything. Not in the same way as other people want things. As a child people asked him what he wanted to be when he grew up. He didn't particularly care. When it was time to choose his major in college he chose zoology for several practical reasons, none of which had anything to do with having an interest in the field. When he asked a woman to marry him it was because he didn't want to live alone and he thought she would say yes. Then he agreed to have a child because she wanted one. His life has always been about following rules and making calculations to ensure comfort.

When his son was born it was the first time he ever wanted something. He didn't know it until the moment the child was placed in his arms. He spent the infancy trying to figure out what it was that made Henry love him so deeply. He never came up with any particularly insightful answer, but it didn't matter why. It had already happened. He wanted the baby to be safe and strong and Henry was frightened every day that he wouldn't be able to provide what he needed. When he discovered his wife felt the same way it endeared him to her in ways he hadn't felt before. They became an efficient team, a loving family. When she died it was left up to Henry. He didn't mind doing it. He liked it and was good at it.

Sitting on the train and not knowing where his son is creates a unique kind of pain which Henry has never experienced. Henry stares straight ahead. If someone is watching him, and Henry is sure someone is, they would not know anything in him has changed. They wouldn't know he has caught on. He looks as clueless as he did a second ago because really, he is. He hasn't gained any kind of great perspective. He hasn't even learned anything tangible. He thinks he is stuck on this train, that if he asks to get off at the next stop he wouldn't be allowed. He also believes he's been drugged. He lost his peace of mind and gained nothing in return. He feels jealous of the untroubled people around him. He turns to the two men sitting next to him. They look abnormal, too stiff, too still, like manikins.

"Benjamin," says Henry, not so much to get his attention, but because he remembers it now. "Ben," he corrects himself.

Ben turns towards Henry but his eyes are unfocused.

"Hello Ben," says Henry. "Do you remember me?"

Ben tries to get up. Henry puts his hand on his shoulder to keep him seated.

"Don't get up. I think they watch us."

"They watch?" says Ben, "Henry."

"Yes," says Henry, happy to have a companion in this.

"We can't lea," says Ben.

"What?"

"We. Can't. Leag." says Ben slowly.

We can't leave. Some words are harder to say than others when you have no lips. "What do you—"

An overhead announcement interrupts Henry. This sudden and unprecedented noise makes Henry jump and his heart shakes his chest.

"Attention passengers of car four. At this time, we would like to invite you all to the dining car for your dinner. Just three cars ahead of you. Come on down!"

The sliding door flies open and Bauman stands on the other side looking worn out. People filter out of their seats and head towards the door.

Henry considers trying to talk to Bauman about what's going on, but he isn't sure he wants to reveal himself. He would probably frighten him anyway.

"The dining car is the third car down," says Bauman without lifting his eyes off the floor. "We ask that you please move quietly, some people in the other cars are sleeping."

Henry stands up.

The old man pushes past him. "I'm starving," he says.

Henry and Ben start down the aisle. Caroline joins behind them and they enter the next car. It has fewer people than car four and most of them are asleep. If it wasn't for all the disturbances Henry may have simply slept through the whole trip too.

"Do you know what is going on?" says Henry to Caroline without fully turning around. He walks forward slowly. He looks at the people as they walk by in case he can learn something from them. They are fairly unremarkable.

"I know we have to get out of here. That's all I know," she says.

"How?"

The next door opens and a man dressed in the expected train uniform stands by. His name tag reads Feightner.

"One more car up," says Feightner.

"It won't be easy, the train seems pretty secure," says Caroline once they are far enough away from Feightner.

"Guns," says Ben.

"We have to take their guns," reiterates Caroline as if the intention of the word was understood only by her.

This idea makes Henry very uncomfortable. He forgets himself and turns around, "and then what? If we got the guns?"

"Then we would have control of the train. We could stop it," says Caroline.

The ideas that have been floating around Henry's head are to try and talk to the man in charge then demand an answer, or to write an S.O.S. sign and stick it in a window. Stealing guns and taking control of the train had not crossed his mind.

They are now in car two. Henry notices a man. Like most people on the train he is fast asleep and is dressed the same. However, he looks like no one Henry has ever seen before. His skin is pink and hairless and alternatively too loose and too tight. Around his neck and elbows it lies in loose piles, but it stretches tight around his forehead and across his hands. His nails look to be an inch long and are solid white. Henry thinks of an article he once read about nail color as an indication of health, but he can't remember white being mentioned. Then again, he can't remember the article very well at all.

"I see you've noticed our resident freak," someone says to him. It's Mick, Henry's acquaintance from the platform. He stands up from his seat and walks into the aisle, blocking Henry's way. "His name's Roland. Gross huh? So, how you doing?"

"What?" says Henry, too distracted to keep up. "I can't talk."

"But you are talking," says Mick. "You're talking fine, that's more than most people here can do. So, you remember anything?"

Henry is frightened by the blunt question. The same topic he felt the need to whisper about, Mick can just blurt out. "Do you?" says Henry.

"What, talk? Sure, I do," says Mick laughing hard and loud. "Hey, they brought us in there a while ago, don't even bother with the food. It's shit."

"Do you remember things?" says Henry, unable to come up with a better way to ask the question.

"Well, I know where we are going."

"Where?" Henry wishes he would quiet down and get to the point.

"If we're lucky, we're all going to hell," he laughs.

Henry sighs. He's not sure what he expected.

"Really though, I don't think there is a person on this train who doesn't deserve it." Mick stares straight at Henry.

Henry looks over at the man with the fingernails, Roland. He looks like he crawled <u>out</u> of hell.

Henry takes a step closer to Mick and whispers. "Do you know what's happening here?"

Mick smiles. "I never know what's going on, I just try to enjoy it. Relax man." Mick goes back to his seat. "The food's shit but a man's gotta eat."

A train employee with a tag that says Phillips steps into the car. He is tall and broad and has a bald and shiny head. He has presumably come to see what the delay is.

"This way please," he says calmly before leaning against the doorway.

Henry enters the dining car. It is arranged like a casual dining room. Rows of tables line the car, each with four chairs. Everything is made of plastic and fastened to the floor. Henry takes a seat at an empty table. Caroline and Ben sit across from him and the old man sits next to Henry.

Philips closes the door and stands in front of it with his arms crossed. He looks like a bouncer at a club.

"How is everybody doing today?' says the old man cheerily without actually looking at anyone.

He is confused, Henry ignores him. He thinks about what Mick said. He suspects Mick knows more than he says but who can tell with that guy. Though Mick telling him to relax bothers him. He hears the critique quite often and has found that when people tell him to relax what they mean is, act in a way that makes me more comfortable.

"It is a lovely day, isn't it?" blathers the old man.

Henry considers Ben and Caroline's idea. The guns. It seems a very unlikely plan. There are too many variables and Henry is not interested in risking his life. Not when this could all be some misunderstanding.

Now that he has thought about it, he sees the plan has no merit. They could ambush Bauman and take his gun but whoever else is on this train will see it and they will have gained no advantage.

"It won't work," says Henry, deflated even though he didn't like the plan.

"I'm mighty hungry," says the old man.

He is getting obnoxious.

"Where are you from?" says Caroline to the old man. She teases him.

"Well, that's funny, I can't . . ."

Henry watches the man closely. He looks at the strange faces around him then out of the window a minute. He stares at nothing, taking in no details and tries to think of an answer to the question. Tries to think why he doesn't know the answer to the question. His eyes bulge slightly, a vein in his forehead pulses, and he looks down at his hands. Then suddenly, he relaxes. His shoulders lower, his face smooths and he says, "I'm mighty hungry."

The front door opens and three men walk in holding plates of food. Through the door Henry can see a simple kitchen. It consists of mostly cupboards and counter space. Secured to the wall are three microwaves. Henry is reminded of something else Mick said. "The food is shit."

The waiters walk the room silently placing pre-assembled plates in front of each person. They go back to the kitchen and come out with cups and pitchers of water. This is not like any other service Henry has received. He feels as though he has done something wrong to have ended up here. When the waiter comes to his table Henry watches him pour the four cups of water. He wears the same uniform as everyone else who works on the train, but without the name tag and with the addition of a black apron tied around his waist. He has red patchy hair and a face that looks as if it has been perpetually sun burnt. Before he walks away Henry touches him on the arm.

The waiter pulls his hand away and shakes his sleeve like a spider has crawled in it.

"I'd like to order a soda," says Henry.

The waiter looks at Henry as if he wants to hit him, then he leaves without saying anything. He hears Phillips quietly laugh.

Henry and Phillips looks at each other. Henry lets his eyes relax. He looks through Phillips instead of at him. This is what the staff on this train expects from the passengers.

Henry looks down at what has been served. A slab of meatloaf drowned in gravy and a roll. The old man is already well into his meal and enjoying himself. Caroline has moved hers around the plate and Ben stares at his.

"Do you think it's safe?" whispers Caroline.

"I don't know." Henry takes a bite anyway. It is cold in the middle and dry on the outside. "I think if they were going to drug this they would make it taste good." Henry proceeds to eat what he can stand.

Ben goes to work eating the food. Henry has never realized how important lips are to mastication. Ben places food on his tongue and closes his teeth around it. He leans his head back and like a baby bird lets the food slide down his throat. This method is not entirely foolproof but he does it with no hesitation or self-consciousness.

The waiters come back in and clear plates.

Henry can hear Philips says quietly, "ending meal."

Henry remembers when he first boarded and talked to Bauman. He heard that sharp noise and saw him grab his ear. They are communicating with each other on the train. It makes Henry furious that they talk about them like this. Henry doesn't know what to do, he can't think of any great plans but the idea of going back to car four with no information and no progress sickens him.

Henry's life has been, by his own design, relatively free of challenges. By having no strong desires or needs and being willing to go with the flow and follow the rules, Henry's life has been smooth. Not unlike this train in fact, diligently sliding along the tracks. The main exception was the unexpected death of his wife. This was Henry's first real challenge. This event taught Henry something interesting about himself which is that in times of stress or conflict, he is not a great man. A life of simple straightforward decisions and low expectations had not prepared him for difficulty.

Henry watches the waiters when he notices one clears a plate that hasn't been touched. The meatloaf lies in its bed of congealed gravy and the roll wobbles. Henry recognizes the man. He is the one who didn't help Henry pick up his coat, the same one who had no reaction to a man being carried out screaming. Henry thought he was a strange individual, but now that he knows a little bit more, he can see he is under the influence of something. This man can't stand up for himself, he can't even eat. For whatever reason, this particular injustice makes Henry get up from his seat.

"Hey." He walks over to the waiter. He stands too close to him and says, "he hasn't finished eating. Put his plate back."

The waiter says nothing and continues to carry the plate away.

This is the kind of irrational thing Henry does when he is upset. He doesn't care about this man in the slightest. He doesn't know his name or anything about him and has no interest in ever knowing these things, but because he is upset he acts irrationally. The man, who is more worried about embarrassing himself than helping himself is, at this moment, gone.

Henry speaks louder, "he's not done."

Without moving from the doorway Phillips says casually, "he's done alright? Sit down."

Henry ignores Phillips. He just keeps looking at the waiter, who stares back at him. Ben and Caroline watch from their seats. They must think he's crazy.

"Take it away," says Phillips.

The waiter turns to leave.

"Hey!" yells Henry. He shoves the waiter and he drops the plate. He grabs the wall to balance himself. The meatloaf makes an unappetizing slap as it hits the ground. Henry recognizes it, it's the same sound made by freshly ripped off flesh. It reminds him of his favorite tiger, who had a tendency to rip and toss the flesh into the air all in one swift movement. For her the process of ripping and destroying a carcass was as important as the sustenance it provided.

The waiter is clearly mad but he doesn't speak. Phillips laughs quietly.

Henry grabs the waiter by his shirt and shakes him. Ignoring the pain in his injured arm he whispers, "why are you doing this?"

Philips is still laughing. The waiter laughs too.

"It's under control," says Phillips. "They don't ever seem to understand. They have no control over this situation, but they're dumb enough to think they do."

Henry shakes the waiter again. "What is he talking about? Who is he talking to?"

The waiter opens his mouth wide laughing.

Henry pushes him to the ground, his fists full of the waiter's shirt.

"Hey, I think they can work themselves up as much as they want, I don't really give a shit about the comfort of their trip. This is all a joke. They're just a bunch of animals. What's that you always say Craig? Herding cattle?"

The waiter practically rolls on the ground he laughs so hard. Henry kneels over him. The waiter's right arm is twisted under his body and Henry leans his weight on him. There is a subtle popping noise and the waiter stops laughing.

Henry recognizes this sound too. The sound of bone breaking within flesh. An entirely different sound than a bone breaking outside of flesh. The waiter screams. Henry gets up and steps back. He had not planned on breaking his arm, he just wanted them to listen to him.

Phillips walks towards Henry. Ben cuts him off. He picks up a cup and smashes it into Phillips head. It's made of plastic but the force makes him stumble. Ben punches him in the gut and he falls to the ground.

The door opens and Feightner, the guard from car two enters. He heads straight to Ben but Caroline intervenes. She grabs him around the throat and jabs him in the eyes with her fingers. Henry is shocked at their quick reactions.

Mick walks into the vestibule and stands at the dining car door. "Hey what's the ruckus? You're having a party and you didn't invite me?" He looks around and laughs. "This is what you're into huh Henry?"

Henry doesn't know what to do now. A man at his feet writhes in pain with a broken arm thanks to him. Two other men are on the ground because of his new friends and still Henry doesn't know what's going on, or why any of this is happening. He wishes he had come up with a plan instead of getting caught up in it.

Mick stands in the vestibule, takes it all in and laughs in his way.

Roland, the man Henry noticed on his way to the dining car steps past Mick and enters.

"Uh-oh, here comes freak show," says Mick. "He's got some plans I bet."

He moves smoothly and calmly through the car toward something specific. Henry can't take his eyes off him. His pink hairless skin glows in the fluorescent lights and he walks steadily toward Feightner, who reels and is blinded by Caroline; his hands cover his eyes.

Though Henry sees animal characteristics in all people, Roland is quite obviously rodent-like and the longer Henry looks at him the more he starts to believe this literally.

As Roland gets nearer, Caroline moves away.

Roland pounces on Feightner. It's a quick and simple movement. Predator to prey. He knocks him to the ground, puts one hand around his throat and with the other rips open his shirt. He lets go of his throat and Feightner gasps. He can't see, he can barely breathe. He kicks his legs and waves his arms. He lands a few lucky blows on Roland's back, but it doesn't help his situation. Roland uses his long white nails to cut him open. He draws thin red lines on his chest turning his skin to confetti.

Everyone watches. Roland takes two fingers and pinches a piece of skin. He pulls it up and admires it in the air. It looks like a beautiful piece of ribbon, red and delicate. Roland opens his mouth wide, pops in the ribbon of skin and holds it there. He savors it, he moves it around his mouth and feels it with his tongue and then he swallows it.

Roland pops a second piece of Feightner's skin in his mouth and the car explodes in noise Gasps and screams clash against each other and fill the room. Cries of disgust and pleas for help ricochet off the walls.

Henry has seen many different kinds of carnivores eat and has made a study of their individual quirks and preferences. He has personally fed a variety of live animals to his large cats and taken a great amount of pleasure in watching the choices they make. Henry can watch a tiger he knows well, a tiger he has become close to, and when he feeds it living meals he can see something take it over. A wild tiger, even one in captivity has hunting instincts. Beautiful and natural instincts. Roland's hunting instincts are warped and disgusting. Unnatural. This man is feral and he cannot be rehabilitated.

Roland swallows another piece of Feightner's skin. Henry throws up. The room smells like blood and sweat when a new smell is introduced. Something unique but familiar to Henry. He looks around for a source. The smell is painfully sweet. The surface of it is artificial strawberries but underneath there is something rotten and rancid. It makes Henry light headed.

The car is suddenly silent. A man behind Henry falls down.

Phillips is on his hands and knees. He yells, "wait," and tries to get up but he falls over like a drunk.

Henry's eyes blur. His legs tingle. He almost falls over but catches himself on a table. He tries to walk but his legs go out and he goes down. He hits his face on the edge of a chair and falls. He is paralyzed. He can feel himself slipping out of consciousness.

The car is silent.

Henry was right. Getting off this train won't be easy.

10.

The door opens and a waiter brings in two plates of food. He hands them to Craig and Lewis.

"How's it going in there?" asks Lewis.

"It's going fine. Just brought in the last ones, car four, then we can start cleaning up."

"They were a little restless earlier but they should be fine now," says Lewis.

The waiter leaves and the door closes behind him.

"Those waiters are freak-ay," says Craig.

"Yeah, where do these people come from?" says Franny.

"I don't know. Where did you guys come from?" says Lewis.

Lewis knows exactly what they mean though he can't say so. Only a handful of positions on this train require experience in the field. Lewis, Franny, and Craig have three of them. The general train staff positions are mainly unskilled and they attract a certain kind of person. People who can be away from their homes for days at a time. People who have little education, who don't mind a somewhat dangerous and atypical work environment. People who are willing to take little money for the job. You end up with people like Bauman who are entirely unsuited, or someone like the waiter who just came in, odd and quiet. It doesn't make for the most cohesive team. Lewis has plans to change some of the hiring practices if he moves up in the company.

Lewis takes a big bite of his meatloaf, "I think this is an all-time low," he says.

"This is bad," says Craig.

Franny opens her thermal lunch bag and takes out a large plastic container of salad.

"That's what you brought? Rabbit food?" says Craig.

"I'm not trying to weigh as much as this train like some people," she says, looking over her shoulder at Craig.

"What this?" says Craig, grabbing his gut. "This is all muscle. I've practically got a six pack."

"A six pack of rolls," says Lewis.

"Oh! Boss man. Thought you would be on my side," says Craig.

"Can we cut out this boss man stuff?" says Lewis.

"Hey boss, we've got some action in the dining car," says Franny.

"Of course." Lewis turns and looks at the screen. "What the hell—" he presses the button on his headset, "Phillips, get that under control now."

"It's under control," says Phillips, "They don't ever seem to understand. They have no control over this situation, but they're dumb enough to think they do."

"Phillips, this is unacceptable," says Lewis.

"Hey, I think they can work themselves up as much as they want, I don't really give a shit about the comfort of their trip. This is all a joke. They're just a bunch of animals. What's that you always say Craig? Herding cattle?"

Craig rolls over to look at the screen. "What is he thinking?"

"He's making the situation worse," says Franny,

"Send in Feightner from two," says Craig.

"Feightner, I need you to get in the dining car now," says Lewis into the headset, "I need you to get it under control."

Feightner appears in Lewis' ear, "I can lend a hand but car two is already a little on edge. I don't want to keep them alone too long,"

A waiter is pinned on the ground and starts to scream. Phillips is hit on the head and knocked out.

"Get in there now," says Lewis.

"Want me in there?" says Craig, his fingers twitch. He's barely able to hold still.

"Let's see what Feightner can do. I don't want to open more doors than I have to."

Lewis and Craig have always disagreed on how to handle situations like this. Craig likes to jump right in, get his hands dirty. Lewis likes to go by the rules. Every situation is mapped out and Lewis intends to follow the map.

"The doors to car two are open," says Franny. "Someone pried them open."

"How the hell did they do that? Close them."

"I'm going in," says Craig.

"No."

"Why the hell not?"

"We have two passengers from car two entering the dining car," says Franny.

"Lewis," says Craig.

"No. I don't want this to spread. There are already too many involved, we have procedures for this."

"What do you want to do then?" says Craig.

"Feightner's down, he's injured," says Franny.

"What is he doing to him?" says Craig.

Roland cuts into Feightner.

"Shit!" says Franny.

"Dose them," says Lewis.

Franny types the command. "They'll be down in forty-five seconds."

Lewis opens the door and enters the service car followed by Craig.

"I need everyone's attention. There's been an incident in the dining car. An Event C, you all know what that means. We need medical immediately, then we'll need all hands to help move them back home."

The volume in the car rises as the workers get up and gather necessary things and prepare to leave.

"Hey!" Lewis waves his arms. "I want to remind everyone the priority of all priorities is to be discreet. We all know how contagious straw moments can be and we don't want this spreading. Okay, get to work."

Craig leaves with two members of the medical team. The rest leave in pairs forty-five seconds apart so not to attract attention from the other passengers. Lewis goes back to watch on the monitor.

He sees the medical team arrive at the dining car. Craig points them to Feightner. They lay him on a stretcher and wrap him in a body bag to carry him safely to the service car. As the rest of the team arrives they break up in pairs and together pick up the passengers. They shake them to wake them up a little so that with the help of the two team members they can stumble back to their seats.

Medical arrives in the service car with Feightner. They set him on the ground near the medical equipment at the front of the car and unzip the bag. His wounds make the room smell like raw meat.

"No major organs are involved," says the medic. "He didn't get through the muscle."

"He was only interested in the skin," says Lewis. It isn't necessary for him to know anything about the passengers, but sometimes curiosity gets the best of him or he learns by word of mouth like everyone else.

"We need to control the bleeding and the pain until we arrive. He has a long road ahead of him, lots of healing to do but I think he'll be okay," says the medic.

He has blood splatter all over his face and shoulders, but his abdomen has the major damage. He has slash marks all over as if someone took a rake to his stomach. Strips of skin and tissue hang by threads across his body and off the table like spaghetti.

"Lewis, could you make sure they have a helicopter waiting to take him to the hospital when we arrive. He'll need to be taken straight there."

"Yes of course."

Lewis ranks all the violent events he witnessed at this job. He moves this one into the number three position bumping the time someone ripped off their own pinky finger. He's exceedingly happy that Feightner isn't going to die. Since they started using the trains there have only been four deaths and only one while Lewis has been in charge and that was a passenger. He pats Feightner on the shoulder and goes back to his work station. He closes the door behind him. It's time for him to make a call he has been dreading since he instructed Franny to dose the passengers.

He takes a cell phone out of his desk drawer and dials.

After a single ring the line is answered.

"Bergen."

"This is Lewis. We've had an Event C during feeding with one major personnel injury. We're going to need a helicopter evacuation at arrival."

"Hold."

The line clicks back on and a different voice speaks. "Event C are you fucking kidding me?"

Lewis dreaded this. The first voice was Bergen, the second Vanveen. Both are Lewis's supervisors. Bergen is Head of Security, the same side of things as Lewis. Vanveen comes from research and doesn't quite understand what Lewis does. On top of that he's a real jerk who feels entitled to a certain amount of respect Lewis doesn't feel like giving him, and has never received in return.

The first time he met Vanveen he was introduced as 'the genius inventor of the compound that keeps us in business.' His hand was sticky when they shook and Vanveen said to him 'it's your job not to screw it all up.' Lewis laughed politely to what he thought was a joke and has since learned was actually his personality. Every time Lewis sees Vanveen he has food on his face or clothes. Lewis feels a little nauseous just thinking about what filth Vanveen is covered in at this moment.

"I don't believe this," says Vanveen.

He's being dramatic.

"Were you tracking straw moments?"

Straw moment is a conveniently cute name the researchers gave to the biggest flaw of their beloved compound. It is the moment when something happens to a passenger that brings them back to reality. An event jars them, or a memory surfaces and they slip out of the drug's control. The researchers call it the straw moment as in, the straw that broke the camel's back. Though Lewis prefers the term Craig has coined, "that big, huge, gaping flaw in Vanveen's dumb ass compound."

"We've talked about this, we cannot track the straw moments. I wouldn't even know how to do that," says Lewis.

"You could if you got off your fat asses and paid attention," says Vanveen.

Says the man whose wide load is constantly parked at his desk chair.

"We can talk later, right now Lewis needs to get back to the train," says Bergen. "We will let you get back, Lewis. Just a reminder though to not dose that group again or we won't be able to hit them at intake."

"Don't dose any of them. Just do your job," says Vanveen.

"I understand," says Lewis, "and the helicopter?"

"I'll arrange it. How is he?" says Bergen.

"He's going to be okay."

"Glad to hear it, goodbye."

Lewis hangs up the phone, he tosses it back in the drawer and slams it shut. Lewis's ambitions to move up in this company have required him to embrace, or at least outwardly embrace the use of the compound. Though as someone with a security background he is fully aware of how dangerous it is.

"Craig wants to know what to do with Phillips," says Franny.

Lewis rolls over to the monitor. "How is he medically?" he says into the headset.

"Medics bandaged his face, say he'll need stitches at some point, but otherwise he's fine," says Craig.

"Give him a seat in car four. I don't want him up here."

"Got it."

"How's Vanveen?" says Franny.

"Oh, he's great. We're going out for drinks after if you wanna come," says Lewis.

"Oho, boss man makes a joke. You're alive in there after all."

11.

Henry is at work. It's the early morning shift and he is doing his rounds. He goes to all the exhibits and takes breakfast orders. He unlocks the gate and walks into the jaguar exhibit. It's one of the zoo's largest with wall-to-wall foliage and a variety of climbing structures. Henry wanders around for what feels like hours until he finds her. The jaguar sits on a rock near the front of her enclosure, she squints her eyes against the sun. Henry climbs over and under branches to get to her. Even though it's early, the zoo is packed and a crowd of people watch. Children squeal and cry trying to get a better view of the regal jaguar. He smells fresh popcorn and French fries and hears a snow cone machine shaving ice.

Henry is next to the jaguar now, he holds an empty tray and an order pad.

"What can I get you today ma'am?" he asks her.

She turns slowly towards him and with a raised nose she flicks her eyes up and down evaluating him. Unimpressed, she turns away.

"Excuse me, what would you like to eat?" He reaches out and touches her coat. It's thick and soft. It feels like touching a cloud.

She flinches and snarls, disgusted by his touch.

"Sorry, I—" begins Henry.

She pounces on him. He feels her teeth on his face and her claws in his arm. She drags Henry, still alive, up a tree and drapes him over a limb. She feeds off his body shaving the meat off his bones with her evolutionarily perfected teeth. She grips his arm and shakes him hard.

The shaking train wakes Henry up. He is startled and disoriented.

He blinks to adjust to the light. He clears his throat and stretches. His muscles are sore and his head pounds. What a terrible nap. He doesn't feel well rested, he feels worse. He turns to the window to figure out how long he was asleep. The sun hovers above the horizon as if staring at him. He grabs the water bottle from the pouch and sips. His throat is raw and he has a sick acidic taste in his mouth. He drinks more water and thinks about an article he once read about public transportation and the spreading of germs. He must be getting sick. He can't wait to get home and go to bed.

He touches a spot on his face that hurts. His right cheek just below his eye. It stings when he touches it and he can feel a scab. This surprises him. He can't remember how he got the injury. He looks around the train car and everyone is asleep. He tries to think about what happened before he fell asleep but all he gets is an instant headache and nausea.

His stomach twists and bubbles. He puts his hands on his knees and breaths deeply. He tries to think about something besides his stomach. The sun is bright and harsh and wears him down. He feels an urge to run to the bathroom, but can't gather the energy. He just needs a good meal, something hearty to settle his stomach. This thought makes him laugh. It's straight out of his parents' mouths. As a boy and even as an adult the importance of a good meal was discussed almost daily as the key to living well. Every day, hours were spent preparing and discussing their meals. On weekends, they would drag him to the farmers market and discuss the benefits of eating organic. One day Henry figured out why they talked about food so much. It was the only thing the three of them had in common. It was safe and there was no exhausting the subject since they had to eat every day. Henry played along though he never had a great interest in food. He ate whatever they put in front of him, but the concept of eating well always stuck with him. Not just in his personal life but with his work as well. No one at the zoo cares more about what those cats eat than Henry. He works overtime to ensure they are well fed and healthy. He even started his own program.

The Greeneville City Zoo has a fairly successful enrichment program. Enrichment can be almost anything that mentally stimulates a zoo animal. An animal that spends its life in a cell, even a very expensive, extensively maintained and impeccably decorated cell can become frustrated and an animal can quickly deteriorate. They express their frustration in unhealthy and sometimes disturbing ways. One of the chimpanzees, Darla will swing her head from side to side faster and faster until she falls over, sometimes banging her head into the wall and knocking herself out. The sun bears spend all day vomiting little piles of white foam onto the rocks then licking it back up and repeating.

Enrichment activities include freezing an animal's favorite foods in a bucket of ice, or placing new toys around the exhibit. They are ways of distracting a wild animal from its life sentence. These kinds of exercises are fine for the polar bears and elephants but Henry's tiger requires more. She is too smart for that other stuff and Henry could not sit around and watch his beloved friend deteriorate.

His personalized enrichment program is to feed her live animals. This lets her exercise her natural hunting instincts. The whole ordeal is entirely against zoo regulations so he has to make sure no one finds out. After work, he finds prey for his friend and late at night when the zoo is empty except for a couple of dispassionate security guards, he delivers the gift. In a way, it is a gift for both of them.

The train rocks on its tracks and Henry throws up into a motion sickness bag. In the few minutes, afterwards Henry feels good. He looks at the people sitting nearby. The old man in the middle seat sleeps and breathes loudly through his gaping mouth. The man at the window seat is far more interesting. He's also asleep and he rests his mutilated face against the window. His long greasy hair hangs in his eyes. Henry observes him closely trying to think of how such a thing could happen to someone. He thinks of his own mutilation, his arm. He looks at it. He's lucky that in long sleeved shirts he looks normal. He's not sure what he would do if he had to wear his scars on his face.

Most of Henry's trauma is between his elbow and shoulder. He lost a lot of the muscle and can only move it because of a series of surgeries. It was a silly mistake. He got too close to the tiger's cell during feeding. He crossed the red line on the ground that marks the place not to cross and the tiger noticed. She was over stimulated. She reached her massive paws through the steel bars and cut his arm as easily as slicing a pear. Her strength was amazing. He fell to the ground and his arm bled badly. It was a stupid mistake and he only blames himself.

Henry looks at the man's face and is dying of curiosity. Maybe if Henry tells Ben his story he will feel comfortable sharing his own.

Ben. His name is Ben. Henry is sure of it but can't explain why. He has never met him. As far as he remembers.

His moment of clarity is over and he feels sick again. His forehead sweats and his body feels cold. He takes the motion sickness bag out of the chair next to him. His body tightens and releases, he hunches over and puts the bag to his mouth. His abdomen is sore from the effort. He looks around for a garbage can. He grabs the two bags and walks to the front. He presses a button and it buzzes back at him, waking the woman in the front row. Her name is Caroline. They stare at each other a moment. She doesn't seem to recognize him. He doesn't recognize her either; he just knows her name.

The door opens and a man says, "I can take that." Henry hands him the bags and walks back to his seat. He isn't feeling well at all.

12.

Jamie Vanveen's head pounds and not metaphorically. It feels as if there is a kick drum behind his eyes. He checks his bank balance. He writes down the exact amount to the penny and subtracts his estimated expenses. He does the math himself, then checks it with the calculator. If he lost his job today he'd have enough to last him just under a year. He wishes it was enough for a full year, it would make him feel better. This is a common exercise for Jamie who ever since being hired by SCG and starting work here at The Vault, has felt his situation to be fragile. He has never made this much money. He spent his whole career in laboratories drawing his salary from grants and fundraising which didn't always pay out regularly. He likes having this extra money, but the idea of someday not having it causes him great anxiety. He obsesses about it. He makes these calculations almost every day accounting for different life events. This habit is only made worse by the fact that he has virtually nothing to do at work all day. M-F, 8-5. This feeds the fear it could all end and gives him loads of time to reflect on it.

Jamie being hired was really about SCG purchasing the compound he invented, CP8+B2. It keeps this place and three others in business. Right after he finished it, when he was figuring out its potential, Jamie envisioned it being used for chemical warfare. Imagine being able to disarm an enemy using non-lethal methods.

Make them docile and suggestive, all with a vapor. But it was deemed too inconsistent.

Jamie opens his bottom desk drawer and takes out a box of éclairs from an Italian bakery he passes on his way to work. He buys a dozen every Monday and eats them throughout the week. They are nothing special but he likes the way they turn sour a little bit every day until Friday when they are tangy and tart.

He takes his first bite and his phone rings.

"This is Vanveen."

"We've got a call from the train."

Jamie recognizes Bergen's voice. Head of security for The Vault. Jamie has always liked him. He's smarter than he looks and he's one of the only people who listens to him.

"They just had an Event C. Thought you would want to be on the call."

"Yes, I would," says Jamie. An Event C is not the biggest deal but Jamie's heart rate picks up a little at the opportunity to criticize someone. Especially Lewis. The line clicks on and Jamie is connected, "Event C are you fucking kidding me?"

Jamie has always had a problem with Lewis and since his promotion he can barely tolerate him. He's supposed to be this great young man, and is expected to go far in the company. To Jamie he is just another meat head making him and his compound look bad by not effectively handling the train.

"Were you tracking straw moments?" says Jamie.

"We've talked about this, we cannot track straw moments. I wouldn't even know how to do that," says Lewis.

"You could if you got off your fat asses and paid attention," says Jamie. For a minute, he thinks maybe he's gone too far. He glances over at his financial calculations.

Bergen jumps in, "we will let you get back, Lewis. Just a reminder though to not dose that group again or we won't be able to hit them at intake."

Jamie can't help but to take one more jab.

"Don't dose any of them. Just do your job." He hangs up the phone.

Every passenger receives a dose of CP8+B2 prior to boarding and again at intake. Lewis has given them an extra dose because he couldn't control them. The real reason Jamie is so mad is because doing this makes it look as though the compound failed to keep the passengers in check.

Jamie redoes the math on his latest calculations. He hits a decimal point at the wrong moment and loses most of his fortune. He tosses the calculator to the far corner of his desk.

Jamie's contract is up in three months. He doesn't know if SCG will renew it and can't see why they would. They own the compound outright. He isn't allowed any money to adjust or experiment with it and they won't let him discuss his work with the public no matter how much media attention SCG and their trains get. He is effectively useless and invisible. He shoves the remainder of his éclair in his mouth, and licks his fingers.

Bergen walks up to Jamie's desk and leans against it. "You were pretty hard on him."

"He screwed up. What should I do? Bake him a cake?"

"He handled it exactly like he should have done," says Bergen.

"He should have caught it earlier," says Jamie.

Bergen rolls his eyes. "You have to understand what it's like for them on the train."

"How could I? I've never been allowed on one."

"I can arrange something," says Bergen with a smirk.

Even the idea of getting on one of those trains gives Vanveen a migraine.

"The bottom line is the compound wants to do its job, they just need to let it."

"You know it's not that easy. They can't just sit back and wait for the compound to kick in when people are getting hurt."

There was so much Jamie wanted to say to this. Who cares? So, what? Why should it matter? The fact that these people occasionally hurt each other doesn't bother him, and he doesn't understand why it bothers anyone. They deserve whatever they get. As far as he is concerned they are all specimens in the CP8+B2 experiment and to interfere with that is criminal. To step in and affect the outcome, to slow the research, all to save one of these animal's lives is utterly ridiculous. Jamie doesn't say any of that, he knows it would make him sound mean hearted and cruel. So, he says nothing. He tamps down his feelings and silences his opinions. Just another day at work.

"Anyway, I guess we'll talk about it later," says Bergen.

13.

Back in his chair Henry feels restless. Something eats at him. He clutches his arm and looks down the aisle. He feels trapped. He strokes his injured arm. The pain is grounding, but not enough. He gets up to walk the aisle. He goes to the back, leans against the wall for a minute then walks to the front. He trips over someone's leg. He turns to see who. It's a man he hasn't noticed before. He has huge broad shoulders and a shining cue ball head resting on his chest. Henry leans over and looks at his face. He has a bandage under the left side of his mouth and a crusty trail of blood down his chin. The sight of him is upsetting and Henry doesn't know why. He leaves the man and paces. He feels as if he will be consumed by this gnawing anxiety.

A woman in the front row gets up. She pulls her coat down from the overhead compartment and reaches her hands into the deep pockets and comes up empty. She lets the jacket fall to the ground. She pulls down a duffel bag and pulls everything out of it. Henry watches her. He's seen this before.

She looks over at him, "Ben."

"No. I'm Henry."

She walks past Henry and goes to Ben. She shakes him by the shoulders to wake him up. He jumps out of his seat and puts his hands on her face and stares at her for a long moment. She stares back. They look like mangy and beat up long lost lovers. Quite worse for the wear.

"Caroline."

Ben releases her face and walks into the aisle. "Henry," he says, as if they are old friends and he is happy to see him again. He pats Henry on the shoulder, then continues down the aisle until he reaches the bald man. He yanks the bandage off and reveals the wound. His bottom lip is hanging off, totally removed by about an inch and a half.

Ben looks at Henry, then Caroline. He laughs then pokes the liberated skin gently. Phillips moans quietly and twitches in his seat but he never opens his eyes.

"I can't believe they brought us all back here," says Caroline. "What do you guys remember? What happened after the dining car?"

"The dining car?" says Henry. The nagging discomfort has a face now. In a flash, it all comes to the surface of him. The things he did. How could he have behaved like that? He was such a fool. These people must hate him. He must have looked like a maniac. His body gets hot with embarrassment.

"I remember," says Ben.

He remembers how Henry acted.

"Everything," says Ben.

"Everything?" says Caroline.

"Before train."

"What? Really?" says Caroline.

Ben and Caroline smile at one another. Henry doesn't know what to say. He doesn't understand.

Towards the front of the train they hear the painful sound of metal against metal. For a moment Henry thinks there is something wrong with the train, but it continues. He hears the bellows of a familiar voice. Mick.

They are too far away, he can't make out any words, but he can hear several people yelling. Then a gunshot and silence.

"What the hell?" says another far away voice.

Henry can't tell what happens next but after a minute, or less maybe, he can hear people coming towards car four. He can hear them enter the vestibule. There is laughter then a muted thud. The door opens and Mick stands with a gun in each hand. Bauman is on the ground and bleeds from his head. He is unconscious and takes dying breaths.

Henry doesn't care about Bauman, he is obviously part of whatever scheme keeps him on this train, but looking at Mick in the doorway sporting two guns; he doesn't feel like the best man won. Bauman's eyes shoot open, they are wide and wet and he gasps for breath he'll never catch.

Mick steps over Bauman and enters the car. A young man that Henry doesn't recognize enters behind him. He must be in his early twenties. He looks like a nice, clean, ordinary young man, but Henry knows this must not be true because someone like that would not be with Mick.

Mick stomps into the car and looks around. He's just killed a man whose body is still cooling, and he doesn't seem to care. In fact, he barely even noticed. He's crazy, a monster, and now he's in Henry's car with two guns.

"Henry!" says Mick cheerily before continuing to look around.

"What are you doing?" says Henry, unable to take his eyes off the two guns.

"Oh these, don't worry. Look," he puts the muzzle of a gun to a passenger's temple. The passenger doesn't understand, he moves his head from side to side trying to get a better look at it. Mick pulls the trigger. The noise rattles the windows. Henry looks away to avoid the bloody scene but there isn't one. The man hasn't been shot.

"See, just blanks," says Mick. "Yeah I was surprised too. I wonder what else around here is fake." He continues down the aisle.

Henry moves past Mick and walks over to Bauman. His chest still moves slightly. His head is surrounded by a pond of dark blood and ringed by a clear fluid. Now that Henry's closer he can see the man was not shot. His skull is cracked from his hair line to the top center of his head. Henry looks around for a murder weapon. On the door handle that Bauman had been so careful to lock when they first boarded, there is a smear of blood. They must have bashed his head on the metal door.

Henry looks down at the dying man and feels a profound loss over the wasted body. At work one of his first and most important lessons was how to keep from wasting resources. How to use every part of an animal for one purpose or another. Bauman for example, could probably see his way to feeding two lions or up to four smaller African animals. This is no small thing. Henry could even trade Bauman's entrails, brain, and eyes to the woman who feeds the scavenging birds and maybe get some fish in exchange. That would be a fun treat.

"What's the deal with this creep?" says the young man who came in with Mick. He watches Henry linger over Bauman's body.

"That's my pal Henry. Don't be disrespectful," says Mick. "Don't mind him Henry, he's a funny kid."

"My name is Alex," says the young man, his arms crossed at his chest.

"Did you do this?" says Henry.

"Yeah," says Alex laughing it off. "Why was he a friend of yours or something?"

"No. But you didn't have to kill him," says Henry.

"Have to? Are you kidding?"

"Hey, Alex back off. He's not like that. He's a different kind of guy," says Mick.

"He doesn't look different," says Alex.

Henry takes great offense at this. He hopes very much he does look different.

14.

Peter Bauman lays on the ground in the vestibule thinking about his cat. Something is wrong with his head, it doesn't feel right and he can't move his body to figure it out. It hurt at first, just for a second. The moment his forehead hit the metal door handle, that hurt, then falling and hitting the back of his head on the ground that hurt too. After that it stopped. He realizes blood must be pooling around him. It feels warm and thick. He has never bled this much. He's never even gotten stitches or broken a bone. His first real injury in life and it kills him. He's admitted it now. He is dying. It makes him cry. Tears puddle around his eyes and blur his vision until they fall in large drops down his temples. He feels pathetic for crying, but no one else will, so why not have at it.

He wonders if he was anywhere else and had this injury if he would live. Say if he had fallen on an icy sidewalk and cracked his head and a good Samaritan called an ambulance, would he live? He suspects he would. Not that it matters. He knows from training that he will not live. To save him the train security would have to leave their bunker in the front of the train, walk all the way back here. Then they would have to deal with the people who did this to him, keep them at bay which they have failed to do this whole trip so they would probably have to kill them all. This would attract other passenger's attention and before you know it there would be a full out riot and the security team would be no match for them.

A man kneels over Peter. He recognizes him by his pathetic way of standing and his weak injured arm. The man stares at him in a way that makes Peter feel exposed. He wants to say something mean to him but finds he isn't able to talk. On second thought, that's okay. He doesn't want his last words to be hateful ones. Peter wonders if this man has intentions of hurting him. His eyes suggest so. Part of Peter wants to feel bad for these people on the train. The way SCG treats them, but looking up at this man, not to mention the ones that have killed him, he can't bring himself to even pity them. Finally, he stands up and goes away. Peter is happy to be alone again, he would rather do this alone.

In some ways, he is very glad to die. Death means freedom from the things that held him back all his life. His sentimentality, his homeliness, his aimless ambition, which is worse than no ambition, his suicidal cat, his bike with the flat tire, his rented home that smells like decades of paint and rotting wood. In many more ways, he is not happy to die. The parts of him that thinks he can make something of himself, that he can fix that bike, that keeping a cat alive is worth the trouble. Those parts are not happy to die.

Lying on the ground in the vestibule Peter is just about numb. The only thing he can feel is the train's vibration. It feels like a cat purring. Peter's cat never purred.

The cat. He should have let her die years ago. If the cat didn't want to live anymore, then what right has Peter to tell her otherwise? He knows that when he doesn't come home the cat will find a way to end her life. There's no one to take care of her anyway.

Peter wonders if he ever made anyone happy. Perhaps his mother in the beginning. Also, one time, a girl at the nursery when he showed her what a Venus fly trap is known for. Small things like that. Not real happiness. His life, despite the effort, has been incomplete and now that he has come face-to-face with the end of it, he doesn't feel like fighting. He doesn't want a second chance. A second chance would not make him a different or better person, he would make all the same mistakes. He wants an ending, sad and incomplete as it may be. Dying on this terrible train puts one thing in perspective. He can relax and be happy that unlike all these people, he never hurt anyone in his lifetime. He never caused pain or sadness.

Except for an empty lot brimming with bamboo, he'll leave the world no worse than he found it. From Peter's point of view, that's pretty good.

15.

"Hey, I recognize this guy." Mick points at Phillips who is still unconscious.

Mick walks over to him and shoves his head with the gun. He doesn't wake up. "This asshole is one of them," he says. He lifts his foot and steps heavily on Phillips crotch. His eyes open and bulge out of his head. His mouth opens wide and he gasps, but he doesn't scream and he doesn't make any attempt to defend himself. Mick lifts his foot and Phillips closes his eyes and his head flops back over.

"Poor guy can't hold his CP whatever, whatever," says Alex.

Mick laughs hysterically.

"CP?" says Henry.

"Oh yeah, I guess you don't remember all that," says Mick.

"C ee us ee two," says Ben.

"Dude, your face," says Alex.

"CP8+B2. He remembers things before the train," says Caroline.

Mick smiles at Caroline. "Does he huh? So, go on and tell us then."

Ben must understand what he means because he launches into a story.

"Aae ooolo," he says.

"You've gotta stop," says Mick. He walks over to Bauman and reaches in his pockets. He pulls out a pen and hands it to Ben. "Here man. I can't listen to you talk."

Ben seems to take pleasure from disgusting Mick. He pulls a motion sickness bag out from a chair pocket and writes on it. *Cut people like this.* He points to his face.

"What do you have against lips?" says Alex.

He writes, *they say lies.*

"Well big fucking surprise there," says Mick.

This conversation has gone entirely over Henry's head. These people are starting to scare him.

16.

Benjamin Croft was raised by a pair of well-meaning innocent bystanders. The kind of parents that ask a lot of questions but don't stick around to hear the answers. If they had stayed and listened they might have been impressed by his intelligence, they might have been frightened by his cruelty. On paper, he was the child they had wanted. Smart enough, athletic enough, handsome enough. The middling child of their dreams. Unfortunately, their lack of personal investment did not go unnoticed.

When Ben turned twelve the family moved to a new bigger, nicer, more expensive house. The move coincided with his parents each receiving promotions keeping them busy and absent. In this new neighborhood, they had an elderly neighbor who took it upon herself to mind Ben when no one was around. She invited herself over with baked goods. Ben found her intrusive but her parents told him to be polite and he did enjoy her baking. Before handing over her homemade treat she required a wet kiss that left him with a moist waxy purple stained mouth.

On one particular day, he arrived home to a note tacked to a box of Mac and cheese saying neither parent would be home for dinner. Having had his fill of lemon squares and Bundt cake Ben decided to end the daily nuisance of washing off purple lipstick and spit. When the doorbell rang that day, he didn't answer it. He waited for her to go back to her house and he followed her in. He selected a sharp knife from a block on the counter and grabbed her from behind by the neck. He pulled her to the ground and cut off the offending lips. The knife was sharp and he was quick, but precise. She had stopped moving about halfway through and never woke up. When he was done he wrapped the bloody purple lips in a cloth napkin and put them in his pocket. His hands were sticky with blood and lipstick so he washed them in the kitchen sink before he left but he couldn't remove the tacky purple stain under his fingernails. He looked at them proudly all night, happy that he took care of his own problem.

No one found her for three weeks and by then her cat had eaten most of her face and one of her eyes, so it was impossible to tell what Ben had done. Her death made sense to everyone. Just the timely natural death of an old woman. Ben had not considered what would happen to him if someone found out what he had done, but it seemed quite convenient that no one did. He kept the lips for a year in his bedside table, then he buried them in his front yard, though by then they looked more like shriveled up caterpillars than a body part. His mother watched him dig the hole from the kitchen window and she was happy to see him playing outside like a normal boy.

Throughout his schooling Ben had been told he had many problems. The source of all of them was his lack of interest in pleasing anyone, or caring what they thought. Most children do what is expected to please their teachers and parents and to not stand out, but Ben didn't care about that. He really, sincerely never cared. So, when he got bored at school, he left. When he wanted something, he took it. So much of a person's life is dictated by what they are supposed to do and simply by not doing those things he made waves.

When Ben reached his teens and started failing classes his parents were forced to involve themselves. Suddenly their easy-bake life required more attention than they were prepared to give. The attention and intervention of his parents was new and jarring but didn't change who he was. They soon abandoned the effort and left him alone. They made excuses to themselves about why he wasn't like the other boys in the neighborhood. It's a phase, he'll grow out of it, he's an artistic type. A free spirit.

When Ben was seventeen he fell in love with a homeless woman and brought her to live at his house. She was in her forties and had been homeless most of her life, even as a child. She spent her days outside the 7-11 holding out a paper cup as strangers walked by. Ben liked her immediately because she didn't expect anything from him. She held out that paper cup but whether a person put something in it or not she had the same reaction. She existed in a blankness he admired. One day Ben gave her a stolen packaged pastry and they started talking. He did most of the talking, which was new for him. They talked every day, and both of them unused to being listened to, fell in some version of love. He asked her to move in and she initially declined, saying she couldn't because his parents wouldn't approve. He went home that night and when they fell asleep he cut their throats. He didn't hate them, he actually felt very little for them, so he killed them quickly and cut off their lips afterwards. He saved them in a small wooden box of his mother's. He wasn't sure why he did that but he wanted to, so he did. He put their bodies in plastic storage boxes in the garage.

When she moved in it was the happiest day of his life. They lived together for two weeks and had a wonderful time. They had everything they could ever want. But when she found the bodies in the garage she did not handle it well. Ben tried to calm her. She wouldn't listen. They couldn't see eye to eye on this. He caught her trying to sneak out and his heart was broken. He couldn't bring himself to hurt her at first. He kept her for three days trying to convince her to stay, but in the end, he couldn't trust her and he couldn't kill her. If he couldn't have her, he needed at least a piece of her.

He let her get very drunk first, he thought it would help. He didn't want her to move around too much. He wanted to do a good job. She would have to live with it for the rest of her life. He took his time choosing a device and decided a simple razor would do the trick. Two quick cuts, the top and the bottom and it was done. He then did the same to himself. He was less precise, didn't even look in a mirror, but he was happy with the result. They couldn't speak to each other for weeks because of the pain, but just looking at her he felt unspeakably happy. He added the four pieces of flesh to his collection and the two of them healed together.

Three months later with pink and tender scar tissue outlined faces they broke in a routine. Ben tied them together at the wrist so they couldn't be separated. They adapted well until police came and took him away. He doesn't know who called them, maybe the paper delivery guy, or the gardeners. Maybe the neighbors or the plumber. When they took her from him he was truly sad. His one comfort was that he had been able to take something from her. Something that made her his forever.

17.

Ben's writing covers both sides of the bag and Henry doesn't understand a word of it. He tries hard to connect these dots.

"Dude, you didn't even try to hide it? Any of it?" says Alex.

Ben furrows his brow. He doesn't understand.

"He didn't think he had anything to hide," says Caroline.

"What happened to the girl?" says Mick.

Their conversation becomes white noise to Henry. It frightens him that everyone else, Caroline, Mick, and even Alex know more than him.

Not actually everybody. In fact, most of the people in the car and most of the people he saw throughout the train are worse off than him. He wonders how they calmly sit there despite everything that's happening. Not caring or even noticing the dead man in the vestibule or what these people are talking about.

"Do you feel bad for them, Henry?" says Mick.

"What's to feel bad about?" says Alex. "They earned their seats here."

"I wasn't talking to you," says Mick.

"What's wrong with them?" says Henry.

"They're just a bunch of sheep. Look, I could kill them easier than opening a can of beer. All I have to do is plug their little greasy noses. They wouldn't try to stop me." Mick pinches the nose of a nearby man.

"Stop it," says Caroline. "This isn't helping."

Mick lets go of the man's face. "Oh, sorry. Does the girl need some help?"

"My name is Caroline."

Mick holds out his hand. "Delighted."

Caroline folds her arms, rejecting the handshake.

"You're the only girly type here. What did ya do? Microwave your baby?" says Mick.

"No, I bet she cut off her husband's dick, blended it into a smoothie and fed it to him," says Alex.

"Don't mind him. He's a sick kid," says Mick. "He's this lousy thief, then one day he steals the wrong girl and before he can get across the border she swipes his own pocket knife, cuts off that finger there and runs off."

Alex shows off his right-hand index finger, half of which is gone.

"This idiot is so stupid, he goes back for her and is immediately arrested of course. It's a good thing though, if it wasn't the cops that got him it would have been the mob. I hear those eastern Europeans don't take kindly to late shipments." Mick's laughter fills the car.

"They would have loved her too, blond, blue eyes," says Alex.

"That's disgusting," says Caroline.

"Go on then, what about you?" says Mick. "I mean, if you even remember."

"I remember now," she says, looking over at Ben.

"So?" says Alex.

Caroline takes a breath.

18.

Caroline Rigby was her father's daughter. Apple of his eye and all that. Although she respected her mother greatly and loved her deeply, her father has always been her inspiration despite his dying when she was only a child. He was an artist and he taught her to be open to the world. To go beyond the superficial, to look, listen, and feel it. Early in his career he had gotten critical recognition for his sculpture but when he switched mediums the attention did not follow. He spent ten years, the whole length of time Caroline knew him, creating elaborate and highly detailed paper cut outs. He was an incredibly focused man who had a tendency to talk to himself, though Caroline assumed he was talking to her. She spent every day after school in his studio with him. He talked about his cut outs, explained every artistic decision he made, spoke of his perspective. His ideas on how to see and live. He was prolific, and no one but her cared. She saw what the lack of recognition did to him, how he would get frustrated and rant about the people who failed to see his art for what it was. He said they deliberately refused to see it. That they didn't understand the world and they might as well be blind. Caroline was young when she learned these lessons but she paid close attention and these ideas fed her being. She learned to hate those people too. The faceless majority who failed to see the beauty in her father's work.

One day he declared his intention to spend a full week in his studio doing nothing but work. He packed up a week's worth of food, water, and art supplies and locked himself in. When he didn't come out Caroline's mom broke in to find him dead. The autopsy was inconclusive. He had not eaten or drunken anything. He had amphetamines in his system and had cut himself around one eye with his scissors. Caroline knew the real cause of death was his art, and the people who refused to see it.

When she was allowed back in the studio she found an envelope with her name on it. Inside she found his scissors. The ones he used for his cut outs. They were beautiful eight inch blades with a sterling silver handle. A note said, "See the truth, share the sight."

After her father's death, her mother moved them to New York City where she worked as a teacher at a local community college. She taught Caroline the importance of getting a good education and finding a way to contribute to the community. She worked hard to keep the memory of Caroline's father alive while avoiding the subject of his strange death and his strong opinions.

She took Caroline to work in the evenings and made her tag along to social occasions. On the weekends, they walked around the city aimlessly browsing the shops. Caroline's mom loved to chat with people. She had spontaneous little conversations with just about everyone she met. Caroline never cared to join her mother in these conversations. She hung back and watched the interaction with her signature intense stare. She put people ill at ease. She judged them as her father would have done. Her mother's co-workers and friends avoided her. Even as a child she noticed this.

Her small, thin frame and her almost total silence kept people seeing her as a child even as she graduated high school and went to college. On her own she didn't know how to meet people or make friends and the staring didn't help. At school, she saw that everything her father told her was true. People don't understand the world, not like the two of them. She felt as if she was continually under attack.

She repeated her father's message like a prayer. "See the beauty, share the sight." Sometimes it felt as though it was all she had.

She stopped going to classes then stopped leaving her room. She grew dangerously thin, weak, and pale. When she looked in the mirror she could see every vein under her parchment skin.

About a month into this a bright-eyed older girl with a bouncy pony tail knocked on her door. Caroline had never seen her before. She said she was a recent graduate and the head Residential Advisor. She expressed concern for Caroline. Caroline sat at the edge of her bed and didn't say a word as the girl talked through all the college freshman cliché issues. She started with anorexia. When that didn't connect she talked about boyfriend problems, social anxiety, academic issues and then landed on depression and seemed to like it there. The twenty-two-year-old performance art major diagnosed Caroline with depression without needing to hear a word from her. She told Caroline to find her passion, to explore her interests, that's what college was for. She explained how she too was lost as a freshman until she decided to pursue her dream of acting.

Caroline really looked at this girl. Her chin protruded aggressively making her head look like a crescent moon. Her eyes were a flat brown color, too close together, and just a tad crossed. Her nose started low on her face giving her a weak profile and accentuating that ridiculous chin. This girl wants to be an actress. She thinks people would pay money to look at her face.

Suddenly, despite the ridiculous and offensive things she had said to her, Caroline wanted to help her. "See the beauty, share the sight." She wanted her to see things as Caroline did. She wanted her to understand the truth.

The girl talked about the importance of going after what you want in life when she caught Caroline looking at her in her particular way.

She stepped into the hallway and made a vague promise to come back and check on her soon, then she left. Caroline never saw her again, but the pep talk worked. She went back to classes. Declared a major of criminology and graduated a year early.

After college, she moved to a small apartment in the city where she was prepared to practice her father's message. Using the education given to her by one parent she could progress the message and legacy of the other. A city full of people who refused to see. It was her privilege to teach them.

She took her father's scissors and she hit the streets. Being a slight and unintimidating woman she found she could get very close to her victims without frightening them and in most cases without them noticing her. She started slow, the first night she only did three.

She picked a person, any person then stuck the blades of her scissors, her inheritance, into their eyes. Two quick jabs with very little force and her work was done. They would never see the same way again.

Everything was random. The location in the city, her mode of transportation and the people she chose. She wore clothes that were a little too big for her and muted in color hiding anything distinct. She chose people based on vulnerability but wasn't precious about it. If they slipped away, she let them. Her education prepared her for this, she learned how to beat the system. But she knew it couldn't last forever. She figured if she worked carefully and precisely she could avoid being caught for up to three years.

For a while she sat in on therapy groups for physical and emotional trauma which some of her victims attended. She listened to them speak about how their lives had been irreparably changed. How they had been forced to live differently, to adapt. She did that. She was very proud. She had proof it worked. After a few months, she stopped going to the meetings. She knew it was a connection that could be traced. It also became more difficult as their number grew. Some of her victims were tourists. A fortunate turn of events. By working in New York City, she shared the sight with the world.

Her actions did not go unnoticed. At times, she felt the pressure was too great and the investigators were too close. When that happened, she stopped. She had no problem stopping as long as she knew she would be able to continue at some point. Her motivation was different than the average serial assaulter. She was in it for the long haul.

Her estimation of three years was a conservative one. She went just under five before her name appeared on a list of suspects.

19.

Henry listens to Caroline's whole story. In the context of her confession he can better understand what Ben wrote and what Mick said about Alex. They are supposedly criminals. But it makes no sense. He wishes everyone would shut up for a second and let him think. He can't shake the feeling that some piece of information is being kept from him. That everyone else knows something he doesn't.

He goes back in his head to how the day started. He remembers boarding the train.

His headaches.

He remembers the accident in the dining car.

He feels dizzy and unstable.

He remembers Roland. What he did in the dining car. The memory of the smell comes back to him. Blood and sweat then something sweet.

CP8+B2. That's what Alex said earlier.

Like a fever breaking Henry feels good again. Normal. He remembers the old man boarding, how he reminded him of his son. Where is his son? He remembers that he has been drugged. That sweet smell. He can't remember the first time he smelled it and he can't figure out why. What everyone is saying, these horrible stories, they must be related to the drug. A side effect.

Henry wants to comfort them, and to tell them what they're saying isn't true. He wants them to know they are good people in a bad situation and it will all get straightened out in the end. Henry wants everyone to calm down. He wants Mick and Alex to go away. He wants the train back to normal. He wants to relax and think about home. He wishes he were there now.

He imagines what his family is doing. He thinks his wife is just getting home from work and will start cooking dinner soon. His son is in his bouncer chair chirping nonsense at her. This memory is from years ago, but it comforts him. A time when his life was consistent and made sense. The time before his wife died, before he spent long nights away from home. Before he was on this terrible train. It wasn't that he was happy. Happiness was never an aspiration of his, he had always required more tangible goals. He was comfortable, which is better than happy.

"Hey Henry?" Mick waves his hand in front of Henry's face. "Hey buddy where you at?"

Henry's body tightens and he wants to punch Mick. If he thought he could hurt him he would have done it, but he suspects it would be like punching a giant potato. Why won't Mick leave him alone?

"Henry you've got to try harder than that if you wanna stay with us," says Mick.

"We have to make a plan, something to get off this train," says Caroline.

"Got any ideas, babe?" says Mick.

"We need—" says Caroline before she is cut off by an overhead announcement.

"Attention passengers of car four," says a voice coming from the speaker. "My name is Lewis, I'm in charge of this train and I want to ask you all to please take your seats."

"Or what?" says Mick.

"Maybe you would all be interested in knowing there is absolutely no possible way for anyone to get off this train before we arrive, and Mick there . . ."

"Hey, look at me, I'm famous," says Mick laughing.

"Mick maybe if these people knew the things you did they wouldn't be interested in being buddies with you."

Mick is still laughing. "Alright alright." His laughter is more out of place than ever. "I guess it's my turn for story time."

20.

Michael The Deceiver was born into greatness in the hills of eastern Oregon, the thirteenth member of the second generation of The Great Deceivers. His father was their leader and someday Mick was to take over. With his birth, their population was brought to eighty-two. By being born into the society he would not have to suffer the rest of the world as his father and the other founders did, he would inherit the community. A great privilege.

The Deceivers were not a well-known group. The locals spread rumors amongst themselves often referring to them as a cult when in actuality the deceivers were realists and survivalists who had done away with the artificial and shallow world.

They had a small homestead in the otherwise uninhabited hills where they farmed and provided for themselves. They prepared for the day The Great Deceiver, also known as Satan, would rise up. Many people mistook them for Satan worshipers but that was also a lie. They never worshiped anything but focused on survival and the inevitable day when they would have to live beside Satan. Rather than being forced to give into Satan, to trade with him, they would be self-sufficient. They lived independent from the rest of the world. They were off the grid. They would never be indebted to Satan in any of his forms. They would deceive the Great Deceiver.

As a child Mick loved his life. He was told how important and special he was daily. He was treated better than the other kids, he got better snacks and was never punished. He developed a habit of crafting the most blatant lies just to see how the adults would handle it.

He loved to lie and he loved it when people got hurt. His specialty was to convince other kids to hurt themselves; then when they tried to tell on him he wriggled right off the hook. Who were they going to believe? The kid who drank the dirty river water or the leader's son?

He once convinced a kid two years older than him to touch an exposed electrical wire on a lamp. Mick held the base of it and shoved the socket in the kids face daring him to touch it. He told him if he wasn't brave enough to touch it then he would never be able to stand up to Satan. The kid got zapped pretty badly and when he woke up he didn't try to tell on Mick. He said he didn't remember what happened.

Mick's greatest childhood lie was the simplest one. While climbing a tree with a friend he reached over and shoved him. The kid fell about twelve feet and broke an arm. When they asked Mick what happened he said he wasn't there. He had sap on his hands and feet and other kids had seen him, but nobody questioned him. Nobody dared to confront him or his family. He had a fun childhood in which he could do no wrong, but as he got older the responsibilities added up and he started to get bored.

He believed in The Deceivers whole heartedly until he was twenty and doubt crept in. He remembers the specific moment. He taught the refresher class on semi-automatic weapons monthly and the thought appeared. For some reason, in that moment, it all seemed stupid. He looked down at his pupils, they were all ages, children and adults. These people had no business learning about guns. They would never need them, and if they did no amount of theoretical training would prepare them. When it came down to it he wasn't sure why the community had such a large selection of weapons. He began to look around with his new skeptic's eye and he developed fresh opinions.

The two pillars of The Deceivers were:

1. Solidarity: support each other and stay united in our singular goal.

2. Preservation: the importance of maintaining the community and beliefs for generations to come.

Mick viewed these differently. Instead of solidarity he saw solidarity conditional upon compliance. Instead of preservation he saw foolhardy people preparing for a future that would never come.

He privately discredited the philosophy but held firmly onto his entitlement and grandeur. Those were rooted deeper.

Mick saw himself leading this group. Telling them to work hard, to prepare for a future that's just around the corner while knowing that it's all bullshit. He could lie to them, he'd done a version of that his whole life. He could follow in his father's footsteps. It would be easy, but it would be boring. He considered his options. He thought about leaving, but he recognized that he was probably ill prepared for whatever went on in the rest of the world. He decided to stay, but on his own terms.

One Sunday morning Mick skipped out on a mandatory weekly lecture given by his father. He knew everyone would be there. He loaded himself up with his family's personal collection of guns and ammunition. Mick quietly waited in the back. No one noticed him. His father was up front spewing predictions and advice for the millionth time. Mick shot him in the head from the back of the room. The rest only took a minute or two. It was as he expected. Despite all the weapons training they were not prepared for an actual confrontation.

Over the next three days he dug a giant hole in the woods and dumped them all in. As his future was somewhat uncertain he decided to leave the grave open. He might need it again.

He spent the next months alone. Then he went into town to recruit new members. He kept the name and the pitch essentially the same. He told people that he was a member of The Deceivers and they prepare for the arrival of Satan. He handed out fliers and leaflets.

People wandered in. After a few weeks, he had fifty new members. He realized there are many lonely desperate people out there. People who were willing to drop everything, people who had nobody to look for them. They were all vastly different. There was a grade school teacher, three nurses, a stock broker, a few college students and a handful of homeless people and child runaways. They all needed something that they weren't getting. Mick used his skills of persuasion and manipulation to make sure he was that thing. He filled the gaps in their lives and when he did, they were loyal to him.

Rather than lead as his father did, preaching and making predictions, he helped them with their present. He taught them to defend themselves, he taught them the art of thievery and made them excellent con-men. They were strong and self-sufficient. Mick started to feel comfortable.

His one mistake was taking a wife. A sixteen-year-old single mother who, it turned out had people looking for her.

The day they were raided was his proudest day as leader. His people put up a noble fight against the police and The Feds. His followers killed more than a few. Mick knew then that he did right by them.

21.

Mick shared his story with a touch of pride and self-assuredness. Henry cannot come up with a way to rationalize this. There is far too much detail and truthfulness in Mick's story.

Henry believes Mick's story is true. So, the others must be true as well. Caroline and Ben look different to him now. They look frightening and ominous, they no longer look human. Henry thinks of an article he once read about group psychosis. If he recalls correctly there is very little actual proof, let alone any studies that prove it exists.

"Well now that we've suffered through that story, can I convince you all to take your seats?" says Lewis through the speaker.

"We're not going to just sit and wait," says Caroline.

"Doesn't make much difference to us. It's really about your comfort," says Lewis.

Henry wants to call out to Lewis, to ask for help. He doesn't know who Lewis is or where he is but Henry knows he needs help and anything would be better than where he is now. He needs someone to know he doesn't belong here. He needs them to know he's different.

He decides against yelling out. He's afraid these murderers would turn against him.

"Very well. You're on your own until we arrive. Try not to kill each other." A click and Lewis is gone.

Henry is certainly alone.

He has dozens of questions most of which he is too afraid to say out loud. One comes to the front because of what Lewis said. A question far overdue.

"Where are we going?" says Henry.

The train enters a tunnel and the car goes black.

22.

Jamie Vanveen sits in his cubicle at The Vault. He hasn't done a speck of work since Bergen left him. He finished off his box of éclairs and its only Wednesday. Now the train is so close he should try to look busy. But first a snack. He goes to the elevator and gets off one floor down at the administrative cafeteria. It is a beautiful modern kitchen with comfortable seating and an excellent chef, but Jamie doesn't like to eat here. The guards and the security team members take their lunches up here and he can't stand to be around them. They stink. They smell like the company they keep, like sweat and mildew, and despair. Jamie is a scientist, he doesn't care for metaphor or drama, but even so he doesn't know another way to describe the very real smell that comes off of them. Maybe it has something to do with working underground and the lack of sunlight but there is something more to it. He doesn't know how they can work with that smell.

He steps off the elevator to buy a bag of chips from the vending machine.

An automated message goes out over the sound system, "Train arriving in thirty minutes. Train arriving in thirty minutes."

The handful of guards clean up their things and head out. Jamie is thankful to see them take the stairs. He won't have to share the elevator. While Jamie tries to negotiate his chips out of the machine's plastic door, someone says his name. He turns around. It's Kari, a young doctor who is a member of Jamie's team.

"Hello," says Jamie.

"Are you ready for arrival?" she says.

Chit chat. Boring.

"Just about," he says, forcing a smile.

"Have you heard anything about how the trip is going?"

"They had an Event C," says Jamie.

"That should make things more interesting." She presses the button to call the elevator.

While he waits, Jamie opens his bag of chips and eats them by the handful.

He doesn't think much of anyone who works here at The Vault, but he thinks especially little of the doctors. Why would a young smart doctor choose to work here of all places? He assumes it must be for bragging rights or a sense of adventure, which he finds deplorable.

"Vanveen how are you?"

Jamie turns around with his plastic smile already in place. Reagan Duff is on the entirely other side of the cafeteria. His voice booms. He can have whole conversations miles away.

"Good, and you?" says Jamie.

Duff is on his way to the elevator, he straightens his blue pastel colored tie and grins. "It's great to see you. It's been a while."

Duff divides his time among the three vault locations. He's quite high up in SCG. He's known to be a charmer and even though Jamie recognizes that, he is not immune.

"It has. I'm glad to see you. There a few things I'd like to talk to you about. Do you think you'll have any time during your visit?" He's going to get to the bottom of this contract issue. He deserves to know if he has a job.

"You know what? I'm going to make time. Right now, I'm on my way to the staff meeting. You're coming, right?"

"I wasn't aware of a staff meeting."

"Oh! Well. Good thing I caught you," says Duff.

"Great," says Jamie.

"And who's this?" says Duff looking at Kari.

"Oh sorry. This is Kari. She's a doctor. She's on my intake team."

"Hello Kari. I'm Reagan Duff, VP of Operations." He shakes her hand.

"Wow. You must be very busy."

"It's a busy time for SCG. Lots of growth. Big things happening we couldn't do it without people like yourself."

Kari smiles wide. "Well I hope I do my part."

The elevator dings and the doors slide open. They step in, Kari presses A which will take them to Arrivals. The lowest level, where the train will pull in.

Jamie wishes he never came down here for the stupid chips. Now he's being drug to a meeting in which no one wants him and he has to go down to Arrivals, which he hates.

Just as the doors begin to close someone yells, "hold it."

Kari sticks her arm out to hold the doors open.

A guard hustles from the bathroom to the elevator, "thank you," he says, as he fastens his belt and tucks his shirt in. He presses P2. Could this day get worse?

The elevator opens to P2, Jamie holds his breath and the guard gets off. The fluorescent light and the cold wet air pours into the elevator. He hears Mozart playing over the sound system. A so-called perk for the residents but nothing here is that straight forward. Nothing here is just one thing. From the elevators you can't see much but Jamie hears them shuffling around in their cement boxes and yelling at each other through the walls. The doors close and Jamie breathes again.

Duff's cell rings, "Duff." A pause. "I'm sorry to hear that. Right, I'll brief them at the meeting." He hangs up the phone. "There was a casualty on the train."

"A passenger?" says Kari.

"A staff member," says Duff.

Kari gasps and covers her mouth.

So naïve.

"What a pity," says Duff.

"It probably had something to do with the Event C they had earlier," says Jamie feeling defensive and worried Duff could interpret this as a failure of his compound.

"We'll have more info soon I'm sure. Don't worry Kari. He'll be taken care of. We'll do right by him."

She nods.

"You know this is only the fourth death on one of our trains which is really quite impressive considering what it was like before. When we transported them without Vanveen's miracle compound."

The elevator opens at Level A. They all get off.

"Kari, it was wonderful meeting you. Have a pleasant intake," says Duff.

She smiles back at him. The death of a fellow worker seemingly wiped from her mind.

"We're this way," says Duff.

They turn down a hallway.

"You want to talk about your contract, right?" says Duff.

Jamie is caught off guard, "well, yes."

"Okay. You are an important part of our team here. Invaluable really. So of course we will be renewing your contract. Feel better?"

"Um, yeah, that's great."

"And there's more news. We're in here."

They turn into a conference room. Jamie takes a seat next to Bergen.

"Hey, look at you out of your cubicle," says Bergen.

"I'm an important part of the team. Invaluable really," says Jamie, only partly sarcastic.

23.

The train car is pitch black and silent except for the running engine and its industrial era moving parts. The ruckus of outdated steel which propel this mad train forward.

Marble sized lights come on and line the aisle, then two large over head lights flood the car with white light. Henry shades his eyes until they adjust.

"Are we in a tunnel?" says Alex.

"You are a smart guy aren't ya?" says Mick. He walks over to the vestibule, steps over Bauman's body. "Come help me with this," he says to Alex.

Ben and Caroline follow while Henry stays behind. They bang around, hit things and grunt with exertion. Henry looks to the back of the car. There is no door, no window, nowhere to move but forward. He joins the others. Mick and Alex try to open the door. They yank and pull and shove on the metal lever. Ben and Caroline are on the other side and take turns slamming the window with the butt of the guns.

Henry can't help but think that Lewis was right when he said there is no way off this train. Even if they did break through a window or open the door they would have to climb out of the pitch-black tunnel then walk through miles of desert. The last town they passed was hours ago.

Henry has come to a decision. He opens the door to car three. "Nobody follow me," he says. Then he walks out.

"Where ya going buddy?" says Mick.

"Henry, relax," says Caroline sternly.

"Stay away from me," he yells at her before he leaves. He enters the next vestibule and closes the door. He wishes he had a way to jam it closed, but there is nothing. He moves forward. In the next car, he is quietly observed by a new bunch of glossy eyed people.

In the next vestibule, he stops for a moment and leans against the wall. He is tempted to go back to the group. He should be eager to get away from those people, but now that he is alone he feels vulnerable. He is alone to make his own decisions. His own life in his own hands. Why should he trust himself with his own life?

The only time he has ever been free to make his own decisions was after his wife died. She died on a not so special day when she was hit by a car outside of their house. It didn't look like you might expect. Death isn't always bloody and this death was quiet and quick. Henry went outside and she lay on the ground looking like she could hop up at any moment. Nothing was out of place except her hair was a little messy. He stared at her while waiting for the ambulance and the longer he looked the more she looked wrong. They took her to the hospital and he was surprised to hear that she was dead. She just got hit, fell, and never got back up. Simple, clean, fast, and bloodless. Henry was a little sad, though his most prolonged feeling was one of injustice. He had done his part, made his commitments, and fate had not followed through. He was annoyed. He found himself alone and forced to make his own decisions. He gave it an honest try, he thought he was doing well, but if he was doing so well how did he end up on this ridiculous train?

He is confident that if he still had his wife she would have seen to it that whatever events lead to this would not have happened. He may not have loved her much, but she was an efficient leader and she guided him soundly and that's all Henry had ever wanted.

Henry resolves to fight to get off this train and when he does he will find a new companion. Someone to see him safely and smoothly through the rest of his life. He will no longer allow himself to be put in these perilous situations. But for now, he has to get off the train.

Henry knows it isn't enough to separate himself from the murderers. He needs to find the people who run the train and prove he isn't like them or with them. His only choice is to continue to move forward. He passes through another car full of sleepy drugged people. Next, he passes through the dining car, which hasn't been cleaned since the incident. There are slabs of meatloaf on the ground, broken chairs and glasses and a congealing puddle of blood soaked into the thin carpeting.

He walks through the kitchen which has also been left dirty. He expects to run into the train staff, but so far there isn't anybody. This is what Lewis must have meant when he said they are on their own.

He walks through another car full of passengers. Some of them look right at him with clear focused eyes. Henry wonders what they know, what they remember, but he is set on moving forward alone. He can't trust anyone. Henry enters the next vestibule and comes to a stop.

This must be it. He stands in front of a completely different kind of door. It's metal and is flush against the wall. It has no handle. He has no idea how to open it but he must open it.

He needs to get inside that car. He needs to explain that he is different. He needs to find out what's going on and how he can get home.

He bangs on the door with his fist. It makes the most unsatisfying muted thud. Whoever is on the other side probably didn't hear a thing. He hits it again harder. He kicks it and yells, "Let me in. Lewis! Let me in."

He rams his body into the door ignoring the shooting pain in his dead arm. He stops for a moment and puts his ear against the door. He hears nothing but the sound of his own labored breathing.

Some part of his brain gives a little twitch and a thought comes to him; it makes him laugh. He thinks of the prey he gave to his tiger, the enrichment. He fed her different things, whatever he came across, but it all had something in common. They yelled, screamed, whinnied, barked, and moaned. They made a pathetic plea to not be eaten. Henry laughs because he behaves just like them.

If he is the victim in this situation someone observes his slaughter. He finds the camera. Then he hears voices behind him.

"Henry, come back, we should work together."

"Get the hell back here asshole."

They've followed him. His stomach twists. He doesn't want to see their disgusting faces, he doesn't want to be in the same room as them. The scenario is complete, he is the prey. He follows the rules. He screams, he pleads, he kicks and hits and tries to get through an impassable door.

"Stay away! I don't want your help. Don't come down here!" he yells over his shoulder.

"Henry, we should stick together," says Caroline.

He hits the door as hard as he can. "Let me in, you owe me an explanation. I don't belong here!" he repeats this mantra. "I don't belong here."

The nearby passengers take notice of him. One stands up and looks at Henry as if he is a foreign object, an animal in the zoo. Henry hates this look, he wants to kill the man for looking at him like that. Other passengers leer at him.

The metal door shoots open.

24.

"Can I get five minutes of peace!" says Lewis. He throws a sleeve of crackers down on his desk.

"We should let him in. He's attracting a lot of attention," says Franny.

"We're almost at The Vault, let's just leave him," says Craig.

"A lot can happen in twenty minutes," says Franny.

"Alright, bring him in," says Lewis.

"Righty-o," says Craig. He walks through the service car to the door.

Franny types a command into her computer and the door shoots open.

Craig grabs the man by the shoulders and yanks him into the service car. The door closes.

"Welcome to Oz. I'm Craig, I'll be your man behind the curtain this evening. Can I get you something to drink?"

"What?"

"Take a seat."

He looks around but doesn't sit.

"What's your name?" says Craig.

"Henry, I—"

"Henry, when I tell you to sit, you sure as hell better sit."

Henry sits on the ground and leans against the door.

Craig walks to the front. "I sat him on the ground. Since all the staff is up here we're out of seats."

"Great," says Lewis. "I swear each trip takes longer than the last."

"The old job getting to you?" Says Franny.

"It's just the home stretch. Kind of drags on. And I'm expecting Vanveen to have his panties in a bunch today so de-briefing could take a while."

"Hey," yells Henry.

"Well our stats are fine if that's any comfort," says Franny.

"They're okay," says Lewis.

"No really. They're average, compared to other trips. One death, two personnel injuries and a handful of straw moments and an Event C. The only thing special is the death and under the circumstances . . ."

"Those are pretty good numbers," says Craig.

They've left out the fact that it has gotten so unsafe and the passengers have been so out of control that they had to pull their staff out.

"I don't belong here," says Henry.

"Too bad about that Bauman guy," says Franny.

"I want to talk to someone," yells Henry.

"Good god," says Lewis. He pulls out a plastic box from under his desk and takes the lid off. It's full of file folders. He leans forward in his chair, looks down the aisle, and yells down at Henry.

"What's your last name, asshole?" says Lewis.

Not moving from his work station, Craig laughs.

"Fritz. Henry Fritz."

Lewis sifts through the files and pulls one out, "Henry Fritz." He throws the file at him then walks back to his workstation.

"Vanveen would love that," says Franny.

"Like he has any real idea of what happens on this train," says Craig.

"How much longer?" says Lewis.

"Fifteen minutes," says Franny.

"Thank god."

"Hallelujah," says Craig.

"Where did my crackers go?" Lewis fishes around under his desk and finds them on the ground.

"This doesn't make any sense," says Henry.

"This fucking guy," says Craig. "Let's knock him out."

"We can't. He was dosed in the dining car, it would be against regulations," says Franny.

"So, what?" says Craig, smiling.

"Well," Franny chuckles, "he might die."

"I might not care," says Craig.

They laugh together.

"I need to talk to someone," says Henry.

Lewis is annoyed by their jokes and their laughter. Or maybe he is jealous. Neither of them is responsible for this train, neither of them is going to have to explain themselves. They aren't asked to make decisions that get a man killed.

Franny's attempt to comfort Lewis with statistics was unsuccessful. Lewis aspires to be better than his predecessors, not just as good. Lewis wants a train with no incidents, no reports. He wants a train with a full, well prepared staff. He wants the ridiculous compound to work effectively and for no one to get hurt. He wants to be in this job for no longer than a year. He wants to move up and out. He doesn't want to herd cattle for the rest of his life. He doesn't want to end up like Vanveen.

He's done this trip five times now so he sees the deck is stacked against him. The compound, which this whole charade is built around, is only so effective, the staff is inexperienced and the true nature of the passengers always wins in the end. There is no way for him to stand out, no way to succeed.

"This thing doesn't make sense," says Henry.

Henry gets up and walks towards Lewis. "Listen to me."

Craig once again opens his desk drawer and removes a pair of zip tie reusable flexi-cuffs. He secures Henry's arms behind his back.

"My arm!" he screams.

Craig pushes Henry to the ground.

Henry wiggles around until he can sit up. "Please. Help me."

"Jesus this guy is exhausting," says Craig. "You got him all riled up boss."

"You think he'll report me?" says Lewis with a smile.

Franny and Craig don't laugh which annoys Lewis even more.

Lewis goes to Henry. He crouches down to eye level. "Did you look at this file?" He picks it up off the ground.

"It's not true, not any of it," says Henry. "I've never killed anyone."

25.

He sits on the ground like a child. The metal door on his back makes him shiver but overall the car is warm. He hadn't realized that he's been cold this whole trip. This car has better lighting, the windows and the seats are bigger and a TV plays a movie. At the front is a separate room where Lewis and two other people sit. It's full of monitors and electrical equipment and glows with an electric blue light. Henry holds a file with his name. He holds it gently with both hands as if it were dangerous. It feels like a trap. These people have no interest in hearing him out. This folder is meant to delay and confuse him. He opens the folder. Pages and pages of text, with transcripts of conversations with people he doesn't recognize. In the back there are pictures, violent, bloody pictures. He closes the folder.

"I need to talk to someone," he says.

This is disgusting. These pictures. He quickly looks at them again. There are pictures of the Greenville City Zoo. He doesn't understand what these pictures are or why these people have them.

"This thing doesn't make any sense."

He gets up and walks down the aisle. Now he sees people's faces. They aren't drugged like the rest of the passengers. Their eyes are clear and judging. Many of them wear the train uniform like Bauman and Phillips. They don't notice Henry much except for an occasional glance. The man who was carried out screaming is gagged and cuffed to a chair. His grunts are muted through a gag. Henry passes the waiter whose arm he broke. His arm is in a sling and he's passed out leaning against the window. The front half of the car has no chairs but is full of equipment. A woman crouches and works on something. As he gets closer he sees she is changing the bandages on a man's wounded stomach. He's from the dining car. Henry had forgotten about him. Henry turns around looking for Roland. He's tied to a chair bound at the hands and feet. He has a canvas bag over his head but Henry recognizes him by his long nails which are crusty with blood.

Henry turns back towards the front and looks at Lewis in the attached room. "Listen to me."

The man who let him in, Craig, cuffs him and pushes him to the ground before he even has time to react.

The pain in his arm is like an electrical shock that ricochets up and down his right side.

"My arm!" his vision gets spotty. The pain is so acute he feels he might pass out. "Please. Help me."

Lewis walks over to Henry and crouches down. Henry can tell he is in charge of the train but not necessarily of Henry's future. He is surprisingly young especially for how worn down and haggard he looks. His face is oily and shiny and he needs to shave. He has chapped lips and thinning hair around his temples. He is handsome, but he won't be for much longer. In fact, he is the perfect age to go to slaughter. His muscles are fully developed and strong but he is not old enough to be a tough cut of meat. He is not overly large but supplemented with kibble and veggies Henry could stretch him to feed his three large cats for a whole day.

"Did you look at this file?" he asks Henry.

"It's not true, not any of it. I've never killed anyone."

Lewis opens the file to the first page. "Henry Fritz. Purchased by

SCG, my employer," he says, pointing to himself, "to be housed safely and securely in The Vault for the remainder of his life. This transfer approved by Judge Barth, blah blah. After being convicted and found guilty of eight counts of murder and related crimes. List attached. Do you have any questions?"

He looks ugly to Henry now. His bloodshot condescending eyes stare down at Henry. His skin looks clammy and grey. He looks sickly, he wouldn't feed meat like this to any animal.

"I didn't do that," says Henry.

"So, you didn't . . ." Lewis rifles through the paper, "lure people after hours to the zoo you worked at, sneak them in a backroom and feed them, alive, to a tiger?"

Not lure exactly, they must have known. Deep down Henry thinks they knew.

"You didn't watch as the tiger ate them alive?"

Half of his job was observation, that's true of any zookeeper.

Lewis reads further. He laughs. "Your mother says you were always a good boy. Ate your vegetables, did you? What do they say? A child only a mother could love," he smiles.

"Ten minutes," says the woman in the adjacent room.

"Thank you, Franny," says Lewis. "I just want to know one more thing," his eyes search the paperwork. "Here it is. Henry was caught when he got a piece of his own medicine. The tiger bit the hand, or arm, that feeds. Gave you this," Lewis pats Henry's injured arm reviving the pain. "They found you the next morning, nearly bled to death, lying on the floor, a woman's purse on the desk and a very full tiger in a cage. What happened?"

She fought back. That hadn't happened before.

Lewis slaps Henry's face lightly. "So, what happened?"

"I didn't do anything wrong," says Henry.

"You're saying your innocent?"

"I am."

"You're telling me you don't remember any of it? The trial? Being sentenced to life at The Vault? Killing eight people?"

There were twelve actually. He never mentioned that.

26.

When Henry started work at the Greenville City Zoo he was an assistant feeder. He went around with another person to deliver food to keepers. He lugged around buckets of fish and tubs of carrots for eight hours each day. It was hard and thankless work. He worked his way up though, and within the year he was assistant butcher for the red wolf exhibit. Soon after, a head feeder position opened for the large cats. Henry jumped at the chance and got it.

This new position required him to feed the smaller carnivorous and the African animals but his main responsibility was to the large cats. The zoo had three. Two sub-Saharan African lions, a male and female. They had been at the zoo for many years and were fairly tame and dull. The third was Henry's favorite, the Amur tiger. Amur tigers are native to Russia and are alternatively called Siberian Tigers. The one at the Greenville Zoo was named Nicole.

Henry had always been satisfied with his job, but he had never been very interested in animals. He is as interested in animals as he is in people which is to say, minimally. However, the first time Henry fed and observed the Amur she took his breath. Finally, Henry understood what other people saw when they looked at these animals. She made him understand that this is something worth preserving. She was like a god, and Henry was her faithful follower.

Amur tigers are the largest living cats on earth. Nicole weighed almost four hundred pounds and was ten feet long from head to tail, very large for a female. Her last feeder had her eating feline carnivore chow for seventy five percent of her diet, a cheap alternative to fresh and frozen meats. Once Henry got to know her he knew this was not right. Amurs are exquisite hunters. In the wild they start as early as seven months old and they'll go after anything they can overpower. They drag their meal to a quiet place and eat the whole thing in one sitting, no matter the size. From day one Henry saw the difference in her behavior when he fed her real meat. She savored it. It made her happy. Which made Henry happy.

He had a budget to keep in mind and the fresh meat was expensive. He started by skimming from his other departments. He stretched the other animal's food with veggie pellets and hay and spent their budget on Nicole. Sometimes he skipped a day of feeding the other animals if he thought he could get away with it. Even by doing this he didn't always have enough money to feed fresh meat to Nicole. Sometimes he had to give her chow and it made him feel terrible. He knew he had to do more but he didn't know exactly what. He wanted to feed her live animals but it was against regulations. He didn't particularly care about regulations but he needed his job.

Then, his wife died and he didn't have to explain his actions or account for his time to anyone. It gave him more time to focus on Nicole. He experimented in ways to enrich her feeding experience. He went in after closing when everyone but a couple of security guards were gone. He moved her to the backroom tiger enclosure and gave her treats. He started with rats and raccoons but her movement was limited by the cages and if the animal squeezed through the bars before she got it, Henry spent the rest of the night trying to recapture it. Next, he tried cats and dogs. That went well, but people at the animal shelter started to recognize him.

The solution came to him early one morning when he was up with his son. It was almost three AM and out of the window he saw cars driving around. He couldn't imagine why anyone would be on the road at three in the morning. He realized humans were invasive. Taking up every inch of this world. Doing whatever they want. Eating whatever they want. While Nicole sat in a cell eating dry flavorless kibble. So, he began giving Nicole humans. Nutritious and hardy, too big to slip through the bars, but not so well looked after as dogs and cats.

He picked them in the day time, someone he vaguely knew. The woman who made his coffee, the guy who delivered his pizza, anyone with whom he could strike up a conversation. Once their polite friendship was established he took things to the next level by telling them he worked for the zoo and if they wanted, he could show them around. A special tour. Behind the scenes. This special offer was never refused.

The backroom enclosure is a series of four cells all connected with gates that can be opened to adjust the size. It's intended for medical procedures and checkups. Henry enclosed Nicole in the first cell so his guest saw her right away. This, he learned, was key as the first impression of the beautiful imposing tiger just feet away ensured that they would enter the room. Henry waited for the right moment then gently suggested that the person enter the fourth chamber for a better view. Often, they entered it themselves, that's how safe it looked. Once they were in he locked the door behind them. After that they were no longer people to Henry. Some of them laughed at first thinking it was a joke, some immediately got furious, but all pleaded to be let out. Next Henry opened the two gates separating the tiger from its meal. He loved to watch. The concentration in Nicole's eyes and the satisfaction afterwards were things of beauty. She drug the body to the corner and ate the whole thing taking short breaks or even naps, but she didn't get up until the evidence was gone. It was a team effort; a team Henry was most proud to be on.

His last one, the one that got him caught was a woman who had approached him at the grocery store. She was dressed professionally and a little older than Henry. She was very forward. Henry didn't realize until afterwards that his big mistake was allowing himself to be chosen rather than do the choosing.

After suffering through a dinner date, he took her to the zoo. When she saw the tiger, she refused to enter the backroom. She was used to being in control. Henry had put his time in and Nicole was hungry so he had to leave his comfort zone and engage in hands on violence. He forced her into the room and closed the door. The woman was quick to respond. She ran over to the desk and hurled a textbook at Henry, hitting him in the head. The joy he took from these nights lay in the passivity of it. Now this woman insisted on engaging him.

He wasn't angry, he felt nothing except for the weight of his obligation to Nicole. Forcing himself to hurt this woman was hard for Henry. He didn't have a murderer's heart. He grabbed both of her arms and drug her into the cell. She kicked him in the shin with her stiletto then jabbed him in an eye. She shoved him and he fell to the ground. On the ground, he looked up at her and she backed away from him. She dialed her cell phone. She was too frightened and too busy dialing to think about where she was. She backed up until her fashionable gray linen suit jacket was pressed against the tan painted, steel bars of Nicole's cell. The swift paw of the beautiful Amur reached out and wrapped around her waist. From Henry's view, it looked as if Nicole was going to hug her. Then the claws extended and she pulled her paw back taking much of the woman's skin and stomach. The woman screamed in shock once but then fell and didn't make another noise. The phone rattled to the ground and

Henry lunged for it; he needed to make sure it did not dial out. His mistake was moving so quickly. Nicole was over stimulated from her successful kill and Henry's movement attracted her attention. She reached her paw out for a second time and caught Henry's right arm. To Henry it felt as if his arm had been ripped off. He threw himself against the back wall to safety. He slid to the ground and watched Nicole savor the woman he brought her. He fell over and lay on his side, his arm poured blood until he lost consciousness.

He woke up in the hospital after surgery. He manufactured excuses. He told them he went back at night because he forgot to give Nicole one of her medications. He could tell when he started talking that the police officer didn't believe him, that she already knew the truth. She let him finish though, and then told him. They found the purse, then they found traces of blood, then when they couldn't find the woman, they killed Nicole and examined her stomach contents. Right there in that hospital bed Henry's heart broke. All he wanted was to make her happy and he got her killed. How could he ever forgive himself?

27.

Who the hell is Bauman? Reagan Duff can't remember meeting him, or hearing about him ever before. Bauman must be new. That's good. If anyone tries to make a big deal about his death they can blame his lack of experience or his inattentiveness during training. Maybe they can even blame the Event C on him.

"He'll be taken care of. We'll do right by him," says Reagan. He just spews this stuff. Finding the right thing to say to people used to be challenging, but after twenty years he can sweet talk anyone.

"You know this is only the fourth death on one of our trains which is really quite impressive considering what it was like before. When we transported them without Vanveen's miracle compound," says Reagan.

Miracle compound. He almost breaks character and laughs out loud. They'd have better results knocking them unconscious. The only miracle that compound is responsible for is getting the public to believe in it. Since using the compound SCG stock has increased more than the five preceding years combined. The passengers would presumably be safer if they were chained to their chairs, the way they've done it for years, but that has been deemed "inhumane." This compound makes the public feel better about taking people to the middle of the desert and leaving them in a hole in the ground. Whatever. It makes no difference to Reagan.

"Kari, it was wonderful meeting you. Have a pleasant intake," says Reagan. Another simpleton working away in the bowels of The Vault. At least this one's good looking. "We're this way."

Today is supposed to be a good day. The train's arrival will bring The Vault up to one hundred percent capacity. Another location at peak profitability. He does not want to waste time talking to Jamie Vanveen.

"You want to talk about your contract, right?" says Reagan.

"Well, yes," says Vanveen.

He makes a stupid surprised face. Why are some people so disappointingly predictable?

Vanveen is not worth the paper his checks are printed on. On a day to day basis he offers nothing. But keeping him under contract keeps his lips sealed. It keeps him away from the press and any number of people who want the details on CP8+B2. Vanveen is just the type to seek attention and praise so it's absolutely worth keeping him on contract.

"Okay. Well you are an important part of our team here. Invaluable really. So of course, we will be renewing your contract. Feel better?" There he goes again. Saying exactly what needs to be said. Sometimes he blows himself away. "And there's more news. We're in here." They turn into the conference room. He takes a quick survey of the room. Seems like everyone is here.

"Hi everyone. Thanks for coming. I know the train will be here soon so we will make this short. I just wanted to get everyone together because of how big today is. As I'm sure you all know today's arrivals brings us to one hundred percent capacity."

Everyone applauds. "Yes! Due in no small part to all of you. Congratulations everyone." He looks around the table. "The other VP's and I have been discussing how we're going to move forward here at The Vault and keep us profitable and strong and we've come up with a few ideas. First, we have a new contract with KitchenKuisine which Jackson over there will be handling. Now that we're at full capacity it should really be explosive."

Reagan is quite proud of this contract. Within the next five years one hundred percent of KitchenKuisine's kitchen stoves and portable induction cooktops will be assembled right here at The Vault.

"Whoo! Jackson. Put those animals to work. Mama needs a new stove," says Heidi Creitz a hillbilly type of woman who manages the overnight guards.

"Secondly, Eileen will be heading our new wellness program which will vastly improve our resident's lives." And comes with a hefty tax break.

They applaud Eileen. "Looking forward to it," she says.

"And the big news, this one's for you Vanveen so listen up. We're ready to invest a not insignificant amount of resources towards improving the compound."

The look on Vanveen's face is hilarious. He looks sickly in this fluorescent lighting but Reagan can see the news makes him happy. There was a time when Vanveen was a real scientist. A really smart man. Reagan hopes very much that Vanveen can make significant progress on the compound. Maybe make it almost as good as Reagan has convinced people it is.

"That's right Vanveen, we're looking to get you back in the lab to patch up a few of those pesky issues in order to streamline our transportation services."

Bergen pats Vanveen on the shoulders.

"The last thing, and I know some of you are already aware, but the train has had a fatality of one of our staff members. It was Bowerman, a vestibule attendant I believe."

"You tell me who did it Mr. Reagan Duff. You tell me and I'll take care of the guy," says Heidi.

"That's enough Heidi." Reagan shuts her down with his perfect white toothed smile. He wouldn't normally speak to someone like this, especially in front of other people, but comments like Heidi's needs to be shut down quickly. If anyone outside of the corporation heard something like that, being said by an SCG employee, there could be major fallout. Enough to derail their entire public image. Though it may seem mild, Heidi's threat of reciprocal violence, and even her comment before, referring to them as animals, harkens back to a kind of industry that SCG has spent a significant amount of effort distancing itself from.

"The train is getting close. I know you've all got jobs to do. I'll let you get to it," says Regan.

The group disperses. Bergen shakes Reagan's hand. Bergen is one person here that Reagan really respects. He runs a tight ship, or train, and he's always a calming presence.

"Glad you're here Duff. This is a big day."

"I wouldn't miss it for the world," says Reagan. This is actually true.

"I'm going to watch the train come in then go meet Lewis and the team at the tracks. Would you like to come?" says Bergen.

"Absolutely," says Reagan.

Bergen turns to Vanveen who is in his seat, evidently twiddling his thumbs. "Coming Vanveen?" says Bergen.

"Sure."

They enter a room down the hall where they watch the train pull in and come to a stop. Reagan watches closely. He thinks it might be the most beautiful thing he's ever seen.

28.

The train slows down. They go deeper underground. Henry yawns
to pop his ears. His arm aches worse than it did after he first hurt it.
He wonders why they didn't just cut the whole worthless thing off.
Maybe the doctors left it as a punishment.

Henry doesn't remember much about his time at the hospital. He
was on a lot of pain medication. He recalls pieces. Men and women
in uniform coming in and out asking essentially the same questions.
A doctor explaining, he would have limited mobility in his arm. His
mother and his son visiting and giving him a headache with their
cries and whining.

If he'd known it would be the last time he was going to see them
he would have been more kind. He would have tried to be more kind.

At some point during all the hoopla of his trial Henry got his
hands on a newspaper and read an article about a man who worked
at a zoo and fed living people to the Amur tiger. It was a good article.
Fair. Henry hopes someday when his son is older he will find a copy
of it and that he'll be able to understand what Henry was doing and
why. He hopes his son finds purpose in something as Henry did with
Nicole.

The train grinds to a stop.

Lewis makes an overhead announcement.

"Thank you for traveling with us, please exit on the left side of the train." He turns off the microphone and says, "go ahead and dose them for intake and open the doors."

They keep up the idea that this is a normal train and they're drugging them again. No one stands any real chance of getting off. He feels foolish for trying.

"Alright." Lewis claps his hands once and stands at the doorway, "all passengers are off the train and dosed with our beloved compound. They have all reached processing so let's unload and go home."

The staff grabs their things and leaves the train.

"We need to get Feightner out first thing. There's an evac. team waiting for him," says Lewis. A pair of people pick up the stretcher and carry him off the train.

Franny and Craig walk out of the front compartment. They step over Henry on their way out. Franny stretches her arms then leans over to look out of the window.

"Hey boss man," she says, "your boss man is here."

"Duff is here?" Lewis looks out of the window. "I didn't know he was coming today. Let's get our friend Henry here off the ground. If Duff wants to come in we don't need people all over the place. Craig, who's in charge of clean up today?"

"Gene, I think."

Lewis presses a button on his headset, "Gene, let's get Bauman cleaned up as a priority."

Craig lifts Henry off the ground and onto his feet. He undoes his cuffs and Henry feels instant relief in his arm.

"Let's go check in with Duff and Bergen. Then we can finish moving these ones out," says Lewis.

"Fine by me," says Craig. He puts Henry in a chair by the window and cuffs his injured arm to the seat.

"Vanveen's out there too," says Franny.

"Oh joy," says Lewis.

The three of them leave the train. From Henry's seat he can see them. They all shake hands and smile.

Henrys arm tingles. The cuff is around his wrist and pushes his shirt up to expose the beginning of the scar. He touches it with his other hand and thinks of Nicole. He's sad that she was killed but it's probably for the best. Nobody would take care of her the way Henry did and it would upset him to think of someone trying. Yes, it's better that she's dead. Henry wiggles his fingers and watches the little bones and tendons dance under the skin. It's such a small hand. The muscles have all but abandoned it. He moves his thumb across his palm making his hand small enough to slip out of the cuff.

Looking out the window he sees Lewis and the others chatting. He wonders what they're talking about. He thinks of how hard he used to work trying to find the right things to say. He supposes he won't have to do that anymore. He could, but for who? What would he gain?

Henry stands. The only people left besides him are the anxious man, the waiter with the broken arm, and Roland. The anxious man is tied and gagged, the waiter is unconscious, they probably knocked him out, and Roland is bound at the hands and feet, tied to the chair with cord and with a bag over his head. Henry goes over to Roland. He slips the bag off his head and they look at each other. Henry sees something different in the man than he did before. He sees an animal in captivity, a caged tiger. Henry unties the knot in the chord.

Roland smirks showing off blood stained teeth. He bends over and uses his sharp fingernails and a good amount of sheer force to break his legs free. Roland holds out his bound hands to Henry. Henry looks at the thick plastic and knows he won't be able to break it. He goes into the front compartment and finds a nice pen, black painted metal with the words "Secured Communities Group:

Industry leader in safety". Henry shoves it in Roland's cuff at the joint. He pushes it hard. Roland uses his long fingers to crank the pen while twisting his wrists. They come apart.

"You don't have long," says Henry.

Roland understands. He goes to the injured, sleeping waiter and pets his face until he wakes up. He puts one hand over the man's mouth muting his screams and with his other hand he slashes his face and neck. Back and forth and across. Blood drizzles down his neck and chest like warm icing.

Henry is ecstatic. He is beautiful, a truly amazing creature. Unique and gifted. It's a pity he'll be locked up for the rest of his life. Henry takes a seat across from the action. The waiter has lost consciousness but he's still alive. Roland eats pieces of him. What a peculiar predator.

Henry thinks back to the resolutions he made to himself less than an hour ago. He was going to get off the train and find a way to have a simple life. He was going to find someone to get him smoothly through the world. He wanted to go back to his life of simplicity and ease. A decisionless existence. Though he wasn't able to get off the train he feels this may be the right place for him.

Henry leans back in his chair; he is exhausted. This has been one of the most hectic days of his life.

Roland seems to be slowing down. He's not going to kill him. Another interesting choice by a fascinating predator.

Some part of Henry feels relieved that he doesn't have to work so hard anymore. He doesn't have to fit in, doesn't have to survive or provide. He doesn't have to worry about his son or his mother or his tiger. He can live out the rest of his life in passivity. The way he's always wanted. He can be free.

Bio
Miranda Manzano

Miranda is an attendee of the Yale Writers Conference and a quarter finalist in the 2017 BlueCat short screenplay competition. She lives in the Pacific Northwest where she sells hot dogs to support her writing habit. Please contact her @Miranduh_M to let her know what you're having for dinner.

Sodom & Gomorrah on a Saturday Night

by Christa Miller

CHAPTER ONE

When the government outlawed empathy, no one protested it much. It was a skill that had been in decline for some time; most employers argued that it, like unionizing, diminished productivity. Others, like teachers, therapists, and supervisors, thought that being able to read one another's emotions got in the way of good old-fashioned communication. (Therapists even went so far as to differentiate between empathy as a quality, which was good, and empathy as a skill, which demonstrated a distinct lack of boundaries.)

As a result, few young people had ever had the chance to use or even develop theirs. So a skill that had taken two generations to flourish all but died, and those of us who remembered how and why to use it could only try hard -- often aided by inhibitor drugs — to forget.

Most days I didn't meet people who stirred my desire to connect with them. As a residential security officer, I was responsible for enforcing homeowners' association regulations, which meant facing down people for infractions involving lawns, curtains, wind chimes, fencing, and other minor issues. When heftier matters, like today's missing person, appeared, they were supposed to be treated in exactly the same way as the rest.

Except that missing persons weren't lawns, and neither the ban on empathy nor the inhibitor drugs killed all emotion. This just meant people were dealing with fear and despair and doubt on their own. By the time I responded early that Saturday afternoon, the missing person's husband was nearly out of his mind.

I pulled up to his house expecting irate, the typical response to the fact that his call had been queued in the order in which it was received. What I got instead from that tall, athletic, self-assured caller was respectful to the point of deferential. "Thank you for coming out, sir," Ian Rafferty said, as if he'd realized that getting abusive with me was no way to find his wife.

Which only unearthed the cynicism I'd cultivated over the span of a career in law enforcement: he'd killed her and he knew it was only a matter of time before I found out. Just last year, a husband had snapped and shot his wife over not keeping their home up to code. It was the first time I'd questioned my place in this system.

That was why I ignored the tendrils of Rafferty's consciousness reaching out towards mine — in moments of extreme duress I could give that a pass, even if others wouldn't — and went through the checklist of questions while he stood in front of me, massaging his own fingers. Last seen when? "Ten p.m. last night." She went where? "Across the street to her friend Liza's. Regular Friday night gathering." She ever stay over there? "Sometimes, but not often. And not last night. I checked. Twice." Anything that might motivate her to leave? "No. God. I hope not. Joni never said — but then people don't —" He shut up. I knew then, because he projected it so powerfully that I didn't need an empathic link to feel it, that he was legit; he'd had nothing to do with her disappearance.

"Mr. Rafferty," I said as gently as I could, "you're going to need to watch what you project."

I saw it then, in his face, what I used to see in my own, shortly before I stopped looking in mirrors: he didn't care anymore. I could do what I wanted with him; the worst had already happened.

The residents I dealt with usually made it easy to cite their code lapses and empathy ban violations. The empathic part of my brain sometimes reminded me that all of us simply tried to survive this new, lean-government, corporate system, with its relentless drive for peak productivity and agile decision-making. We had no room for the time or emotional strength to maintain property according to the rules. Fear and isolation, however, had a way of bleeding through the inhibitors to make for a lot of pissed-off residents. I told myself I was citing attitudes, not the people themselves.

Ian Rafferty was something rare, one of the throwbacks who had opted to dispense with inhibitors in favor of simple self-control. I found myself wanting badly to flout the system, to pull out all the stops to find his wife Joni, the way I would have once, in a different uniform, productivity and efficiency be damned.

Those were seditious thoughts, though; around a citizen who wasn't using inhibitors, I needed to watch what I myself projected. I merely thanked him and shook his hand. Then I walked across the street to the neighbor's.

I was allowed to interview a maximum of two witnesses, at my discretion, for context on any given call. On most calls, any witnesses were anonymous informers, and neighbors had a habit of being out of earshot when I rang the doorbell.

Liza Hill contrasted with this in two ways. Not only had Rafferty named her; but I already had a rapport with her, one I didn't recall until I set foot on the walkway leading to the front door. Three months ago, a nuisance-animal call: I was supposed to trap and kill the mother and four baby raccoons Mrs. Hill had found in her attic, but I was newly assigned to her neighborhood and wanted the chance to cultivate some goodwill. I borrowed a trick from an old animal control officer friend and showed the Hills how to evict the wild family through loud music and bright lights.

The Liza Hill I'd met then had been gracious, thrilled to have a humane solution in a cultural climate that seemed to be growing more callous by the day. Her thanks had been full of smiles and light that gave me hope. Even her blonde hair had seemed to capture and radiate sunlight.

The woman standing on her doorstep now barely resembled her. The blonde had gone brassy. The smile had sunk into a sullen droop. The sparkling brown eyes had turned as dull as a puddle of churned-up mud. She was holding a tall glass that held what looked like white sangria, golden liquid keeping a few listless pieces of citrus afloat.

I had to force myself not to gape, especially after re-introducing myself. She seemed not to remember me at all. What had caused this in the space of three months?

"I haven't seen Joni since last night," she announced, loudly enough so that Ian Rafferty might have heard her. "She left sometime after midnight."

"Any idea what time, exactly?

"We were in the backyard." She gestured behind her. Sangria spilled over her glass onto her hand. "She said she needed to get home. She just walked around the side of the house, where the grass is soft. She likes to walk on it in her bare feet, she says it feels like carpet." She took a drink. "But she was very careful so she wouldn't slip and fall. The sprinklers had just gone off, she was waiting for them to stop. She didn't want to raise a fuss. Make the neighbors come to their windows and shout at the drunk housewives." Liza's lip curled. She took another drink.

I guessed that wouldn't have been the first time the women had raised a fuss with the neighbors. "How much would you say she had drunk?" I asked.

Liza didn't seem to have heard me. Her eyes had lost their focus. "The moon was so bright," she said. "Like some kind of guiding message. Joni said to me, 'Isn't the night just filled with possibilities?' I don't think I'll ever forget that. Would you?"

Did you forget about the raccoon family? I wanted to ask, but I didn't. Instead I stuck to the important facts to thumb into my phone: Joni Rafferty. Left this home for her own two doors down, on foot, sometime after midnight. Drunk. Much like her friend was now.

Since the early days of the empathy ban, inhibitor delivery had evolved from pills — which the cheap still used – to wearables: wigs or skin implants laced with the same drugs that were in the pills.

Whether Liza Hill had decided to double-dip on inhibitors, pills plus a wig or implant, or how the alcohol might interact with the inhibitors, was tough to tell. What that might mean for her statement was even tougher. I squinted down at her in the midday sun. "And you watched her go towards the street and turn in the direction of her own home?" I had to work at the sound of impartiality. One slip in the way you treated these people, or in the way they perceived you treated them, and you could be shipped to a labor facility that same week.

Mrs. Hill was, however, too happy to care how I sounded. "Of course not, love," she crooned. "I was on the divan."

I wanted to ask her to show me, but it wasn't as if it was technically a crime scene. Besides, I'd again forgotten to carry sunscreen with me, and the sun had started to sear the flesh of my nose and cheeks. I needed to wrap this up. "Mrs. Hill, when Joni first came over, did she seem at all upset or worried?"

A big sip of her sangria. "Not in the least. Joni is a happy person. Beautiful family, beautiful house. No reason to be upset or worried." Defensive, I scribbled in my notebook. Tried not to be unsettled about why she would feel the need to be that way with me, why she might withhold information that would get her friend found. "You have no reason to think anyone would target her?"

"Of course not." She flapped her hand as if the question needed to be swatted away. "She used to be a nonprofit director, for god's sake. They don't have enemies."

That depended on the nonprofit. I made a note. "Was anyone else with you?"

Blinking this time. Then, slowly: "My next-door neighbor, Brooke. But you don't need to talk to her. She left before Joni did."

I'd learned as a rookie that the people I "didn't need to talk to" usually had the most crucial information on cases. "Next door on which side?" I asked.

She gestured to her right. The sangria in the glass again slopped over the edge onto her hand. She raised it to her lips, took another big gulp.

I opted to deflect. "Any chance she would want to escape? Take off, leave it all behind?"

She gave a short, cynical bark of a laugh, again so at odds with the bubbly woman I'd first met. "Where would she go?" Another big sip of sangria. The glass was half empty in just the span of a ten-minute conversation.

That left some kind of opportunistic crime, but I didn't think Liza Hill was in any shape to help me work that out. Besides, my time allotted for this interview was about up. I turned off my phone screen. "Thanks for your time, Mrs. Hill."

She regarded me as if she'd just noticed I was here. "Bit different from raccoons, isn't it?" she said softly. Then, before I could answer, she turned and shut the door.

About as different as you could get. I headed back down the walkway to the sidewalk, checked the side yard for signs of struggle, anything dropped behind. The grass was unruffled, though, the border hedges undisturbed. As if Joni Rafferty had vanished into thin air.

I paused beneath the shade of a big maple tree that grew at the front of the hedgerow between the Hills' property and the neighbor's. Even though loitering in between interviews meant flirting with half an hour's docked pay, I wanted time to go back over my notes. If Ian Rafferty was, despite my earlier sense, the threat Joni had gone on the run from, I had one more chance to find out. Even though her friend Brooke had left early and would be able to offer no insight into Joni's actual disappearance, she might be more inclined to talk about Ian. Sweat trickled from my neck down my back as I considered different lines of questioning.

Rubber screeched on pavement, and then a Jaguar convertible roared past me, around the corner and up the Alberinis' driveway. It was my cue to get a move on, even though I wondered how much information I might reasonably get from a person who felt such a great need to dominate a quiet suburb.

I followed the Jag up the driveway. The owner, a tall, dark-haired, distinguished-looking guy, had lingered in his garage, looking over a workbench as if deciding whether to take on a hobby project. He glanced up as I hovered outside the door. "Help you with something?" he called to me.

I held up the identification badge that hung on a lanyard around my neck. "May I come in?"

He beckoned. I followed him into the garage's belly, up two steps and through the door into a kitchen that looked recently photographed for a cooking magazine, gleaming pink granite countertops and cherry wood cabinets, not a pan or utensil out of place. Its professional feel gave it a sort of edge, as if I didn't watch my step, I'd knock the whole thing out of place.

The Jag driver waited on me with a steady practiced gaze, as if I were a subordinate about to deliver a presentation. I ignored it. I didn't even present to my own boss. "Sir, I'm investigating the disappearance of your neighbor, Joni Rafferty."

The managerial demeanor gave way for a moment. His jaw hung open; his brow furrowed in a way that appeared genuinely disturbed. He said, "Joni's missing?"

"Her husband reported her missing this morning after she failed to arrive home from her friend's."

"Liza's, right? You mean Liza's." The frown deepened. "They're my wife's best friends, but Brooke left early last night."

"Any particular reason? Mr...."

A blush crept up his neck into his face. "Alberini. Sorry. No reason in particular. They'd been drinking, she was feeling..." He motioned in a way that could have meant anything; tired, sick, horny, bored, pissed off. "She came back around eleven. We went to bed not long after."

"Joni never came back here?"

"No. She'd have no reason to." Some other emotion came into his face, something almost like wistfulness, but it was gone before I could pin it down. "You don't think anything happened to her?"

"There's no sign of foul play, if that's what you're asking."

He snorted. "Yeah. They're good at leaving no traces."

He was practiced at hiding his less diplomatic gaffes. The corner of his mouth quirked in what could have been a wince; he adjusted his posture. This was my cue to ignore what he'd said.

Thing was, while he could report me for lack of deference, he knew I could report him right back for sedition. And so, for the moment, I had an upper hand that might help an investigation. I said, "They?"

He shifted again. "You know. The foreigners down at the beach." The words slid off his tongue as if they tasted bad. "No offense. I know they're the reason we're able to live here." He didn't seem to be able to help his lip curl; I thought it was meant to be in irony. Now that the initial shock of the news had worn off, he regained his poise, including a touch of impatience. He continued, "I've heard sometimes they come up here and kidnap our women and children. Just because they can, because they're protected. They keep them for themselves instead of auctioning them. That's what I thought you were investigating."

Just like that, my upper hand came back down to earth. I had no real authority, not like that, and he knew it. Even without following me home, down off the hillside into the veritable company town below, they all knew I was as much a part of this system as they were. They thought the way the public had always thought about cops: a mix of fear and resentment, and always, always trying to find the advantage.

I kept the charade going. "All lines of inquiry are open." My tone pleasant. "Do you know anyone else who's lost a wife or child to them?"

That blush again crept up his neck to his chin. "No. Not personally. Just seen them up here, cruising around, like they're looking for property. Like they'd ever be allowed to move up here with the decent business owners. We figure they're here looking for something else." His chin jutted with self-righteousness.

From what I'd heard, it was entirely possible they were up here looking for property. I'd heard the Russian enterprise executives had purchased or at least squatted in the palatial mansions that lined Route 1A. Correcting him, however, would only get us into a pissing match; Tom Alberini was playing a role from times long gone by — the tough-upper-middle-class-manager I-make-enough-to-pay-your-salary act, back when police were viewed more as "public" than "servant." Now, all I could do was maintain patience. "Can you tell me when and how often you've seen them?"

The blush kept creeping. "Not often. Not so we'd feel the need to call you folks, but often enough that we'd notice."

Which meant once, maybe twice. Maybe even not at all. And not to the point where he felt threatened. "When was this?"

"Over the last year or two." He gave a short, sharp nod, as if to confirm this to himself.

"Have a vehicle description?"

"Nah, you know what kinds of beaters they drive. Miracle they ever get them off the cinder blocks in the front yard."

Now that was interesting. The Russians didn't drive beaters. I made a mental note rather than a digital one, turned my phone screen off, shoved the device in my back pocket. "Is your wife home? I'd like to speak with her as well."

"What for? I've told you she came home early last night. She's got nothing to do with this."

"Nothing to do with what?" A woman's voice from the doorway. Practically cued, she drifted into the kitchen. Her poise suggested a start as a model or actress, either of which she might still be doing, or might have given up in this new world. Tall, skinny, dressed in a short pink silk robe, long dark hair piled neatly in the kind of intricate beehive that indicated it could only be a wig.

"Brooke. You shouldn't be up so early." Alberini held out his arm. His wife fit her waist into it for a kiss on the cheek. Then she pulled free. His fingers trailed over her hip like a promise. She went to open one of those cherry wood cupboards.

Her husband said to her back, carefully, as if to test her reaction, "This officer has some questions for you, if you're feeling up to it."

She turned back around, glass in hand, and raked her gaze over me as if deciding whether I was worth speaking to. "Questions about what?"

I took a gentle approach, pulled my phone back out of my pocket. "Your friend Joni's husband, Ian, reported her missing this morning."

She froze on her path to the refrigerator, snapped her head around and locked gazes with her husband. "Joni? My God! But I just saw her last night!"

I couldn't decide whether it was an act, whether the two of them were violating the empathy ban through that channel their eyes had established, even though the wig meant inhibitors. I was supposed to probe them, but it always felt wrong, intruding on private marital connections. "I know. But she went missing shortly after midnight. Her husband said she never came home."

She resumed her deliberate steps. Opened the refrigerator, pulled out orange juice, poured herself a glass. "I can't believe it. I just can't. She'd never go off and leave the kids. Never."

"You have no thoughts about where she might go at that hour, if not home?"

"No. None. You're sure she's not still at Liza's? We both stay there sometimes."

The thought crossed my mind, whether Liza Hill or her husband had ever taken the time to go room by room. "I'm sure."

Sipping at the orange juice, she came to rest by her husband's side. He said, "I was just telling the detective that I think the foreigners down by the beach had something to do with this."

At that she rolled her eyes. "Oh, Tom. You and your foreigners." She smiled sweetly at me as if including me in on the joke. "Tom and his friends find a blade of grass out of place, they blame the foreigners. Which ones, dear? Serbians, or Russians?"

"It's not like that." Tom removed his arm from Brooke's waist, sulked.

"I suppose." Something beyond the window captured her attention. I followed her gaze. On deck a pool-boy had started his slow walk around the pool's perimeter. Not a foreigner, as far as I could tell, though I wondered whether he was a local kid encouraged to be entrepreneurial, or had been bussed in from the Stratham labor facility. Regarding him, Brooke pursed her lips as if measuring whether to say something else. I waited.

Eventually she turned her back to the pool boy, gave a small shake of her head, another brilliant smile. "I'm sorry I can't be of more assistance, Officer."

I wasn't done. "This is the first time Joni's gone missing, correct?" If life was going to give me better witnesses than Liza Hill, I wanted it to mean something.

Brooke's face clouded over. "Of course it is. Don't you have records of calls for service?"

I mirrored her. "Of course. But you said sometimes she's slept at Liza's, or I presume here —" I didn't miss the fast glance between the Alberinis — "so couldn't she have 'gone missing' in the past, only to end up in a new place you didn't know about previously?"

"No." Brooke's voice was firm, insistent. "This feels different, this time. It just does."

You get a sense, working in law enforcement long enough, of when people aren't telling you something. Especially when it's something crucial to your case. Maybe I might have to come back in the evening, try to get Liza Hill and Brooke Alberini alone and drunk, to find out what. Maybe I'd have better luck sacrificing a chicken and asking the water gods for an answer. I was welcome here in the day, when I had a reason to be here; by night, showing up would mean a one-way ticket to a labor facility. I shut my phone screen off once more, nodded to the Alberinis. "All right. Then I think we're finished here. Got what I need. Thanks both for your time. I'll be in touch."

Mr. Alberini eyed me as if wondering whether I wasn't suddenly "them" in disguise. Followed me back through the garage, possibly so I wouldn't snatch anything small and valuable. The door slammed behind me.

Walking down the driveway back to my car, I could feel a gaze heavy on my back, as if Brooke had telepathically leaped aboard and was trying to whisper something extra in my ear. It took everything I had not to turn, not to try to establish that link. I made it to the car and slipped into the driver's seat before I snuck a quick glance up at the hill their house sat on. No one was there.

#

I'd parked under the shade of an oak tree near the Raffertys' house. I sat in my assigned vehicle now, a Crown Vic so old I swore I'd driven it back in the day, to complete the necessary checkboxes for a missing person. I started with a quick review of the surveillance video feeds from overnight. There were three: one at each end of the street, a third on the corner. To be thorough, even if it took a few extra seconds, I ran each one from 11 the previous night through 3 this morning. None showed anything out of the ordinary. It was as if Joni Rafferty had disappeared into thin air.

I shook off the terrible sense of deja vu dropping a stone in my gut, turned my attention to filing reports: missing-persons report. Be on the Lookout notice, also known quietly as a "Diamond Alert" because the reports only went out for the landed gentry here in Hampton proper. The beach establishments' private police forces would search, too, would get everything I posted and would, over the next few nights, use their biometric scans on both their clientele and their new merchandise for any matching Joni's description. Whether "foreigners" had indeed kidnapped and trafficked her depended on their risk tolerance. Both the Russians and the Serbians had high tolerances, but legalization of their "entertainment" industry had turned them more towards business than danger. Unless they had a plastic surgeon who could do enough of a job to screw up the face matching, we would find her. I had to believe that.

I wrapped it up. Missing-persons reports, the same checkboxes as all our other reports with only a few lines for limited free text, weren't supposed to take any longer than 15 minutes to finish and file. If they did take longer, that would be docked pay plus a penalty fee. Enough to miss meat for a week, but it wasn't like I fed a family these days. Once upon a time I could've made up for it by staying later, but shifts were strict now because resources were limited — a half-hour spent canvassing would mean someone on the evening shift wouldn't have a vehicle, and my poor decisions would impact someone else's earnings. It wasn't as if the extra time could make a difference.

I checked my phone for the remainder of the day's assignments. No new calls were queued up — they rarely were — but the rest I had been assigned in the morning needed to be done. The next two were in this neighborhood, queued based on their geography, the efficiency of going from one place to the next. Maybe I could develop a few good leads on Joni Rafferty, like in the old days.

I put the car in gear just as someone shouted "Officer!"

I should have taken my foot off the brake, cruised down the street as if I'd never heard a thing. Out of the corner of my eye, though, I spotted a figure standing at the top of Ian Rafferty's driveway. I shifted the car back into park, but remained in the vehicle. If I got out, I knew, I might be here for much longer. Better to stay seated and let him know I didn't have time to compare notes.

He crossed the road towards me. Behind him, his daughters huddled together on the sidewalk like small wild animals dumped in a new and unfamiliar habitat. Suddenly I felt wrong about not spending more time with them.

He reached my door. "Anything?" he inquired.

I said, "Some information, but no real leads."

He nodded, lifted his chin to survey his neighbors' houses up the hill to my right. Useless, I could practically hear him thinking. "What now?" he asked.

"I've got a few other calls. I can ask those neighbors if they heard or saw anything."

"No, don't do that," he blurted. "I don't mean because — look, you're already there to get on them about code violations, they're not going to be in any frame of mind to cooperate with you. Are they?"

"If they don't cooperate, they'll have more to worry about than code violations." It was bluster, one of those things I wished I could take back as soon as I said it. "No. You're right. I don't know what now. There'll be some resources to commit to a search, but not a lot, and not for long."

His face closed itself over, a weary acceptance of how things were. "I'm an actuary for the businesses along the boulevard," he said. "I tell them how to keep their risks low. Their risks." He snorted, a tight bitter sound. "Years ago, college, I worked summers on the beach lifeguarding. Saved lives, helped find missing kids. Please. Tell me how I can help find my wife."

A question, do you remember, rose like a bubble up the back of my throat, only to burst in my mouth. The answer didn't matter anymore. I told him much the same thing I would've said in the past: "Stay home with your kids. Keep them secure. Let them know they still have a dad." Closing off that little bit of connection, the thing that might, once upon a time, have made me move heaven and earth for as long as I needed to find his wife. Things didn't work that way anymore, and we both knew it.

CHAPTER TWO

In a lot of ways the empathy ban made life easier. You couldn't miss what you didn't have a connection to; you no longer had to worry about making yourself vulnerable. Days like today, when a single call had the power to make me feel like a real cop again, were a bittersweet mess of memories and mislaid plans. I chose this life, I often reminded myself. After Election Day three years ago, six months before I'd planned to put in my papers, knowing I was never going to move to Costa Rica the way I'd wanted to — would never open a bar for other American expats, never find a good woman with whom to live out the rest of my days — I'd taken the deal that was offered to me: keep your salary, work for the foreseeable future, give your retirement fund a chance to build up.

Except I wasn't sure there was a retirement fund. The job itself was pretty easy, but the ripple effects of how it had come about swirled around my brain. In the first six months under the newly elected president and cabinet, government as we knew it had been completely dismantled, all the departments privatized. Lifelong bureaucrats found themselves unemployed, downgraded to less prestigious roles if they couldn't produce measurable results; recent retirees were forced out of retirement to "pull their own weight." That had happened to my former police chief and a couple of the local sheriffs. Worse, one or two of the other near-retirees I'd known had tried to retire anyway. I didn't know if they had planned to leave the country, but I never heard from them again.

This was why finding Joni Rafferty was especially attractive to me. Apart from her husband's actuarial sensibilities, I knew what "measurable results" meant in my world of lawn care and fence type enforcement. Results from the kind of police work I did back in the day, though, were on much shakier ground. At times like this I counted my blessings that I hadn't been assigned to work security for the businesses along Hampton Beach. You couldn't get much further from old-style police work than that.

I signed out at my next assigned residence, a couple of blocks over from the Raffertys' house. All it took these days were taps on the dispatch app. Dispatchers had been inefficient for years before Election Day — on a busy day it could take several minutes to get them on the radio, especially if they worked the phones, radios, and computers alone — but I missed the radio sometimes, the snap of an annoyed dispatcher's voice or the unspoken "who loves you" when they found a piece of info we needed. They'd known how to make an over-the-air empathic connection, and patrol felt isolated without it.

My next call after the Raffertys' concerned lawn care: a lawn that had gone brown and "scraggly in spots," the app informed me, and indeed it had. I walked up the front walkway of an angular, 1960s-style ranch, and knocked on its door.

A woman answered. She was almost as tall and as old as I was, willowy, swaying in turquoise silk pajamas — did everyone up here spend Saturdays in their pajamas? — as she opened the door. Her head was wrapped in a turban that matched the silk. Her sharp brown eyes went from curious to fearful as soon as she saw my identification. Her hand went up to her ear to fiddle with a hoop earring. "May I help you?" she asked.

I didn't know her name. Our reports didn't offer names, just addresses, and I hadn't been assigned to this zone long enough to get to know anyone. Policy dictated I wouldn't be.

I shook it off. "Good morning, ma'am. I received a report about your lawn." I gestured behind me. "Something going on with your lawn care service?"

Something like defiance lifted her chin and made her eyes flash. "We canceled it," she announced.

I waited for more, but none came. "You were going to care for it yourselves?" I asked.

"Yes, and for the first few weeks of spring, the organics we were using did wonderfully," she said. "Then my husband had to travel, and the sprinklers stopped working, and that heat wave..."

"When did the sprinklers stop working?"

"About a month after we canceled lawn care."

"You know lawn care fixes those?"

Another lift of her chin. Any higher and she'd be sneering down at me. "Of course we know. It isn't worth the chemicals they use." With that the chin came back down and a frightened stare widened her eyes, as if she thought she'd said too much.

I didn't have a ready answer for her. Weren't there organic lawn-care companies? "Ma'am," I said, "please consider this your first warning. If the lawn isn't on its way to greening back up in one week, the HOA will have to start fining you. It'll be the cost of lawn care plus your penalty."

She shook her head. "We can't have that lawn care service. I'd hire a different one, believe me, but none seem to deal with organics. Do you know of any?" Her voice bordered on desperation. I felt it, too, dark and heavy around the edges of my mind. Apparently she, like Ian Rafferty, had dispensed with the inhibitors.

I kept my tone even to try and keep her calm. "I'm sorry I don't."

I didn't even know if any had existed before Election Day. "Ma'am, the chemicals don't get into your home water supply or anything. You realize that, right?"

Fury crept into her gaze, leaked out around the edges of her mind. "No? Well, they must be getting into something. Explain this." She unwrapped her turban. I held up my hands, a weak attempt at stopping her. The long turquoise fabric spooled at our feet. Before long she stood in front of me, head bald, patches of what looked like eczema sprinkled like pink nonpareils across her scalp. "Just a year ago my hair was as thick and shiny as when I was 20. Now this. My doctor is useless, but I've got friends dealing with the same thing. What else could it be but chemicals?"

"Ma'am." My allotted time on this call had started to run out. I tried not to let my exasperation show. "I'm just the messenger. I'm explaining that you need to find a way to green that lawn back up. You can do it yourselves, find another lawn care company, whatever, but I'm going to need to see the start of a greener lawn by this time next week. And for god's sake," I lowered my voice, "if you're not using inhibitors, watch what you project. Understood?"

She stared me down as if it was four years ago when she had a choice, snarled, "Understood." Then shut the door in my face.

In my app I noted "first warning" and "advised subject to get lawn care service" and that was that. Ian Rafferty had been right: she hadn't been in any frame of mind to respond to questions about his wife.

My next call was to a corner lot that had garnered a complaint last week about a playset that was too large. The homeowner had solved that by breaking the set down into its component parts and distributing them around the backyard. Now it looked cluttered, but it was below fence level, and besides, his kids seemed happy. "You ever find out who reported us?" he asked, but I told him I didn't have access to that information — I truly didn't — and he said he hoped the person would be happy now. So did I, though I was reasonably sure that the cash reward for informing on his neighbor had settled things.

"Hey," I said as I got ready to go. "You see a woman walk down your street, last night around midnight?"

His eyes narrowed. "I was in bed at midnight."

"Of course. Sorry to trouble you."

"Although," he said then, "I did hear something that sounded like screaming."

"Screaming?"

"Yeah. But I thought it was probably just animals mating."

Given the surveillance videos' feeds, he was probably right. I thanked him, went back down his walkway to the street and my vehicle. I marked his call "Resolved" and continued on. I had five minutes to get to my next call, and that was in another neighborhood entirely. I got moving. This was how the rest of my day went: warnings about pets, wind chimes, hedge heights, some I noticed en route, most called in by neighbors with the best of intentions. By the time it was time to go home, my midday burst of feeling like a real cop had broiled away under the summer sun.

#

Adding insult to injury was a request from my supervisor to talk after I turned in my vehicle. Praise never got doled out unless it was for exceptional service that made good business sense, and that wasn't how I operated, so this had to be a reprimand. Between the heat and the reminder of what my job used to stand for, the day had felt like a death march to nowhere. All I wanted was to get home, crack an ice-cold beverage, and relax underneath the ceiling fan on its highest setting. Then, let the cold numb the bubbling memories, let the breeze blow them away, until only silence and darkness was left.

Instead I threaded my way through hallways en route to the supervisor's office. Years ago, before Election Day, the tiny, garrison-like structure that had served as Hampton PD's beach outpost was replaced by a bigger, more corporate-looking building. I was grateful for that. It allowed me to focus on the strange silence in a space that should have been alive with keys clacking as cops typed incident reports on drug busts and drunken scuffles and missing daughters. Now it was like a tomb. I focused on the hollow sound of my footsteps.

The supervisor's office was in what might have been an interrogation room back in the day, before checkboxes and drop-down lists replaced human interaction with even our suspects. The room lacked windows and air, and like all good interrogation rooms, closed in as soon as I stepped inside.

The supervisor, a young guy named Will who looked barely old enough for his goatee, offered me a seat in the dowdy corporate cushioned chair in front of his desk. I opted to stand. I didn't expect to be here long.

"Talk to me about this missing-persons report," Will said. The words "missing" and "persons" sounded like he was speaking a different language. That was probably accurate. It wasn't only that the three times I'd met him, he seemed bemused, as if he couldn't figure out how he'd ended up here. It was also on my end: this was the first such report I'd taken in this new world, and he'd been assigned here less than a year. I had no idea where he'd come from, where the previous supervisor had been sent.

I gave him the rundown on Joni Rafferty, her habits, her neighbors, her inability to have left any indicators behind.

He said, "Is that why you spent an extra twenty minutes up there?"

Inwardly I cursed. I thought I'd remained under my limits, but that pause to talk to Ian Rafferty hadn't helped. I said, "This was my first missing-persons report since — well, given the circumstances, I fell back on prior experience working those kinds of cases."

As soon as the words were out of my mouth I wished I'd chosen differently. I'd learned that "the way we've always done it" was frowned upon, if only because the new government was trying to establish a new way of always doing things.

Will scowled, so bemused gave way to annoyed. "Taking extra time isn't going to find her any faster."

"I know." I narrowly avoided tacking on a "sir" at the end.

"I'm docking you half an hour's pay. The twenty minutes plus ten extra for thinking you know better than our efficiency experts who programmed this app. You'll be able to work this case in between your other calls?"

That meant ask for information about this missing woman from people I warned or cited. "Sure," I said. "How long am I being given to find her?"

His mobile device chimed. He reached for it, thumbed his passcode into the screen. "She'll turn up," he said. "Biometrics will catch her, alive or dead. You can go."

I left. Probably a good thing to cut that short: I could argue that biometrics meant nothing on a badly decomposed body, on a live woman who had been given plastic surgery, or traded on markets which used no biometrics at all.

Officially, though, none of those possibilities existed. I'd only been docked half an hour's pay, which wasn't great, but meant I could have meat every day if I skimped. The chewing-out hadn't taken long at all. I began my walk home.

CHAPTER THREE

Freedom or no, I felt every hour of that shift. I'd traded five eight-hour days with considerable risk for five ten-hour days with much less risk, but it was a lot at my age. That, and the creeping sense that Will was either hopelessly naive, or had downplayed concern over what might happen if this woman was never found. The email that had introduced him had made clear that he was there to drive better, more efficient results. I hadn't thought our results were bad, but then again, it wasn't as if I talked to the other residential security associates. Part of the empathy ban, and especially our ability to enforce it, were work structures, including schedules and routes, that made it difficult for us to congregate. I had no way to know if I had been asked to piggyback the investigation on other calls because it was overall more efficient — or because it was me they wanted to test.

I pushed aside the worrying thoughts. My walk home, like my morning walk to work, was designed to ground me, to help me keep a sense of sanity. All I had to do was ignore the transition from the daylight beach tourism activities to the evening ones. No matter what people like Tom Alberini said, up in the hills, time and distance insulated the residents. They never had to be aware that Ocean Boulevard existed, except most people didn't know what it had become. During the day, they still saw the same concerts, festivals, family friendliness as ever; by sunset they went home. Then came nightfall and curfew.

Knowing this, although tempted to sit on the seawall and sink my aching feet into the cold saltwater, I kept going. This time of year, another few hours would pass before sunset, but already the Maseratis and Porsches had begun to assemble in the long, central parking lot strip, awaiting the start of their owners' evening entertainment.

I did, then, what I always did on the walk home: kept my chin pointed to the east, gazed out over the Atlantic surf rumbling ashore, remembered the days when an actual beach had been accessible from the seawall. Sometimes, at high tide or in rough weather when the waves lapped over the concrete onto my shoes, I took comfort in knowing that in the not too distant future, the rising sea level would make all of this inhospitable.

The day's heat had baked into the sidewalks and buildings, but the humid salt air felt good. I breathed it deeply.

A pair of ATVs turned onto the boulevard from G Street, not too fast, but their blue lights flashed Enterprise Security, Code 3.

In three years, I'd only seen a Code 3 response a handful of times. My pace quickened in spite of myself. I turned to watch. From here I couldn't see any crowds gathering. Whatever it was, must have been happening at the far end of the boulevard, past where I'd come from.

More vehicles rushed by: a fire engine, an ambulance. "... shark attack?" a woman speculated to her husband or boyfriend or sugar daddy, equal parts fear and hope as they stood together by the railing.

I wanted to go home. Climb the few steps to my tiny three-roomer, shut the world off, sit on my sofa and think about nothing. I almost kept going. I knew, though, that I wouldn't last long at home, not the way my instincts tingled. Will's dressing-down aside, this felt like I needed to go check it out. I turned around.

I took another fifteen minutes to reach the Marine Memorial and see the crowd. It pooled around the sidewalk near what was left of the granite jetty that my daughter had once loved to traverse. The boulevard had been blocked off in one direction, traffic rerouted through the parking lot across the street. My gut tightened. They had set up like a crime scene.

I couldn't imagine Enterprise Security doing that for a sex worker, though, not these days. I touched the plastic card on its loop around my neck, made sure my ID was easily accessible. If that was Joni Rafferty washed up on the beach, I didn't want to wait for the facial-recognition notification to tell me, hours too late to get in front of it.

I reached the small crowd, which lined the metal railing. The uniformed security team had started to tie on yellow tape. I scanned faces reflexively to see if anyone was wound up or excited or in tears. No one was. I turned my attention to the scattered granite stones. The tide was out; plainclothes types stood on the stones, all looking down at something that lay at their feet.

I retraced my steps, leaned over the railing from an acceptable distance. At first the object of the plainclothes types' attention seemed like a blue blanket or rug. Then someone snapped a photograph, and in the flash the blue blanket fractured into glittering shards. Of course it was a dress, not a blanket. A blue sequined dress. Not likely Joni Rafferty, not the last thing she'd been seen wearing. I couldn't figure out whether to be relieved or disappointed.

I caught a detective's eye. An unexpected flash of recognition: where did I know her from? I broke down her features one by one: long dark wavy hair, pulled into a loose ponytail and flipped over her shoulder; slim runner's body; heart-shaped face, narrow nose. Almost Latin, if it were possible to achieve a position in Enterprise Security with that ethnicity, and if most with that ethnicity hadn't been deported.

None of her rang a bell, and she'd turned her attention to a colleague. I returned my attention to the crowd.

That was when I saw Joni Rafferty.

Pale skin, white-gold hair, ice-blue eyes, a square jaw: beautiful if her expression hadn't been so vacant, if her appearance hadn't given the sense that she'd been out on an 18-hour bender of booze and stimulants. Before I could work out what this meant, she evaporated along with the morning haze.

Shit. I'd moved too slowly. I walked toward the crowd once more, stepped into the street, scanned the backs of heads, the parking lot to my left, the sidewalks ahead and behind me. No one else, Mrs. Rafferty or other, went there. My neck crawled: what if that was her on the rocks? Had I seen her haunting her own crime scene?

An ambulance pulled up. A set of EMTs carted a stretcher down the cement steps, scuffed through the sand on their way to the jetty. No medical examiner; that meant the victim wasn't Joni. Her facial structure would've been a hit on the scanners, and there'd be stricter crowd control and secrecy. Instead what we gawked at was the aftermath of a deal gone wrong: probably sex, maybe drugs, definitely business.

Normally these outcomes were confined to the motel rooms and alleys where transactions were completed. Not out in public like this, not in a way that would capture attention. I couldn't imagine what message this was meant to convey.

I started to head back to the sidewalk. It was long past time to get home.

"Help you with something?" My path, blocked. The female detective from the rocks; she must have climbed up the shallow concrete lip, swung her long legs over the metal railing. Close up, my sense that I knew her grew even stronger, but I still couldn't place her. The mirrored sunglasses she wore didn't help.

I held up my ID. "I was on my way home from work. Saw the

activity, walked up this way in case that was the missing person I was assigned to find this morning." I nodded at the zipped-up body and stretcher being moved up the beach towards us.

She eyed me. "Not your property, then," she muttered, almost to herself.

"I look like an establishment owner?" I couldn't keep the snark from my voice.

A slow smile spread across her face. I couldn't figure out if it was a nice one or not; the rest of her was unreadable. "Guess not." She held up her own ID, pulled off her shades. "Suzanne Costa. Enterprise Security. Who's your missing person?"

Our eyes met. Hers were a bright, clear blue. In that instant I saw us building a partnership, like in the old days, bantering while we ran down leads and identified suspects and rescued victims.

My mind had acted of its own accord to establish an empathic connection I hadn't actively sought. I tamped it down, nodded towards the spit of land that jutted out of the north end of Hampton Beach. "Woman from Hampton proper. Husband's an actuary for the enterprise." At least until artificial intelligence replaced him and he got three months to retrain into a new job.

Costa's eyebrows went up. If she'd noticed my empathic slip, she didn't let on. "And she's missing-missing? Not just on a bender at her friend's or something?"

"No, that's where she left from. She's missing." I avoided her eyes, thought of the ghostly face in the crowd. In my memory it had started to float, bodiless, even though I thought I'd seen a red hoodie where its shoulders would've been.

"You know the first thing I ran was facial recognition, and I didn't come up with any hits. So good luck with that. Do you have any — " Her words were cut off by a silver Audi allowed through the roadblock, rolling up to the scene. "There's my establishment owner.

Again, good luck. See you around." She shoved her shades back on her face, unblocked my path, went to meet the Audi. The crowd had dissipated as soon as the stretcher went into the ambulance. The sidewalk stretched long and deserted in front of me.

Costa's good-luck wish unsettled me; she may as well have echoed Will, talking about his faith in biometrics. She had been about to ask if I had any leads, and I couldn't think of a way I would have told her — delusions of partnership or no — that Joni Rafferty had been in front of me, and I moved too damn slowly. I hunched my shoulders and walked home, fast against the sea breeze.

#

After about twenty minutes, when I'd passed the Seashell stage, a car slowed before it pulled up next to me. Black vehicle, one of those distinctive unmarked Challengers, with their shark-like grille grimaces. Enterprise Security had definitely gotten the better end of the deal on vehicles. Like house slaves, they were afforded more privileges; they had a more discernable effect on the bottom line. The window glided down. "Offer you a ride home?" said a female voice.

I peered into the vehicle's interior. Costa, the detective from the crime scene, grinned at me.

I shouldn't have been astonished that she could clear a crime scene so soon; but once finishing with the establishment owner, that had probably been the end of it for her. I wanted to be righteously indignant on behalf of the dead girl, but the fact was, Costa had no more control over her place in this system than I did in mine. That didn't mean I was comfortable accepting her offer. My paranoia said that predator's grille was pointed in the wrong direction, and breaking from routine could only lead to ruin. "No, thanks," I said.

The grin widened, became something else. "You down here looking for something?" she asked knowingly.

We were across from what had once been the Casino Ballroom, now a meat market, mostly for younger merchandise. "No! Jesus."

"Come on, now," she said. "I know you don't live with anyone. You should milk that discount."

I shut her off. Stared straight ahead, resumed my walk. If this was some kind of test, it was a sick one. Even if Residential Security did get the kind of discount she meant, I wouldn't use it. I couldn't think of a bigger slap in the face.

The engine roared; the car pulled away. Good.

She must have circled back around, though, because within another few minutes the Challenger was once more in front of me. This time Costa got out, waited for me to catch up. Knowing I wouldn't cross the street to get away from her, not with the ballroom right there.

"Come on, neighbor," she called. "Don't you recognize me?"

"From the crime scene, sure," I said. Neighbor? Was that new language, the way comrade or brother had been once upon a time?

I stopped. We stared at each other. No inconvenient delusions this time. No illegal empathy. Thank God.

"We're literally next-door neighbors," she said. Sounding put out.

Her comment about knowing I didn't live with anyone took on an extra edge. She'd been watching me? That wasn't, however, the sort of thing you challenged Enterprise Security with. "Okay," I said. For myself, I'd made it a point only to notice enough about my neighbors to determine whether they were threats, real or potential. After years of being the "neighborhood cop," I had liked the anonymity; it didn't pay to notice many details. At least, if you weren't trying to gain pretext over people you lived nearby.

She kept going. "I thought I recognized you, but it took me some time to place you. Seriously, can I offer you a ride? You look beat. I'm headed home myself."

I couldn't help tossing the grenade back at her. "Sure you aren't down here looking for something, yourself?"

She smiled then, a beam of mirth that made me, in spite of myself, want to get to know her better. "Nah, I prefer to keep the paychecks I get, not give portions of them back." She winked. "Anyway, I found you, didn't I?"

I reeled from the joke. "Is that how it is," I choked out.

The grin grew wider. "It's however you want it to be." She burst into laughter. "You should see your face. Come on, sometimes a ride home is just a ride home."

I found myself climbing into her car, better judgment be damned. The banter had thrown me; my earlier vision of us as partners -- I refused to think of it as a bond, or the result of one — roared back into my head. Even so, after that opening, I tried to keep it professional. "You identify your victim?"

She glanced at me sidelong, swung the car into the parking lot for a U-turn. "I haven't even identified my passenger."

This time, in the confined space, I felt the blush spread from my neck to my face. "My name's Ray. Ray Trueman."

She nodded, satisfied. "Okay, Ray, Ray Trueman. I did ID our victim. Or rather, the establishment owner did." Her voice took on a cast I couldn't identify. "Biometrics saves the day."

"And? Any ideas on what happened to her?"

This drew out a deep sigh, as if she'd personally been assigned to protect this girl or boy and lost. "I saw ligature marks on her neck. To me it looks like one of the customers got too heavy into roleplay. We'll have to investigate, of course, this girl wasn't rated for roleplay."

Rated? I kept my mouth shut. Our phones, more specifically the apps, had microphone access. In the first few months after the Hampton Beach Business Consortium had been incorporated, we had heard about employees who had disappeared after questioning the system. Rumor, but no one took the chance anymore. Instead I said, "At least it shouldn't be too hard to figure out who the customer is."

She took the corner onto M Street, our little slice of company town, harder than she should have. "Here we are," she said. Pulled into her own driveway. "Tips appreciated, but not necessary."

We both got out. I couldn't shake the sense, empathy ban be damned, that my question about the customer had crossed a line. I tried to cover. "Did you at least find out if the girl had a name?"

A tch of disapproval, or frustration. "I said biometrics identified her." She clomped up the stairs to her own place. End of discussion, I thought, and stepped onto the sidewalk. The banter had been nice while it lasted, although maybe crueler. It reminded me of how things used to be between people, the connections we had made through shared experiences. I'd shut it down between Ian Rafferty and myself; now, Costa was shutting it down between herself and me. It was too dangerous for all of us.

Then she stopped. "Ayana," she called down from her porch.

I stopped, too. Costa wasn't looking at me. She remained on that top step, stared out into the darkness across the boulevard and the Atlantic. She said, "I was standing there when her ... handler ... called the house to notify them. The victim was called Ayana."

A chill in the sea breeze caught me off guard. Names still had power, perhaps even more in this era of quantification and catalog. This name felt especially electrified, as if speaking it had brought Ayana's ghost to our street.

The corner of her mouth quirked sadly. "She was lucky, you know. Not all the establishments let the girls have their names. Anyway. Good luck with your case. See you around." She walked the rest of the way to her door.

"Good luck to both of us," I called, my voice stronger than it had felt in the last ten minutes.

She didn't appear to have heard me, as she went inside. I watched her shut the door. She didn't turn on any lights. I imagined her dumping her stuff, kicking off her shoes, heading straight to her kitchen for a stiff drink of whatever her paycheck and her Enterprise Security perks enabled.

I hauled myself up the steps onto my own porch. Opening my door, I held my breath against the initial smell, the sunscreen and takeout meals of families past. The smell, like the banter with my neighbor, was to be avoided; those families were long gone, and the less I thought about them the better.

Instead, I did the same thing I always did: lock the place up tight, even though it meant the indoor dewpoint rose and made my joints swell. I would watch a little television and then go to bed, grateful for the insulation I'd installed on the Consortium's dime. The insulation was a buffer against the wind and the sounds from outside. It would be hard to sleep at night otherwise, hearing what went on in the dark.

Naturally, as I checked locks on windows and doors, a knock sounded at my door. I ignored it throughout two rooms, four windows, and my back door, but it grew more insistent.

If it was my so-called neighbor I was going to have a few things to say, whatever the risks to my job. I was too tired and sore to care. I tried to put as little weight as possible on my aching feet as I made my way back across the tiny cottage to the door.

I stared out onto a curfew-emptied street, ready to interrogate — what? Only the sodium streetlights and the shadowed cottages where other workers lived greeted me. I stood back, started to close the door.

A shadow to my right moved. I backed up fast, reaching my left hand for the screen door, my right hand for my empty belt.

"Please don't turn the light on," the intruder stage-whispered. "<u>Please</u>."

I paused. The figure came no closer. It stood there, swaying a little, shoulders hunched, head bowed, spelling all kinds of trouble. Drugs, an escaped sex worker, an Enterprise Security sting meant to ensure workers reported either one. Nonetheless, I dropped both my hands. "Are you in trouble?" I kept my voice low.

"I need help," the figure whispered. It shuffled forward so that in the dim light I could see its face.

Joni Rafferty stood at my door.

CHAPTER FOUR

I scanned the slumbering houses. People had once walked these streets into the wee hours. Those days I'd have given anything for this moment, another face, home at last. Now all I felt was anxiety that someone had seen her out wandering past curfew, had observed her here, that I might be complicit in a married woman's disappearance, even though of course none of my neighbors save Suzanne knew about my case.

Light spilled onto the porch as I opened the door wide enough to assess her. She wore a red hoodie, same as I'd seen on her just an hour ago — that was good, I wasn't losing my mind — and gray shorts, both dirty and stained, along with her Chucks. Her thick blonde hair was a tangled mess.

"Come on," I said. "Let's get you some help."

She followed me inside, her face as blank as it had been in the crowd earlier. I wondered if she'd somehow been lobotomized. I picked up my phone to make the report. With any luck, one of my night-shift colleagues would be out within the hour and have Joni home to her family by midnight.

I started punching in numbers. Behind me came a little gasp, a cry. I turned. She backed up against my door, her eyes wide. I put the phone down. "What's wrong?"

"You can't send me back to them," she breathed. "You can't. Please."

"Your family?"

Her mouth gaped. She made choking sounds, as if her airway was blocked.

I positioned myself in front of her. "Marlee and Makayla," I said, gently, hoping the names' familiarity would calm her. "Ian."

She shook her head and rapidly shuddered in a way that made me hope wasn't the start of a seizure. "No. No. I don't know who they are. I just can't go back." She slid down the door with her knees to her chest.

Jesus. Amnesia? The alcohol would've worked its way out of her system within a few hours, so what had happened to her between then and now that would account for this degree of shock? Or the slight accent, a tinge of the Spanish that had been all but eradicated from society. I wanted to connect empathically with her, kept myself honest. I held up the phone again. "I just want to get you a doctor," I said.

"No. No! They'll take me. I can't go back."

"All right. All right." I held up my hands. I went to put the phone on the table. Then thought better of it, stuck it between the cushions. Hoped I'd remember I put it there. "No phone calls. Can you —" A thought occurred to me. "Can you tell me your name?"

She gulped, nodded. "Ayana."

Oh. Shit.

"Ayana," I said gently, "My name is Ray. Are you hungry? Can I get you something to eat or drink?"

She stared at me, saucer-eyed. Finally, like a little girl, she nodded, four slow tentative shakes of her head.

"What would you like? I have some leftover canned spaghetti, some sandwich fixings."

Her voice was so quiet, I couldn't tell whether she was talking to me or herself. "Spaghetti? Please?"

I held out my hands. After a moment she took them, and I pulled her up. She gave me a small smile.

I led her to the kitchen. Tried not to think about the fact that she'd given me the same unusual name as my neighbor's murder victim, that I'd have to find a way to get my neighbor over here without spooking this woman, that there would be hell to pay if I did anything except bring her home to her husband and kids. I wondered what reaction she'd have if I simply did that; let them work out whatever she needed to get better.

I pulled the leftovers out of the fridge. Fixed her a plate, heated it in the microwave. "Iced tea? Lemonade?" I asked her.

"Iced tea," she whispered. I wondered if that was a Joni taste or an Ayana taste.

I fixed her a glass. The microwave beeped. I took the food out, grabbed a fork and napkin, set everything down on the table.

She wolfed down the meal, polishing off the spaghetti and the iced tea inside of maybe two minutes. When she was done, she rose and brought the container and glass to the sink. I watched her wash both with the sponge and dish detergent I kept beside the sink, then place them carefully in the drain rack.

Watching a woman do a chore in my home for the first time in years was surreal. "You didn't have to do that," I said when she shut the water off.

She stared vacantly over my shoulder. "Oh."

We stood awkwardly in my silent kitchen. I wished desperately for a way to signal Costa next door. Flick my lights? Pound on the wall? Either would spook Joni/Ayana, and I couldn't afford to let her go. "Ayana," I said, "What do you remember?"

She turned the vacant gaze on me. "Remember?"

I nodded. "About coming here to my house. About where you were before."

She wrapped her arms around herself. "In the salt marsh. So cold when the tide comes in."

She should have been caked with mud, her hair stringy from the salt water, but other than a few smudges she looked like all she'd done was wander the streets for the last 18 hours. "What about before the salt marsh?" I asked.

Her ice-blue eyes rolled away, stared at a point on the ceiling behind me. "On a boat? I think. Dark. Floaty feeling."

I'd have to ask her husband if they owned a boat. "And before the boat?"

Tears welled up. "I can't."

"Please. It could be important."

She squeezed her eyes shut. The tears dribbled down her cheeks. "No. No. They're my friends, they would never do — no, I can't." She began to rock back and forth.

"Who, J — Ayana?" I asked gently.

"Brooke and Tom. I can't. I can't." The rocking intensified, the words faded into a mumble.

The Alberinis? I was in even more of a world of shit if they'd been involved, either with Joni's disappearance, or with the girl on the beach, or, apparently, both. "Who are Brooke and Tom, Ayana?" I asked.

Her head snapped up. She glared at me. "Who's Ayana? My name is Joni." She took in the few details of my kitchen, stood with a jerk that shoved her chair back hard against the wall. "Where am I? How did I get here? Who are you?"

"My name is Ray Trueman. I'm with Residential Security and I've been looking into your disappearance from your home on Hampton Oaks Lane late last night. You showed up on my doorstep about thirty minutes ago, telling me your name was Ayana."

She stared at me, less belligerent now, slack-jawed; she blinked a few times, reached her hand to her head as if to adjust a hat, put it back down by her side. "I want to go home."

I decided to keep her on the defensive, see where it led. "Mrs. Rafferty, you just said something to me about your friends, Brooke and Tom Alberini, being involved in what seemed like a pretty traumatic event. Can you tell me about that?"

More rapid blinking, another reach for her head. "They would never do anything bad. Please, I just want to go home to my family."

No accent this time. "You don't know the name Ayana?"

"No. Why should I?"

"All right." I held up my hands. "Let's get you home. I know how worried your family is." I returned to the living room, plucked the phone back out from between the cushions. Then stood there, twiddling it between my fingers. I didn't want to call a colleague. Who knew how long it would take them to come out here? I could walk to the station to sign one out of the motor pool, assuming any were available; but I couldn't bring Joni/Ayana with me, not after dark. That would mean leaving her here for quite a while, which I wasn't comfortable with, now that she was in my custody.

Unless my newly introduced neighbor could make herself available to keep Joni/Ayana company, to help drive her home and get a sense of what was going on.

"Mrs. Rafferty," I said carefully, "I'd like to take you next door. My neighbor works for Enterprise Security, and she has a take-home vehicle. I'd like to see if she's available to bring you home."

She fixed me with that cool blue gaze again. "I don't care how you do it as long as it can happen quickly."

I gestured toward my front door. "After you."

Even the few short paces from my front door to Suzanne's demonstrated that nothing could ever be simple. Something about the outside environment — the dark, the sharp tang of saltwater in the air, a girl's faraway scream — triggered whatever was locked deep inside Joni Rafferty's brain. By the time I knocked on my neighbor's door, Ayana was back, head bowed, shivering in her red sweatshirt.

It took a few tries to get Suzanne to the door. When she finally answered, something wasn't right. She'd put her long dark hair up in a bun, but it was messy, frayed like she'd been pulling at it. Her face was flushed, but her eyes were dry. And she was restless, watchful, not at all the kind neighbor she'd presented to me on the street a few hours ago. "Suzanne," I said, "I'm your neighbor, Ray. Do you have a few minutes?"

Her steel gray eyes flicked from me to Joni/Ayana and then back again. "A few." She stood aside and let us in, shut the door behind us so quickly I felt the corner whisper against my shirt back. "Now," she said, "what can I do for you?"

She wanted us out. That much was clear. I didn't know if I could reasonably give her that option. I glanced over at Joni/Ayana, who slouched like she wanted to shrink into an inner hidden pocket of her sweatshirt. "She showed up on my doorstep about half an hour ago." I decided to head directly for Go. "She told me her name was Ayana."

The expression on Suzanne's face morphed from closed irritation to wary disbelief.

"I know," I said weakly.

I was useless. Suzanne turned her full attention on the woman beside me. "Ayana," she emphasized the name, "I'm Suzanne. I need to ask you a few questions. Would you like to come on in the kitchen? Can I get you something to drink?"

Joni/Ayana relaxed, a fraction. "Iced tea, please. If you have some."

"I have some." Suzanne led us both into her kitchen. It was done up in summer-beach-house kitsch, all pastel pinks and peaches with a seashell theme. It was an ironic throwback to a carefree time, a contrast that set my teeth on edge. My place remained purely functional with its dark wood paneling and the utilitarian furniture it had come with. I'd kept it that way because some part of me thought it was temporary. Suzanne's decorating suggested the long haul. I couldn't decide which was worse.

Suzanne gestured for us to sit. Joni/Ayana sat; I stood. I didn't want or expect to be here long.

She poured a single glass and without turning around, said, "Ray? Tea?"

"No. Thanks." I wanted to get this over with.

She set the glass down in front of Joni/Ayana, and sat in the chair square to hers.

"Ayana," Suzanne started carefully, "I'm a police detective."

The woman in front of us kept her eyes on her lemonade glass. "I know. Ray told me."

"How did you get to Ray's house, Ayana?"

"I walked."

"From where?"

Joni/Ayana blinked a few times, as if trying to string together the pieces that weren't making sense. I prayed Ayana stayed with us a little longer before Joni came back. She said: "The salt marsh. No — the marina."

"That's great, Ayana. Can you tell me what you were doing at the marina?"

Joni/Ayana shuddered. She drew her heels up onto the edge of her seat, wrapped her arms around her knees. When I thought she wouldn't say anything at all, she whispered: "It was dark. I think I was blindfolded. He did things. When he was inside of me he strangled me. I blacked out. Then I was in the water. It was so cold. Then I was on dry land, walking." She flicked blue eyes up at me, raised a hand in my direction. "I saw him walking. He felt safe. Like he cared. I followed him. I followed the car he got into. That felt safe, too." She reached out a bird-like hand, took her glass and sipped her iced tea. Stared straight in front of her glass at the coral-painted table.

Suzanne blinked a few times. Then she sat back. I watched her form and then discard different lines of questioning over the span of about twenty seconds. She'd rolled with the situation when we first walked in, which, now that I thought about it, was pretty amazing, but her mind needed time to catch up. I wondered whether she was as disturbed as I was at the notion that we appeared to have broadcast our emotions, wondered whether the broadcasting might be the result of two empaths coming together, exactly the sort of thing our schedules were designed to prevent. All she said eventually, though, was: "Who strangled you, Ayana? Did you know who he was?"

"Tom," Joni/Ayana said faintly. "His name was Tom. But he couldn't have done those things. He couldn't."

And here came Joni, roaring back to life. She dropped her feet to the floor and stood in one motion, glaring at me. "You. What is this place? I asked to be taken home."

I lifted my shoulder off the door frame, where I'd been watching the whole conversation. I ignored Suzanne gaping. "I said I'd bring you next door to my neighbor's so I could get you a ride."

That caught her off guard. "I don't remember coming here. Why don't I remember coming here?"

Possibly for the same reason she recalled her friend and neighbor doing horrible things to her, but I didn't say that, didn't even know what that reason would be. "Mrs. Rafferty, I'd like to talk to Suzanne alone for just a few minutes. Would you mind? You'll stay here?"

"I have a choice?" she grumbled, but teenager-like, flopped back down into her chair. She picked her iced tea glass back up, then scratched at her head.

On her way out, Suzanne grabbed my arm, dragged me into the little hallway adjoining her living room and then into her bedroom. It, too, was beach kitsch, with a twist: there was no bed, only a hammock strung across a metal stand.

While I was still processing this anomaly she hissed, "What is going on, Ray?"

"I don't know much more than you do." I leaned my back on the closed door. "You asked if I'd found my missing person. That's her. Joni Rafferty. But she showed up at my door with the same name — and maybe memories — as your murder victim."

She folded her arms. "I think you do know more than I do. Who's Tom? You didn't blink when she said his name."

"Wouldn't you know? Sounds like he was the customer responsible for this girl's death."

At that she blinked as if slapped. She peeked around me, fearfully, as if I'd brought a cadre of colleagues along to listen in. I wondered where she'd left her phone. She said: "Our records were hacked. The customer's name and credit info were wiped from the rental record."

I didn't know how to react. "Hacking still happens?" I whispered.

She gave me a withering, where-have-you-been glance. "A lead would be nice here."

I'd forgotten I was the one holding the keys, at least for the moment. "Tom Alberini is Joni Rafferty's neighbor. You can probably check marina records or even ask if he has a boat." I paused. "Would it lead anywhere? I've never seen those people get prosecuted for anything much more than the wrong color curtains."

Something flickered behind her eyes, then went out. "Destroying company property? Hacking? Either one by itself gets a labor facility sentence. Together? Maybe sedition." She closed her eyes, pinched the bridge of her nose. "So Mrs. Rafferty said she needs a ride. And you brought her here?"

"I don't mind taking her. It's just that I'd have to walk to the station and sign out a motor pool car, and I don't want to leave her alone."

"You guys don't get take-home cars?"

I found it amusing that even in the security services, one half didn't know how the other half lived. "Why should we? We have shift coverage, we're not on call like you guys."

"Good point. All right. But you have to come along. I'll have to justify after-hours use of my vehicle, and I can do it since she's material to your victim, but I'm not taking her home. She needs to go to a hospital."

Hospitals these days were more hit-or-miss than they ever had been. Insurance companies had been buying them and other medical practices for years before Election Day, but now the process had accelerated. Even if your hospital wasn't mired in the paperwork labyrinth that went along with acquisition, it might limit or deny care if it deemed you too high-risk. Black-market clinics had popped up in this void, but Suzanne could be anywhere on the political spectrum, and it wasn't worth risking my job to raise the possibility with her.

I couldn't tell whether she responded to my hesitation or the emotions that caused it when she said, "No way she won't get care at her income level. You have her husband's number, right? We can call him from there." She touched my shoulder. "It'll be okay, Ray." I shouldn't have, but I believed her.

We went back to the kitchen. Joni had drained her iced tea; now she stared off into space. "I grew up, visiting a little beach cottage like this in the summers," she said softly. "On Folly Beach in North Carolina. It was raised up on stilts so it wouldn't be flooded by storm surge, but it was decorated a lot like this."

"You can come back and visit anytime," Suzanne said gently, the way you do when you know it'll never happen. "Mrs. Rafferty, I know you're eager to get home, but we're concerned about your memory loss over the last twenty-four hours. We think it would be prudent to get you checked out at a hospital. We can call your husband from there."

I expected an argument. Instead Joni said, "We have an account at CareBridge. Will you take me there?"

CHAPTER FIVE

The ride to the hospital triggered no more Ayana episodes, at least not that we saw. Suzanne didn't ease up on the gas, flying over roads that had become a virtual no-man's land, dominated by truckers who ran freight for the businesses that ran the country. I'd become so used to the cozy pseudo-village of Hampton Beach that I'd forgotten. Out here truckers had their own laws, their own sense of justice. Perhaps Suzanne had brought me on this trip for more than convenience.

I glanced in the rearview mirror and caught Joni, in the half-light, fussing with her hair as if to straighten it on her head. Wigs again. It was another notch in my theory that the alcohol interacted with the empathy-dampening drugs. I made a mental note to talk to Suzanne about that later. Meantime Joni put her hands down and stayed silent.

We parked in the ER lot. Suzanne let Joni out. Joni checked herself, straightened her wrinkled clothes as best she could, touched her hair to make sure it was in place. Then the three of us walked abreast into the emergency center.

We jumped through all the triage hoops. I led Joni over to a little water cooler while Suzanne stayed behind to talk to the intake nurse, presumably about the split personality that accompanied the memory loss. Irrationally I was glad I hadn't said anything about black-market clinics.

Suzanne joined us in the seating area. "The nurse will call your family in a little bit," she told Jone, "after you've been checked over."

"Why not now? We don't live far. They could be here in ten minutes. Ian wouldn't have to interrupt the girls' bedtime routine."

"They don't want him to take you home before you've had a thorough workup," Suzanne said gently, "and I think they're right. Your memory loss means you could have a head injury."

This satisfied Joni. She might have given us more of an argument if she weren't so tired, but she must have been awake for nearly 24 hours, with most of that time spent walking. She sank into a chair while we watched over her.

In contrast from earlier days, the ER was far from a hive of activity. As quiet ERs often did, it felt preternatural, poised in anticipation of an influx of patients it would likely not see again in my lifetime. Not only did CareBridge not serve the Hampton Beach company town; the people who had once used ERs for primary care no longer had access to them.

I motioned to Suzanne. Together we moved several paces away from Joni, what I hoped would be out of earshot. I said, "She wears a wig. Right?"

"Sure. Doesn't every woman, these days? Besides those of us in security services." She gave me a weak smile and a sense of her internal agony over having to enforce the craven law.

It was like a shot to the solar plexus. I took a step backward. She gave me a rueful grin, took a deep breath, shut the connection down.

I was as dumbstruck by its sudden absence as I had been by its power. It took me a few moments to collect myself before I was able to say, "Joni was drinking with Liza Hill and Brooke Alberini. I helped Liza Hill with an issue a few months ago and when I interviewed her about the disappearance, it was as if she was a different woman." I lowered my voice to nearly a whisper. "What if the alcohol interacted with the inhibitor drugs?"

Interest sparked in Suzanne's eyes, but she cut her gaze away from me, shook her head. "It isn't supposed to. It's made specifically so that it doesn't interfere with lifestyle."

The turquoise woman had complained of lawn chemicals making her hair fall out. I was pretty sure that company would say its chemicals weren't engineered for that, either. But regulation had been dismantled in the first year of the new government, so who knew?

I had kept that thought and its cynical emotions to myself, but Suzanne surprised me. Her own voice pitched lower. "Not that marketing has anything to do with reality now that everything is deregulated. What do you mean, she seemed like a different person?"

The notion that she was responding to my unspoken thought unsettled me. I worked at keeping my tone even while I told her about Liza's shift from a warm, welcoming, humane woman to the blowsy alcoholic I'd met that day.

Suzanne focused on a spot on the floor, listening intently. "That's a pretty drastic change," she said when I finished. "I thought you meant that she seemed disconnected. Cut off from herself."

"It's not that much of a leap, is it? Cut off from herself because she somehow took on the persona of one of the trafficked girls." I felt foolish, saying it. "Anyway, never mind the results. If the alcohol is interacting with the inhibitors, it makes it a public-health issue, doesn't it? It impacts productivity."

Her eyes narrowed. "Only for the husbands, and they're not the ones having the problem. As long as they're taking care of the issue on their own time and not work time."

Damn. I'd thought her interest in her victim's name made her less of a corporate lackey. I shut up, returned to the row of seats by Joni. Suzanne stayed where she was, arms folded, gaze fixed out the window, posture straight, as if weighing her options in advance of some momentous decision. If I ended up in Stratham tomorrow for sedition, at least I had a good run.

I didn't think it would come to that, though. That lawbreaking blast of emotion hadn't just been about feelings. With it, Suzanne had given me insight into her character — and more than that, had established the empathic connection that had been teasing at us since we first locked eyes on the beach.

I hadn't truly connected with someone like this since long before I retired. I'd forgotten how it felt, the sense of tethering that could simultaneously ground you and give you wings. At the same time, and for the first time since Election Day, real fear gnawed at my gut. She'd shut off the tap in much the same way I had with Ian Rafferty, but the connection had established itself anyhow. I would have to be extra careful in spending time with her, no matter how much I wanted to let the bond grow.

It took another twenty minutes for us to be called, enough time for Joni to fall asleep. I watched Suzanne gently wake her, then walk her back to the nurse, through the doors and to the exam rooms. I felt her avoid my gaze. I couldn't figure out if we were independently worried about inadvertent empathic exchanges, or if something had leaked through.

As considerably shorter as ER waits were these days, it was late, a lot had happened today, and my joints were stiff. I walked around the small, empty lobby with its stark white plastic chairs and linoleum.

The front lobby doors swished open. A small family rushed inside. It took me a minute to recognize Ian Rafferty; his arms were full of sleepy toddler girl, and his older daughter trailed him, her expression dull and uncomprehending. Why he hadn't left them with a neighbor? Stupid question; I spent my days investigating people whose neighbors informed on them over the smallest details. I wouldn't trust any of those people with lawn equipment, much less children.

Maybe more importantly, how had he found out? My money was on the intake nurse, though what her motivation might have been, I couldn't tell. No one acted altruistically anymore; everyone was too busy surviving.

Rafferty charged over to me. His hair and clothes were rumpled; he was considerably more agitated than he had been when I first met him. He seemed distracted by his kids, directing his older daughter in one direction, then in another. I got the sense that he relied on Joni almost entirely to deal with them. He confronted me with a look of betrayal. "Why didn't you call me immediately when you found my wife?" he demanded.

I thought about inviting him to sit down, decided against it. I'd slammed the door on the bond that might have allowed me to speak to him like a friend. "Because she had the symptoms of a head injury, and we thought it better to get her checked out so that by the time we called, we'd be able to tell you more."

"Head injury? How bad? I want to see her."

"Mr. Rafferty, she's part of a police investigation. I'm going to need to ask you to wait." Technically he could see her, even take her home, get their own doctor to deliver care. He had every incentive to do so: an overnight stay could mean a higher rate, which would come out of his pay. The hospital wouldn't argue with him; it would be able to cut its own costs, and the risks were potentially lower with a provider who knew her.

"What police investigation?" he demanded. The little girl in his arms started to wake up. He let her gently slide down to the floor. "Marlee, go get your sister to get you some water. Makayla, help her."

He glared at me, but I waited for the kids to walk away before I spoke. "Your wife appeared to know some of the details of a murder investigation that began late this afternoon, before she turned herself in."

"Turned herself in? She isn't a suspect, is she?" A terrible realization dawned on his face. To him, a head injury could mean days or weeks or months of disruption, therapy, lean times. A murder charge was something else entirely: social stigma, a tax on him for her care in prison.

"No, sir, I meant just that she came out of hiding or running to ask for help. We're still piecing together who exactly was involved."

"You don't have any idea where she was or what she was doing while she was ... was on her own?"

"No, Mr. Rafferty, I'm sorry we don't." I badly wanted to ask what he thought his neighbors Tom and Brooke might have been up to during those hours, but the investigation wasn't there yet.

"What about the surveillance cameras?"

"Sir, if you wanted us to review those for information about your wife's movements — and there would be hundreds to review — you'd have to pay us to do that."

"Who came up with these rules, anyway," he grumbled. I bit back a comment about the price of low taxes. I couldn't be sure about what I'd said, now that his wife had shown up acting and talking like this morning's murder victim. She'd implicated her own neighbors, Suzanne didn't have anyone to pin the murder on, so it was entirely possible that Enterprise Security would want to scan the footage to learn more.

Ian Rafferty's shoulders slumped as a sigh drew out from deep within. I followed him across the lobby to a bank of chairs, where he dropped like a weight. "You said she was found. Where?"

"At a private residence."

"A residence? But we don't —"

"We think she'd been wandering for a long time before she needed a rest. She observed one of the workers coming home from a shift, and followed that person to where she could ask for help."

His eyes narrowed. "And they knew to call you?"

He was good. Any other person's doorstep, the responding officer would have been under no obligation to call me once the biometric scanner identified the missing person. Joni could even have been home tonight, strange behavior and all. "It was my house," I admitted.

"Your house? Why you?"

The suspicion he projected, like any good interrogator's, had me mentally scrambling to recall my own experiences. "I don't know. She only said she'd followed me, walking home from the station."

He regarded me, equally speculative and wondering. I met his gaze, tempted to let my defenses down, to let him feel that I had nothing to be ashamed of. Whatever he thought, whether I'd found her and kidnapped her for myself, he was wrong. I hadn't asked for any of this.

Or maybe I was projecting, because he finally backed off. "I want to see Joni."

He said it the way suspects had once asked for their attorneys. I stood. He didn't deserve to be held off any longer. "Come on."

We headed for the intake nurse. At that moment the exam area doors opened. Joni Rafferty came out, flanked by Suzanne and a doctor.

The doctor buttonholed Ian and Joni. Suzanne joined me. "No sign of a head injury," she murmured. "She's the picture of health."

We watched Joni's kids hug her, by turns, watched Ian's gaze turn almost rapturous. "My God, Joni. I didn't know if I'd ever see you again." He pulled her into his arms, buried his face in her neck. It would have been sweet if she hadn't been so stiffly unresponsive.

"Could the doctor explain the Ayana stuff?" It certainly didn't fit an insurance code. But Joni brought her arms up around her husband's shoulders, and when one of the kids said something she smiled a bright, wide, if tired smile. As far as our supervisors were concerned, our cases were over.

We stuck around and observed to make sure Ayana didn't reappear. If the thought of her friends doing terrible things, and her need to protect them, had driven Joni's reappearance, then the sight of her family would certainly ground her.

I wondered if seeing the Alberinis could trigger Ayana to come back. "Mr. Rafferty," I called, as they made for the door.

He stopped, turned, tight with impatience, a far cry from the family man who had tried to establish a connection with me. "Yes, Officer?"

"Let me know if you see or hear anything … strange. Call it in, request me personally. Will you do that?"

I felt him wondering about my motivations, wondered if he was deliberately projecting to test me. Finally, he said, "I doubt we'll need to. But thanks anyway." With that, one arm around Joni and his daughter curled in the other, he trooped with his family out the door.

#

We followed. Ian Rafferty had parked as if it were a hotel registration deck. The whole family piled into his SUV without so much as a backward glance. No great surprise. Suzanne and I strolled back to her car, neither of us in any rush to get home, despite my best intentions to cut off this nascent bond. We drove, more silently and awkwardly than I expected, through darkened and silent post-curfew roadways to the 101 interchange.

"What happened in the exam room?" I felt a little dirty, intruding on female conversations.

She paused as if metering what to say. "Pretty much what you'd expect," she said. "Rape kit. Head exam."

I waited.

"Both clear. And Ayana didn't show up again." Disappointment weighted her voice.

"You were hoping she would?"

Suzanne scowled at me. "Yeah. I was. You know how that doctor treated me when I followed her out of the room to tell her what we'd observed? Like I was making up excuses to keep this woman in custody. Why in God's name would I do that if I didn't have a good reason?

"I didn't even mention the real Ayana," she continued. "I tried to keep it as care-oriented as I could, split personality and shit. I even mentioned your theory about the alcohol-inhibitor interaction. But the doctor sneered down her nose at me and told me to stick to pounding skulls. She literally said that. Can you believe it?"

A female doctor, sneering at a female enterprise security officer whose job it was to keep other women in line? Sure, I could believe that, even though I would never say it. Instead I played it safe. "Didn't you ever encounter a doctor who didn't like you encroaching on their territory?" I teased.

At last she laughed. "Guess not," she said. "Mine always treated me with respect."

"Not mine," I said. "I'd tell them my knee hurt, they'd say no, it had to be my back. Once my elbow bounced off the pavement when I fell during a foot chase. I had witnesses and everything. Still the doctor said it was my shoulder."

She laughed again, a little mutter that made her sound like bigger, more expansive mirth lurked underneath. I wondered what it would take to bring it out. Wondered why I wanted to deepen this bond, when I should have worked harder to kill it.

She asked, "You were a cop before?"

"My whole career."

She fell silent, as if considering. Then she said, "This entire system must drive you crazy."

I wasn't sure how to respond. Both our phones were still switched on. Before I knew what I was doing, I grabbed hers out of the cup holder, pulled mine out of my pocket, switched them both off. "What did you do, before?" I asked.

She smiled slow and wide. I couldn't tell what she thought, if anything, about my switching the phones off, engaging in conversation that our overlords and their entire system discouraged. If she'd asked, I'd have told her I thought we were way past that. "Portsmouth PD," she said. "I had just started in detectives. I'd been doing that for about seven months before Election Day."

"Good gig," I said. "Were you liking it?"

"I was loving it. I got to work with some great people." Her voice turned unbearably wistful.

"Work there long enough to catch any good cases?"

"A few." Her face closed off. She didn't want to talk about it. I didn't blame her. A lot had changed in three years, even if talking about times before wasn't frowned upon.

Before long we passed underneath 95, where the tractor trailer traffic transported goods and people between the labor facilities in Maine and the Boston business center. Long ago I'd traversed truck stops up and down that corridor, hoping for any sighting or even secondhand information about my missing daughter, but Suzanne didn't need to know about that. It was already a lifetime ago. I kept my mouth shut, let the silence stretch out across the dark tree-lined stretches and eventually, the marshes.

Far in the distance, as we got closer to the beach, the Seabrook Nuclear Power Station loomed, the reactor containment dome lit up like a warning. I wondered whether deregulation would cause a meltdown that would end this place, or the enterprises would find a way to justify filling the marshes in and building back here, or the sea would rise up and claim it all first. I was rooting for the sea.

Suzanne didn't say another word until we were on Ocean Boulevard, turning the corner and coming down the hill. We passed where the cliffs sloped down into the beach sand, and the houses went from the owners' mansions to the single-family blocks.

Suzanne glanced sidelong in my direction as if she expected me to strike up a conversation. "These houses," she said, at last turning her attention fully to the road. "Sometimes, I look through their windows and I think we're in a time warp. That if I look closely enough, I'll see women with beehive hairstyles and tailored dresses serving canapes and highballs to dinner guests. It sounds dumb, I know. But look at these places' architecture. It's, like, steeped in the early sixties. In some ways it's still there, you know? Like pockets of a simpler time, the years this town was growing."

"I know," I said, because I did: those were the years I'd come here as a kid. For the first time I thought perhaps part of the wig craze was a way to recreate those simpler times. "We used to spend a week here each summer. Stayed in one of the little motor inns off the beach," I told her, even though I wasn't sure why. "My mother had one of the hairstyles you mentioned. And my father used to drink highballs. Remember those little plastic chairs in front of the motel rooms? They were supposed to be there for show, but he figured if they were there, they should be used. So he'd sit there and nurse a drink for a few hours."

She smiled. "Yeah?"

"Yup." The memories I'd tried, and only briefly succeeded, to recreate with my own family. In spite of having powered down our phones, I wondered if anyone was actively listening to this conversation, decided for just once, I didn't care. "Simpler doesn't always mean better, but this time…"

Suzanne stared straight ahead. Her grip on the steering wheel tightened. "Ayana was — well, they call it 'promoted,' but what it really means is she got a year older and they moved her from being merchandised out of the casino arcade, to being merchandised online, for the higher paying customers, the ones from Boston who are looking for their own party and not just buying one for their kids' first experience. Ayana didn't fit particular profiles for the porn — she was biracial, so she was saved for the race fetishists online."

Her tone soured with disgust. I wondered where she was going with this. She talked about this girl like she'd been a human being, not just a piece of merchandise. Enterprise Security never talked that way, whether or not anyone else listened in.

She kept talking. "That silver car you saw pull up to the scene? That was the operations manager, the woman who runs the business, keeps an eye on the girls, keeps them in line. She laid into me for not keeping business interests in mind. I don't even have anything to do with customer vetting."

"Customers get vetted?" I didn't mean for it to be an ironic question, but Suzanne burst out laughing nonetheless.

"Yeah, asshole, they do." Her tone said "asshole" was a term of endearment. "There's this small squad of former computer cops who check them out, make sure they don't post on S&M boards or streaming snuff or things like that. If they are, they get access to the appropriate merchandise."

That sounded a lot more like Enterprise Security. If it wasn't so dangerous to be on Ocean Boulevard after dark, I'd ask her to let me out so I could walk home. I would take a good long, hot shower when I got home, metered water be damned.

"Look, I'm sorry." She sighed. Glanced at her phone as if to be sure it was off. "I hate talking about human beings like this. I started my career being an advocate for girls and women, and now I'm protecting the abusers' interests. Sometimes I dream about walking off the job, you know? Especially when people like that doctor judge me. But you can't just quit, not these days."

I opened my mouth to agree, to toss off some mindless crap about how I didn't know what I'd do with myself anyway. Instead what I said was, "We haven't seen the last of Joni Rafferty." I didn't realize I believed it, that I'd even thought it, until I said it.

"Sure we have. Next time Ayana comes out to play, she'll get committed. Most we, or you, anyway, will hear about it is a formal complaint lodged against you for releasing her back to her family without correctly identifying that there was an issue."

She was probably right. She hooked a right on Ashworth so that we drove around the business district. This way we wouldn't have to see its sleazy inglory. Even so, she focused straight ahead, and her jaw tensed as we stopped for customers and merchandise in crosswalks, headed to and from the motor inns that lined Ashworth. A few girls stepped our way, as if thinking to look for a score they didn't have to work too hard for, but Suzanne accelerated past them. "They're expected to service us, or at least the guys, for free, since it keeps them on our good side," she said quietly. Then she didn't say another word until we were on M Street and she parked behind her house. "Come on over anytime," she said. "I have nothing to do in the evenings, and I'm sure you don't either."

She was right. I didn't. Even so, I couldn't imagine becoming buddies with someone from Enterprise Security. With friendships discouraged, the only other possible alternative was recruitment, a "networking" move that could get me promoted if I played it right. It wasn't just the pecking order that made her my superior; it was the cost of that superiority, what Suzanne herself had said: she protected the traffickers' interests. I had double if not triple her years on the job, and much as I'd found people end up doing the very things they said they would "never" do, I could honestly say I'd rather have died than work for Enterprise Security.

She headed up the steps of her back door. "Hey." I jammed my phone as deep in my pocket as it would go. "What would you do instead? If you quit?"

A dreamy smile ghosted onto her face, then passed. "Still working on that. I'll let you know when I figure it out, though."

Sure she would. "Until then?"

Her back turned to unlock her door, she cast a backward glance at me over her shoulder. "Why?"

"No reason. Let me know when you do, though. Figure it out."

She got her door open, turned and faced me. "Will do."

In spite of my resolve to avoid friendship, a bond, any sort of attachment, it felt as if I'd entered into something bigger and deeper. I walked the few paces back to my place, the surf whispering secrets only it could understand.

CHAPTER SIX

A reunion turned out to be closer than either of us could have imagined. I spent the next day in a fog; the night's events had thrown off my bedtime. I got through the day groggy, no matter how many cups of cheap weak coffee I drank.

Days like that had a way of kicking you when you were down. In the old days you'd get a string of feuding-neighbor calls the shift after you were up all night with your sick two-year-old, or one major call — the fatal collision, the major burglary — that took up most if not all of your day. The adrenaline was usually enough to get you through those, and if it didn't, you had overtime to look forward to. These days, not so much.

About an hour before my shift ended, of course, the dispatchers sent me back to Hampton Oaks and the Raffertys' for what they called a "disturbance."

Even though I should have been a good little robot and spent the fifteen-minute drive thinking up different property codes to enforce, instead I backtracked to the public servant days and prepared myself for any scenario: Ayana had told Joni's kids she didn't know who the fuck they were, and they were crying and scared while their mother cowered on the bathroom floor. Ian Rafferty had mentioned something about going boating over the weekend and had triggered Ayana to relive her murder, though hopefully not as graphically. The

Alberinis had shown up for an impromptu dinner party, with the same result.

I was close on the last one. Ian Rafferty waited for me on the street. "She's in the backyard." He pointed. "Jesus, she's crazy. What happened to her?"

I jogged down the hill, back into his yard. The tableau would have been funny if I didn't know its backstory. Three hysterical upper-middle-class housewives; two, screaming, pointed at the third who crouched on the ground, her back to the shed, brandishing a broken wine bottle. I wondered if it was the weapon, or the waste of good wine the others were screaming about.

Put my cynicism aside and approached the screamers: Liza Hill and Brooke Alberini. Resisted the urge to slap them both. It was too damn hot to scream. "Ladies. Settle down. Can one of you tell me what's going on?"

"She's gone crazy." Liza Hill spit her words. "Just look at her. Didn't you notice she was crazy when you found her? Or did you just dump her back on her husband and figure it was his problem now?"

Nice how Ian Rafferty was absolved of responsibility for his wife's condition. "Has she said anything? Hurt anyone?"

"She was fine until I walked in the yard," Brooke Alberini said. The confident, borderline flirtatious woman from the other day had been taken down a few notches, though whether from guilt or simply faced with the stark reality of mental illness, I couldn't tell. "As soon as she saw me, she freaked out. Started screaming about how she wouldn't let me finish the job, broke the bottle, started waving it around. We cornered her by the shed and called you."

As if she were a wild dog or a rabid raccoon. "Who cornered? You and Mrs. Hill?"

"No. Me and Tom."

The two people who had attempted to murder Ayana, locked

deep within Joni's mind as if she had been another personality, not a human being of her own. I spoke directly to Mrs. Alberini. "Did she say anything else to you and Tom?"

Her arms folded across her midsection, her hands clutched her elbows. She looked everywhere else but at me. "No. Just that she wasn't going to let us finish what we started." She scratched at the side of her head above her ear.

"Anyone call an ambulance?" I asked.

"No." Liza Hill again. "Isn't that your job?"

"It's my job to assess the need for one and I have. Your friend — " I emphasized these words — "is going to need a safe place for transport. The back of my car isn't it." We had a policy against transporting the mentally unstable in motor pool vehicles, but she didn't need to know that.

Her nostrils flared. "Ian." She addressed Joni's husband, who had followed me down the driveway and remained on the periphery of the backyard, apparently hoping no one would notice him. "Call an ambulance." She swung her glare back around, leveled it at me. "I hope we won't be fined for something out of our control. Our property values have dropped enough because of the water issues."

Brooke Alberini gasped. "Liza! No!" She turned wild eyes on me. "Please don't mind her. She's been drinking, she doesn't know what she's saying."

"I don't know what I'm saying? Little Miss Pill-Popper? Look at you, all—"

I shut them out. Ian Rafferty had fled, looking only too happy to have something useful to do. I took a brief glance around. No sign of either Mr. Hill, or Tom Alberini. That was interesting.

I made sure I was in Joni/Ayana's line of sight. Then I advanced slowly, cautiously.

She scrambled back a few inches, fell back on her rear, shrank into the shed wall. Otherwise she stayed put. Watching. Defending.

"Ayana," I said softly, when I got close enough that I thought the other two women wouldn't hear me. "Do you remember me?"

The ice blue eyes had roved the grass behind me as if seeking an escape route. Now they focused on me, wide, unseeing.

"Ayana, it's Ray. Remember? You showed up at my house, and my friend Suzanne and I helped you." I sent the tiniest of connective threads to her.

"Spaghetti," she said, and before I knew it she flung the broken wine bottle aside and clasped me tight around the neck. "Please help me. They came back for me."

"I know." I kept my hands away from my sides, spread out where they could be seen rather than embrace her back. I could fine these people, and they could report me right back for putting hands on them. "I'll protect you, but I need you to let me go."

She held on for another couple of seconds. "Please. Get me far away from here."

In the distance I heard a siren. Shit. I should've told Ian to make sure they didn't run code. "Ayana," I said, "you've been through a lot. We'd like a doctor to check you out. Will you take a ride in an ambulance to your doctor?"

Wariness crept in. "All he's going to do is prescribe some antibiotics and send me back to work."

"Not him. A different doctor. Would that be okay?"

"I guess."

I held out my hands. She took them and pulled herself up. She clung to my arm like a shield as we slowly made our way across the yard towards the front of the house. The siren wailed closer, then stopped. It couldn't be far, then, maybe even as close as the neighborhood itself.

The reactions were interesting. Liza Hill stared at us as if we'd personally insulted her. Brooke Alberini had found some patio feature to be fascinated in. Ian Rafferty took a step towards us, arm raised, like a groom prepared to take his bride from her father. I felt worst for him: treated like a lackey, and even his wife didn't recognize him.

But Joni wasn't far beneath the surface. As we passed by him she loosened her grip on my arm. "Let him," she mumbled. "He's nice to me." She took the arm Ian offered her. I followed them as they made their way up the driveway to the street, where the ambulance pulled up.

Getting her on board was straightforward. Ian Rafferty made sure they headed to a hospital that handled mental health cases. I agreed to file the necessary paperwork within the next two hours. They would need the police report for billing; anything that wasn't in the patient's control would be billed for less.

The ambulance driver shut the doors, returned to his cab and pulled the rig away.

"What happened to her?" Rafferty asked quietly. His face was drawn, closed in on itself. He couldn't believe the world could encroach on his suburban utopia. I wondered when he'd realize utopia was an illusion made through enforcement.

I ran with the idea that had occurred to me before. "When you consult with her doctor about her case," I said, "find out whether the dampening chemicals in the wig could be interacting with the alcohol. I know they aren't supposed to, but it's worth asking." I paused. A new thought had presented itself. "Also," I said, more slowly, "be sure to ask him to dig for past trauma. Ongoing abuse by a family member or friend, something that might make a child want to disassociate from what happened to her, make up a — almost an imaginary friend for it to happen to." But there was still that small, crucial detail of her sharing a name with Suzanne Costa's murder victim.

Rafferty shook his head: he didn't believe it. "I've known Joni since we were in grade school," he said. "I'd have known it if anything like that was going on with her."

Not necessarily, but I let it lie. "It doesn't hurt to tell the doctor, and let him use that as a basis for inquiry along with whatever information you can give him."

He nodded. This made more rational sense to him. Unexpectedly, he stuck out his hand. "Thanks," he said. "For taking care of her. Today and last night."

I understood: a crazy wife was better than a missing wife. I shook his hand. "Good luck."

He climbed back up the hill to his home. I headed to my car. I had paperwork I needed to file if I expected to get home and rest tonight.

From behind me, the direction of the backyard, a shout. "Tom, wait," I thought I heard, and I hurried. I'd had enough of this community's drama. I hadn't planned to fine any of them, but that would change if they kept up like this.

I succeeded in getting into the driver's seat and turning the engine over when Tom Alberini charged up the hill. I did my best to ignore him, put the car in gear, but he waved his arms at me. As he came closer I could see this wasn't any random citizen's question: his face was red, agonized. As I shifted the car back into park, turned off the engine, then got out, he slowed to a halt. About twenty paces away from me, agony turned to uncertainty. He had the look of a man who felt moved to confess something, but had started to weigh the implications.

At that moment it hit me: the story I'd heard from Joni's lips the night before was right on. Tom and Brooke were guilty of killing Ayana, and Joni Rafferty somehow had a direct line into what they'd done.

I wondered if she'd be at peace if they confessed.

I came around the side of the car. At that moment Brooke Alberini ran up the driveway. She stopped just behind Tom, clung to her husband's arm the way Joni had with mine.

"I don't know how she knows." Tom Alberini's voice was quiet, gravelly. "She knows. Joni knows, Brooke."

"Shut up!" Brooke hissed back. "Joni's delusional."

He shook her off. "I don't believe that. And neither do you." He faced me once more. "Joni Rafferty freaked out today when we showed up to a last-minute dinner party. You heard her. Somehow she saw us, or she was told..." He shuddered. "We killed a girl, Officer. We rented from the arcade's website, and then we hacked the system to cover it up. My wife has unusual tastes, and it got out of hand, and the girl we rented died." He sounded truly regretful. I wondered how many of his "tastes" he had dumped onto Brooke.

Enough, apparently, for her to let go of his arm, to pummel him, slap and kick with her dainty flats. "You asshole! My tastes! You got me into this shit!"

He cast his gaze upward as if seeking inspiration. He said: "I got you into things consenting adults do. Not bondage with kids, and certainly not snuff." His lip curled with true disgust for his wife. "For Christ's sake, Brooke, what happened to you?"

Her lips trembled. She backed away with a look of hurt, betrayal and fear. For the first time I had the sense that she didn't know what had happened to her, either. Now the one person she counted on for stability had backed out of their contract.

Nonetheless, I'd have to put them into custody. And I'd need backup to do it. No way would I transport them both in my vehicle. I took a few steps toward them, locked eyes with Tom Alberini.

He reached up under his shirt.

In the time it took my brain to process the word gun, he pulled it out, stuck it into his mouth, and blew the top of his head off. When he fell, he took Brooke down with him, collapsed onto her legs like a great bloody domino.

Her screams went from anger to horror and shock and raw grief. By turns she pushed Tom's body away, tried to drag it closer. Eventually she worked her legs free. Then, howling, she embraced him.

In thirty years of law enforcement, it was one of the worst things I'd ever seen.

The last thing I wanted to do was touch that mess. Blood and gray matter and voided bowels had splattered all over the grass and Brooke herself. The gun was still in play, though, and there might be consequences if I let Brooke off herself. I punched the codes for "suicide" and "arrest" and "officer needs assistance" into my smartphone. Then I pulled a couple of pairs of nitrile gloves out of my pocket and doubled up.

The gunshot had brought the neighbors out of their houses, and people gawked from their front lawns as if some invisible property barrier protected them from the drama. I ignored them, made my way to Brooke. The grass was slippery as hell, and I couldn't see the gun anywhere. "Mrs. Alberini," I said gently. "Come on. There's nothing you can do for him."

At least she had stopped screaming. She held onto her husband's body, whimpered something about all the things they had left to do.

By that time I should've heard the ambulance coming. Then I remembered: cost containment meant there was probably only one on duty, and they were busy with Joni Rafferty. I prayed there wouldn't be a next call. A busy evening could mean Tom Alberini stayed out here on the Raffertys' lawn for half the night.

My phone chirped. My supervisor, Will. "What've you got, Trueman?"

"A mess." There were no codes for the entirety of this kind of situation. Will was going to have to limit or extend my time on his own. "A man just shot himself in front of me and about a dozen other people. His wife won't let go of his body. I need an extra set of hands to help take her into custody for involvement in the murder — I mean, destruction — of enterprise property."

A pause. He was used to denying people resources for incidents like this down along the boulevard; nothing like this ever happened in these hills, and now he'd have to show that Residential Security could be counted on to assure citizens' comfort. Otherwise our business would be out of a contract by year's end.

Finally he said, "You need to turn the wife over to Enterprise Security anyway, right?"

"Yes, sir."

"Don't call me sir. Let me call someone from there to come up and assist. Got an ambulance on scene yet?"

"No. I called, but they aren't here." Narrowly avoided another "sir."

"Tied up." He sighed. "Let me see if I can get volunteer fire to come help."

Volunteer fire: one of the very last vestiges of pre-Election Day society. The apparatus and its operators were ancient — the younger volunteers had been conscripted to bigger and questionably better things — and the service would probably go away once enough of the old-timers, or their vehicles, died; but they were better than nothing. "Sounds good. Thanks," I said.

"One other thing. I don't see any fines entered into the system. I assume you haven't had a chance to file your report?"

"I don't even have the scene secured."

He snorted, as if my use of old terms was quaint. "You have a sense of the fines they'll be liable for?"

"Sure do." Disturbing the peace was a Tier I, among the heaviest offenses, right up there with altering one's land or structure without the correct permits or getting into a neighbor dispute over, say, a property boundary. Had it happened on the Alberinis' or Hills' properties, I'd have no trouble fining either of them. But the Raffertys were victims, in over their heads on higher insurance costs and the danger of losing insurance entirely. I had no intention of fining them, contract be damned.

"I'll look for those when you're clear, then. And just come back to the station. I'll send someone from night shift to oversee whatever's left of the cleanup."

With that Will hung up. The distraction had, counterintuitively, done me a favor: Brooke Alberini's grip had slackened, and she'd zoned out. "Mrs. Alberini," I said again. "Let me help you up."

She seemed to have forgotten about the gun. This was good for me. Not so good for me was the fact that she was nearly catatonic. I pictured having to lay hands on her, her freaking out, both of us going ass over teakettle on this bloody, foul slip 'n' slide. I didn't want to have to spend part of my food stipend to purchase new clothes.

I compromised by crouching down in front of her. "Mrs. Alberini. Can you look at me, please?"

Blood had spattered her face. A thin line of it trickled down her neck into her bra.

"Mrs. Alberini." I touched her hand.

That got her attention. She stopped humming and looked at me. I couldn't tell whether she had any idea who I was.

God help me if she was having some kind of weird Joni/Ayana episode. "Mrs. Alberini, it's time for us to go. Let me help you up."

"Go where?"

"Someplace safe. Get you cleaned up, into some dry clothes." Finally, far off in the distance I heard a siren.

"What about Tom?" she asked.

She wasn't going to make this easy. "Right now we need to focus on you. Can we do that? Can you take my hand?" I stretched it out to her.

She appeared to be inspecting it for warts. Reluctantly, she took it. I levered myself off the ground, knees cracking as I went.

She stayed on the ground. "We're just going to leave him here?"

"I'm sorry. We have to." The siren got closer. With any luck it would be the ambulance and she'd be able to see the cleanup crew at work, help convince her there was nothing more she could do for him.

She pulled herself up, held tight to my hand. She'd been sitting on the gun.

I helped her down the lawn to the street. The next tricky part: get her into custody. I pulled out my plastic handcuffs. "I need to put these on you," I said. "For safety."

She'd zoned out again. By the time I got them zip-tied and could breathe once more, the siren had again gotten closer. It felt like it had been several days, not just an hour or so, since I'd waited for the ambulance to come for Joni Rafferty. I lifted my head, searched for the red volunteer truck.

Instead one of the Enterprise Security Dodges zipped around the corner. Just great. They'd get to ride off into the sunset with their suspect, and I'd be stuck here bodysitting through nightfall.

The Dodge parked behind my Ford. After a beat, the door opened and Suzanne Costa got out.

If anyone was going to respond to this scene, I wanted it to be her. Still, it had been such a long time since I trusted anyone enough to be my partner, I startled myself into silence. She came around the car to greet us.

Today she looked more official than she had at yesterday's crime scene. Her hair was pulled back into a bun, she wore the mirrored shades. Perhaps that was why I went official on her: "I'm releasing subject Brooke Alberini into your custody. The charge is destruction of enterprise property."

"From yesterday?" she said in a low voice. "All wrapped up in a neat bow. Jesus, Ray."

"We'll talk later." I let go of Mrs. Alberini. "Her accomplice is dead. She's going to need an evaluation."

Suzanne's expression was unreadable behind the mirrored shades. She said, "Meet me at the hospital when you're through?"

"I'll try," I said. "I have no idea when I'll be done here."

Her lips twitched. A moment later, disappointment surged, then retreated, behind my ribcage. "I understand," she said. "We'll catch up another time then. Thanks. See you on the flip side."

I couldn't help feeling I'd missed an opportunity as I watched her escort Mrs. Alberini to her car, fold her suspect inside. Whatever it was, I had no idea what would happen to Brooke. Incarceration in today's world meant forced labor or prostitution, but I couldn't imagine someone from the upper echelons being sentenced like that, especially not for someone as replaceable as Ayana. Besides, there needed to be a way to prevent Brooke from destroying future girls.

In the silence that followed the Dodge's departure, most of the neighbors went back indoors. A few turned to their hedges or landscaping as if to check for blemishes.

Before long the old ambulance hauled around the corner, its diesel engine strained, as much of a contrast from the Dodge as could be. Probably needed an oil change. Hopefully it wouldn't break down on its way to the morgue. Like Suzanne, it parked behind my car; unlike Suzanne, the old volunteers took quite awhile to get out of their cab. I'd be lucky to make it to the hospital before dawn.

CHAPTER SEVEN

One hour later Tom Alberini was on his way to the morgue, Ian Rafferty had been advised (not by me) to hose off the mess or wait for the next good rainstorm, and I was headed back to the motor pool, one hour late. I was sure my evening shift counterpart was out of his skin by now. His pay would be affected, too.

I was tired of being responsible for other people's pay. I wanted to go home.

Pulling into the chain-link lot, instead I got another phone call. "Are you still meeting me at the hospital?" Suzanne's voice, breathless.

I had never agreed to begin with. "No. I'm late as it is, turning in this motor-pool car." And there was still inspection to do. "Can you come by later?"

She was quiet on the other end. I wanted her to be contemplating how much worse we Residential Security types had it, but in reality, she probably wondered how she'd gotten caught up with a jerk like me. "No," she said at last. "You really need to see it. I have to supervise Brooke Alberini's medical exam. Come by before I have to book her."

My counterpart buzzed out of the station door, headed straight for me and the car. That gave me an idea. "Let me see if I can get a ride." I hung up.

The other officer wanted the $10 for the hour of pay he'd missed, but he agreed to the ride if I helped with inspection. That was supposed to be a two-step process, one done by the outgoing officer, the other a validation done by the incoming. Helping seemed like a gray area of corner-cutting, but my counterpart was practically bouncing to get on the road, and I needed a ride. We completed inspection together. I made certain I hadn't brought any bits of Alberini into the car with me; he dealt with the exterior. When we were done I flipped him the keys and swung into the passenger seat beside him.

"What's this about, anyway? Sick relative, or something?" he asked.

"Something." It would be too difficult to explain. Meeting Enterprise Security for a case that should have ended as soon as Tom Alberini's body was loaded onto that ambulance. Joni Rafferty was in her own doctor's care, Brooke Alberini was in custody. I wasn't sure what the consequences might be of getting involved beyond my station, but I refused to let some kid I barely knew be a part of them.

Neither of us spoke during the fifteen-minute drive. As we pulled into the parking lot I thumbed through my phone, pulled up Suzanne's logged call to get her number. "I'm here. Where are you?" I asked.

"Emergency. Show your ID to the triage nurse when you get here. And hurry up."

My counterpart must have heard her. He pulled up in front of the ER doors. I thanked him, hopped out. "How you getting back?" he called.

"The person I'm meeting will give me a ride. Good night." I waved him off.

Suzanne waited just beyond the double doors. In the glass's reflection I saw my counterpart in the old Crown Vic, watching to see who waited for me. I had no idea what the implications of me going off course to meet an Enterprise Security officer might be. I'd worry about that later. "What's so important that you're interrupting my evening now?" I teased.

She flipped me the bird. "Just getting you back for the way you interrupted mine last night. So listen, thanks for coming down. I needed to show you something."

"What? Brooke Alberini has a tattoo that marks her as some secret undercover society member?"

She gave me a look. "I made Hospital Security babysit her for ten minutes so I could visit the ladies'. On my way back I saw Joni Rafferty being evaluated. Ray, I think you were right about the wigs." She ducked down a corridor. "That door, Number Five. Take a look in there and tell me what you see."

I walked down the corridor, feeling like a kid about to play an especially hard prank on a maligned teacher who probably didn't deserve it. Number Five's door was closed. As Suzanne had asked, I peeked in through the window.

Joni Rafferty sat cross-legged on her hospital bed, looking bored. She was in the standard johnny — no straitjacket, at least not yet — and her face had been scrubbed of makeup, so that she looked like a high school kid. The one thing missing was her platinum blonde tresses. Her own hair was more of a thin strawberry-honey blonde, pulled back at the nape of her neck in a very short ponytail. Patches of scalp glowed under the fluorescent lights.

I beelined back to Suzanne's side before anyone, including the patient, caught me gawking like a zoo tourist. We walked back the way we had come. "What'd you think?" Suzanne murmured.

"What makes you say I was right about the wigs?"

She gave me a look like she thought I, too, was missing a few marbles. "Didn't you see how she's acting now that she isn't wearing it?"

"I wouldn't imagine that she'd be screaming and crying in a hospital."

Suzanne pursed her lips. Either I was being dense or she couldn't figure out how to convey what she wanted to say. Without empathy, she had to know, of course it would be harder for me to figure out what she meant.

I tried anyway. "You mean her behavior changed as soon as the wig came off. Like instantly?"

She pulled me around another corner. "Brooke is down this hallway. Joni stopped crying as soon as the wig came off. She settled down gradually after that. Like something worked its way out of her system."

I started to understand. "You think instead of an inhibitor, her wig was treated with something else?"

"Not treated." Suzanne's expression went faraway, as if accessing a place I couldn't follow. "Ray, don't you know where wigs like that come from?"

I did my best exasperated-blank face.

"Oh. Well, Jesus. They're made from the hair of workers. All workers, not just the sex kind. The idea is that it cuts down on the amount of hygiene the owners have to be responsible for. During intake they shave heads. That hair gets made into a wig. The wigs either end up being used by the higher-priced sex workers, or more often, sold to rich women like her."

She believed what she'd been told, that it was a hygiene thing? She seemed satisfied, though, by her own explanation. Perhaps she really was too young to ever have learned about other "workers" throughout history whose heads had been shorn at intake. For myself, I'd had no idea that was happening. A little cold stone flipped, sank deeper in my gut.

I kept my tone steady. "Why do rich women get the wigs? Some bizarre status symbol?" That seemed safe.

A wry smile curled her lips. "Synthetics are crap. You should know that."

I had to admit they looked plastic, mass-produced. "Okay, so they get real hair from the heads of workers." Again I bit back a history lesson. "What would change the way Joni's wig was treated? It should still get inhibitors, shouldn't it?"

We reached the end of the corridor, the last door. Suzanne opened it, stuck her head inside. "I'm here. You can leave."

A uniformed hospital security guard shuffled out. I stayed where I was until Suzanne beckoned to me.

In contrast to Joni Rafferty, Brooke Alberini was stretched out on her bed, passed out. "She was given a sedative, not that she needed one that badly," Suzanne said. "They're swamped tonight and didn't want her bitching while she waited for her exam. Anyway, so here's what I'm thinking. I don't think Joni's wig was treated at all. I think somewhere along the way, Joni Rafferty ended up buying and wearing Ayana's hair. You know how objects can be haunted by the souls of people who were especially attached to them? I think the trauma of being ... subjugated made Ayana project herself into her hair. And then whatever the Alberinis did to her, the murder, the trauma of it was enough for Ayana to project it, for something that used to be a part of her to retain enough psychic energy to — where are you going?"

I'd heard enough. Whether it was the political climate or the nature of this particular tourist town since Election Day, something was fucking with people's heads. "I don't have time for drama," I snapped over my shoulder.

She followed me. "It's not drama," she said. "I know it sounds nuts. But if you stop to —"

"I don't need to." I turned, walked back to her. This wasn't something I wanted to holler back down the corridor. "Even if it was true, the coincidence, Suzanne. The best friend of a woman who committed a crime ends up wearing the hair of a worker she killed during some bizarre sex game? Who just happens to have strong enough empathic skills to project herself onto that hair? To <u>haunt</u> it? No. The only way this makes any logical sense is if Joni Rafferty was in on whatever the Alberinis were up to."

Her slate gray eyes turned gunmetal. "If she was in on it then she'd be in on the cover-up too. Not wandering around town at all hours, not turning up on your doorstep with some bizarre story about being thrown into the salt marsh. Which makes sense, by the way. I checked the tide tables from that night. Whoever killed Ayana fucked up and dumped her body in the salt marsh just as the tide was turning back, so instead of being washed out to sea, she ended up on the beach."

That actually squared with Tom Alberini's guilt trip, but I wasn't going to let her change the subject. "Being in on the murder doesn't mean able to handle it. Obviously her mind snapped. I just think whatever games they got up to with that girl, the only way Joni could have known was if she was there."

"Except that she knew her name." Suzanne's voice went quiet, almost reverent. "One thing I've seen over the past two years: the customers don't care about their merchandise like that. The girls' names are the only thing they've got left of themselves. They don't go telling their clients."

"Not even if they're house whores?" I regarded Brooke Alberini, unconscious on her bed. "If Ayana thought she was going to get more stability by living in a house, she might give it up."

Suzanne shifted around. "Ayana was a call girl, not trained to be a house whore. The establishments don't offer a try before you buy, and anyway, the online auction sites are full of ads for trained ones. I doubt the Alberinis dangled that in front of her."

Behind us, Brooke Alberini stirred. I peered over Suzanne's shoulder. Brooke shifted on the bed as if uncomfortable. Her heart rate and blood pressure had gone up, but her eyes remained closed.

"Anyway," I pitched my voice quieter, "I saw Joni at your crime scene. She was drifting around the edge of the crowd. I tried to catch her before you pinned me down. I think she heard the name when you did, when the handler made the call."

Suzanne shook her head. "No one was near us when she made that call."

"You're sure?"

She glanced down at the floor, quickly enough to look uncertain.

Brooke Alberini started to mutter from her bed. Suzanne and I exchanged a look, then hurried to her bedside. "What was that, hon?" Suzanne leaned over, gently brushed the dark hair back from Brooke's face. Her gaze flicked upward at me; she pointed at the other woman's hairline. I couldn't tell what I was looking at, but if I had to guess, Brooke wore a wig.

"… got out of hand," Brooke mumbled.

"What did, hon?"

"… games we played with all our girls. Tie them up, choke them, sometimes knife play or heat scares them. Fear makes it hotter."

"Was Joni there, Brooke?" Suzanne said, quickly. "Did Joni see the games?"

Brooke frowned. "No. No Joni. Don't know why she … freaked out."

"What did you do when it got out of hand, Brooke? What did you do with the body?"

"We were on our boat," Brooke slurred, "so Tom … said the tide would take it out to sea."

Suzanne's crazy scenario worked better than my logical one did. "Name," I mouthed at Suzanne.

She nodded. "Brooke," she said, "did the girl at any point tell you her name?"

The corner of Brooke's lip curled up in what might have been a smirk or a sneer. "Silly," she said. "Those girls don't have names."

With that a nurse came bustling in. He didn't look at either of us. He adjusted something on Brooke's IV, checked the machinery and went right back out. Within a few seconds Brooke was sound asleep.

We retreated to a corner of the room. We leaned, shoulders on the wall, facing each other in a mirror pose. Suzanne's attention remained on the sedated woman. "I don't get it," she murmured. "That's a real-hair wig Brooke is wearing. Why wouldn't she show the same signs of possession? Whatever you want to call it."

"Because that's not what it is." I tried not to gloat.

"Did they say anything? Before the husband shot himself? Maybe anything about those games she mentioned?"

I thought back. It had been such a straightforward suicide that I hadn't thought there was anything there worth noticing. "He blamed her for the murder, her tastes. She blamed him right back, said he was the one got her into those tastes. He said he'd gotten her into some things, but not ... not child bondage or snuff." Saying the words made me ill.

Her eyes widened. Equal parts horror and triumph laced out around her professional boundaries. "Jesus, Ray. I wonder if her wig was haunted enough to make her see things, just like Joni, but instead she coped with it by becoming the abuser?"

"That makes no sense."

"It makes perfect sense. History is filled with people who perpetrated acts of violence as a way to gain power over the violence they themselves experienced."

"Yeah. But not because they're such powerful empaths." There, I'd said it.

235

She stared up at me as if she couldn't believe my gall. Then, before I knew what she was doing, she grabbed my hand. "What do you feel?" she asked.

I yanked my hand away. "This is illegal." Of course I felt a sense of loss. I couldn't deny that any more than I could deny the power surge of the first time she'd ever projected at me.

"When we first met," she said, "there was something about you. More than recognizing you. I knew I could trust you. I knew that, without knowing anything at all about you. I didn't even remember we were neighbors until later."

For something like this, I had the power to arrest her. If I could only shake the vision my brain had concocted, us as partners, our easy banter that had blasted through the artificial barriers of mistrust and suspicion that living this system had engendered.

She lowered her voice. "The empathy ban is bullshit, and so is making us enforce it. We're cops. That sixth sense that warns us something is off about the driver you stopped, or the apartment you're knocking at. It's intuition squared. The same sixth sense extended to others. And they make us use it to keep people in line, instead of protect them."

The sense I stopped believing in when it failed to identify the danger my daughter was in. I almost said it. Swallowed the words instead.

"When the ban went into effect," she said slowly, "I took the inhibitors. I had this ... friend that I used to joke with, that we were so empathic, we were downright telepathic. Because before that, sometimes I would think I could hear her voice in my head. I thought I was going nuts, missing her, having these conversations. But when it was gone, that was when I felt like I was going nuts." She paused as a pair of nurses walked down the hall. "I stopped the inhibitors, but not so that I could enforce the law. It was because she keeps me on an even keel. She gets me through the worst days on my job."

My wife had been like that. Eventually feeling my grief had become too much for her, and in those years before the inhibitors were available, she'd left. Her absence from the back of my mind for the first time in twenty-two years had, as Suzanne described, felt like a spiral into madness.

Then I realized what Suzanne was really saying about this friend of hers. Jesus. If anyone ever found out that not only was she violating the law, using empathy for herself personally, but also that she was gay, she'd be on the other side of the Casino wall faster than I could stand for her.

I covered. "You're not wearing your friend's hair. Are you?"

She sighed. "No. We had a bond before all this. Anyway, that isn't the point. I mainly want to find out how it's possible. What makes one person react like Joni, and another react like Brooke. I mean, we know nothing about their backgrounds. Right? Even if Brooke was just hallucinating or having visions or whatever — remember, Joni's visions only messed up her mind once they involved her friends — they could've somehow titillated Brooke, made her want to explore what she was feeling. Maybe she was abused as a kid, and there was some overlap."

"You see her as just as much a victim as the girl she killed."

"No. Maybe. I don't know what kind of past trauma she did or didn't experience." She lowered her voice. I had to strain to hear her. "I think she'll be paying for it in the most brutal way possible. I don't care if prison was already a brutal environment before. To sentence her to legalized brutality this way…"

It was a seditious thought. We both fell silent.

"Besides," Suzanne said, "if Tom got her into kink, any other personality joining in would've seemed like role play to him."

"That's not what I meant." I was glad for the change back to the subject. "I mean, if this were a problem, why wouldn't we have seen other women having it by now?" As soon as I said the words, I knew: I had seen it. "Never mind," I said. "Liza Hill's personality change."

She nodded, once, a sign of approval.

"So what, though? Where does it get us? This isn't an investigation. It isn't like we can rescue anyone." I sounded more desperate than intended, but maybe that was okay.

Suzanne pursed her lips thoughtfully. "We know Ayana's name and where she worked, her ID. From there we should be able to trace back her entire timeline, when she entered the system, where she came from, who she came in with. If we can use that information to find out where the raw hair went…"

"To do what? Identify a bad batch? Arrest the manufacturer? Try to identify and warn other purchasers, about how hair might make them feel?" I shook my head. "Just with these three as a test case, do you really think other women could be convinced to chalk up funny behavior to wigs? I don't know about you, but a complaint would be filed against me faster than I could predict it. Which would only reinforce our employers noticing our activities."

"Yeah. I guess." She turned so that the backs of her shoulders rested on the wall. "I forgot I'm not working the same way I used to." In her voice, a tinge of sadness.

The door opened. A doctor strode in, followed by the nurse. "Exam time." The doctor scanned us both up and down. I wondered if she wore a wig, too. "They sent two of you for this? Who's the lead?"

Suzanne lifted her shoulder off the wall, raised her hand. Without looking at me, she said, "Ray, why don't you go grab a cup of coffee. We'll catch up in a few minutes."

The last thing I needed was to be up half the night. I found a water fountain, took a good long drink. Then I sat in a waiting room chair, breathing the cool dry antiseptic air whose artifice was such a contrast to the wild humid eddies of seabreeze.

Suzanne's idea felt the way it had years ago, when my wife first approached me with her fear that Dani was being groomed by an online predator. Dani's smart, I'd told her, she knows better, you worry too much.

Except that Dani hadn't been smart, her mother's instincts had been right on, and if I thought about it in that context, then what Suzanne had told me meant a group of my constituents desperately needed help.

That propelled me to Joni's room. If I could get her to give me insights on where they'd gotten the wigs, Liza's and Brooke's personality changes, how widespread was this thing? If it was a bad batch of inhibitors, which seemed the most likely scenario, then in spite of Suzanne's misgivings about it primarily affecting women, that could make it a public-health issue. Identifying it could seal our job security, maybe even for life.

I turned the corner. This time her door was open.

I walked past, glanced inside. She sat alone in a wheelchair, the wig in her lap. She ran her fingers through its strands as if caressing a child's head. Or comforting the dead victim whose head it came from, which was more disturbing than I wanted to credit. I put more power into my step, prepared to hurry by.

Her chin lifted; she caught my eye. The intense emotion on her face, far beyond recognition, made me stop. The expression on her face blended fear, gratitude, compassion, and even a little anger. I could sense none of these, though. The hospital had dosed her with inhibitors.

We regarded each other for a few moments. Finally I advanced on the door. "Mrs. Rafferty," I said.

"Officer Trueman. What brings you to the hospital?"

Shit. She didn't know about the Alberinis. "Your friend, Brooke, had a little meltdown after you left." It seemed like a safe version of the truth.

She looked back down at the wig. "Brooke could never stand someone else being the center of attention."

Brooke was within her rights this time, but I kept my mouth shut. "Mrs. Rafferty," I said instead, "if you don't mind my asking, when did your and your friends' hair issues start?"

She gave me a sharp look, but then relaxed. "About a year ago. Liza and I talked over wine one night about how it was like right after we had our kids, all our hair falling out. But then Brooke spoke up, she has no kids, you know, and said it was happening to her too. Our doctors said stress. We're afraid it's something we have no control over. Like something in our food or water."

Then she caught her breath, eyes wide; she'd let slip a borderline seditious thought. I stopped short of asking her whether she'd spoken to her neighbor, the woman with the turquoise turban. Changed the subject instead. "That's terrible," I said sympathetically. "You're not able to petition the HOA board or anything, find a new lawn care company?"

She snorted. "Where do you live? The HOA is an enforcement body only. Like before, only no community gatherings. And if the doctors say stress, then who else do we have?"

I let it drop. "Mrs. Rafferty, where did you and your friends get the wigs?"

She picked at the lace that edged the wig. "Online, of course. What of it?"

"I have a neighbor whose hair is starting to fall out. You purchased human-hair wigs through one particular seller. Can you tell me about that?"

She picked at a pill on her blanket. "What's there to tell? We found her, we found some merchandise we liked, we purchased it, it came to our homes."

"How'd you find the seller?"

"Through an online ad. Nothing special about it. It popped up at the top of search results." Her tone questioned why this was such a big deal compared to other transactions. "It said it was local, so I assumed targeted. I wanted something fast, so I clicked."

"Did the ad, or the website, say where the wigs came from?"

"Does it matter? Real hair is what matters." She ran her fingers through it. "Why are you so interested in our hair, anyway? Aren't there better things for you to be investigating?"

I tried a different tack. "You've been experiencing things, haven't you? Memories that don't seem like your own, things that seem like they come from another life? Before the last couple of days, did you ever find yourself blacking out or thinking you were in a place you weren't? Unusually vivid nightmares?"

Her hand stilled and dropped into her lap. "You're talking crazy. Empathy is illegal." But her voice quavered.

"Mrs. Rafferty, the events of the last few days have been pretty crazy, haven't they?"

Her tone grew sharper. "The stuff with Brooke and Tom didn't start until a couple of days ago."

"The stuff with Brooke and Tom would've been the worst of it." I waited.

"No." But her answer was too abrupt and short. "I don't even know why I — I thought they had done something to me, but I can't think why, I've known them for years now. Such sweet people. Always so kind to my children."

"What did you think they had done?"

She squeezed her eyes shut. "Horrible things. Please, I — I don't want to get them in trouble."

"Mrs. Rafferty, nothing you tell me here tonight is useful in a court of law," I said gently. "But if you think Liza or any of your other friends are in trouble — if they're experiencing the same, I'd like to help them."

"No. Jesus. We're not a bunch of hysterics. I mean, Liza started falling apart, but the hair thing, alopecia, whatever, really messed with her head. That's all." She fell quiet, but she stared at a spot on the floor near my shoes. "Although."

I waited.

"She seemed to feel like she was being punished. I don't know if that's the right word. That was when she started drinking more." She fiddled with the lace on the wig. "She was always a drinker, but it accelerated over the last few months. She started drinking until she passed out in her backyard. People avoided her at her parties. She'd talk about how she didn't feel like she fit in her own skin. About never being able to get anything right, deserved what she was getting, stuff like that." Her voice was downright gentle. I started to wonder if rich-bitch Joni hadn't been part of the armor she wore, a useless defense against her mind turning Ayana on and off like a light bulb. "We joked about it," she continued. "'Sure, you deserve another glass of wine,' that kind of thing, but we never..." She closed her eyes. "We never connected it to our own issues."

"Oh?"

"I didn't wear my wig much. But on shopping trips or at a park with the girls, the strangest thoughts would pop into my head. Almost like memories, but not. Things like fighting with my foster sisters, when I never even had siblings. Or I'd find myself making plans for running away. But I would never leave Ian or the girls." Her eyes filled with tears.

I started to get a picture of who Ayana had been once, how she had come to this life and death. Why she was in Joni's head, though, was another question entirely. "Mrs. Rafferty, how long has this been going on?"

She hiccuped, swallowed, blinked. "It started maybe nine or ten weeks ago. Not long after we got the wigs. What are they? Some kind of weird radar?" Her voice pitched lower. "Will I get in trouble for violating the ban?"

Was she responsible for failing to identify what had been going on in her mind? How would that work? I didn't know. "That's why I'd like to find the seller."

She picked up the wig. Showed me a wisp of a silk tag. "Here. New Moon Creations."

I came closer. She whipped the wig at me. "Take it. I never want to see it again."

I didn't want to touch it, either. I grabbed the personal-effects bag, pulled the wad of clothes out of it, laid them on the bed, stuck the wig in and rolled the whole thing up to make it as unobtrusive as possible. "You take care of yourself, Mrs. Rafferty," I said.

CHAPTER EIGHT

I rejoined Suzanne in the hallway. "We're done and ready for booking," she reported. "Nurse is helping Mrs. Alberini dress. Where were you? Why are you holding that?"

"Wanted to see if Joni Rafferty could lend any more insight."

She did a double take. "And did she?"

I shrugged. "See what you think." I told her about the women's alopecia and Liza's punishment complex, about New Moon Creations, Joni's memories. I held up the bag I couldn't help but think of as evidence. "I want to find a way to get it tested," I said, "for some kind of hallucinogenic drug, or bad inhibitors."

Suzanne regarded me for a long time, as if trying to figure out whether my drug theory helped or hurt hers. Before she could speak, the nurse came out of the room and nodded once at Suzanne. Then she paused, stretched out her arm. Brooke Alberini emerged, trudging as if the sedative hadn't quite worn off. She wore scrubs and paper slippers. She didn't look at either one of us.

Suzanne stepped briskly behind her and zipped a pair of cuffs on her wrists. We perp-walked her through the emergency room and out into the parking lot. If anything Joni Rafferty had hallucinated was true, Brooke probably deserved it, but it was hard not to feel sorry for her after the way her husband had gone out.

The night air was warm, thick with humidity, the kind of night you'd spend driving with the windows down because 2 a.m. felt as warm on your skin as 10 p.m. and you knew you wouldn't be able to sleep. Like she had the other night, Suzanne drove fast along Route 101, virtually the only car on the road, blue lights flashing. The spark of danger crackled.

Both Enterprise and Residential Security used the old Rockingham County Sheriff's Office and Jail as a base of operations. Even though most of the security staff worked out of whatever business or district we were assigned to, criminals ended up there. I'd brought in exactly one person, back when all this started, before the people who lived in the hills learned to fear arrest rather than avoid it. I booked a teenage boy for vandalism after I'd caught him spray painting the street with anti-government slogans.

These days, our arrests were enough evidence of guilt, so there was no processing. Suzanne would turn Brooke Alberini over to Central Booking and that would be that. The AI would handle the rest, weighing the evidence and returning a judgment.

We walked into the building. Brooke, still out of it, stood in a daze as Suzanne, hands shaking, punched her information into the tablet and signed her digital signature. I wondered if Brooke realized what was happening, whether the hospital had dosed her with anything beyond what she'd been given when she first arrived, whether that made a difference when it came to the AI.

Suzanne paused in the entryway as we left, as if to gather herself. "You okay?" I asked.

If Joni had armored herself against another identity, Suzanne did so now against her own. "We've spent the last, what, twenty-four hours dealing with victims of a system of slavery, and I just turned over a woman to become part of it." She looked me in the eye. Her anger flared, molten in my chest. "I don't care what she's done against the enterprise."

We started walking again. "You've never arrested people under this system?"

"Of course I have. Men. Not a lot. My job is to track merchandise throughout the enterprise system, investigate if there's an interruption in the flow of traffic — that's how we find if someone's trying to steal an extra hour, or steal a girl, or if a girl is trying to escape."

"People actually attempt those things?"

"Well. Not so much anymore." She was quiet. "I've never stopped to think about why. Haven't you?"

"Thought about it? No."

"Arrested people?"

"Sure." I told her about the teenager.

"You thought he deserved hard labor for that?"

"I didn't think about it," I admitted. "It was back when this all was still pretty new. I remember thinking how convenient it was to bring him up here and just drop him off, let an algorithm judge his case."

"You assumed he was getting his due process, and that was the end of it?"

I had to admit that it was, but I didn't let her dwell. Instead, I said, "Brooke Alberini probably raped and murdered a young girl. How is it different?"

She stopped again. "Did you see her, Ray? Really look at her? She's gorgeous, young. No way she'll be sent to a labor facility, which means that for her crime, she deserves the same as she gave. Is that really justice? Especially considering the enterprise doesn't consider that rape-and-murder victim a real human being. To them what matters is the loss of revenue that girl would have generated for them. Is that worth this woman's body and soul?"

With that she stalked away. I followed after her like a lost puppy.

She drove with her whole body, leaning into the curves, her movements smooth and expert, as if the driving helped her control her rougher emotions. Near the Route 1 interchange she slowed as if preparing to get off the highway. I took a sidelong glance over at her.

She said nothing, just sped up again, on across the salt marshes.

Finally we were back in the village. Suzanne turned all her lights off. Instead of taking the right on Ashworth that would bring us home, she brought us to Ocean Boulevard, took a right across from the remains of the stone jetty, where Ayana's body had been found. I tensed.

She drove us very slowly down the boulevard, on the southbound side where I couldn't stare out over the Atlantic the way I did to avoid the sights. The daytime businesses were shuttered and gated, their innocent summer wares — beach clothes, trinkets — locked tightly away. The remaining businesses had turned into a veritable red light district. Girls and women shrieked down from motel balconies, Mardi Gras-like with bared breasts and gyrating hips. Women and men simulated sex acts in plate-glass windows of buildings that had once been restaurants. What had once been arcades were meat markets of mostly young, mostly brown, mostly naked flesh.

"This is what we're casting Brooke Alberini into," Suzanne said. "It's not that we're taking her out of her comfortable environment. It's that we're sentencing her to that." She pointed, like the Ghost of Christmas Future, across the street at what appeared to be a gang-bang — or rape — in progress that took everything I had not to leap out of the car to stop it. "We're told that all these women and men are working off some debt to society. That now they can't leech off the system anymore. But they can't work their way out from under this system any more than they could under the old one. Remember when we used to roll our eyes when some prisoner yelled about cruel and unusual punishment? This really is."

I turned my face away, cowardly as always, trying to preserve the memories I'd grown up with, that my daughters had known, spending hours racking up points on arcade games I played as a teen. There had been no gateway to get inside, no cashier to sell tickets or change dollars for quarters/tokens, so you could walk in and walk around and do almost anything you want. Play games, hook up. That people could now exploit teenagers wasn't much of a stretch; in spite of the good memories, all I could think of were the last few hours I'd spent here, frantically running from door to door searching for Dani.

All my lame reminiscences about our summertime traditions went out the window. I wanted to vomit, but not for the reasons Suzanne might have thought. "My daughter, Danielle, went missing from here," I said quietly, gesturing to the old Casino Ballroom building on our right. "Years ago. She was only thirteen. I was joking with my wife about how the arcade was like some cursed building from a Stephen King novel, how you could separate the faces from the clothes and hairstyles, but you'd see the same people if you took pictures of them at the same time on the same night every decade. Kind of like what you said about time warps. It took us a good half an hour to realize Dani wasn't just off in some corner."

She was quiet for a long time. "I'm so sorry," she said. "She was never found?"

We were about to turn onto M Street. I couldn't figure out if I wanted to go home or keep driving. "No," I said. "We eventually found that she'd been groomed by some guy from Mass. She arranged to meet him during one of our family trips. We never found another trace of either of them. I can never figure out if I want to look at those faces, keep looking for her, or not."

She turned down M Street, but instead of turning into her driveway, she accelerated once more. Hooked a right on Ashworth and kept going. For one crazy moment I thought she would know exactly where Dani was. Before long we were back on 101, speeding across the salt marshes. "I want you to know," Suzanne said, "what I'm doing now could cost me. These cars are tracked, apart from our phones. My supervisors will want to know why I came all the way back out here in the middle of the night."

She again slowed at the interchange with Route 1. Took the steep curve a little too fast, brought us out onto a completely deserted Route 1. Then hung a right into an overgrown parking area. I couldn't read the old entrance sign.

We passed a set of rundown buildings, a collective that looked like a set from a horror movie about zombies or angels and demons. Eventually the paved road turned to dirt, and we came up on a set of trailers. Suzanne parked the car and got out. She left her mobile in the car, motioned for me to do the same.

"I know it doesn't look like much," she said. "But this is the rescue operation I told you about, that my friend runs. She operates this one little cell of a whole network of rescues. Has since all this started. I've been wanting to join, but I haven't found a way to make it work. Anyway, this is just the base, and I think she tries to move around every now and again." She said the last words in a rush, as if they were part of a script.

That crackle of danger came back to me now, as if the woods around us were alive, electrified the same way my street had been the night Joni Rafferty appeared on my porch. I followed Suzanne to the steps of a camper, still carrying the bag with the wig inside. I hadn't let it go since taking it into custody. Suzanne knocked on the camper door in a pattern that could have been a code. After a few seconds the door opened. We went inside.

The camper was ablaze with light, but the windows had been papered over. I wondered how many others were active at this hour. A small window-unit air conditioner chugged away, sucking out the heat generated from a bank of computers along a kitchen counter. A laptop sat open on the small dinette.

But the words "What is this" died on my lips as I tried to catch Suzanne's eye. She was planted in the middle of the trailer, eyes locked with an older woman whose wide eyes and dropped jaw indicated she thought Suzanne might be a ghost. The two of them stood like that for so long, they had to be communicating telepathically. Eventually they embraced, holding on like the long-lost lovers they were.

"So good to see you," the older woman murmured as she released Suzanne. Her eyes were bright with tears. "I sensed you coming but I hardly wanted to believe it."

Suzanne's eyes had gone misty as she gestured toward me. "This is my neighbor, Ray," she said. "Ray, this is Callie."

We shook. Callie had bones like a sparrow and a grip like a hawk, short salt-and-pepper hair and brown sharp eyes. "Pleasure, especially if you had something to do with her coming here." She gazed at Suzanne with fondness.

I opened my mouth to give Suzanne some credit, but Callie gestured at the dinette's padded benches. "You look rough around the edges. Feel that way, too, all grief and angst. Please, sit. Get you anything to eat or drink?"

Callie had pretty precisely pegged my current state of mind after barely laying eyes on me, but I couldn't take the time to appreciate what that meant; I'd had nothing to drink since the water fountain at the hospital. "I'd love some water," I rasped, and sat on one of the benches, Suzanne opposite.

Callie gave us both a bottle, sat down beside Suzanne. A shared look told me their clasped hands on the table were only what I could see of a much broader, deeper story.

"It's time," Suzanne said. A quick glance at me. "I want out."

Callie stared at her. I couldn't read her face; it seemed to shift from annoyance, to calculating, to wistfulness in the space of a few seconds. She said, in a way that made it difficult to read her voice, "What changed your mind?"

Another glance at me. "Remember how I told you I could manage not to become part of the system?"

Callie snorted, an awkward, harsh sound that brought her down to earth. "My naive Su."

Suzanne reddened. "Yeah, well, it's not that simple. I could show up and give you information for one rescue and be done with it, right? But I want out, Callie. I'm ready."

Callie regarded her as if contemplating whether this was an impulse, or the real deal. She said, "Back up. Why don't you tell me what it was that changed your mind."

Suzanne told her part of the story, starting with the discovery of Ayana's body on the beach, then moving to that night when I brought Joni Rafferty over. I picked it up from there, how Joni had spoken like Ayana and how her memories of the Alberinis had triggered her to come back, unable to process the two sides of them. That led me to Tom Alberini's confession and suicide, Brooke's trip to the hospital in custody.

"Here's the thing," Suzanne said. "This is the crazy part, and I'd never talk about it if I didn't have backup." Another glance at me.

I pushed the bag with the wig in it over to her. With a small nod to me she started to unroll it as she talked. "The wigs weren't the cheap synthetic kind they give the establishment women — they were the real kind, the human-hair kind." She pulled Joni's wig out of the bag. "Both of those women at various points showed signs of split personalities. But not just any personalities — they were talking like victims. And I think somehow, instead of being treated with inhibitors, these wigs are — haunted, in a way. That somehow the women whose hair this is came with them."

I jumped in once more. "Joni Rafferty told me that all three women bought their wigs from the same source online, a business called New Moon Creations. You can see the tag on that one. We need some way to track down that source. Find out what they're doing to the wigs, if it's some hallucinogen they're adding, or just a bad batch of inhibitors."

"New Moon," Callie murmured. "That sounds like Kirsty."

"Who?" Suzanne asked.

"You never met her. She briefly stayed with us, but she moved on. Her empathy was too powerful to keep the group safe. Wouldn't surprise me if she'd found a way to tap it somehow."

"I wondered if you'd heard of any other victims who had the same symptoms," I said. "Victims who showed up acting strange, talking like they were someone else, that kind of thing."

"No," Callie said bluntly and a little too quickly. "It doesn't make sense. Our victims don't end up wearing one another's hair. The trafficked women get synthetic wigs, like Suzanne just said. They're heavily dosed with inhibitors. Only rich women like your patrons end up with real hair, and they don't come to us."

She was right. Only the real, physical women and girls who were being bought and sold online would turn up here. Women like Joni would end up being medicated for mental illnesses.

"Then help us track down more victims," Suzanne said. "Spare a hacker to find New Moon Creations. We find the wigmaker, we might be able to rescue more victims. Starting with Brooke. Now that she's in the system, they'll use her hair too. I know it's a long shot, but it's all I've got. Then I can be with you. God, Callie. It's been so long and I've been so stubborn, I don't know why I didn't see it before."

How did she plan to find more victims? Wear the wigs herself?

Coerce someone else to wear them, to experience what the victims experienced?

"Love," Callie said gently, "I think you've been misunderstanding me. I'd love for you to join me here, but at this point we need someone on the inside."

Suzanne's head snapped up. The rapturous look fell away. "You're kidding me, right?"

"I wish," Callie said. "We can only rescue so many per night." She glanced at me. "We've got operators — Suzanne called them hackers — who go on the trading sites. They purchase victims, then another volunteer meets them at some prearranged location, gets them in a car and brings them out here. We house them for a couple of days, long enough for them to get some uninterrupted sleep and a chat with a counselor. Then we move them along." She eyed me. "You'd be a good mover. Set you up with a semi cab, no one would look twice at you."

"People shipping? In containers?"

Callie's eyes twinkled. "No, silly. Put a couple of girls behind the curtain in the back of your cab. Act like they're your property, get them up to Maine or near the border. We'll talk about it another time." She turned back to Suzanne. "What I want is someone to identify the women who are about to be retired. Catch them before that point."

"But you got into this because of the kids." Suzanne's voice pitched higher. "What about the kids?"

"I've already got insiders working on finding the kids." Callie's eyes went flat. "Which you'd know if you were involved."

Suzanne opened her mouth, but Callie cut her off. "That woman you arrested tonight. She's no less important than the others, and I'm not arguing that she in any way deserves what she's getting. But I have no more operators to spare to focus on one person. The best way you have to help that woman is to set up a way to identify women who are about to be retired and shipped to labor facilities. Do that, you can have a whole machine set up to spare her and other women like her."

"I only have access to the databases for the Casino Ballroom, not the labor operations. I don't even know who runs it." Suzanne seemed about to say something else, but then she snapped her mouth shut. "I just miss you," she said softly.

Callie caressed her face, then pulled her into another hug. I got up so that they could have some privacy.

Mover, Callie had said I could offer her group, had laid it all out like a turnkey operation that I could pick up as soon as I walked away from my job. Had to be something she wasn't telling me about that too-easy scenario, like surprise inspections or perhaps the risk of getting shanked by other truckers who wanted "my" merchandise.

Then again, her words about "retired" workers had tweaked a thought I hadn't been willing to allow myself: what would happen when I was ready for retirement? In the old days a government pension and maybe a part-time job would've seen me into my twilight years; now, I wasn't so sure.

"Come on," Suzanne said behind me, grabbed my sleeve and pulled, hard. Then she opened the camper door and led me down the small wooden steps, back across the hard packed earth towards her car. When we got there she flung herself around my neck and sobbed. I held her, absorbed her grief into my own skin, let it drain away into the ground. I thought back to last night in the car, driving me home, when she told me she was working on a way to do something different with her life. I wondered if she was out of options.

CHAPTER NINE

I needed to find that wigmaker. It was on me, since I interviewed Joni Rafferty, gotten the details.

What stopped me, then, from following those same steps Joni had laid out, thumbing "real hair wigs" into the search bar? As always, things that seemed like good ideas under the cover of a waning moon seemed terrible by the light of day. If Suzanne's vehicle usage was being tracked and monitored, likely my phone activity would be. In fact, since we were held to stricter standards in Residential Security than Enterprise, a reprimand on my record might even carry heavier weight.

My schedule was also a problem. I had a full shift today, barely any time to complete my check-box reports, much less run a questionably legal search. That would be two strikes.

In each neighborhood, though, all I could see was Brooke Alberini screaming, blood-soaked, on the Hills' front lawn. I'd been aware of people's fear of me, but for the first time I felt their fear as my own. I could threaten liens on their houses all day and it wouldn't make a difference: what they feared was the inability to rearrange their budgets to make the payments, or some other situation that would get them arrested. Having seen what happened to Brooke last night, I could no longer believe that anyone "deserved" a corporate penalty. By the end of the day I was so pissed off that my walk home nearly became a jog that might, if I let it, carry me far from the rising tide and all that went with it.

For once, Suzanne left work on time and was already home, I saw when I walked up the block. I was so fired up from dealing with the corporate puppets that I didn't bother going home first. I sprang up her steps, banged rapidly on her door.

She took a few seconds to answer. When she did, I stepped back. She looked like hell, eyes sunken, red from crying, lips chapped raw. Skinnier, even. "You're sick," I said. "I'll come back."

"I'm not sick." A wave of self-loathing washed over me, in contrast to the invitation of her open door. "Come on in."

I followed her in. She turned the tap off, as she had earlier in the hospital, but its effects lingered: revulsion for who we were, what we'd become. I shut the door behind me, stood in her cool summery living room, trying to ground myself. "Did you even go to work today?" I asked.

"I went." Her back to me. She padded into the kitchen, returned with a mug of steaming beverage. "Offer you something?"

"I'm good, thanks." I could've killed for a beer, but alcohol was reserved for the establishments' paying customers; bigger profit margins than from employees. I still hulked by the door. "You look — really, I can come back."

She sat on her couch, curled her legs under her, the mug in her hands like it had been sent from heaven. "I could use the company." She pointed her chin at the opposite end of her couch. "Please, sit."

Maybe I should've asked for a beverage. I was going to be here for a bit. "Well, what happened?" I asked, afraid of the answer: Callie had been arrested, Suzanne had had to do it, the campground had been torched, there was no more rescue.

"Nothing," she said. "I'm a big goddamn hero."

I opened my mouth to question why, but she got there first. "I went the extra mile," she said. "I didn't have to, but by God I tracked down that rotten scofflaw who thought she could destroy company property and get away with it." A sob escaped her throat, harsh and choking. "They're already talking about promoting me."

I didn't know what to say. Suddenly my fearful housewives and reticent breadwinners seemed pale by comparison. Still, her raw anger all but mirrored my own.

More tears slipped down her cheeks. She sipped at her mug as if she wanted, but couldn't quite drink the scalding liquid.

The last time I had seen a woman cry like this, a detective told her that all leads had been exhausted, and we might never know what happened to Dani.

My phone was in my hand before I knew it. I turned it on. Then thumbed "real hair wigs" into the search bar.

The first ad that came up, Joni Rafferty had said. I tapped it. Action felt better than empty comfort.

The website was a single page with a three by three grid displaying "blonde," "medium," and "dark" tints in "short," "medium," and "long" lengths. At the very bottom was an Ocean Boulevard address all the way down in Seabrook Harbor. That close to the Massachusetts border, I wondered if it might be fake. A "ship to" notation preceded the address; maybe it was only a drop point, a place to pick up the raw materials.

"Suzanne." I showed her my phone. "See that address?" Powered the phone down. "Even if it's a drop point, it's our best shot at finding Brooke Alberini's hair."

Incredibly, she started to shake her head. "I know that address. It's not good down there. Shit. I should've thought an operation like that would run from there."

"Why? What's wrong with it?"

She sighed. "We were supposed to be housed there," she told me.

She stared over her mug, across the living room towards the door. "Enterprise Security," she clarified, "was going to have all our housing down there, Seabrook Harbor. Bigger housing, probably we'd have had to share, but we were told the company town was expanding and we were going to get first dibs." She was quiet, sipping. "When we cross that drawbridge you'll see, right on the water where the ocean opens up, this block of houses. Blasted, burnt to a crisp. The first thing the enterprise found when they got in there was a secret mosque. They firebombed it, but the sea breeze carried the sparks to surrounding houses and about leveled two blocks. That still wasn't enough. They went through all the remaining houses, looking for other illegal activity. They found a couple of pirate podcasters, an old-fashioned paper newsletter operation, some hackers. A few gay couples, a shelter for transgender people. Maybe all the arrestees figured if they holed up close to the enterprise, they'd be overlooked." Her voice shook. She drew a deep breath. "They almost found Callie. If they'd come only a few hours earlier. But she was down further, closer to the Mass. border, she had the chance to figure out what was going on and clear out. She only had a few rescues then. The shelter was her idea, but she wasn't running it. She got everyone up and out and that was the last time I saw her. Until the other night."

I hadn't been expecting any of that. "It's the memories you want to avoid?"

She turned her face toward me. In the half-light her eyes were sunken dark pits. "Don't be ridiculous." Her tone was sharp. "Ever since they killed that place, they've been monitoring it for subversive activity. They left the drawbridge up for ages so no one could even get in or out, but I guess they let it down again when they were worried about the gears corroding, or something. They certainly won't let us live there, in case we try to unionize or something. I don't know how that wig-maker is avoiding detection." She took a long, slow drink of her tea. I realized she was jonesing for a beer as badly as I.

"You said <u>when</u> we cross that drawbridge. Not if, but when."

"Did I? I shouldn't have." She drew a breath as if to say more, then stopped.

"Suzanne, last night you couldn't wait to find this wig-maker. Now we've found her. What was so important about her? How were you planning to find Brooke?"

She didn't answer right away. "I was gonna wear her hair, see if I recognized any details. Assuming I got any visions to begin with."

"That's what I was afraid of," I murmured.

"Don't worry. I'm not in so much of a hurry, now." She paused. "Maybe the best we can do is what Callie asked. Set up a way to identify women going to labor facilities, and catch Brooke that way."

"After she's already been used up? What would be the point?"

"Rescuing a lot of other women besides her. Jesus, Ray, we got into law enforcement to help people. I mean, do I identify with Brooke? Sure. I'd have loved to live in her place, a nice neat neighborhood filled with neighbors making nice with the dykes while excluding us from parties and shit." She sipped at her tea some more, regarded my phone as if it dripped with blood.

"One problem with Callie's plan," I said. "You told her you have nothing to do with the retirement system. Okay, so the hackers have access to all that stuff. But identifying women who are about to go to labor facilities would only be the first step. Don't you see? You'd need an entire network of people to help you divert the women, regularly, going from here to the facilities. Those kinds of relationships are like deep undercover, they take years to build. We don't have years. The only other alternative would be transport records — the database of people on their way to labor facilities. If there were a way to intercept the trucks, rescue entire groups of people…"

"Doing raids on the interstate system would be hard," she said. "Like suicide-mission hard. So forget that."

"What about the records you have access to? Are there flags on individual records in the worker databases?"

"No." She shook her head. "I'd have seen that, would've made it easy. I don't know how they track retirements."

Maybe this was Callie's way of keeping Suzanne at a distance, a latter-day equivalent of breaking up with her. "The new moon rises tonight," I said. "If our wigmaker gets hair shipped to her at night, this is our shot." I let her feel my own sense of urgency, my unwillingness to wait the four weeks until the next new moon.

Her interest feathered around my chest, but she continued to hold the tea close. "Assuming it would be shipped there tonight or tomorrow, that it hasn't already been shipped. Assuming we can afford to stake the place out — that's another night out, you know, maybe a few of them. Not to mention, why would we be doing this?"

Because I wanted all this to be worth something, this time. "Is there something else we can do with the info?"

"Like what?"

"Get her to tell us what's going on. If she's the one doing it, get her to stop whatever it is she's doing to those wigs."

She was quiet. Then she said, "You remember my car is tracked, don't you? Even if they were too busy jacking themselves off over my so-called solve, they'd notice all this extra activity at some point."

I'd forgotten what it was like, having a partner who could read your mind. I said, "Yup. I remember. Was going to go out there myself if you didn't want to."

"With what? A bicycle? And then what? Bring that wig back for me?"

"Sure. Or the wig-maker herself."

A small smile twitched at her lips. She placed her mug on the table. "Senseless letting you go out there yourself. Never know what subversives might do to you."

"That was a fast mind-change." I followed her into the kitchen, expecting some smartass comment.

Instead her eyes were faraway, worried, as she placed the mug in the sink. She said, "It's not. I still don't want to go. But I can't stand the idea of letting you go alone."

Now I got it. Callie had disappeared on her once. We weren't lovers, but she cared enough not to let me get arrested on my own. "Last chance," I said. "We ride back out to Callie's and grill her again about hacker resources. Find out if there's a way to hack the tracking system."

She smiled faintly. "No. Thanks, though."

It felt strange getting into a car on a mission without carrying anything, not a go bag or a breaching tool in sight. We took the left on Ashworth, drove it until the merge with Ocean Boulevard, at the edge of the company town.

Flashes of light caught my eye, heat lightning from a storm over the Atlantic. Before long we crossed the little drawbridge that separated Hampton from Seabrook Harbor. I practically heard the license plate reader camera on the old control house snap an image of Suzanne's car.

From here I could barely make out the charred ruins at the mouth of the inlet. The rest of the place, at least that we could see from the road, had an in-between, borderland feel. I hadn't been down here in years. The houses had been nice at one time, well-kept, well-to-do. Now, weeds grew tall and strong around the foundations, trees sprouted through decks, telephone poles and power lines lay in tangled forty-five-degree angles. I couldn't tell whether a good storm had brought them down, or the response to the rebellion.

The address for the wig-maker brought us all the way to the border of Seabrook Harbor, to a block of what had once been a gas station, a realtor's office, and a couple of restaurants. "Drop point," I said to Suzanne, driving past. "An intersection. Of course, it would have to be. She probably gets hair from the establishments in Saugus and Lawrence, trucked up Route 1 and 495 to this road right here." I turned on to 286, then made a U-turn.

"Great. But how do you want to stake it out? You on this side, me on the other?"

The skin at the back of my neck prickled. "No way. We both stay in the car. Look." Across the street was a house with a deep driveway. I backed in until my rear bumper tapped a fence. "We don't need to see the actual transaction. Just see the vehicles, who goes where."

"Assuming anyone shows," Suzanne said quietly.

Two nights of little sleep was going to take its toll on me. Probably her, too. "So," I said, "How'd you and Callie meet?"

She smiled faintly. "On the job, of course," she said. "She was actually a DCYF social worker. She had just transferred from the Foster Care program to the Juvenile Justice program. She didn't really like it, it was a lot harder on her. She was trying to get into Child Protection, bless her. Anyway, we met on this one case I was working, this set of convenience-store armed robberies, and once we worked out that our perp was a juvenile with a record ... That was five years ago."

"You were together for two years?"

"Only for a few months, before Election Day. It took us a bit to establish that we were both gay."

"How'd you vote, anyway?" I asked.

She regarded me carefully. "Democratic socialist. You?"

"Conservative."

"Oh? And how's that smaller-government thing working out?"

"I don't think anyone could've foreseen just how much smaller." I could hear the defensiveness creep into my voice.

"That shit's for damn sure." She wriggled around so she faced me. "How about you? Were you with anyone before shit went down?"

"Kind of. I was seeing a nurse who worked an opposite shift. We hardly ever saw each other. I thought I liked it that way."

"Don't know what you've got till it's gone," she murmured.

"Not really. More like, once it was gone, I realized what I didn't want."

"And then you got this job, which doesn't make it easy to meet anyone. And when you do, she's gay." Her tone teased me.

"Exactly right. You get me so well. It's criminal."

"Literally."

That ended the conversation, but instead of devolving into awkwardness, silence sat comfortably between us like a third partner. When Suzanne started to drowse, it was on my shoulder.

Close to midnight, headlights appeared up 286. I shouldered Suzanne awake. "Anything coming from your direction?" I said.

She mumbled something, struggling to wake up. I handed her the coffee thermos.

The vehicle was a van. It pulled into the lot across the street and idled, lights blazing. In contrast was the car that came to meet it, a dark-colored minivan, lights out entirely. The two vehicles went around the back of the buildings.

Suzanne came fully awake. "I hate that we can't see them," she said. "What if there's another exit we can't see?"

"Stands to reason that the way in, is the way out," I responded. "All that's on the other side are marshes. But keep watch on your side."

After twenty minutes, the van left, exiting to 286 the same way it had come in. Suzanne squinted. "There," she said. "Way down where that other lot is."

The new moon made it difficult. I turned over the engine, slowly made our way out of the driveway. Ahead we could see taillights. I sped up, lights off, until I was satisfied we weren't close enough to spook or far enough to lose the other driver. That vehicle could go to any one of these side streets or houses, and I was prepared to slam on the brakes.

Instead the car disappeared around a corner. I sped up, took the same corner a little too fast. In front of us the road stretched away into blackness.

"Where'd the car go?" I panicked just a little bit. If the wigs were haunted; if they were coming from a ghost in a ghost factory, I was going to turn myself in for hard labor. I slowed way down, unwilling to drive us into the salt marshes, and turned on my parking lights. The road, half drifted over with sand, glowed amber a foot or two in front of us. I barely made out the faded yellow center lines. We crept forward. I contemplated a warren of houses to the right. I didn't want to go door-to-door.

Suzanne pointed to my left. "There."

"I don't see anything." I sounded like a cranky old man.

"That road, right there. That turnoff."

I saw. The signpost was gone, but fresh tire tracks had cut into the drifted sand. I turned.

The tracks, along with the sand, disappeared within a few feet, but no matter: we were close. The tracks reappeared from time to time along a largely deserted road. "This wigmaker couldn't be living out of her vehicle," I started.

"Ssh." Suzanne pointed. "Look. That house. See that light?"

I slowed. Sure enough, a faint chink of light came from some structure, a mobile home or bungalow, alongside the road. More tire tracks turned into what was probably its driveway. I cut the lights and followed them, praying we wouldn't get stuck. The dunes had slowly retaken where humans had once built. When we parked and got out, what might have been flat, three years ago, tripped me and got into my shoes as I scuffed through it. Suzanne switched on a tiny LED flashlight, beamed it around enough to see the structure.

It had a front door, but the steps were gone, scavenged or deliberately removed. Suzanne's beam picked out more tire tracks, which guided us around back.

The engine still ticked. Beside the vehicle, wooden steps led up to a small deck. One floorboard squeak could give us away. I felt the familiar adrenaline surge that came before every raid, the body's way of prepping for what could seriously go wrong. Suzanne moved ahead of me, positioned herself at the bottom of the steps facing the door. She expected me to slice the pie upwards, to cover her at the top step while she came up the stairs, even though she was the only one armed.

The back door opened, spilling bright yellow light onto the deck. A backlit silhouette stood there, hands on hips. "Why don't you come up here and come in," said a woman's voice, "instead of getting bitten out here by marsh mosquitoes?"

I felt them suddenly, sharper than regular mosquitoes. Like a pair of kids competing for who got the shower first, Suzanne and I rushed up the stairs and into the house. It only occurred to me that it could be a trap after I was inside and the door was shut, as we examined our hands and arms for welts and found nothing. Suzanne and I exchanged glances, anchoring to one another before dealing with whatever came next.

The woman in the room with us was older. She wore a sleek black exercise ensemble, the kind favored by upper middle class suburban women, draped with a large paisley shawl. Her long curly dark blonde hair faded to silver; she gazed at us sharply, with stormy gray eyes in a delicate heart-shaped face that was beautiful even in spite of — or perhaps because of — its lines.

Emotions slammed into us, a rogue wave with no time to break. She wanted to give us a tongue-lashing, but she didn't want to drive us away. She was more curious than angry or scared. "So," she said, "you're here to ask about my wigs."

We gaped at her, this time like kids caught stealing cookies. The part of me that missed the comfort of an empathic bond wanted to reach back out. The pragmatic part kept my feelings tightly under wraps.

"Oh, come on." She sounded amused, but put out. "Smart move on your part, tailing me. Normally my spells keep people out, but you two. I could sense you were there to help. I'm glad you followed the path I laid for you." She raised one long finger, wagged it between us.

"You mean your tire tracks?" I snipped. Covering for my seditious thoughts.

She laughed. "If you like. Just know that if, after we speak, you decide you can't or won't help, then by tomorrow I'll be gone, and I'm changing my pickup address."

"How did you know what we were here for?" Suzanne squeaked. She cleared her throat.

The woman squinted. "So much for trained observers. I'm Kirsty, by the way. Not my real name, in case one of you gets it into your head to run me through the system." She flashed us a sudden, wide smile filled with delight. "The spirits only give me a general sense of what's going on, so why don't you tell me more specifically why you're here?"

Kirsty. Callie had spoken about Kirsty.

"Actually." Suzanne cleared her throat. "May we have some water first?"

"Of course." Kirsty turned, left the room on feet as light as a cat's. The shawl swirled behind her.

As soon as she was out of the room I could think more clearly, as if her departure broke whatever spell she'd put on us. That let me observe more, too. For the first time I noticed that the walls had been painted with unusual symbols, patterns that curled and flowered and spiraled.

"Your wall art is very unusual," I said when Kirsty came back, holding two glasses of water.

"I know." She handed me one. "Those are my spells."

Suzanne caught my eye, gave me an unspoken warning. She accepted her water glass with a small smile and a nod.

"You didn't come here about that, though," Kirsty continued. "You still haven't answered my question. Oh, stop looking at each other like you can't hold an independent thought between you. What about my wigs brought you here?"

"Kirsty. Some very strange things have been happening to women in the residential district," Suzanne started. "It's as if they're living lives that aren't theirs. In one case, a living woman appeared to experience being murdered at the hands of friends of hers. Her mind couldn't handle the strain of it."

"I see. And she was wearing one of my wigs?"

I held up the bag with Joni's wig. "It has your tag and web address on it."

"So it's working," Kirsty murmured. "Then if this woman understands what is happening to her sisters in body, what's the issue? She is prepared to help them now, isn't she?"

"What are you saying? You made this happen?" Suzanne's brow creased.

Kirsty sighed as if unwilling to explain much. "I use a spell and some herbs to draw out the essence of the spirit the hair comes from.

Its wearer then has a line on its woman of origin. She can see things more clearly, not take so much for granted. Hopefully be inspired to help."

I could see Suzanne's rope beginning to fray. "Kirsty, one of those 'sisters' was murdered by a woman wearing one of your wigs. The visions she was having titillated her, made her seek control by acting out those visions herself. She killed one of her own 'sisters.'"

Kirsty's face blanched white. A few seconds later, a wave of shock and horror tinged with regret washed over me.

"We came here," Suzanne continued, "to find the hair of the woman who was put in custody for that murder. To try to find her. Surely even you can agree that she doesn't deserve a sentence for the same fate as her victim."

"Of course she doesn't," Kirsty murmured. "But then, none of them do."

"What is all this?" Suzanne said. "What kinds of spells are you casting? What kinds of herbs?"

A new wave of defensiveness hit me. "That's not for discussion. My faith is private."

"Your faith is getting people hurt. Did you never hear of unintended consequences?" Around the edges of Suzanne's rising voice I felt her righteous indignation, the sort of thing that had gotten our society to where it was.

"Kirsty," I said gently, though I couldn't bring myself to project calm, "how long does it take you to make a wig?"

Her lip curled. She continued to glare at Suzanne when she answered. "Six to twelve weeks. Depending on style and demand. I try to keep them simple so that they don't take as long."

"The woman we're trying to help doesn't have a lot of time. Is there another way?"

"Other women have been in the system for years. Why don't you rescue them first?" A bolt of weariness from Kirsty. I struggled to keep up with her emotions and her words; I was badly out of practice.

Suzanne uncrossed her arms. They lay at her sides like dormant swords. "How many wigs have you got? How many have you sold?"

"Dozens. Every week, new shipments. High demand, you know."

A year had passed since the last of the illegal immigrants had been deported, since the poor had been given their mandatory skilled and unskilled labor assignments and the system as we now knew it had come to be. The tide was unlikely to slow if the rate of our enforcement kept up.

"The more chemicals go out into the environment," Kirsty continued, "the worse the hair and skin conditions get."

"You've got to stop," Suzanne said in a rush. "Let them deal with their bald patches. Maybe that's what will make them rise up. You can't keep letting them hide the problem."

I could see why and how she and Callie had disagreed over how she could best serve the rescue's mission. "Kirsty," I said.

She held up her hand to me. "Rise up? Where do you think they end up? You think those women have any power? You think we still live in a democracy? They're as much prisoners on the hill as women down here. But hair is power. I give them hair, I give them a little something extra too. They get sick, maybe encourage their husbands to stay home instead of patronize the establishments."

Suzanne pinched the bridge of her nose and swayed a little. Fatigue had hit her like a semi; my own truck wasn't far behind. "You won't help us find this woman."

"I meant what I said before. If you want to help, it can't be about one. If it's an uprising you want, you have to involve more." Kirsty turned to her sofa. A stack of boxes sat in the corner where a television might have been. "Tonight's shipment. A collection from over the past month. Each box contains maybe 25 hanks of hair."

She opened the boxes one at a time, lifted out plastic gallon bags filled with shorn hair. With some red or blonde exceptions, most of it was dark. No great surprise; the establishments and labor facilities had "employed" the Black and Latino and Asian laborers who were ineligible for deportation. The volume unsettled me. The week's shipment had included ten or twelve boxes. Nearly 300 women were out there, heads shorn, awaiting and experiencing God knew what, and we thought we could save one?

The truck hit me. I sank onto the couch.

"There is another way," Kirsty said. "Help me get these wigs into the hands of the trafficked women. By remembering who they are and where they come from, it will disrupt business."

"How?" We asked simultaneously. Suzanne added, "We can't possibly match the hair to each original owner."

"No, that would be impossible," Kirsty agreed, "but by replacing the synthetic wigs with these, by reminding the women of memories and emotion, perhaps that is how the revolution will begin."

"How is that even possible." My tone was flat, short-tempered, an approximation of how I felt.

A blast of confusion as Kirsty shifted her gaze back and forth between us. "The inhibiting drugs the synthetics are treated with make the women compliant, make them forget, but the effects are transient. Once the wig is off, it only takes a few minutes for the wearer to return to herself."

"You made those wigs," Suzanne breathed.

Kirsty shook her head. "I worked for the company that came up with the idea. After I escaped, I tried to come up with a plan to turn the idea around. Two years." Her voice was quiet.

"Your herbs and spells work the same way? Absorption?" Suzanne asked.

Kirsty nodded. "Can you get them into the women's hands?"

Suzanne hesitated. "I'm Security. I don't work directly with them. I'm not sure how the supply chain works."

"You don't have to. Take my van. Make deliveries to the motels where they're housed."

"Duplicate deliveries will confuse them," Suzanne said.

"We have a mutual friend, don't we? Who can hack the system? Substitute my name for another supplier's?"

Doubt on Suzanne's face. I recalled, as I was sure she did also, Callie's admonishments about Kirsty's character and being unable to spare hackers. Then again, for a mission on this scale, maybe Callie would help.

"It would take time to set up," Suzanne said finally.

"You can set it up tonight. Take my van. Go to your friends. Explain what you're doing. Make the deliveries tomorrow afternoon."

"Will you cast a spell to help us?" Sarcasm sharpened Suzanne's tone.

Kirsty's blue eyes remained clear. "Yes. I will. Go, now. And take the wigs." She began to pick up boxes from a different stack beside the doorway, loaded us both up, and gave Suzanne the minivan's keys.

We stumbled through the dunes to the vehicles. "We're going to have to call in sick tomorrow," I said.

"Yeah. Which means I have to get my car back to my place. I can say I tracked something out here, maybe a black market operation, but I can't leave it here all night and all day."

"I'll follow you," I said.

"Too risky. I can get away with being out after curfew. You can't, not in that vehicle. You're going to have to drive back to Callie's and explain the situation, then come get me in the morning. Will you do that?"

"I don't think there's much of a choice, is there?" I said.

Her lips compressed into what might have been a thin, tense smile. Then she reached up, kissed my cheek. "Thank you."

"You take care, now. Get some rest." I deliberately tried to sound nonchalant, like I expected to see her tomorrow morning. The fact was, as we drove back along to the coast road, as she turned left in front of me to return to Hampton Beach, I couldn't shake the feeling that it would be the last time I ever saw her.

CHAPTER TEN

To get back to the old campground where Suzanne had brought me the night before while avoiding curfew required me to drive back to the drop point, then take a right on the old Route 286 and drive along the Massachusetts border back towards Route 1. I rattled along the darkened roads in Kirsty's old minivan. Shocks, brakes, steering all felt like they needed work.

The lights of Route 1 only brought temporary relief. Even though I hated to leave her, I was thankful that Suzanne wasn't with me. I wasn't sure I wouldn't be meat if I broke down out here. Parts of this road had always been sleazy, especially the Saugus area a few miles south, all strip clubs and porn shops. I shuddered to think of what that had become under today's system. Here, the small businesses that had once supported Hampton's upper classes, and the few houses on the main artery, had been abandoned. Tractor trailers idled in their driveways and parking lots. It didn't take much to guess what they were up to.

Back when Dani went missing I'd spent entire nights around the big traffic circle that connected Route 1 to 95. I feared she'd been enslaved, wired up on heroin or meth and sent to give blowjob after blowjob to the truckers en route to and from Maine. After a week or so down there I couldn't take it anymore, the endless transactional highway life. I only went back a few months later, when a girl was found murdered in a dumpster behind a gas station. It wasn't Dani and I never returned.

Before Election Day I'd held that all lives mattered, and I'd never treated anyone differently, no matter where I worked as a cop. I'd also never expected slavery to become legal once more. Somewhere deep in the back of my mind I wondered whether it had simply remained underground, waiting for the day it could again be justified.

I juddered my way through the truck traffic, sweated past a couple of Enterprise Security vehicles who, I was sure, had cottoned to our plot, had arrested Suzanne, and were on the lookout for me. As I made my way out of the business arena and back onto quieter, more familiar marshland, they didn't follow.

Alone out here I wondered: what was the campground's risk of being raided? Was their hacking activity traceable? Would I arrive to find the place as abandoned as it appeared?

Driving through the gates, though, I noticed a detail I hadn't picked up on before: the presence of old-model vehicles, a Toyota Tercel, a Honda Civic. The kind that might once have been up on cinder blocks, that Tom Alberini had sneered at. If those were still here, it was a good bet the place was hardly abandoned.

I carefully made my way to the trailers I recalled from the other night. Parked, got out, tried to orient myself. I didn't have the empathic connection with Callie that Suzanne had, that had guided her the first night we'd come out here.

Behind me came a soft snick: a screen door closing or a gun cocking, I couldn't tell the difference anymore. I turned.

Callie stood on a trailer's wooden stoop. "Mr. Trueman," she said softly. "Lost your way?"

"Found it." I made my way to where I could see her in the faint starlight, craning my neck to look up at her. "Suzanne sent me."

"I know. Kirsty sent a message. No, not with technology." Callie sounded dryly amused. "Why don't you come on up. She only told me you were coming, not what you were here for."

I came up, even though I was unwilling to leave the van or its cargo. Callie opened the door wide, gestured me into a different trailer than the one we first visited. This one was hot, running a good dozen computers. At the dinette sat a couple of younger women, one with green hair, the other with blue, sporting multiple piercings and tattoos. They spoke in whispers, in a foreign language I couldn't recognize.

"Now," said Callie, "what brings you back here?"

The other night I hadn't been able to read her, to get a sense of who she was or what she wanted. Perhaps that had been because she was focused on Suzanne. Now, her request seemed like a demand, and I felt compelled to respond. I told her everything, how we found Kirsty, what Kirsty had asked of us, where Suzanne was, and what we needed from Callie.

"She'll be out of a job if we do this," I said. "She won't be able to learn anything about the women heading to labor facilities. But this might be even more disruptive to the system. If it works."

The two women at the dinette had gone silent, listening. Now they burst into a chatter that strained my nerves.

Callie turned, hands out, palms down, seeking to quiet them. Then she turned back to me. "I see." Her voice was toneless. Whatever telepathy she and Suzanne shared, was walled off from me. "Have you considered all the risks?"

"I'm not sure I'd know where to start." Suzanne would have a better sense of those risks. She should be here, even though I knew it had never been possible.

"One of those things where you can't anticipate them all," Callie mused. I was grateful for that piece of wisdom, even though it felt as if she had let me off the hook. "All right," she said. "We'll do it. You sit tight until I give Suzanne the signal. Got it?"

"Signal?" I said stupidly.

"She'll know it when she gets it. Look." Her face softened. "I can't promise exactly when we'll get into the system and make the changes. That's why I need you to wait. Can you do that?" She looked me up and down, showing rather than projecting her uncertainty that I could pull it off.

"Sure," I said. "You're in charge."

A faint smile, or grimace; I couldn't be sure. She waved me off. "Go find our Su."

"One other thing," I said. "The cars I saw out here. Do you ever drive them into the hills above the town? Where the middle managers live?"

Callie's sharp brown eyes measured my words, my presence. "No."

"Never in the last few months?"

For the briefest of instants her eyes flicked up at the ceiling. She sighed. "I told Sam she was taking a big risk," she muttered.

I waited.

"One of our rescues," Callie said, "grew up back there. She was twelve when her family lost everything in the great recession. Her mother left to find work in another city. They never heard from her again. Her father fell into a depression. She went to live with her grandparents. They died in a car crash shortly after Election Day. She ended up in the system, down on the beach. She told us she wanted to remember where she came from. On her way out from the rescue we took her back there, against better judgment."

"One of the residents thought you were foreigners looking to steal their girls and women." By now, that resident's home was surely already on the market, waiting for a new paranoiac to move in.

Callie held up her hand. "I can't even begin to unpack the sheer stupidity of that statement."

She was right, on levels I couldn't begin to fathom, and it was time to leave. I did so quietly.

The fresh cool 2 a.m. air felt good on my skin and in my lungs after the stuffy heat of that confined cabin. Curfew in downtown Hampton Beach would still be in full effect. I made my way back to the old van, crawled into the back seat, did my best to stretch out and sleep. All I could manage was a light snooze until dawn.

During the night I woke enough to call in sick. I wouldn't be paid, but at least I couldn't be fired for forgetting to notify Will that I would be out. Somewhere between sleep and waking I wondered if they could trace my location, if they'd come looking for me, if they'd find Callie, raid the camp before the hackers did their magic. Then I fell asleep and forgot again.

By sunrise a second wind hit me and I was able to sail down Route 101, windows down, ready to face the day.

Of course that was when my phone buzzed. It was work, my supervisor's supervisor wanting to speak with me. At least I was sufficiently strung out, on four hours' broken sleep, to look sick.

I parked on the far side of the lot, where fewer people were likely to see the minivan, and walked around to the employee entrance. Irrationally I wondered if my thumbprint would even work. The scan glowed green on the first try, though, and I was in.

Not far from the supervisor's office was a break room I hadn't known existed. Inside were two other Residential Security goons, neither one last night's ride. Still they eyeballed me. I was about past them when one of them spoke up. "What are you doing up so early? Trying to get yourself a promotion to Enterprise?"

"Nah, too old for that crap." I didn't know him, didn't want to know him, nor how he jumped to that conclusion. Stayed focused on the supervisor's office door.

"Not too old to bone one of them," the other one said. They both snickered.

Unease crept from the base of my spine up to the nape of my neck. Not only had my colleague seen me with Suzanne; he'd talked about it. Nothing said you couldn't do whatever was needed to try to get promoted, but like in the real world, things that made other people look bad — showing up early, being productive in a sea of slackers — tended to result in the wrong outcomes for people who "didn't want to be here."

I shook it off. Knocked on the supervisor's door, waited for the invitation to walk in.

Where my supervisor's office was cramped, windowless, and airless, the big boss had (of course) a corner office, with huge windows and the kind of nondescript faux-cherry furniture that was supposed to communicate "high-class executive." My stomach twisted. Nothing I had done since Will had spoken to me could count as making good business sense. If I got laid off, at least Callie seemed like she had space for me.

Will, my direct supervisor, stood behind the big boss, his rump against the windowsill, arms crossed, looking distinctly uncomfortable. I almost felt badly for him. He wasn't a bad guy; he was paid to manage resources, not bust balls.

He started the ball-busting anyway. "Thanks for coming in on a sick day to meet us." The tone of his voice, overly solicitous.

I gave a little cough into my hand. "What's this about, sir?"

He rolled his eyes at the "sir," but chose not to engage. "You didn't fine the residents at 12 Hampton Oaks for their disturbance of the peace."

"That's right."

"Why not?"

"They were already worried about paying additional insurance for

Mrs. Rafferty's medical issues. I felt that a fine would be adding insult to injury."

"You felt? But it was Mrs. Rafferty herself who was disturbing the peace. Don't you think if she was that worried about money, she might have kept it to herself?"

"She wasn't in her right mind."

"Still. It wasn't your call to make. You understand that, don't you?"

"Yes. Sir."

His eyes narrowed. "Next topic. Your search activity on your mobile has been a little unusual."

Gravity started to suck me down into the floor. "It was part of an investigation, sir."

"I see. One that couldn't have waited until the start of your next shift?"

"No, sir. I wanted to be sure to have the time to run it down."

"Are you saying you don't have adequate time on your shifts to follow up on leads?"

"Time was of the essence. I had intelligence that a possible public-health hazard existed for the residents in my subdivision."

"From a woman's wig-maker?" They both snickered.

Shit. Since when had they been able to look at a person's browsing history from their login? "Yes, sir. She uses real human hair, not synthetics. That makes it a potential matter of public health."

The big boss spoke up for the first time. "And what hazard was it that you were investigating?"

"Bizarre behavior, sir." I thought fast, back to that hospital conversation with Suzanne. "I was afraid the inhibitors in the hair might be a bad batch."

"You wanted to find the location of this wig-maker so you could obtain a sample for testing?"

His tone was too snotty, an abusive boss trashing an employee's carefully considered project pitch without respecting the work that had gone into it. "Yes, sir," I said anyway.

"You brought one of the residents to the hospital. Did you have any indication from her doctor that she was affected by a bad drug?"

"No, sir."

"No, they didn't give you any indication, or no, there was none to be given?"

"They didn't give us any indication."

"Did you ask?"

"No, sir."

"Then your search was baseless."

"I don't know if I'd —"

"I'm docking you another day's pay besides this 'sick' day," he snarled, "and locking down your privileges. From now until a time to be determined, you will seek your supervisor's permission before performing any further searches. Is that understood?"

"Yes, sir."

"You're on notice, Trueman. One more fuckup, you're on the next bus out to Stratham. Now, go take your day off." He sat back, looking smug.

"No, wait." My direct supervisor spoke up. "Is it true you've been spending time in the company of Enterprise Security personnel?"

I paused. "Not personnel, sir. One person. My neighbor."

"Are you unhappy here, Trueman?"

"No, sir. The other investigator is my neighbor."

"Interesting choice of friends," he murmured.

"We were both sworn law enforcement. We understand each other." The moment it was out of my mouth, I wondered: was it seditious to spend time with a person from the old days?

"I see." He motioned with his fingers. "All right. You can go."

With what Suzanne and I had planned, the confrontation hadn't gone as badly as it could have, but it hadn't gone well, either. Paranoid about the van now, I walked around the neighborhood after leaving the station. Half an hour passed before I felt comfortable driving it home.

By the time I got back, Suzanne had crouched on the top step of my front porch. "I called in sick and took my time getting back from Callie's," I told her before she could say anything. I hopped up on the porch, unlocked the door, let us both inside. I wouldn't tell her about the reprimand. She didn't need to know, and it had no bearing on what we were doing. The inquiry about our friendship was more of a concern, but I'd have to wait for the right time to bring that up.

As soon as the door was shut Suzanne flung herself at me, much like she had the night Callie had told her she wanted her to stay in the system. I held her close, feeling her tension bleed into the space around us. Before long she broke off, stood at arms-length. She said, "I was called into a meeting this morning."

"On a sick day?"

She blinked at me. "I didn't call in sick."

"Oh." I felt like an idiot. "You young'uns."

She tried to smile. Couldn't quite make it happen.

"So, seriously. What's wrong? You look like you've spent the morning having your knuckles rapped." I went into the kitchen to start making coffee, toast a couple of bagels.

She followed me. "Not far off," she said.

That sense of unease crept back along my spine. Whatever she was about to tell me, I hoped it wasn't about to put me off my breakfast.

She didn't respond right away. The coffee brewed before I told her, "Out with it. You're acting like you were suspended."

She nodded slowly. "Close, I guess." She breathed deeply, in through her nose, out through her mouth. "I was called in first thing this morning to justify my travels last night. The day after telling me I might be promoted, right? The best I could come up with was that I'd received intelligence that a black-market service operating in the harbor was undercutting enterprise business, that I'd spent time walking around to verify the report, and found nothing."

Her shoulders had ratcheted up around her ears, and she regarded the coffee pensively.

I pulled out the bag of bagels, gave them a sniff. No mold. That was good. I pulled a couple out. "So you found nothing. They'll be less likely to investigate?"

She still didn't look at me. "I was reminded that there is a special squad for black-market investigations and I should stick to my own patch. If I received future intelligence about such operations, I'm to distribute it through the proper channels. And if I want to be a part of that team, I need to use the proper channels to seek promotion. I can't even remember if I knew about this squad or not. Like, maybe they mixed in the announcement with all the crap notifications and I missed it."

I opened my mouth to answer, to tell her about my own experience, but she raised a finger to her lips. Pulled out her smartphone, dropped it on the coffee table. Motioned for me to do the same. Once both phones were out, she pulled me back out the door.

"Remember the old days, when we thought it was bad enough that some social media app was listening in on our conversations and showing us ads?" she tried to joke as we walked up M Street, towards Ocean Boulevard.

I didn't. "Didn't use many social media apps," I said. "Asking for evidence from them put me off using them."

She let out a short bark of laughter. "Fair point. Anyway. I fucked up, Ray. I should've come up with a better story. Now I'm stuck feeling like I just opened my big mouth and put C — the rescue in danger."

I recognized her dilemma: she couldn't warn Callie without taking the vehicle out there again, but if Callie got raided, she'd never see her again.

"Tonight," I said. "When we're done making our deliveries." Then I remembered Callie hadn't been able to promise we could do that today.

"Did you get her to agree to use the hackers?"

"Yes, but she wasn't sure about their timing." I paused. "It wouldn't make sense for your people to raid the campground tonight. It'll take more time than that to verify your story and determine if they even want to spend resources. Rushing back out there tonight is more of a risk to the rescue if cars show up after dark."

"I guess." She didn't sound convinced.

"If you don't mind my saying so, I think you're worried about her because you're having a hard time with the uncertainty of not being together."

She pursed her lips. "I guess you're right. You'd think I'd be used to that by now."

"I don't think anyone ever gets used to being without someone they love." I'd never thought about it, but it felt true: I'd used the empathy ban as an excuse to enforce my own loneliness, though whether in self-defense or self-punishment, I couldn't be sure.

We crossed Ocean Boulevard. The sun was already high and strong. From across the street I saw the high tide lapping over the concrete, spilling onto the roadway. I didn't want to walk through that. Instead we took a right on Ocean Boulevard. "Have you eaten?" I asked.

She shook her head. I laid an arm across her shoulders. "Come on,"

I said. "I was about to toast some exciting raisin cinnamon bagels."

We crossed back over the roadway. Neither of us said anything until we were back down M Street, climbing onto my porch. "Stuck here waiting," Suzanne said. "For what, by the way?"

"She said she'd signal you. She said you'd know it when you got it."

"Ah." Suzanne smiled, a small private thing. "How many bagels and how much coffee have you got?"

CHAPTER ELEVEN

In late afternoon she left to start packing. I used the time to pack a few clothes and toiletries of my own, along with the last of my food. Then I walked over to Suzanne's.

Her living room was a mess, trinkets pulled down from walls, things I remembered from one surface misplaced or on the floor. "I can't decide what to take," she told me.

"Take what matters," I said.

"Right." With that, she disappeared into her bedroom. Within a few seconds I heard the clank of metal, realized she was dismantling her hammock frame.

I followed her. "Help?"

"Grab that black bag. It has some sleeves in it. Slide the parts into the sleeves."

I picked up the bag. "We should talk about how we're going to work this. What if it goes bad? If the van breaks down, or if someone gets suspicious?"

She unscrewed a bolt. "Floor the gas and drive like hell."

"That van is a rattletrap. It's one loose hose or belt away from disintegrating." I needed to look under the hood. "If that thing breaks down on the other side of town, we need a way to get out." I paused. "Access to your vehicle preferable."

"My vehicle that sticks out like a black and white? What, you want me to follow you like an escort?"

"That's what I'm asking. Does it make sense to you?"

"No. For one thing, I work days. I'm already on the hook, and if my vehicle locator comes up tonight with more unusual activity ... did you check all the belts and hoses in the van?"

"I'll do that now." I put the bag down, left her to finish with the metal parts.

I exited by the back door. Behind her car the minivan baked under the risen sun; the dark paint that concealed it under the new moon would absorb all this heat and make it murder to drive. I opened the driver's side door, popped the hood.

Everything, amazingly, checked out. I wondered whether Kirsty, or her hair supplier, knew enough about cars to do basic maintenance. In any case, the car seemed like it would be all right. I closed the hood, went back in the house. "We should eat," I called.

"Not hungry," she called back.

I felt out of joint. Whatever connection we had, that had leaked out around the edges of our vigilance, had been disrupted by some unknown force. I didn't want to go out bickering. I went back to her room, prepared to make whatever apology I needed to make.

She was curled in a ball on the floor, sobbing silently. Her shoulders shook. Every few seconds she took a long breath inward.

"Hey." I sank to the floor beside her, pulled her into my arms.

"You should go pack," she choked out.

"I'm done. You shouldn't be alone." I rocked her gently.

"I don't want you here."

"I can't go. I'm in this thing too deep. I can't go back and still live with myself."

Before long her sobs abated into longer, deeper breaths. Not long after that she sat up, met and held my gaze in a long, deep stare. She spoke silently. This is it, Ray, her voice said in my mind. The end.

<u>We do this, we're done. We'll be fugitives. Are you okay with that?</u>

I reached out, touched her face. <u>I'm with you,</u> I thought back to her.

She kissed me then, full on the lips, but it somehow wasn't a sexual thing; it was more like a seal, a bond. Then she retreated, eyes still closed. She said, "You should pack."

"I told you I was done."

She fit the last of the hammock into its carrying case. "That was fast." She didn't look at me; it was as if we hadn't had a moment.

"Didn't have much that mattered."

"You were ready for this day, weren't you?"

"Nah. Ready more for a labor facility." Saying it, I realized it was true.

She picked herself and her carrying case up off the floor. "Let's stack our stuff together so we can just grab and go."

I followed her to the living room. "I brought food, too. Just in case."

"Dinner party once we're out," she said.

"And then? I guess I'll be a mover." Callie's proposition made sense, even if it meant more time on the road.

"Probably the best place for you. Traumatized women don't need to see some guy skulking around the campground." She smiled thinly; it seemed like she'd been trying to joke, but it fell flat.

"What about you?" I said. "Where would your place be in a system like that?"

"Honestly? I never thought about it. I always thought there would be a spot for a former cop. Tracking down abusers, or something. I guess that doesn't make too much sense." She was quiet. "I always thought Callie let me stay in the system because she'd eventually need me. Then time went on and I was still doing the same." She picked up a seashell trinket, put it back down. "I don't care if she and I are over. I'm ready to make a difference."

"We will." I'd rather get caught or die trying, anyway.

I mentally calculated, several times, how long it would take us to get all four of our bags out the door and into the van. "Why don't we sit in the van to wait," she snarked, but it was the same stress I felt. When I came back in she put a couple of sandwiches together.

I'd taken a single bite when the word <u>GO</u> resounded in my brain. I stopped chewing, met Suzanne's eyes.

"You heard that?" she said. Nodded, swallowed her bite. "That was our signal, all right. Nice." She winked at me, but her face was pale. We finished our sandwiches in record time.

We both found ourselves hyperalert, checking the yards and houses for a secret sting. No one surrounded the van as we got inside, or pulled up as we backed out of the driveway.

We started with the motor inn down the street. "We don't look like delivery people," I fretted. I should have cut the patches off a uniform.

"No one does anymore. Relax. You're projecting. That'll get us noticed faster than anything else we might do."

"How many boxes, you think?"

"Start with two. If they say they ordered more, we give them more. Till we run out."

"I wish we had the app we needed to know for sure."

"Not all the suppliers use apps." Suzanne regarded me as if speculating whether I was up to the task, but her encouragement bloomed behind my breastbone.

I forced myself to breathe deep, lock my emotions down. I estimated the place had about 30 units, which might mean 2-3 women per unit. I started with four boxes.

"You're new," said the woman behind the counter, tonelessly.

For an instant I wished I had popped a couple of inhibitors. "Just started," I told her.

She shrugged. I wondered how often the enterprise changed suppliers without telling the recipients. I set the boxes on the counter.

She frowned. "How many wigs per box?"

"Ten."

She did a quick calculation in her head. "That's right."

"Have a good night," I told her, a courtesy I was used to offering with the residents, which took an ominous meaning in this setting. The handler only waved her hand in response.

We drove up Ashworth. One motel had never requested a delivery. The rest seemed to accept what they were given. It was almost too easy.

Our last stop was the large motor inn across the street from the police station. This place had more than 100 units; we managed to save about seven boxes. The number, though, was the least of our worries.

The woman whose house I'd responded to the day Joni Rafferty went missing, the one who'd canceled her lawn service because her hair was falling out, stood at the front desk. Same turquoise turban, same upper-lip sneer. I reminded myself of Kirsty's words: she was as much a prisoner of this, probably one of the most lucrative operations, as the women she sold. I did my best to avert my eyes.

She recognized me anyway. "How the mighty have fallen," she commented.

"Yeah. Didn't fine enough residents." I set three boxes on the counter. "More outside."

She inspected the boxes. "New Moon Creations? I never order from them. Not since the wig I got from them for myself arrived at my house reeking, some strange herb I couldn't place."

"Your business name and order were in our system." I felt the first beads of perspiration break out on my back. Joni Rafferty had never mentioned how the wigs smelled. Hell, I'd handled her wig, never noticed a smell. I bet this woman had spent her life complaining about perfumes and deodorizers.

"No system I'm a part of," she grumbled. "I order direct."

We'd miscalculated, assuming everyone was on the enterprise delivery app. Just because not all suppliers used the app didn't mean not all customers would. Of course there would be outliers, an especially lucrative business like this one, located near the hub of Casino activity. Why hadn't we accounted for that? "Ma'am, I just go where I'm told to go."

"That's what I'm telling you. You'd never have been told to come here. I don't. Order. From here." She stabbed at the name on the box.

"Look." My heart hammered. All Suzanne needed was for me to drop dead of a heart attack. "You're not happy with the current system. I'm not, either. Me and a friend of mine, we're doing something about it. That's what those wigs are."

She peered at me. The pink tip of her tongue ran its way across her bottom lip. "I don't know what you're talking about. I ought to call the enterprise, find out what's going on with their system."

Unlike app usage, not being happy with the current system didn't mean abandoning it for the unknown. I rubbed at my upper lip. Grabbed the boxes on the counter. "No need. Sorry to trouble you."

"Wait," she said. "What do you mean, 'doing something about it?'"

A second chance? I rushed through an explanation of what the wigs were, why they "reeked," the effect they had had on her neighbors, what we hoped they would do to wake the women up.

She recoiled. "First you threatened to fine me. Now you want to take away whatever livelihood I have left?" She grabbed for her smartphone.

I grabbed the remainder of the boxes, got the hell out of the office.

"Drive," I told Suzanne. "Fast."

"What?" She pulled out onto the roadway.

"We got made." I told her everything. In the rearview mirror, I saw the woman on the curbside, holding up her phone, probably giving a vehicle description.

She listened, lips compressed. "Can we make it to Callie's without being followed?"

"Maybe. Take your car instead?"

"What about the rest of these wigs?"

"I don't think we can risk it."

"We sure as shit can't risk going all the way back to M Street." Route 101 was up ahead. She sped up. "Jesus, Ray. Why'd you tell her what we were doing?"

She was incensed. I felt that plainly. "I thought she'd want to help. I thought she'd have incentive. I was wrong."

She was silent. We hooked a left on 101.

"Anyway," I said, "Why didn't you tell me some businesses get special breaks?"

"I'm supposed to know all there is to know about those businesses? I've responded to complaints at that place, they seemed legit to me."

She drove fast. The van rattled. "Isn't it a risk to go straight to Callie's?" I ventured.

"We're not going straight there," she said tightly.

It was high tide, or close to it; the marshlands had all but flooded. Near the interchange with Route 1 Suzanne took another left.

This area was woodsier, populated with a few nice, well-kept minor mansions. "Some of the enterprise people live here," Suzanne said, her voice still unnaturally tense. "You come out here to parties when you're looking to get promoted."

At the end of the road was a boat slip. I counted four boats bobbing in the water. Suzanne parked. We got out. "Leave the wigs," she said. "Grab our stuff."

"Where are we going?"

"See that boat?" She pointed to one at the far end of the dock. "I know that owner. He leaves his keys under a mat."

As we walked onto the dock I examined the lettering on the boat's stern. It appeared to be Russian. Even better: stealing from a mobster.

"What's the tide doing?" she asked.

"Not sure. I think it's on its way out."

"Of course it is." She was the angriest I'd ever seen or felt her. At me, at the mobster, at the whole situation. "We'll take it as far as we can and hope we don't run aground."

Was this how it ended between us? A narrow escape, a few days or longer of living in tense silence, each of us going our own ways? And yet, continued apologies seemed too weak.

"We need to go back." I tried to project my voice, make it much stronger than I felt.

"Excuse me?"

"Put the wigs in the boat. Take the boat downriver instead of up."

"And then what?" Her tone had softened some.

"Kirsty didn't say how long it would need to take effect. What if we handed them out to the girls behind the Casino?" My voice faltered. It was a dumb idea and I knew it. We'd be in labor facilities by tomorrow.

"No," she said. "We'll take the van, go back around. The long way, via Seabrook Harbor, where they won't look for us."

"The long way? Down Route 1, where your colleagues will be posted?"

"After dark? Please. We'll get my car, and we'll go to the Casino with my credentials. We'll hand the wigs out there."

"In the Casino?"

"Not on the floor. There's a staging area behind the game room where the girls dress and get ready." Weary lines creased her face. "We'll hand them out there, say it's a surplus or something. Then we get out."

I could only nod. This was suicide; we both knew it. But it was the only thing that felt right.

#

We rattled down Route 1 towards the Massachusetts border. Suzanne couldn't keep her eyes off her rearview; her nervousness joined mine, amplifying each other's mood so that she startled when my hand brushed against hers. Before long we left the truckers behind and entered the dark wooded roads along the border. Here, if anywhere, was where Kirsty's van would give up the ghost. But we made it through the harbor town, across the bridge and into Hampton Beach, where it seemed as if nothing had changed.

Suzanne parked in the tiny lot behind what had once been a miniature golf business directly behind her place. We unloaded the boxes. She hopped the small fence that bordered the two properties. I handed the boxes to her one by one, then carefully climbed over the chain link. Together we loaded the boxes, and our belongings, into the trunk of her car.

For the first time in weeks, a chilly breeze kicked up, the kind that made you want to throw on a sweatshirt even if your legs still felt okay in shorts. Ages ago that had meant fall was on its way, but it was only July.

"If your car is tracked," I said, "then do we use it to get back to Callie's?"

"Haven't thought that far ahead." She didn't think we'd get out of this any more than I did.

"Wait." I stopped her. "Is this stupid? Do we really think it will work?"

She was quiet, her eyes downcast. "It's all we've got."

"We've got each other. You've got Callie."

She smiled sadly. "Who do those women have?"

I put the last box in her trunk.

The Casino parking lot was almost full, but a few spaces, where the tour buses had once parked for concerts, had been left reserved for Enterprise Security. Suzanne pulled into one. "Wait here," she said.

I waited, slouched low in the seat, tried to block out the sounds of clicking high heels and pubescent girls' voices. Before long Suzanne came out with a two-wheeled dolly. No one paid attention to us as we loaded the boxes. I grasped the dolly's handle, followed her into the building.

I hadn't expected the memories to return, not back here where there were no arcade games or families, but the way the rickety wood creaked and bowed under my weight brought it back: the way I had shepherded Dani from game to game, inhaling the sweet summer smells of sunscreen, sweat, fried dough torn off and eaten as we chose between arcade games, the clacking of skee ball or air hockey pucks. Somewhere nearby an auction was going on, and even that reminded me of the patchwork of motley voices: shrieking toddlers and squeeing teens, conversations, competitions, straight-up cons.

We had never come back here to search for Dani. Never even thought to ask. Trusted that the Casino Ballroom staff and the police would have in hand whatever we missed. If we hadn't trusted, if we'd demanded access, would we have found her?

I forced my emotions into neutral as a woman came into the corridor to greet us. "Renata," Suzanne said. "I'm escorting this deliveryman. He's had some trouble with robberies. We wanted to make sure these hairpieces got into the right hands. You good for us to distribute them?"

Renata's gray eyes shifted between us. "We just got a delivery yesterday," she said slowly.

Had she heard about us, perhaps via backchannel app, from the motel owner? My palms began to sweat. I said, pitching my voice lower so it wouldn't crack, "This is a last-minute order from a patron, who's asking for a more natural look for the auctioned property."

I couldn't see Suzanne's face, but Renata's turned from guarded to exasperated. "A patron," she muttered. "All right. Bring it on back."

Suzanne elbowed me as we followed her deeper into the belly of backstage. I glanced down at her. She wore the tiniest of smiles. I felt a little better.

We set the dolly down, cut open the first box. Renata lined up the girls.

The inhibitors were powerful stuff, as if they suppressed emotion as well as empathy. These girls' eyes were dazed, dull. It would take longer than a few minutes for Kirsty's herbs to kick in, wash away whatever else was in the girls' bloodstreams. I scanned each girl's face as I handed out black, red, blonde, brown wigs. Dani would be about their ages.

My heart pounded as Renata helped the girls replace their synthetics. I focused on wigs and boxes; we might have enough.

"Like some really fucked up beauty pageant," Suzanne muttered under her breath.

She was right. Girls wore sparkly gowns like the one on Ayana's body, as well as lingerie, bikinis, and little-girl outfits. I focused on their faces, on doing what I came to do.

We were down to our last box when the first girls were sent onstage. I listened hard for any signs of protest, but the girls didn't make a peep. Tears pricked at my eyelids as I pulled wigs out of their plastic bags and gave them to the last two dark-skinned girls. "Let's go," I muttered to Suzanne.

We hustled out the way we had come. "Did you hear that?" Suzanne murmured. "Raised voices. A girl's."

I hadn't. We moved down the corridor, as close as we could without touching.

Suzanne had parked her car in a space next to a tall staircase that led to the upper level ballroom. The first tuxedoed men had begun to emerge with their purchases. "Wait," I said as Suzanne turned the engine over.

"No. I'm finished here. I need a shower. Maybe some bleach."

The man and girl crossing behind us forced her to wait before backing out. I watched them in the side rearview. The girl leaned away from the man as if resisting him.

At last we backed out. More auction patrons had begun to emerge. One girl wrestled her elbow out of a woman patron's grip. Another hesitated on her walk down the stairs.

"Look." I nudged Suzanne. "They may not know why, yet, but they're not in the mood to comply."

"Shit acts fast," she said. "Kudos to Kirsty. Wherever she is." She shifted the car to Drive, revved out of the parking lot.

What we saw as we left amazed me. An hour had passed since we distributed the very first wigs. Driving back towards 101 along Ashworth, groups of women confronted patrons and shielded one another.

Suzanne stayed focused, guided the vehicle north and, finally, west. "I didn't expect to get out of that," she said grimly. "Nice one, Ray."

"What's next?" I asked. "How do we rescue these women?"

"I don't know. They seemed to be doing all right rescuing themselves."

"Organized criminals run these places. They won't stand on rebellion. They could kill these women, have new ones out here within the week. With new synthetic wigs."

"Yeah." Suzanne went quiet. "Maybe we transmit Kirsty's formula to other places like this one. Maybe we get it into the labor facilities' water supply." She paused. "Maybe rally the women on the hill. Or document the rebellion, make sure word of it gets out. Maybe inspire others. The empathy genie is out of the bottle. Systems like this don't crumble overnight."

I didn't answer her. Even if we succeeded, the women we empowered wouldn't have voting rights, nor the power to run things.

"It doesn't feel significant right now," she replied. "The start of big things rarely do."

We didn't speak again until after she made the left turn that would take us to the boats. As we got closer, lights appeared. A motor thrummed on the river.

Suzanne took her foot off the gas, her face serene as she moved the car closer. At the mouth of the river, the tide indeed going out, she parked. "Grab your stuff," she said.

I did, hers too. I followed her to the water's edge, near where the Russian mobster's boat bobbed. In the middle of the river a big houseboat idled.

"What took you so long?" Suzanne called.

Callie appeared from a room. "Me? What about you?" She was smiling. "We going to make some rescues, or what?"

I felt totally out of the loop. Suzanne waded out ankle-deep, then calf-deep, into the water to greet a little rubber dinghy. She put one foot in, turned. "Ray. You coming?"

I walked down to the water's edge, handed her her things. "You're going to need someone to transport the girls to wherever you dock. Aren't you?"

Her dark eyes regarded me, as if she worried I might play her. Then she said, slowly, "We'll dock at the slips near the bridge to the harbor. You know where I mean?"

I did.

"You can't use my car," she said. "They won't trust it. And you can't use the minivan."

"You know what you said about rallying the people on the hill? I'm going to try that. Starting with Joni Rafferty." I did my best to smile. "Maybe once I explain the situation, she'll be up for rallying."

She got out of the boat, sloshed ashore, reached up and hugged me, the kind of long, tight hug I had longed for when I'd first met her. Then she let me go, handed me the keys. "Better go while you can," she said.

I watched her slosh back to the dinghy, but I didn't go to her car until she reached the bigger boat and climbed over the edge. As it chugged away I sensed her, deep in the back of my head, a new strength I hadn't wanted to believe was possible until now. I turned the car engine over, backed up, headed back east on 101 toward the Atlantic.

Bio
Christa Miller

Too goody-two-shoes for the rebels and too rebellious for the good girls and boys, Christa Miller writes fiction which, like herself, doesn't quite fit in. A professional writer for 15+ years, Christa has written in a variety of genres ranging from crime fiction to horror to children's, but her favorite stories to write — and read — are those which blend genres. She has an affinity for the dark, psychological, and somewhat bizarre, but doesn't let that stop her from snuggling baby animals at a local wildlife rescue, adventuring with her two sons in rivers, swamps and salt marshes, or relaxing with a good book and a cold beverage in her hammock. Christa is based in Greenville, SC. Learn more at https://christammiller.com/.

Time to Quit

Tom Rinkes

Chapter One

Date: 7 July 1865

To: Mr. William H. Doster, Attorney at Law.

To be delivered to 1289 Prospect Road, Richmond, Virginia 23219 on or about July 11, 2014.

I fought the good fight. I came to this era with the noblest of intentions. To right the grievous wrongs of a distant relative; to clear my family name and derail the event that became one of the darkest days in American history, yet I failed miserably. I fashioned this as "my sacred mission" and indeed it was, but I had no plan of forethought nor proper direction to guide me. As the dawn approaches, my date with the executioner is set and I will not protest my fate for I have done murder, and for this I must pay the ultimate price.

My name is Ryan James Anderson. As I draw my last breath today it will be thirty years, one hundred forty-five days and three hours since my dear mother gave me life and I am so grateful that she is with our Lord and Savior Jesus Christ. She may plead my case before Saint Peter, if he will hear it, and I might be permitted to reside with her in Paradise. I slew my distant uncle in self-defense at first we engaged, nonetheless his blood is on my hands, and it haunts me to this day. My only defense before the Almighty's Court, if I am so allowed, will be to say the whole sordid plot was the concoction of that devil Booth and we were told, or should I say deceived, that the premise of his plan was a kidnapping, not an assassination. If I had done the proper research on the subject beforehand, instead of ignoring the truth, I would have known what a liar he was and planned my scheme accordingly. I know I should have heeded the consul of my pathfinder, a learned man named Endras, when he told me my cause was sublime, but may prove to be fruitless.

This may well be my last will and testament; that I have nothing to bequeath but my sorrow and guilt for the calamity I helped force on my Nation. I labored as best I could to stop the inevitable but have learned that every man's destiny is sealed and a mere mortal such as myself can never derail the forces of the Universe. Abraham was martyred for a reason I know not, but accept all the same.

One jailor of mine, who I will only identify as MacMillan, has secretly garnered a typewriter, stood watch as I penned my last thoughts and will be kind enough to see it delivered at the appointed time. My lawyer, William Doster, is a good man whom I have treated in an uncivil manner. I finally told him the whole truth of my life thus far and for that he has classified me a madman and argued my case with an insanity plea. I did not come into this world as such, but fear I will leave it that way.

I must tell you that I have argued and prayed for Mrs. Surratt's sentence to be commuted to life without parole so she will not suffer the same fate as we, for she is a good woman converted to an insane plan brought forth by a master manipulator. To this conclusion I stake my honor, such as it presently is.

As to my Family; I love and miss you all. To Hailey, my beloved sister to whom I have confided much; this pilgrimage that I freely took was conceived with the best of intentions. It did not evolve as I had wished but I want you to—privately—tell Father and Pap that I tried to right the wrong but got caught up in a set of circumstances I could not control. If you are reading this then you know I am dead and will not be at your wedding. For this, I am truly sorry, but I wish you a long and fruitful union with your betrothed.

In closing I say to those in the future who will undoubtedly try to untangle this web I have woven, a journal of my trials, from start to finish, can be found at these coordinates. It will be buried by my confidant in a lead box wrapped in three layers of heavy canvas, approximately three feet deep, and can be readily found by the people who knew me and will understand the numbers below.

Longitude: 40.1017802

Latitude: -80.82205

Chapter 1.5
A Drive to Destiny

The Virginia day was warm but not especially sultry that seventh of July, 2014 when I cruised through Richmond with my windows down. My mind was awhirl with the significance of this date due to a curse brought upon my family and its good name by an uncle of mine. I didn't know how many three, five or nine times back he was and I didn't care. He was a deserter, a scoundrel and attempted to murder the standing Secretary of State as the helpless man lay in his sick bed, by stabbing him seventeen times. By the Grace of God Mr. Seward survived the attack but Lincoln did not and the rest is one of the darkest days in United States history.

His name was Lewis Thornton Powell and I loathed his memory.

"Ry, why you look so sad?" Hailey asked.

Hailey was my baby sister, five years my junior. She sat on the porch swing, moving slowly back and forth looking like she hadn't a care in the world and really, she didn't. "Toots", as we nick-named her, was tall with a slim but shapely build, dark brown eyes with long, wavy hair to match. She had caught the eye of many an eligible bachelor and was engaged to be married this coming August. I was glad that one of us might make dad a grandchild. Lord knows it won't be me if my life keeps going the way it has.

"Awh … nothing really, Toots. Just the same old same old."

I put the car in park and grabbed the six pack from the front seat. I sat beside her, popped the tops on two cans and gave her one. I sat silent, moving with her rhythm as we went to and fro. Finally, she broke the ice.

"Ryan, are you thinking about him again?" she asked.

"Yeah I am. It's been a hundred and forty-nine years since he took the big swing and people still look at us funny, especially when that damn History Channel keeps running the stories about the whole thing every year at this time. Why can't people just forget about it?"

"I don't know, Ry, but can't you just ignore them? I mean that was then but this is now. We didn't have anything to do with that so why do you let it depress you so much?"

"Toots, he was a relative of ours and did some heinous things. Things I just can't get past. I wish I could go back in time so I could stop him. I really don't care how, just get it done."

"I'm sorry for you." She laid her head on my shoulder. "I never realized it bothered you so much."

I put my arm around her, hugged her and gave her a quick kiss on the forehead. I loved her so. She was the best friend I'd ever had and probably ever will. As we swung in silence a small envelope fell onto the porch floor.

"What's that," I asked.

"I's a letter that came for you today."

"Who's it from?"

"I don't know. I ain't opening your stuff. That's against the law, but I did notice it didn't have a return address. That's only a misdemeanor."

We both got a chuckle out of that crack. She always knew how to make me laugh. I picked it up and looked it over. It was a tan color, the sign of very good paper. My name and address were printed, nice and neat. I took a big swig and opened it. Inside was another tan sheet folded three ways. I read it not once, but twice because I couldn't believe what this man tried to tell me.

Dear Mr. Anderson,

I sense that you need a friend. You are a much-troubled young man caught up in a calamity not of your doing, yet one that weighs on you heavily. There are many ways to rectify this situation and I desire to help you. If you wish to discuss them I can be reached at Temple Shalom, Manassas, Virginia anytime and any day.

At your leisure,

Rabbi Menelek Endras

What can a rabbi do for me? I thought. *I haven't set foot in a church since mom died, let alone a synagogue. What is this craziness?*

I left the note on the small table by the swing and went in the house to take a nap. I thought it was someone playing a prank because they knew how irate I'd get this time of year, and maybe they thought it would cheer me up? I failed to see the humor and five seconds after I laid on the couch I was out.

***

I awoke to the sound and feel of a dull thud on my feet.

"What, Pap? That hurts."

Grandpa Anderson—a.k.a. "Pap"—was eighty-four years old and a spitfire. At his best posture, he was over six feet tall, always thin. A railroad worker for forty years before a bad back forced him into retirement. He always wore a white shirt and the tie of the day, of which I think he had hundreds. His oak cane slapped my flat feet twice. Since my mother died young of cancer, Pap was my number one. Little did I know that I'd be tested.

"Git up, Ryan. It's time for supper."

I walked behind him to the dining room out of respect and to make sure he didn't fall in one of his unstable moments. He sat at the head of the table; Dad at the foot with Toots and I across from each other. Pap always said the grace but today he was off a little as if his mind was elsewhere. We finished, Toots and I cleared the table and set things up for Dad to do dishes in which he insisted on doing himself. Dad was never the same after Mom died, and none of us could cheer him up or bring him out of his depression. Pap retired to the back porch to smoke number two in his three-cigarettes-a-day regiment, his only vice. I joined him, making sure I was upwind.

"What's up Pap?" I asked as I set down. "You're not yourself today."

"It's the same thing that gets you down every year this time. It's just today some smartass young punk left a message on the machine and it really pissed me off, pardon my French."

"You're excused. What did it say?"

"He sang—now git this— 'hang down your head little Lewis, hand down your head and cry. Hang down your head little Lewis, today you will surely die'. That made me so dadgum mad I erased it and even went on that thing called the internet for the first time ever. By the way, what's malware?"

"Something real bad in a computer."

"I don't know what I did but the sign said you got a few of 'em now. Sorry."

"Don't fret it, old man. I'll fix it. Why'd you go on the internet?"

He put out that Lucky Strike and immediately fired up another one. "Because I wanna see what it'd cost to move all of us to Alaska. I hear there's a whole bunch of people that went there a long time ago to escape stuff like this. We all could git a cabin out in the boonies somewhere and not have to take no shit off nobody."

Gramps was serious and very angry. He never used profanity unless he'd get mad at the Redskins and only then would he let a few fly. And then I remembered the letter from that rabbi and wondered if this was all planned by someone.

"Pap, put that thought on the back burner for a while. I'm going up to Manassas tomorrow to look for work. We'll talk about it when I get back. Okay?"

"Okey-doke. Only if you promise not to tell Toots about this extra smoke. I don't want her up my ass about my quota. Agreed?"

"Agreed."

I don't know why, but it *is* funny when young boys and old men swear. My age bracket gets the lectures and the others get a pass. It's not fair, but it is what it is.

-2-

MapQuest—after I cleaned the virus's out of my Toshiba—said the drive from Richmond to Temple Shalom would be approximately ninety minutes. I've always hated the word approximate. It tells you nothing. I want exact, but I guess I'll have to live with app … that word. Anyway, I left at nine in the morning, got a large Mickey D's coffee to go and hit I-95. Around eleven I pulled into Manassas proper and found the Temple amongst the hustle and bustle of Kruger Street. I sat in my still-running car and tried to talk myself out of this. *Do you know what you're doing?* I asked my brain and better judgment. *What can a "man of the cloth" possibly do for me? What can he— or anyone for that matter — say to ease my mind?* I finally gathered some nerve, put the car in park, shut it off, walked to the front door and hit the buzzer.

"Yes? My name is Abraham. I am the Shamash (attendant). How can I help you?"

"Yes, sir. My name is Ryan Anderson. I'd like to talk to Rabbi Endras, if he's in."

"He's *constantly* in. Come with me."

As I walked down the long hall to his office I noticed pictures of congregation members with Endras; some with Shimon Peres and other Prime Ministers shaking hands with Endras.

And then I came across one of Endras shaking hands with what looked like a Zen Master or some other kind of white-cloaked weirdo.

"Shalom, Mr. Anderson. I am so glad you decided to visit me." He rose from his huge and cluttered desk. Endras was about five feet nine or ten inches tall, of slim build but with a set of muscular forearms that would've made the average biker jealous as they didn't seem to fit his snow-white hair and aging eyes. As he extended his right hand I accepted the greeting without thinking and I swear I heard at least two knuckles pop, and neither one was his.

"Sit down, young man, and let us talk. I understand that you and your family have a stain, for the lack of a more gentle term, on your family lineage. Is that correct?"

"Yes, we do. Yet, I'm curious. We live ninety miles away and I don't recollect ever meeting you before. How do you know all this?"

"Oh, we have people all over this country—and the world for that matter—that know when others are in need. They stay, how should I say, behind the scenes? Suffice it to say it has been brought to my attention that you and your grandfather are in much distress this time every year. I may be of some service to you."

Now what kind of service can he do for something that happened in 1865? I thought. *The only kind of help I need to erase this scourge. End this and hammer back home.*

"Rabbi, I appreciate what you may think you can do for me against my long-lost wicked uncle, but you can't help me. Nobody can. I'll be on my way now."

I rose, nodded my head in a "thank you" and headed for the door. Just as I reached for the doorknob he calmly asked me one strange question.

"My son, have you ever heard of Kabbalah?"

Chapter 2
Paranormal Plastic

I'd heard of Kabballah before but paid it no mind. I thought it was some of that new-age nonsense going around the net, and we all know you can't believe everything you read there. Something made me stop and release my hand from the doorknob. I stalled for a second or two before I answered.

"Yes, I've heard something about it, but that mumbo-jumbo is for dreamers, sir. I need a solution, not smoke and mirrors."

"Ah yes, I agree with you. Yet, you have day dreamed about the concept of travel back in time to right the wrongs, have you not?"

"Yes, yes I have."

"Please Mr. Anderson. Sit back down and allow me a few minutes of your time," Menelek said calmly, matter-of-factly.

I walked slowly over to the chair and eased back down. I took a deep breath and gave the man his due.

"Please forgive my bad manners, sir. I was raised better than that."

"Not a problem, Ryan—may I address you as such?"

"Yes, sir, you may. I don't rightly know what to say, but I'm all ears."

"Now," Menelek said as he leaned back in his chair. "Kabbalah is an ancient study of the Universe, our relation to it and the things we can do if our thoughts are genuinely focused on changes for the common good. The 'Powers That Be' will allow this if one's cause is righteous in nature. Do you understand so far?"

"It's sinking in. But how long has this practice been going on?" I asked.

"Kabballah is as old as our King Solomon. You have heard of him?"

"Oh yeah. Everyone knows the wisest man in history."

"And that he was, but only because he requested it above all other things. Wisdom and understanding of more than governing our people was afforded him and he passed much of his secret knowledge to those deserving of it. Very, very few people obtained that status and I must tell you truly that I am one of the 'Select'. Do you wish me to go further? Do you require a glass of water?"

The man was a mind reader. I was dryer than a box of popcorn at a Sahara theatre. As he talked his aura was almost hypnotic and part of me was mesmerized and the other scared to death. *This man actually believes what he's saying,* I thought.

"Yes, I could use one," I said.

Endras walked over to a mini-fridge and got me a chilled Avian. I gladly accepted it and downed half of it in three gulps. I rubbed the cold bottle across my forehead because I started to sweat just listening to him. I composed myself and asked the Master something.

"Okay, I'm alright now but help me to understand. First, I am not a righteous man and I know little of all things God and certainly don't know a thing of Solomon or anything of the Old Testament. My dear mother—God rest her soul—tried to teach me about those things but I was bull-headed and wouldn't listen. Are you saying that I can go back in time to rectify this?"

"Absolutely; you can try. Your cause *is* sublime and honorable, but I must warn you. Sometimes things cannot be changed if your cause and morality is found to be lacking. Nonetheless, that shouldn't stop us from trying. Wouldn't you agree?"

"No, we shouldn't. But I promise before you and the Almighty that I will do my very best to change my family's history for the better. On this I give you my word."

"Good then. First, I must ask you some questions. Do you have a Smart Phone?"

"Yes." I was getting a little mystified...what a poor choice of words.

"Does it have Nav Clock?"

"I don't think so."

"Then download that app. It will be a must for you. Let us meet at five pm, two days from now at the coordinates I will give you. Wear your normal wardrobe for the day but bring all the personal grooming supplies that you'll need for one hundred days. Food, water and clothing will be up to you and your wits to provide. Thank you for coming and may peace be with you."

When he rose I knew the meeting was over. As we shook hands he handed me an envelope of the same type as the one he sent in the mail. I didn't open it there but waited until I got in my car. The numbers meant nothing to me but there were two words I understood.

A longitude and a latitude.

I hurriedly left and went straight home, only stopping long enough to get a Mc-Meal; # 3 to be exact.

-2-

After supper that Monday night Pap and I retired to the back porch again to have a coffee, him a smoke, and lollygagging the evening away. We did a little small talk; he asked about the work prospect up in Manassas with me lying. I brought the "Lewis" subject up for the last time, I hoped. I told him that one never knows what will happen and maybe, just maybe, things wouldn't be so bleak every year.

"That's funny, Ry. That's the same words those two strangers said to me this afternoon."

"What two strangers?" I asked.

"Two young men—well everybody is younger to me—but they came a calling about one o'clock dressed prim and proper, looking like two Dandies from the big city somewhere. They never did tell me their names except the taller one said he was a Jehovah's Witness and the shorter one was wearing one of those harmonicas on his head."

"You mean Yarmulke?" At least I knew that much.

"Whatever. Anyway, I think the shorter one was Jewish and he was carrying a big, black book about something torn, or another word that I couldn't see right. You know, sonny, the eyes now ain't what they used to be."

"I bet it was the Torah, Pap. That's our Old Testament. What'd they say?"

"They started off talking about the weather and other things in life that can make a man's day look bleak. Then they said that maybe things would get better for us and it'd be like nothing ever happened. The first thing I thought was these shysters were looking for a donation or a hand out and I was about to kick them outta here with this cane. But they made me feel all peaceful inside. They bid me their adieus and left as quick as they came. Ryan Anderson, come here."

I moved closer until we were face-to-face.

"Boy, whatcha know that I don't?"

"Nothing, Pap. Nothing at all." Then I thought it best to change the subject. "Is that your third cigarette of the day?"

"It is."

"Then fire up another one and save one for me. I'll be back." I thought it proper to smoke one, seeing as how I hadn't had any for three years.

I got out of my chair and started to walk away.

"Where you going?" Pap asked.

"Down in the basement to snatch that bottle of bourbon you been hiding behind the furnace."

"You're the one that's been thieving my hooch. I shoulda known."

"Ever since my arms got long enough to reach it. Now you don't tell Toots and neither will I. Deal?"

"Deal. Now hurry up. I ain't gettin' any younger."

I would cherish that little buzz I shared with my Grandpa.

-3-

I started that morning like all the rest with toast and coffee and more coffee and some more coffee because I didn't sleep well, but who could in this situation. I Google-mapped the numbers Endras gave me, got the Nav Clock app and narrowed it down to a farm field outside of Richmond. It was only a mile from here but I went upstairs to pack early. I found a raggedy-looking "traveling bag" of Pap's in the attic the night before and in it was an old, rusty-looking straight edge razor that was all the rage years ago. A little CLR and a Brillo pad made it look like new so I packed it and a bar of shaving soap I borrowed from Pap's stash. Then I got down to it.

Let's see, I thought. *I'll take two...no three tubes of toothpaste, two bottles of shampoo, my last bottle of Old Spice, fingernail trimmers, a good pair of scissors...my nose and ear trimmer...better get a twelve pack of AA batteries, my blow dryer—no idiot, leave it here. Electricity ain't even been invented there yet. My comb, favorite hair brush...better get two more tooth brushes, I'd say four...no five bars of Life Buoy and a shaving brush. What you better get is your ass to Walmart.*

And that I did.

-4-

At four I told Dad, Pap and Toots I was going out to see some friends and not to wait up. This I usually did and they were none the wiser because I didn't let on like anything was up. I knew I was on a "secret mission" but I didn't know how long it'd take. Maybe all day; maybe an hour of 2014 time. I was so naive.

As I drove slowly down that dusty township road I kept checking my phone. Longitude 41.104, 41.103, 40. 127....40.110. I stopped and turned the phone left and right until my left side said - 81.923...something. I drove slowly into what looked like a freshly mowed field and eased forward a foot at a time as things started to come together. Another foot...the numbers came down...a little farther and I was almost there...a little bit—OMG...

In front of me was a shed. Not a wooden model but one that looked like the Rubbermaid kind you'd get at any home store. I slammed on the brakes and stopped about six inches from knocking it over. I looked at my phone, and I was there.

Exactly 40.1017802—Longitude. -80.82205—Latitude.

I grabbed the phone, my bag and walked cautiously around the shed. It was a standard eight feet by four wide by four feet deep model, green with a plastic, black roof and something on top I'd never seen before on any model; a sky light. I didn't know whether to yell, knock or hi-tail it out of there until I heard the unmistakable squeak of the door opening. That's when I unzipped my bag, because if this wasn't going to go down right I had to find that straight edge razor. As it swung fully open I put my weapon down.

"Menelek." I pointed to the building in question. "**This** is my time machine?"

"It is today, Ryan. It is your portal and your point of origin. It is here where you must return to your time if you choose to do so."

"Well, there's no 'ifs' about that. I'm going there, do what I need to get done and come back home."

The Rabbi stoically stood in front of me and said not a word.

"Then let me tell you a few things beforehand. After you arrive in 1865 you are to leave this structure, walk one hundred and twenty paces straight ahead and there you will find rest, warmth and reprieve as you regain your strength. This is not negotiable; you must recover first. Please, explore you chariot," Menelek said as he put forth a hand towards the door.

I peeked in and saw a five gallon, clear plastic jug of water with cup, maybe ten towels and a bench seat across the length. Lying on it was a huge and flowing blanket that looked like the one Buffalo Bill wore in all his pictures but appeared to be a sleeping bag.

Do I get to take a nap while I'm traveling? This may be a piece of cake.

"Stand right here in front of me, Ryan."

I complied, and found myself about a yard in front of him.

"Stand up straight and rest your hands at your side."

I did.

"Now, I will recite to you the theory of the Third Song and the Two Threads."

And *now* I was looking for my car keys because I didn't come here for a fairy tale.

Chapter 3
Cabin Fever

"At the end of each Day's Creation, the sounds emanating from this Heavenly Act became as a song to our Lord God's ears. On the Third Day, our sun was strong enough to shine its Light on Planet Earth for the first full period of one of a human's day and also created the First Darkness. These two entities are as a string; a thread of Light and Rest, eternally moving to and fro; never ceasing, never changing."

Menelek removed his hat, folded his arms together and bowed his head.

"Oh Great Sovereign of the Universe, I call upon you today in great humility, because I wish to ask Your help in a mission of mercy. Your servant, one Ryan James Anderson, desires to right a great wrong done in the distant past by his bloodline. He wishes to purge that man's cruel actions from history and Ryan's intentions are honorable; his intent beyond reproach. I beseech You now to allow his ears to hear the beauty and wisdom of Your Third Song, and guide him through his journey between Your Two Threads."

Then I noticed a cloud bank rolling in from the east. It stretched from one edge of the horizon to the other and I heard a most enjoyable noise. From nowhere—or everywhere—the sounds of a limitless choir started to sing a song that I didn't recognize. The language was foreign to me, yet it had meaning. Something about it was comforting and I felt as if I could do no wrong. I was suddenly at peace with myself. I closed my eyes and dreamed of a happy place with my family beside me and smiling at me. My eyes opened when I heard the loud hum of something that I can only describe as electrical. I looked to my left and saw a thin, blue string or thread from the ground up as far as I could see. And then to my right the same anomaly but with a bright, white tone. The two threads of wonder compressed and closed in on my shed. I looked at my travel agent but couldn't move or even take a deep breath.

"Are you ready, Mr. Anderson?" he asked.

"As ready as I'll ever be. Let's get started," I said as I gained my composure.

"Then enter, lock the door behind you, sit as comfortable as possible and I will begin. When you arrive it will be Monday, January second, 1865 at eight am. Godspeed."

I went in, sat my bag down and rested on the big robe, looked straight ahead and tried to relax. All was well until Menelek spoke and his voice changed into something very low and scary.

"Omnis Verto Masvenit Pro Redintegro Pro Elista"

The beautiful gathering of angelic voices continued, and I really enjoyed that, but my eyes fixated on the square beam of sunlight passing from the front door. I noticed a moonbeam—same size—as it did the same thing. I stood and looked up as far as the bubble-type skylight would allow and behind me the sun was rising again, but faster than I'd ever seen. I knew instinctively that behind me was west but the sun moved so it would set in the east? That's when I began to lose it.

As the "magic rays" of light intensified speed I felt dizzy and sat down. *Am I going crazy?* I thought. *This is like nothing I ever imagined.*

I feel like I could throw up. As the speed of the light flew by in what seemed like a black and white circle I breathed hard and panicked. When my exhale turned to steam I grabbed the buffalo robe and covered myself from head to toe and then I'd shed it as quickly when the temperature inside my crypt became hot and sultry. I sweated profusely and then froze as the atmosphere went from one extreme to the other. I looked up to see sunshine and then rain, then sleet and snow and back to balmy, over and over and over again. My clothes were wet with perspiration and then became as stiff as a January wind. I fell off the seat and poured a glass of water to quench my unearthly thirst and after gulping half of it I felt a terrible pain in my teeth as the hot liquid froze to my tongue. I passed out. I came to in God only knows what century to the loud hum of the threads moving towards each other. The white changed places with the blue and my torture started all over again. I learned to shake my covering and take a big gulp of water in record time before everything went Antarctic on me. And then, my time machine changed atoms.

The all-plastic capsule was now made of weathered and rotten-looking wooden planks. I eased myself up to the bench, sat down and immediately half my rump sank into a small hole. I jumped up not knowing, with what I'd just been through, if it was something that was trying to eat me or worse. The wooden bench seat had not one but two holes cut in the top and the aroma coming out caused me to throw up. After I finished I lifted the cast iron latch and stumbled outside. I couldn't believe that Menelek—with all his so-called knowledge and wisdom—had seen fit to deposit me in an old-fashioned outhouse.

At least it was a two-seater, and I should've been grateful for that, but I wasn't.

I turned around three sixty to survey my surroundings. The open field was now totally covered with leafless trees and a cold wind chilled me to the bone. I went back in and retrieved my coat, bag, water and the only towels that weren't soaked or frozen. I turned to see the most welcome sight of all. In what I knew would be one hundred and twenty paces straight ahead was the homiest-looking log cabin I'd ever seen, and I gladly walked to it.

I stopped at the entrance to the one-step-up front porch and took a good look. It was not a shabby abode but a well maintained, one story structure of logs and "chinking" between them. It had two windows, I assumed for the only two rooms there. The door looked heavy and huge, but at that point I didn't care if it was as solid as a bank vault. I was going in even if I had to pop a window and crawl in. On each side of the door were piles of split oak, cherry and dried locust. I was grateful to whoever set this up because I was getting hypothermic and was in dire need of warmth and rest. I knew then that Endras was not joking about the non-negotiables.

I knocked three times and got nothing. The door was unlocked so I sheepishly opened it and peeked in. Nothing was there but a huge wood stove, one bed, a table and chairs made of roughhewn wood and two large floor cabinets. I made myself at home, gathered kindling from a wooden box by the hearth, grabbed a tall match from a round, metal can and started a blaze using the locust first because that burns much hotter than the others. After an hour or so I filled the stove up, banked it down a little as it would last longer, threw off my filthy clothes—BVD's and all—and dove head first into the huge, feather bed. I covered up with my trusty robe and I didn't know how many hours—or days—I slept, waking only to relieve myself in very quick trips at the master bathroom right off the front porch and reloading the stove. I had never slept so well in all my life.

Tuesday (I guessed) January 3, 1865. Dark outside.

I woke sometime that evening about as ravenous as I had ever been. Walking fully robed and wearing nothing else, I got the fire going again and found a coal oil lantern to light my way. As soon as the warmth caused me to shed my hairy coat I tore into the tall cabinet highboy that would undoubtedly bring thousands someday at an Antiques Roadshow. I found a metal "tin" of brown flour, some dried meat that was either beef or deer jerky and flour. I had the water and the appetite so beef and biscuits it was, with water for dessert. I cooked the meat in a cast iron skillet and the biscuits on the wood stove. As I almost inhaled the feast I took a good look at myself. I stood there, in someone else's home, buck naked and barefoot.

Time to clean house. With the help of a hand-pumping well off the front porch I filled two buckets with ice cold water, found a big cast iron pot and put the water on the stove to heat. Rummaging through my bag I found a bar of my soap so I washed the clothes, the birthday suit I arrived in and put my wardrobe over the two chairs to dry by the stove. Even though I was a porridge thief like Goldilocks, I made the bed.

In a large, cedar chest was a pair of red long johns—as my Pap would call long underwear—heavy wool socks, knee length leather boots with pointed toes. I chuckled when the phrase "shit kickers" came to mind as that was what Pap would call this style of footwear. I pulled a pair of dark wool pants and a shirt out of the second drawer and heard a sound like change jingling. In a far corner was a small, oak box with a flip-up lid. I gingerly opened it and found a pile of "Gray backs": five silver and six gold coins. I counted the paper and found the owner of this house had $5,200 worth of Confederate dollars which were losing their value daily at this point in the Civil War.

Well I thought. *You're stuck here for a while. Might as well get nibby.*

In the bottom drawer was a long, leather-looking bag that was weathered and dirty. I thought it might be part of a saddle bag it looked so rustic but I opened it to find piles of handwritten letters addressed to—my lucky day—Lewis Thornton Powell. So I was in his home, partaking in all that he had, ready to steal him blind and not feeling a bit remorseful about it. I turned the wick on the lantern all the way up and began to get a real education.

The first one was from Samuel Bland Arnold. His espoused the committed cause of a new Southern Nation totally separated from the north, and his thoughts about the North's leaders were cold and chilling. The next was from Michael O'Laughlin. With the same sentiments as Arnold, he vehemently disagreed with the process suggested by their ringleader Booth. O'Laughlin was contemptuous of a mass kidnapping; he wanted to kill all three. The third was from Edwin Spangler and it seemed to me, by the tone of his pen, that he was not sure of the proper course of action but would support the majority in their plot and do whatever was necessary. I saved the best for last.

John Wilkes Booth. Who in America doesn't recognize that name? I found his phrasing and penmanship exemplary, but he **was** an actor, and could put on a good show no matter what the medium. In his response to all four conspirators he spoke directly to each one, bringing forth his guidance in a manner I thought was soothing for a cold-blooded killer. Booth led them to believe that kidnaping was the main goal, execution was secondary, but his best arguments and compassion were left for Lewis. I took it that he knew he could count on his right-hand man to spirit away Secretary Seward, but in the advent of that being impossible Lewis would use his own discretion on Seward's "neutralization" as Booth put it. I didn't even think they used that term back then, but I was learning a lot about this war and the people in it that I never knew before. As the dawn cracked my dark world open I heard a horse snort outside.

Lewis dismounted from his gray mare and then looked at the roof. He started at it for a second, looked towards the front door and pulled out a pistol with a very long barrel. Instinctively I knew he'd spotted smoke coming from the chimney and knew an intruder was in his home. He slowly walked tall and proud up the path to the house. We looked so much alike it was like watching a hologram of myself with beard, long, dirty hair wearing tattered clothes and stalking me in the High Noon mode. *Did you come here to let him kill you?* I thought.

Out of fear for my own survival and the completion of my mission, I grabbed a large butcher knife from the knife rack, and hid behind the door.

Chapter 4
Felling No Paine

"Hey you in there! You git your trespassin' ass outta my house right *Now! You hear me?*" Lewis yelled at the top of his lungs.

What could I do? I couldn't sneak out the back door because there wasn't one. My robe was in a corner by the bed but I didn't dare move from my vantage point. Never in my wildest dreams did I think I'd meet my uncle this way. He was known as a murderous bastard and would think nothing of killing me. I stayed silent and let him make the next move.

"All right, squatter, you asked for it. Make your peace with Jesus because I'm gonna send you to meet him."

Goosebumps layered my naked body from scalp to shins as I saw the creaky door open. The first to enter was the business end of his wicked-looking weapon and I drew my knife closer. After what seemed to be hours he popped his scraggly mug in and looked right then left. The sounds of his high-heeled boots and spurs vibrated as he walked in. This reminded me of every western I'd ever seen, but was real and frightening. This could be my life or death if I didn't say the right words.

"Uncle Lewis?" I stuttered. "Don't shoot. I'm your long-lost nephew."

He turned quickly towards me with both hands on his weapon

pointed at my forehead. I shook even worse then but he took a good hard look at me. His facial expression said to me he thought he saw a ghost. The color drained from both of us but mine was extremely visible for obvious reasons. His gun dropped just a little as if he was having second thoughts till he looked me up and down.

"That can't be, youngin'. Ain't no kin a mine would run around naked as a jay bird nowhere. Say your prayers *sodomite,* 'cause I'm the last living thing you ever gonna see."

And then he pulled the hammer back on his long gun, and I closed my eyes, resigning myself to the fact all this was for naught. The next sound I heard was almost as pleasing as the choirs of the Third Song.

CLICK.

A misfire saved my bacon, but not for long. I raised my knife up and the seasoned warrior quickly turned his gun around and gripped the barrel. He threw it at me with near deadly accuracy and I turned my head to the left to avoid the impact, but it hit me above my right temple, bounced off and fell on the floor. The pain was intense and the blood immediate. Before I knew it, he was on top of me and we began to wrestle for the knife. I was close to unconsciousness but a surge of anger overtook me. All the years of being de facto aligned with his crimes and the way he'd hurt my loved ones came boiling out. I felt a wave of heat from my feet and then all the way up to my arms as I rolled him over in a move that surprised him.

His momentary lapse of courage was all I needed to grip the knife with my right hand and pull it away from his. He let out an insane war hoop and tried to snatch the dagger from me, but I was ripe for the fight that I always wanted. I grabbed him hard behind his neck and with one quick move of superhuman strength that I knew I'd never feel again I turned the point to him. He stopped his advance as I laid on top of him.

"Lewis Thornton Powell," I said in a voice so callous that it scared me. "Stop this and *listen to me!* I'm here to stop you. Will you listen to me?"

He relented for a split second and we made direct eye contact. It seemed to me as if he knew who I was and knew that I knew what he was. His expression went from total understanding to one of malice and murder.

"You ain't no relative of mine. You sound like one of them darkie-lovin' Yankees and there ain't no way you could be any blood to me. I will end this conversation *NOW!*"

And with that statement he lunged upward at me and I leaned forward with all the DNA that he'd sent my way. The blade went into his sternum to the handle and I watched the life drain from him. As blood began to appear on his lips I knew his time was short and I wanted to leave him with one last thought.

"This is for my Father and my Pap, you filthy piece of shit."

And then I slowly twisted the blade full circle and listened to it tearing his black heart in two.

Oh may God forgive me.

***

I sat on the floor at the other end of the cabin for the longest time, trying not to look at the violence I'd done. When I came to my senses I found my whole body covered with blood. At first, I thought it was from my head wound until I looked across the room. His bloody form lay lifeless with my murder weapon visible as he lay flat on his back. I raised my knees up and tried to hide my face between them knowing that I struck him in self-defense, but also realizing I took delight in his speedy dispatch. The first attempt at my mission had developed faster than I'd expected and had gone so terribly wrong, yet I still had a chance to fix this whole sordid affair.

Number one on my list was what to do with Lewis. I walked slowly over to his corpse, not wanting to look but knowing I had to. After I pulled the knife from his chest I picked him up, laid him on his bed and covered his whole body with the blanket. I put this seamy incident behind me as "what's done is done" and then reheated the water on the stove. It took a while to clean all the blood off as I had to sit down a few times due to my dizziness.

I saved my hair for last. As I slowly dipped my head into the soapy water the pain was excruciating, but I knew I had to man up. One thing I didn't need, in this anti-biotic less age, was an infection so I gritted my teeth and thoroughly cleaned the wound. I looked at it with my round, shaving mirror and found it was about three inches long and deep enough to require stitches. I wrapped my head in the only clean towel left, dressed in the warmest clothes and packed all that I could including his pistol. I knew from previous research that *no* man could be seen in public without a hat so I took a brown, stiff-rimmed derby. As I got ready to leave I took one last look at my uncle's make shift mausoleum.

You can't leave it like this, I thought. *You have to destroy all this and assume Lewis' identity and you can't have anyone finding his body.*

In three hard kicks, I knocked over the wood stove and spread the burning logs and embers around the cabin. I grabbed two logs in full flame with a shovel and put them under the bed. Within seconds the flames grew and spread. I walked out knowing it wouldn't be long before Uncle Lewis went out like a Viking warrior. I mounted his nervous steed, moved back far enough for the horse to settle down and watched his deposition as the flames consumed his tomb. As the wind called to the flames I turned to leave but was stopped by an eerie, crackling noise. The trees surrounding his home were being attacked by the fire and within seconds the pine canopy was ablaze. Thinking this would draw some attention I kicked my ride in the haunches and we flew in the nearest path's direction.

I was bleeding again, and in dire need of a "saw bones".

-2-

Wednesday January 4, 1865

The weather warmed some that day, with bright sunshine and a cloudless sky which lead me into a small town. If a sign named this burg I didn't see it, but I felt "a might poorly" as the old saying goes and wasn't paying attention. The clapboard-clad buildings looked as old as one could imagine, with a boardwalk for a sidewalk and businesses with roofs over their frontage. The first person I saw was a young boy about ten or eleven. We caught each other's inquisitive eye and he walked right up to me.

"Excuse me, mister. Are you all right? Ya' look a bit peaked," he said.

"I need a doctor. Does this town have one?"

"Matter-a-fact we do. Got the best damn—oh Lordy, sir, please don't tell my momma I said that word. She'll whoop my ass with a new switch ifin she founds out—doc in the whole state, right over there by the saloon. You want me to fetch him for ya'?"

"I can make it that far. What be your name anyway?" I said, feeling better already.

"I was baptized on my third day and christened Artimus J. Pyle, sir, the "J" being junior. My Daddy—God rest his soul—used to call me that when he was a-funning me. Can I be so bold as to ask your Christian name?"

"Yes you may, young man. It's Lewis—*do you really need to give that out yet?* I thought. *Your head hurts like hell and your body's in great discomfort*—Paine; spelled with an "e". Can you tell me the name of this town?"

It's Mechanicsville, Virginia."

"What happened to your daddy, Artimus?"

He angrily changed his tone. "He got kilt by one of those shit-eating, wimun-violating Yankees up in Pennsylvania some two years back. You can tell my momma what I called 'em 'cause that's what she calls 'em and I'm thinking she'd be mighty proud of me."

"If I ever see her I'll do just that. Now, what's this famous doctor's name so I can address him properly?" I asked.

"Doctor Mudd."

"…Say again?"

"Doctor Mudd. Don't tell me you've never heard of him now."

"No, I recollect the name. I imagine we'll talk later Junior, but for now I've *got* to meet this doctor. I thank you kindly for your help."

I dismounted, tied off my horse and walked up to Dr. Mudd's front door. What I saw printed on the glass gave me a little sigh of relief, but a little disappointment too.

Dr. George Dyer Mudd

Physician

***

"Can I help you, pardner?" he asked as he opened the door.

"I sure hope you can, doctor."

"Oh my, look at the blood. Get right in here, sit down and let me have a look."

Dr. Mudd was a tall thin man, I'm guessing in his late forties, wearing a long-sleeved white shirt, black tie and pants that looked saddle worn and weather beaten. He stood behind me as he parted my hair whispering a few "tsk, tsk's".

"How bad is it?" I asked.

"It'll only take about five stitches. Can I ask as to how you acquired this?"

331

"I'd rather not say, Doctor. Do you really need to know?"

"No, not really. Just asking in case the sheriff comes round asking if I've patched up anyone because they got into a brawl."

"No. this happened way back. Not anywhere near this town."

"Good enough for me. Now, do you want to lay down while I do this?"

"Maybe. Can you use some of that new stuff ... you know ... morphine first?" I asked, hoping that he did.

"Not a chance. All I had has been confiscated for the war effort. I got some really good pain elixir I use with a fair amount of success. Want some of that first?"

"What's in it?"

"One part good Kentucky bourbon and two parts laudanum."

Laudanum was liquefied opium and was coming into its own. It's funny how your brain can talk you into almost anything.

You're no stranger to bourbon, and you did two years at Ball State, so a little bite of the Buddha won't hurt. Lay down and take your medicine.

I did, and I still don't remember feeling any pain, without the "e".

Chapter 5
Cougartown, 1865
Thursday, January 5, 1895

After drinking a glass of the Big O chased with whiskey I felt this irresistible urge to primal scream, because I'd never tasted anything that evil before. As I laid down on the examining table I started to hallucinate, seeing the Ball State cheerleaders looking down on me and smiling.

This is some pretty good shit, I thought. *Go to sleep and it'll all be over soon*

I was getting used to waking up in strange places, but at least this one was comfortable and I was dressed properly. Outside was dark but bright inside and I found myself next to a huge stove fired fully with wood and coal. My vision was blurry but I made out the good doctor sitting in chair across from me. I was very hot and took the blanket off that he had put on me. He looked up from his paperwork.

"Morning. Want some coffee?" he asked.

"I'd be much obliged," I answered, using the jargon of the era.

When he left for the kitchen I surveyed my surroundings. He had a very comfortable place, with curtains around the windows, solid handmade furniture and a hardwood floor. The sun peeked into the room and the smell of strong coffee filled the air.

"It's black," he said as he handed me a large mugful. "It's all I've got."

"Black's just fine for me, sir."

I hurriedly drank half of it and began coming to my full senses. I was twenty miles or so out of Richmond but knew—seeing as how I wasn't battle-hardened at all—that a horse ride to Baltimore was out of the question. I needed some answers from this man but he was already a little suspicious. I decided a frank conversation was in order.

"Doctor Mudd, I want to thank you for your help. You have been a life saver. I wish to pay you your fee, in cash of course."

He looked me over and his face seemed to get kinder, as if we could have a man-to-man dialogue.

"Let's say three dollars should cover it. By the way, what's your name, just for my record's sake." he said.

"Your fee sounds fair and it's Lewis Thornton Paine, with an 'e'," I said as I tried to rise and get my bag. As soon as I got halfway up I sank back down as fast.

"Hold on, young man. You're as weak as a kitten. Let me get it for you. You need to rest."

He rose and gazed into my half open case. One of his eyebrows raised up in a Spock-style, yet he handed it to me without comment. When I pulled out my money box he said something that threw me for a loop.

"That would be three dollars silver or Union script."

He was very adamant about that. I knew then that the Confederate cause was lost and financially bankrupt beyond repair.

"Well," I said, closing the lid. "You look like a man I can trust. In this box, I have over five thousand dollars Confederate plus some gold and silver coins. Can you give me a wild guess as to how much I *really* have to my name?"

"I heard yesterday the current rate of exchange for one Gray back dollar is about eight cents, so maybe you have sixty good dollars. That's still a pretty fair sum nowadays, ifin' you don't get robbed."

"I carry protection." I pulled my equalizer from the bag.

"Ah yes, I noticed your long gun. That's a Whitney revolver, ain't it?"

"It is," I said, hoping he was right because I didn't have a clue.

"You do know that particular model has a tendency to misfire, don't ya'?"

"I've heard that."

"Then you know you have to keep it clean at all times. If you don't then the next time we meet I'll be preparing you for a burial."

"Let's hope I take care of it properly. I never was any good at paying attention to details."

"Let me learn you how."

I gave him the gun and he pulled a table from the back of his chair. He broke it down into four separate pieces, oiled it and wiped the whole thing down to where it was clean and almost antiseptic looking. He put the paper cartridges back in the cylinder and handed it to me, barrel down and handle upright.

"Where you headed for now," he asked.

"I've got people in Baltimore to see."

"Then son, let me give you a bit of advice. You are completely exhausted and my diagnosis is that you need to rest for a least a week. You might consider selling that horse to Amos Harrison over at his livery station and take a train up there. The Baltimore and Ohio runs there from here once a week. Just a thought you might want to ponder."

"I'll consider it, doctor. But I want to ask you a question. Have you ever heard of a Doctor Samuel Mudd?"

"I should. He's my nephew. He studied with me up in Bryantown, Maryland where I have my main office. He was a good student and I hear he's doing quite well. Why do you ask?"

Why couldn't I have an uncle this reputable? I thought. I had to give him some advice, yet I didn't know how without revealing how I knew, so I just laid it all out.

"Because of this. I know of a man who may make your nephew's life miserable someday. He is a very calculating and vicious individual who can manipulate people to his ends. I urge you to tell Samuel to stay as far away from this man as possible. His life and reputation are at stake."

Dr. George Mudd looked at me funny. I knew he was thinking: *Where does this transient get off instructing me on anything?* He sat up in his chair and took another swig of coffee.

"And just what, pray tell, is this scoundrel's name?" he asked.

"Booth. John Wilkes Booth. Please believe me and take it for what it's worth to you. Now, if you would be so kind as to direct me to the stable, the bank and good lodging for the week, I'll be on my way."

We rose and I was much steadier on my feet this time. We shook hands, I told him I'd be back later to pay him properly and we parted ways. He was right about one thing. I did need to recover some more from this most exciting ordeal.

-2-

At this time in American history you could find any enterprising town or city by the smell of fresh horse shit. I know that's gross by 2014 standards, but this was a different era. True to my nostrils I found Harrison's Stable right smack dab in the middle of this town's business section. There was the livery next to the bank next to the saloon across the dirt street from "Adele's Place", properly named the Mechanicsville Manor.

It was almost like a mini-mall, but I'm sure I'm wrong about that.

Amos offered me five dollars—Union—for my steed and I gladly accepted it not knowing if it was a fair price but not really caring. I wasn't going to be here long; or so I thought. At the bank, I traded my stash for sixty-two dollars good money and put down a week's worth for a room at the Manor. After seeing all the "sportin' ladies" waltzing around with wanton eyes and bosoms galore I knew I was in a high-class whorehouse. I could tell it was upscale because they had a piano in the lobby, and a skinny but well-dressed man tickling the ivories as the male clientele tickled the girls. I made up my mind I would stay clear of this behavior because the last thing I needed was a case of syphilis or gonorrhea.

I was firm on that, until I met Adele, and then I got a change of heart.

Miss Adele Lastrade—pronounced Less-trah-day as the piano player promptly corrected a drunken customer—was a tall woman with flaming red hair and baby blue eyes. I'd say for an experienced Madam she was in her mid-forties, dressed exquisitely with a large bosom and hospitality to match. I was just a bit smitten the first time I saw her as she sashayed softly and tenderly down the steps from her office to the bar. I'd settled into a small room with an ample fireplace and plenty of wood stored by the hearth. After finishing my evening meal of steak, potatoes and bourbon I felt drawn to her end of the long, oaken bar.

R. J., you know what she wants. Did you come her to enjoy yourself or to get a job done?

Outside, a winter storm had rolled in with the snow, the gale winds and the freezing cold. My doctor said I should rest for a week. Whatever his wisdom was it went by the wayside as my hormones kicked in. I stood by the stool next to her and tried to be a southern gentleman.

"Miss Adele," I said softly as I removed my hat. "May I sit beside you and be honored with your presence?"

"You most certainly can, handsome. Come sit, and tell me your story. And if I find yours interesting, I may tell you mine."

My Pap once told me that God gave man two great things; a brain and a penis. The downside was He only gave us enough blood to run one at a time. I never understood that back then, but I sure did that day.

We drank burgundy and I tried to get through a mug of beer so skunky that rednecks would've thrown it out their truck windows. It was small talk at first with a few "How do you like your accommodations?" and "How long have you had this establishment?" to other matters of foreplay this and that's. She was indeed experienced in matters of the heart and other male parts. Her beautiful baby blues read me from my scalp to my toes. I don't know if I fell in love with her right then or later but it really didn't make any difference. All I knew was that I desired this lady like no other woman I'd met. I had but one complaint about my room.

"You know, Adele, I noticed that my room doesn't have a bathtub in it. How might a man clean up properly here? I feel a bit crusty."

"We have a community shower house out back, but it's seasonal and I don't think you want to freshen up in this climate, do you?"

"No, no. I'm not that brave." I cautiously leaned forward and took a quick sniff of her bare shoulder. "You seem to be as fresh as a spring rain. How do you manage that, if I may be so bold as to ask?"

"I have a Parisian bath tub in my quarters."

"What's so special about that, my dear?"

"It will accommodate two people. One male and one female only."

Oh my, my my, my my, my my. Be careful with your next question.

"How much would it cost to experience this pleasure."

She looked at me with those eyes, dropped them long enough to finish her wine and answered.

"That will depend on just how clean you wish to be, young man."

I helped her down from her perch and held her soft hand in mine as I helped her to boudoir.

Chapter 6
Artesian Adventures

Adele's room was the best in the house, as one would expect. There was a parlor complete with two upholstered high-back chairs and a loveseat, a small fireplace with a wooden desk and chair. Ledgers were everywhere and papers ready to be signed. In her bedroom was a small wood stove close to the bathing apparatus that I was dying to experience, and it *was* a large one. What caught my eye were the four black servants carrying hot and cold water in buckets and pouring them in. After their second trip up the stairs Adele ran her fingers in the steaming mixture and dismissed them. Two were young girls, two adult males and I knew then, by the hopeless look on their faces, why we got into this war in the first place; no man should own another man.

Miss Lestrade was not a bit shy with her sexuality as she undressed fully and stood by the tub. She looked at me and I looked at her. For a woman, at least fifteen years my elder she had the body of a maiden—at least that's the way she looked to me—with an hourglass shape that sent chills up my ... you know where. She gracefully entered our little love boat and coaxed me in with one, longing glance. I shed my clothes in Olympiad time and gladly joined her.

Beside the tub was a small three-legged table on wheels that held two fancy-looking glass bottles with lids, plus a few cups. She pulled the table close to her, poured what I found out later to be perfectly prepared and aged bourbon in two glasses. She offered one to me and she started to sip on the other. We faced each other and eventually I placed my legs alongside her outer thighs and squeezed them, trying to say, "I've got you now" but knowing she wasn't going anywhere. After finishing her glass, she reached behind her with both hands— exposing those lovely breasts that made my brain drain—and came up with a large bar of pinkish soap. All this time we'd said not a word and it stayed that way as she turned her back to me and cradled her form against my groin.

"Wash my back and rub my shoulders, would you please?" she asked softly.

Of course, my answer was what any red-blooded American or French man would say.

"Oh, hell yes!"

After a nervous soap, down—the damn bar kept sliding out of my hands, but things worked in my favor as the soap accidently landed in her lap and lower—I cleansed her back and shoulder muscles and then administered a back rub that consisted of thumbs up and down her spine then branching out to her shoulder blades. Her "Ooohs' and "Aaahhs" were more potent to me than a ship full of oysters and on every groan, I rubbed harder. Then she slid under the water—and I was waiting for the ultimate thrill—she came back up quickly, grabbed the other bottle and popped the lid. Immediately the aroma of lilacs filled the air and she handed it to me with another untimely request.

"Wash my hair, you gentleman."

I lathered her up, gently rubbing what fingernails I had into her scalp for the deepest of cleansings and then massaged her temples and the base of her skull all. From somewhere she handed me a very big comb and asked me to remove the soap from her hair and with each stroke I felt my blood begin to boil as the anticipation of what was to come next. She went back under, rinsed her haired, squeezed the excess with both hands and turned to me. She put her arms around my shoulders, locked them onto the back of my head and kissed me as passionately as I had ever been kissed before. I was—at that moment—officially her boy toy, hers and hers alone, and I didn't mind one damn bit.

Unlike them Yankees, a Southern Gentleman never tells of his sexploits.

-2-

I spent the better part of a week with Adele, living in the lap of her luxury, basking in the warmth of her charms bi-daily and we even pulled a tri-daily the following Monday. I just violated my own Oath of Honor by reporting this, but I felt my oats by the fifty-pound bag at a time and I *was* a happy camper.

Anyway, I was invited to play poker with three other gentlemen. Seeing as I was steeped into the online thing back in my time, I graciously accepted. I broke even only drawing my weapon once on another player who accused me of cheating, which I was. I bowed out gracefully, gave him his take back and hurriedly left the room. My sweetheart had been kind enough to give me a blank diary of very fine paper and I recorded things of importance to the person or persons who may read it.

It was time to leave. I knew it, and Adele knew it too by the distant look in my eyes. The storm had abated the day I boarded the train for Baltimore and she walked with me to the dock.

"My dearest Miss Lestrade," I said with a nervous voice. "I want you to know you will forever have a place in my heart, no matter where I go or what I do. But, there are things I must tend to up north and I must leave you. I love you, Adele, and I always will."

She said nothing. As we embraced for the last time, I gave her a sweet kiss on the lips and forehead, and hugged her twice as hard as she squeezed me. With tears in our eyes I turned and made the step up to my destiny, whatever that may be.

-3-
Friday, January 13, 1865

The passenger car heated by a wood stove and comfortable seating. I dozed when I felt the train grind to a halt and marveled at how quick the trip to Baltimore was. I couldn't have been more wrong.

We had crossed over the Union lines in Alexandria, Virginia when the porter ordered everyone off the train. As we exited we were met by two Union troops checking paperwork and whatnot, and I didn't even have an ID. Immediately, one thought came to mind.

Dammit! RJ, this is Friday the thirteenth. Why didn't you wait till Saturday to leave?

After mentally calling myself seven different kinds of dumbasses, I stepped up to their plate like I had nothing to hide.

"Name?" the man with the most stars and bars demanded.

"Lewis Thornton Paine, sir. Spelled with an 'e'".

"Can you prove that in any manner?" he said, like a smartass.

I knew the day would come when I'd have to dig deep into my psychology bag, but it never was much bigger than a tube sock. I thought of all the nights I watched Improv on the Comedy Central, and decided to wing it.

"Well, sir, I could have up till three weeks ago. I was in my cabin, just a stone's throw south of Richmond, minding my own business when this group of ruffians—I think they was part of that Mosby bunch—came bustin' in and stole me blind. They even went so far as to raze my home to the ground with a fire and then hit me in the head with a pistol—looky here at this scar right there by my temple—and left me for dead. The last thing I 'member is those bastards calling me a Yankee 'cause I'm clean shaven and all. Truth be known I ain't neither. I'm just a man trying to get by, that's all."

The Captain, Colonel or Sargent looked at me hard and straight. I didn't blink and he looked away and then swiftly back to me. I held my ground.

"Would you be willing to take an oath to this great nation of ours?" he said.

"I most certainly would."

"Raise your right hand and repeat this out loud."

He handed me what looked like a postcard with writing on it. I took it proudly and recited it with my shoulders back and my head high.

"I, Lewis Thornton Payne—*Damn, he misspelled it. No sense making a fuss about it now*—do solemnly swear that I will support and defend the Constitution and government of the United States against all enemies whether domestic or foreign; that I will bear true and faithful allegiance to the same, any ordinance, resolution, or law of any State, convention, legislature, or order or organization, secret or otherwise. I do this without any mental reservation or evasion whatsoever, and especially that I have not by word or deed or in any manner whatever given countenance, aid, comfort or encouragement to the present rebellion or to those who have been or are now engaged in the conspiracy against the government of the United States of America, so help me God."

He made me sign it and I did just as he'd spelled it. He gave it back to me and shook my hand.

"Good. Where you headed?" he asked.

"Baltimore. Got family up there."

"Have a safe trip and stay clear of anyone that looks like a rebel."

"Not to worry, sir. I will do my best."

I walked hurriedly past him, found the nearest latrine as he nearly scared the piss out of me. After we returned to our seats the rest of the trip went smoothly, and I enjoyed the scenery until nightfall.

-4-
Saturday, January 14th. One a.m.

I knew Lewis would see his girlfriend, Maggie Branson, as soon as possible but I was weary from the trip and spent my first night at Miller's Hotel that was adjacent to the terminal. It didn't seem proper to barge in on the family who'd shielded my uncle in his time of needs. I drank one tall draught and a double shot of whiskey at the in-house bar contemplating my plan. Things were about to get serious and I knew if I didn't convince the players in this barbaric coup that I was who I said I was, I could end up as dead as the real Lewis. Being Uncle Lewis' number one biographer, I knew his every move and decided to jot down my plan in its order of importance.

1. Convince Miss Branson that I'm the lover she knew two years ago.

If I fail here, I thought, *then I'm sunk. Yet, if Miss Branson is half the woman Adele was then this'll be a piece of cake. Enough for one day. Go to sleep.*

For some strange reason, I dreamt I worked in a cake factory and a deranged-looking woman threw forks at me for all eternity.

Chapter 7
Page Six and Seven

I slept soundly until around noon when housekeeping knocked on the door. I stumbled one-eyed over to it, found the knob and opened it. I was still in my long johns and I read somewhere that if a woman accidentally saw a man like this then she had to marry the dude and vice versa if he saw her. Some kind of back woods, home spun, code-of-the-mountains bullshit that was common then in America.

"Mister, is you alive in there? I thought you might have expired in your bed 'cause live people don't sleep this late ... do they?" she said.

She was cute in looks and demeanor, attired in a long, white dress flared out in an umbrella shape with crinoline and a black apron so I couldn't get mad at her. After seeing that young, innocent face with her brown hair tucked tightly in a bun and a strand of curls hanging from each side, I was putty.

"They do when they don't check in till midnight, miss. Give me five minutes and I'll be out of here. By the way, where can a man get a good cup of coffee?"

"Well, sir, right downstairs in our little coffee shop. Best brew this side of Charlotte, South Carolina if I do say so myself."

"Thank you, missy. I'll get dressed and be on my way."

***

After downing three delicious eggs fried in lard and sausage with two cups of coffee I sat back and surveyed the place. It was definitely mid-nineteenth century in décor as everything that hung high or sat on legs was made of wood. Stoves were abundant in this establishment and the coziness stopped my traveling plans for a while. Outside in the bitter cold was a man selling papers. I decided to educate myself.

"My good man," I asked as I tipped my hat. "What publication is that?"

"Why, it's the Baltimore Sun," he said.

"How much would a copy of that cost me?"

The old man, who was dressed in shabby, winter clothes, a fur cap atop a plaid scarf wrapped around his face and flannel gloves with a few fingers missing, scratched his chin and sighed.

"Two ... cents," he answered, almost whispering.

"*Two cents?*" I said quickly, not believing anything could be that cheap.

"I know, I know. I told those nimrods down at the main office that they shouldn't a done it. I said one cent was enough for this rag, but they said they needed more money comin 'in for the new piece they were trying to push."

"What's that?" I asked.

"Advertising. I think it's a crazy notion, but I'm just a cog in their wheel here. Anyway, that's the best I can do, mister."

I handed the man a dime.

"You want five of these?" he said after grabbing a handful of papers.

"No, just one." I said. "Take the rest and go buy some good gloves."

"Well now, that's mighty kindly of you, sir. You from around here?"

"No. Richmond, all my life."

"It is indeed a pleasure to meet a true southern gentleman. That's the trouble with this town now. There's way too many of those damn Yankees runnin' round now. May God bless you," he said.

"Here's hoping He always does. Try to have a good day now."

***

I sat back down and resumed my caffeine infestation. The front page was about the war, second page about more war, the editorial page tore into the Confederacy and the southern way of life unmercifully. Section two had a few elaborate ads with drawings of certain shops pitching their wares and services. One caught my eye.

Branson's Boarding House
**Welcome one and all. Please visit,
try our cuisine and our fine, Southern manners.
All SOBER quests are welcome. Do not enter if you are
afflicted by the spirits in any manner
16 North Eutaw Street, Baltimore proper**

I grabbed my bag, put on my buffalo robe and headed for Eutaw Street; wherever that was.

-2-

After the paperman gave me the "three blocks that way, two to the right and halfway up the next block" directions I stood at the doorway of Branson's place. It was a tall, at least three stories high, brick and mortar building. I contemplated my next move. I didn't know a Branson from a Bratwurst so I had to figure a plan. If I went in and stayed silent someone might recognize me and start the ball rolling. The most important con to work would be Maggie. From Lewis's bio, I knew she and Lewis were an item and I guessed a little carnal knowledge had transposed between them, if you know what I'm saying without me coming right out and saying it.

As I entered I met an older woman sweeping the hallway. She may have been in her fifties with graying hair pulled back in a bun and a lean and slightly humped over frame. From the look of her red and chaffed hands I knew she was no stranger to hard work, but she wasn't dressed like a maid. I froze and hoped for the best.

"Yes sir," she said as she looked up. "The name's Rebecca Branson and I'm the proprietor of this hotel. What can I do for ...? Lewis is that you?" she asked.

"Yes, ma'am, it's me in the flesh. It's been a long time."

She came over to me, put her hands on each side of my shoulders and gazed at me for an uncomfortable period of seconds.

"Well, now, you sure have changed some. I never knew you could clean up so well. When did you find time for a good barber?" she asked.

"I'm traveling in disguise, Miss Rebecca. I'm a wanted man in some states right now and I thought I could stay here for a while, if it's all right with you. If you have a room I have cash Union money to pay for it."

She looked me over as if she tried to search my soul. I wasn't getting the vibes I wanted so I quickly changed the subject.

"Ma'am, where's Maggie?" I asked.

"She's back in the kitchen doing up some dishes. You go talk to her and then we'll talk about your lodgings."

The last vibe I got from Mama Branson was something telling me to bob and weave.

**

I gingerly opened the double kitchen door and peeked in. There she was, bent over with her hands in the wooden sink, scrubbing and buffing the huge, ceramic plates. At about five feet five inches tall, she was a trim woman with brown hair flowing gently across her shoulders and attired like her mom but with a flowery print in her dress. I tip-toed to within six feet of her and said the only thing I could think of.

"Margaret, it's me, Lewis."

Everything about her stopped and I swear she even stopped breathing. I heard a plate drop into the sink and then she slowly turned to me, and I mean like slow-mo style. And I immediately started thinking:

Oh shit!

"Lewis Thornton Powell, just who in blue blazes do you think you are? You think you can just waltz in here looking all clean-shaven and handsome and such and woo me back into your bosom just by showin' up? Why you horn-swogling, moth-eaten, good for nothin' pile of horseshit, it ain't gonna be that easy, mister. I'm here to tell you that."

Back to my psychology bag, which out of necessity, was starting to get bigger.

"Maggie darlin'. I was running with Mosby and that man wouldn't let none of us write to our folks. He claimed it'd be easy for the Yankess to trace us and ifin you crossed that guy he'd just up and shoot your ass. Honest."

That worked for about two seconds, and then she regrouped.

"I'm here to tell ya' that Willie Roberts was with Gilmore's Raiders and he wrote Sally Jenson letters to the tune of once a month and he's still walkin' round. Then there was James Aspinwall and he was with Quantrill for Pete's sake, and that murderous sonbitch let him live. He wrote Elizabeth Hartley once a week and you can't drop me a few lines in two years? Forgive me, but you're a liar. Here's your welcome mat."

And then she started what I jokingly called later the "Silverware Serenade".

The first thing she hurled at me was a big-ass salad fork, but I dodged it. Then came a knife—a steak knife—and it bounced off my buffalo robe followed by a big spoon and that didn't worry me because spoons can't draw blood, but the cork screw thing that sailed end-over-end sure would, and it nailed me on the side of my neck.

As I wiped the blood from the jagged wound I looked at her with anger. An ass-chewing was in order—yes—but trying to kill me wasn't very nice. That seemed to freak her out and she put her hand over her mouth and backed up two paces.

"Oh Lewis, I am so sorry. I didn't mean to hurt you but damn you, you shoulda wrote me. I been worried sick about you for the longest time. Come on over here, sit down and let me fix you up."

I did as she ordered, stayed silent and acted like I was in a fair amount of pain. I really wasn't, but I wanted to milk this as long as I could because if her right cross was as accurate as her right pitch, I might wake up in a hospital. She brought warm water, soap that must've been laced with pure alcohol—it stung that bad—cleaned my wound and applied a fresh bandage.

"Now, this might make you feel better," she said as she patted on my shoulder, "but don't you expect an apology. The way I see it, you done *me* wrong and you're the one who needs to apologize."

Seeing as how she may have been right—and had a whole drawer of weapons that she obviously was not afraid to use—I whipped up a sad and mournful little boy face.

"My dearest Maggie. You are correct in your assumption that I did not treat you right. The only thing I can say in my defense is that I was involved in some clandestine activities that may warrant the gallows, and in no way, did I want you associated with my name."

She looked at me, smiled widely and with a twinkling eye said, "That will do for now. Give us a kiss."

And then I did what any red blooded American guy would do; I gave her a smooch.

***

Even with all that schmoozing I still had to pay a dollar a day for room and board but Rebecca seemed cool towards me; giving me a wary look whenever I entered her space. I hadn't had to dodge anything metal for the last three days so I think Maggie was in my corner although, on the night I snuck into her room as soon as her mama started snoring—and 'Becca could rattle windows—Maggie asked me a question that made me have to think up good lie.

"Where did you learn to do that? Don't get me wrong, because it do feel good, but have you been stepping out on me?"

"No Ma'am. Cheat on a champion knife thrower like you? Surely not. It's just that one of the Rangers had this book on … love stuff …you know …what we been doing."

"What was it called?" she asked as she rolled over and placed her body against mine.

"The Kuma Sutra."

"I never heard of that, but it sounds interesting," she said.

"Good, 'cause that was page six. You wanna read page seven?"

"Yes, I do."

Good night.

Chapter 8
The Game Plan
Saturday January 21st, 1865

I spent the next two weeks wooing the Branson ladies, with Maggie being the center of all my loving intent but Rebecca's concourse posed a different problem. She was still stand-offish and I got the impression she wasn't sure I was who I said I was. Every time I spoke or made a move her eyes were upon me, and her glare was anything but friendly. That morning she pulled me aside.

"Lewis, there is a man you must meet now."

"And his name is?"

"David Preston Parr. He runs a China shop across the street. You may want to talk to him. All of you in the Circle share the same objective and he will be your liaison to the rest of your allies, the bravest of men."

The Circle? I thought. *It can't be what I think it is. It's just a myth thought up by those conspiracy nuts on the Military Channel. Maybe Rebecca is trying to set me up. I better play along.*

"All right, I'll go see him at once," I said.

"No, wait until tonight. David does his best business after dark."

"As you wish, Mrs. Branson. I'll retire to my room."

"Make sure," she said as she walked away, "that it is *your* room. Rumors abound since your advent."

And retire I did.

-2-

Parr's Hall China Shop looked quite charming at its frontage. His fine plates, saucepans and tea cups shone brilliantly in the luster of the nearby oil-fired street lamp. I'd heard about this secret organization from my Pap for years, and he claimed the Knights of the Golden Circle were as real as he was standing there. Their stated goal—which they never tried to hide—was to create a new slave-state nation encompassing our South, Mexico, and the Caribbean Islands. Most of the founders were men of means and meant every word they said, but I privately judged them as "too Masonic" and sloughed it off. Yet, finding out now that it *was* legitimate I surmised there had to be a secret handshake, Occultist writing codes or maybe even a special knock on the door. If I ever needed the advantage of my wild-ass imagination, it was now.

Lemme think here. If their plan was to create a new slave-state nation and it was drawn up in a circle ... then a knock would have to represent that. They're 360 degrees in a circle but it wouldn't be 360 knocks ... no, that'd take too long. Let's see ... 3 plus 6 equals 9 ... it's worth a shot.

So, I tapped on the front door window nine times as my hand went in a circle and thinking this was the dumbest thing I'd ever done. I thought that right up until the door slowly opened and was greeted by the business end of another long gun.

"I didn't hear a tenth knock, stranger. Promptly state your business," a gruff sounding voice said.

So, I missed it by one. What are the odds?

354

"Yankees know me as Lewis Payne, but it's really Powell, and I was sure I did ten. My hands are about froze and numb in this bitter, night air so maybe I missed one, or you heard wrong. Can I come in?"

"Who's the king?" he asked.

Pap told me the name of the man who started this apocalyptic group. What was it? It started with a "B".

"Bickley." I answered loud and proud and ready to run. Yet, some doctor named George Bickley did start this bunch of weirdoes.

"Come on in, brother. Forgive my manners, but things here now are tenuous."

Mr. Parr was a short, middle age man who had curly brown hair, a handlebar mustache and dressed as classy as his product line. I followed him into a back room filled with ledgers, pens galore and a tall, upright safe that looked C-4 proof. He pulled out a bottle of whiskey and poured two glasses, which meant he trusted me because if you plan on killing a man, you don't waste the booze on him. We sat across from each other and both partook in a long swig.

"Tell me, Lewis, have you met our leader yet?" he asked.

"Which one do you mean?" And that was a real question because I didn't know; they were so many players in this group.

"The one who is making the Grand Plan for us is a man named Booth. Ever hear of him?"

"Oh yes, if you mean John Wilkes."

"One and the same. He will be coming into town early next month. He has written me a letter, telling me of your adventures with Mosby and the tenacity of your punishments. If our plan fails we will need a man who is not afraid to commit murder. You do qualify in this requirement, don't you?"

Thinking about my session with Uncle Lewis, the only answer was a true one.

"Yes."

"Good then. We are about to depart on a mission that will determine the course of free men everywhere. There are many of us—the true Knights of our Golden Circle—that cannot bear to live in a world that will be someday dominated by the coloreds. This is an abomination to us, and if our plan works then we can save all of these United States from the tyranny of a dictator such as the one we have now. My thoughts tend to wish the speedy demise of all three men at once, not pirate them away, but if the nation moves toward total chaos men of our character can fill the void. Do you agree with us?"

"I most certainly do. And while we are being frank, whose idea is it to kidnap these men?" I inquired with the conviction I needed to stop part of this.

Parr looked at me suspiciously, as if he wondered why I'd be asking so many questions after we'd just met.

"Why do you ask, Lewis?"

"Because, I'd like to thank the man personally. It's an ingenious move, more practical than killing all three outright. We can parade them all over our land in cages and chains before we try them. We may even get the concessions we need to further our goal. As far as I'm concerned, the North no longer exists."

That statement seemed to soften his tone towards me, and I surprised myself at how revolutionary I could be, yet he gave no answer. Then I thought this may have come too naturally for me, and that was *not* a welcome epiphany. I was daily finding things out about myself that were anything but comforting.

At that moment, we heard exactly ten taps on the front door, and David rose to answer.

"This is your lucky night, young man. I believe a few of our brothers are here," David said.

Two men stood in the doorway and shook hands with David. I

knew the one from previous pictures but the other was a mystery. After they exchanged small talk and hung up their soaking wet coats, David ushered them into our room. I stood at attention waiting for the introductions.

"Lewis, this is John Surratt and Louis Weichmann. They have put in a harrowing night. Gentlemen, please come by the fire while I make us a round of warm rum."

Weichmann was the first to greet me with a handshake and a smile. He didn't fit the mold of the average rebel as he was short, rather stout and nursing a notable limp. He didn't look like he could catch a cold, but Surratt was different. Taller than six feet, he sported a full shock of curly auburn hair, redder than brown, combed straight back with an unkempt moustache as his only facial characteristic. Judging by his appearance he looked like he could've been, at one time, a choir boy, but looks are deceiving.

Our host served up four glasses of the warm liqueur and we sipped slowly, waiting for someone to start the meeting. As it turned out, David was the chairman.

"Lewis, these gentlemen have been traveling for two days now to procure a vehicle that will be paramount in the completion of our plan. John, will you please inform our new brother of your adventure?"

Surratt looked over at me, judgingly, and then back at David.

"With all due respect, I don't know this man from Adam. Can he be trusted?"

"Absolutely. Mr. Powell, or Paine or whatever name he chooses to use, rode for over two years with Mosby. He *is* one of us," Davis answered convincingly.

"So be it," Surratt said as he eased up on his reservations. "I meant no disrespect, sir, but times now are perilous. Louis and I went down to a place called Port Tobacco. Are you familiar with this place?"

Lying through my teeth, and trying to use my best vernacular of this era, I said, "Yes, I am. I have heard that we having many friends there. Am I correct in that assumption?"

"You are indeed," Surratt said. "Louis and I have partially acquired a small boat to be used later if our mission is a success."

David them chimed in. "Lewis—we have too many Lewis's—can I call you ... Mosby?"

"Yes, sir, you may," I said with a smile.

"Capital then. John, Louis, I and the others are open with the plan to kidnap the President, Vice President and the Secretary of State in one fell swoop, sneak them as fast as possible across the Maryland side of the Potomac to the Virginia side. There these traitors will be skirted to Montgomery {Alabama} and tried for treason."

"Why Montgomery, may I ask." Why not Richmond?" I asked.

"Montgomery was our first capital, and to us, it will always be that," David answered. "John, how did we fare on that?"

There was an uncomfortable period of dead air as John and Louis looked at each other and sheepishly to boot. Surratt cleared his throat to answer.

"It didn't go quite as planned."

"How so,' David asked, and his facial expression projected to me as "I'm not real happy to hear that".

"Our man wanted more than we expected, especially for his services," Surratt said.

"How much more?" David asked calmly.

"Three hundred dollars. Two hundred more for the boat and one hundred for his captaining skills."

"So be it," David said nonchalantly.

David went to the safe, turned the tumblers and retrieved a stack of bills, Union script.

"Here is what you need. Do you two feel like returning tomorrow?"

Surratt and Weichmann looked at each other, and they did look weary and worn out. Surratt said something that just tickled me to death.

"David, you know our devotion but Louis and I are next to exhaustion. Can you send someone else? Someone such as Mr. Mosby?"

"Yes, I can. Mosby, will you volunteer?"

"Yes, I will," I said proudly and without hesitation.

"Good then. John, fill him in on the particulars."

"David, if I am successful in this, would one of you vouch for me where Rebecca Branson is concerned? I feel she mistrusts me."

"Complete this, and it will be done," David said.

John Surratt filled me in on the directions to the docks, train trip times, our greedy middle man's name and handed me the money in an old, leather satchel. I went straight back to Branson's to spend the night in the arms and charms of Maggie, my newest love.

I was *finally* in the game.

Chapter 9
The Better Actor
Sunday January 22nd, 1865

The Baltimore and Ohio Railroad, being the corporate types they are, did not bow to Protestant pressures and travel on the Sabbath ran like any other day. My coach left promptly at 7:14 am and after two stops we arrived in Port Tobacco at precisely 1:17 pm. The line ran adjacent to the Potomac River and the docks weren't hard to find. My contact was a man named Amos McGee, and one of his "hands" was kind enough to show me to his office. Via telegram, I presumed, he knew of my coming but didn't seem to know my name. Maybe this was another test.

"Excuse me, but what is your name?" he asked.

I remembered a movie I saw once, *Reservoir Dogs,* about a group of high class criminals who prepared to rob a huge, Los Angeles bank, and the different fake names they used. I looked around his boat-building shop to see long, bent planks, hand planes everywhere with dirt and shavings floor wide. I invented a new alias.

"Mr. Wood, and I assume you are Amos?"

"You assume correctly. Please sit, and let us conduct our business."

Amos could've been a poster boy for *Old Man and the Sea* monthly because he was aged, grisly-looking and smelled like the last time he had a bath was when the final waves of Hurricane Whoever rolled through his shop. I wanted to make this as quick as possible, but I also wanted to leave him with the impression I knew what I was talking about and was no one to cross.

"Now," he said as he pulled his large frame up to the desk. "Before we continue there is the question of the balance owed. Have you been made aware of that?"

"Yes, sir, I have. The two gentlemen who negotiated with you earlier filled me in on all the particulars," I said.

He leaned back in his chair and gave me a long, cold scare.

You know his kind, I thought. *He's nothing more than a back-alley bully. You've dealt with these types before in school. Show him what you're made of.*

"Well now, I would not call our conversations a 'negotiation'. The way I remember it I set a price and they accepted it. If things have changed, then so have the services to be rendered," he answered like a typical smartass.

And this dude had no idea how right he was.

I laid a wad of money on his desk and sat back while he counted it. He almost sang as he clicked off tens and multitudes of tens and one hundred then two hundred twenty, forty, fifty and then he looked up.

"Wood, this is fifty dollars light. The deal is off."

"Well now, is that not a shame?" I said as I pulled my long gun out and placed it directly against his forehead. At once his gaze shifted from the barrel to my stare and I believe I saw total fear in his eyes, as if my glare had murder without hesitation. It was nothing more than a bluff and I hoped my powers of persuasion would always stay that way.

"There is two hundred for the boat, according to plan. Then there is fifty dollars to guarantee that you *do not* guide anything other than a fork to that glutinous face of yours. In terms you may understand, on the night they wire you to be there you never," I said coldly as I pulled the hammer back, "ever show up. Do you understand the language that I am speaking here, Mr. McGee?"

The old prick farted as he shook and may even have pissed his pants as he tried to speak.

"I understand, Mr. Wood. I will heed your instructions to the letter."

"Good. You better, because I know where you live. Now, where is the best damn steakhouse in this shithole of a town?"

"Three doors down. Only Jackson's meat is very expensive." Amos said.

"I needn't worry about that. Is case you haven't noticed, you just gave me a fifty-dollar tip. Live long and prosper, tuna breath."

As I pigged-out on one of the best Porterhouse steaks I'd ever eaten, I remembered a moment in this plan's history. Two weeks later Surratt and Weichmann returned to do a dry run of their midnight voyage thing, but Amos was nowhere to be found. They rowed all night and at daybreak they docked on what they thought was the Virginia side of the Potomac. Turns out they were back at their point of origin, rambling on the water all night long in a big-ass circle. And I thought:

Maybe theses cowboys should change their name, because the circle thing ain't working for them. And that just breaks my heart.

I patted myself on the back for being a bigger smartass than Amos, rewarded myself with another bourbon while thinking Clint Eastwood would've been extremely proud of me.

This, I thought, *was a very rewarding day.*

-2-
Friday February 3rd, 1865

After breakfast Rebecca came by with a fresh pot of coffee. She refilled my cup and as I looked up at her she smiled. The lady had shown me nothing but a hard time since I arrived, and this bit of kindness was a tad un-nerving. She sat across from me and gifted me with a smile.

"Lewis Powell, I owe you an apology," she said quickly.

"Fo ... for what?" I stammered, trying to put on the innocent thing.

"For mistrusting you when you first appeared. I did that as a precaution, on the premise of your last performance with certain members of my household. I have since been corrected by the man you are to see today."

"Apology accepted, ma'am. And just who is this mystery man?"

"David Parr. He stopped by yesterday and told me you were an immense help to him and for me to consider you henceforth an honored quest. That is to say your stay now will be charitable on my part."

"I thank you greatly for the kindness," I said, thinking that was just enough and to shut up while I was in the lead.

"Then it is settled. Yet, I feel I must get something off my chest," she said in anything but a soothing manner.

Oh boy, I thought. *There had to be a catch.*

"I will tell you truly that I know what your mission is now and what it may be in the foreseeable future. My daughter has always been fond of you—for whatever reason—and when you disappeared before you broke her heart. When this time you part—as I know you will—you would be well advised to tell her beforehand. I have friends everywhere and ... well... let's just affirm the Good Book says a man

will reap what he has sown. While I am not saying I am an agent of the Good Lord's justice … I can say I am mighty close. Do we have an understanding, young man?"

"Yes, ma'am, we most certainly do. Rest assured I will do everything you have requested."

"Good. Now be on your way, for Mr. Parr is a busy man."

I couldn't get out of there fast enough.

***

I immediately went to David's shop and waited in the wings until he finished a sale. As the happy customer left, he signaled for me to follow him into his office. We sat and exchanged cordial greetings.

"I've been told that you wish to see me, David. Rebecca was emphatic that I come as soon as possible."

"Yes, and I'm glad you heeded her request," he said.

"After our conversation this morning, I will *always* honor her desires," I stated, raising my eyebrows. We both got a chuckle over that, and then got down to business.

"Lewis, it is now time for you to meet our leader. Mr. Booth will be in town late tonight and would like to lunch with you tomorrow. He has heard of your work so far and your tenure with Mosby. He is most anxious to meet you."

"No more willing to meet me than I am he," I said. "Where and when?"

"John Wilkes stays at the Barnum Hotel when he is in Baltimore. It is at the corner of Calvert and Lafayette Avenues, about six blocks from here in the downtown area. I must tell you that this establishment is very expensive, but the cuisine is exquisite. How are you fixed for funds?"

Thinking about my bountiful trip to Port Tobacco I said, "I have enough money as of now; a loan will not be needed."

"That is comforting. Financing for our cause is becoming less and less now, but we *will* survive it. By the way, do you know what Mr. Booth looks like?"

"Yes. I've seen his face on many marquees. He is an actor, isn't he?"

"The absolute best," David said. We shook hands and away I went nervously knowing that if I was to pull this off, tomorrow would be Act One.

-2-
Saturday, February 4th, 1865. Noon.

The walk to Barnum's took about a half an hour and I used that time to put on my "game face". In case he asked about my uncle's murderous missions with John Mosby, aka the Grey Ghost, I went through every battle and skirmish I knew my relative was in. Studying Uncle Lewis's exploits through the books Pap kept worked in my favor, although at the time I thought of it as an abnormal obsession.

The house restaurant at Barnum's Hotel was packed that lunchtime and the clientele were obviously the wealthy and powerful players of the day. Booth wasn't hard to find as he sat in the middle of the gala sipping a bowl of soup. One tiny sip, and then he blows off the steam of the next dip and the next and I immediately gave him "asshole status" for his pompous demeanor. He wasn't just sitting in his chair, he *posed* with his left fist resting on his thigh, he lifted the spoon to his thin lips in a purely measured move with his right hand. His brown, curly hair was combed and pampered and his moustache was trimmed and groomed. Before I approached him, I had to have a talk with myself. I said, *Self, you know you want to waltz over there and drop kick this asshole right out the door and on to the harbor, but you need to gain his confidence or your plan is nixed. He's an actor, so you have to be one too.*

"Mr. Booth, I assume," I said as I stood by his table.

"You assume correctly, sir, and you must be Lewis."

"Yes, I am; at your service."

We shook hands and I marveled at the strength of his grip. I made a mental note to comment on that for future plans. We sat, and a waiter came quickly. I ordered a hot cup of coffee and a piece of cherry pie.

"Tell me, Lewis. What do you think of our President?" he asked.

Think hard RJ. This could be your last test.

"Sometimes, Mr. Booth, I almost feel sorry for the man. To die for such a worthless cause that we both know as unjust as well as immoral seems to be a terrible waste of talent. Nonetheless, he has had four long years to correct himself and yet he has shown us what a stubborn man he can be. I almost pity him, and probably will, right up to the time you say the word and I slit his throat."

Judging by the way his spoon-holding hand was suspended a few inches from his gaping and wide-open mouth, I was as cold as I needed to be.

"Any more questions, brother?"

Chapter 10
Row Boat Blues

Booth continued with his last sip of soup as I sat there, looking right at him. He brushed his bowl aside, wiped his mouth by tapping the napkin on his lips and lit a small cigar. He offered me one and I accepted it.

"Well now," he started carefully. "That is my plan for all three, eventually. But, my first choice is to seize them and bring them to Montgomery as fast as possible. I covet your thoughts on this, Lewis."

"John, I am in total agreement with you. Yet, traveling with General Mosby has taught me one true fact; things *never* go as planned. We must think this through properly, and have a counter if plan A fails. It would be whimsical to think all three guarded men can be carted off at the same time without flaws appearing."

John Wilkes sat straight up, processed what I said. If I could convince an accomplished actor that I was genuine, then maybe I could win an Oscar for my performance in eighty years or so.

"What you say is true, my friend. Nonetheless, our plans are as thus. Two of us will accost the Vice President, two for Secretary Seward with myself and one more trusted soul for Lincoln. Lewis, do you know of anyone who is qualified in both strength and intellect?"

"Judging by the firmness of your handshake and the tenacity of your resolve, I would say you might be able to pull that one off yourself. But, if it is your plan is to subdue the President and lower him to the stage—"

"Mr. Powell," Booth interrupted quickly as his temperament changed to one of suspicion. "How did you know I was planning to do that?"

Oh shit, RJ, I thought. *You're on the verge of blowing this whole deal. Think fast.*

"I would assume that, with you being an accomplished thespian and preforming at theatres everywhere in Washington, that you would attempt it there. You know the layout of all the finer entertainment houses, their exits, height of the balcony to the stage and of course Mrs. Lincoln is a well-known fan of yours. Who's to say that Mr. Lincoln wouldn't accompany her for a performance? I have been told that she is a hard person to say no to. With the strength, we both possess my first thought was you lowering the President down from his balcony seat—I assumed he would sit up there—and I will cling to him as if my life depends on it, which I am sure it will. Then we will swiftly exit out a back door to the two— no, three—horses I will have tied up there. Please correct me if I am in error here. I did not mean to overstep my bounds, sir."

Now, if his ego is as big as I think it is, and my bullshit was first class, he will eat that up.

Booth eased his tightened posture, took a drag of his smoke and a sip of coffee. His disgruntled face turned to a smile and I had one thought.

Gimme that statue and a bottle of champagne.

"I have found," Booth said, "there are times men think alike when a proper plan of action is required and this may be such a period. That was my thoughts to the letter and I believe you are my comrade in this. Yet, in the event all goes awry I feel I must do what I must do to ensure this tyrant can afflict us no more. If there is found no other recourse, do you accept that eventuality?"

"I do, but I will do my best to see that happens in Alabama. In this, I pledge my sacred honor."

"Then it is done, Lewis. You must travel to Washington to meet the others. How soon can you depart?"

"There might be a problem," I said as I cleared my throat.

Booth gave me an ornery little smile. "I am sure Maggie will let you go for a few days or weeks. As you see, I have spies everywhere."

"I gather that. But, I signed a pledge—under duress—when I got into this territory to not leave Maryland. This might pose a problem."

"Let me see it."

I handed it to Booth, he studied it and slid it back to me.

"Lewis, what type of writing utensil did this Captain use?"

"... It looks like a pencil."

He handed me a block eraser and I caught on immediately, being a little tiffed I didn't think of this myself. A few swipes of the rubber tool and my travel restrictions were null and void.

"Why do you suppose this man used a pencil?" I asked.

"I did say I had spies everywhere, didn't I? Never judge a man henceforth by the color of his uniform. Now, go to your sweetheart, make amends and pack. I will be in touch."

We stood, shook hands and I departed for Barnum's thinking this whole scenario over. But first, I knew I had to stop at a tobacco shop because, eventually, I'd have to stop smoking OPC's.

Other Peoples Cigars.

-2-

Monday February 6th, 1865

Surratt's Boarding House, located at 604 H Street, wasn't the finest bed and breakfasts in Washington, D.C. but it was suitable for me. Creature comforts—other than my Maggie's embrace—meant nothing because my mission had begun and its completion my only thought. I was anxious to meet the proprietor, knowing her legacy would be a topic of heated debate to the present day.

Mary Surratt answered my knock at the door and, at first sight, I found her a handsome woman in her mid-thirties, with long, black hair parted in the middle and tied back tightly in a bun. A set of innocents looking brown eyes complimented her smooth complexion and I detected no malice in her person. I almost choked back a tear knowing she'd be the first—and I say guiltless—white woman to be hanged by the Federal government.

"Yes, sir. Can I help you?" she asked in a diplomatic manner.

"Madam, I was wondering if your son John was here today."

SLAM

The breeze from her surprising answer almost blew my hat off. *RJ,* I thought. *What did you do wrong? You know this is the right place. Do you look threatening? You took a bath and shaved before you came down. Do you still look like a vagabond? Try it again.*

I removed my hat, brushed back my hair and thought of a new plan. I knocked ten times and, after a period of dead air, I heard loud footsteps coming to the door. I was greeted by a man I knew I'd meet eventually.

"Stranger, state your business," he commanded.

Samuel Bland Arnold looked anything like his middle name. He stood tall, well-toned with dark, curly hair, and a slight growth of beard. His hazel eyes had the same devilish appearance that I saw on my uncle. He dressed all in black attire which gave him the semblance of what was referred to then as a "Highwayman". They were indispensable in times of revolution or criminal enterprises because they would do anything to complete their mission. And I do mean *anything*.

"Excuse me, sir. My name is Lewis Powell to you, Lewis Payne to the bluecoats. I was instructed by the actor to report here. If I have the wrong address then forgive my manners, and I'll be on my way."

He then loosened his stiff posture. "Come in and follow me. Do not look at anyone eye-to-eye but do not look away either. Put your hat back on, for any man with their hair exposed is considered suspect."

I did as he said, thankful I'd been schooled on proper male etiquette before someone with a .44 parted my hair. We went to a smoke-filled inner room with a table and chairs, and well-lit with four, large candles illuminating most of the room.

"What's your pleasure, brother?" Sam said as he raised his empty glass.

What would he think if I asked for whiskey? It's too early for hard alcohol. Yet it's noon somewhere.

"How about a cup of black coffee in a bowl filled with good, Kentucky bourbon?"

Sam smiled. "A man after my own heart. Two Irish coffees coming right up."

After he left I surveyed the room and counted six chairs with an ashtray by every one of them. If my count was right then the "Final Solution" would be orchestrated and voted on here. If I did nothing else, I had to steer that meeting towards the kidnaping aspect. Anything else would be a death sentence for all three parties and this whole experience a waste of history's time.

"I received a telegram from the actor telling me of your coming visit. And, by the way, you can say Booth's name here. We all are brothers in the Cause and soon you will meet everyone important. Since you are new to our clan I must tell you that anything said stays in this room. I will caution you just this once, but I've already gotten the impression you know that rule," Sam said in a respectful manner.

"Oh yes, I know. If I learned anything from Mosby it was knowing when to keep still. Tell me about Mrs. Surratt. Why did I get such a cold greeting?"

Sam looked away and tilted back in his chair. "It wasn't you personally, Lewis. She is a careful woman and dearly loves her son, John. She has no idea what we are planning but she is not stupid. Just because John will not tell her anything about our meetings gives her cause for suspicion. I am sure you can understand a mother's concern for her only remaining son. Her other two boys were lost at Antietam."

"Would there be any harm in telling her a little? Maybe that would ease her mind," I said.

"Absolutely not. If John found out woe be it to that man. John is a careful soul, but can become murderous when he is crossed. Do not mention anything to her. It is for your wellbeing as well as hers—what the hell?"

Just then we heard a loud noise that sounded like a whole squadron of jack-booted troops coming our direction. Sam stood—showing no fear—and drew his weapon. So, I did too, knowing full well I'd miss if I had to shoot. My killing days were over as far as I was concerned. The first man through our door was Louis Weichmann, looking mad, bad and glad to yell at somebody.

"Samuel!" Louis yelled. "By God we better start to rethink this thing again, 'cause that low-life, snake eatin' smelly sonofabitch was nowhere to be found!"

"Who?" Sam asked.

"McGhee, that's who. John and me rowed all night tryin' to find Virginia in the dark. We ended up goin' in a big damn circle. Wouldana happened if that catfish-fuckin' ingrate had showed. And why the hell is *he* here?" Louis said.

Tempers softened as John Surratt walked slowly in. Weichmann looked no worse for wear but John was a different story. Visualize anything the cat would drag in, and that was he.

"Now settle down Louis," John said as he eased him to a chair. "Ain't nobody's fault but McGhee and he will be compensated for his betrayal; mark my words. Mr. Powell or Payne or Mosby or whatever the hell your name is this day, did you arrange this with McGhee like we asked?"

How could I answer that?

"He agreed to follow all my instructions to the letter," I said, lying through one orifice or another, yet knowing that's just what he did.

"This is your responsibility to correct. No one can double cross the Circle and get away with it. What say you?"

"... I say ... first thing in the morning I head for Port Tobacco. Will that suffice?" I said.

"Only if Amos receives his just—and last—rewards." Surratt said with the same set of eyes as Samuel.

I spent a fitful night at Mary's House, wondering if my conscience would allow me to do what I knew they expected from me.

Chapter 11
Blood on My Hands
Tuesday, February 7th, 1865; mid-morning

I skipped the train ride down to Port Tobacco because the weather was warming and I detected a thaw in the air. John Surratt lent me a fresh horse and I was becoming an accomplished horseman, only falling off my steed three times in as many weeks. My buttocks and pride were bruised, but not my determination. I even thought about a cushion for comfort. Then I imagined General's Mosby or Custer seeing me like that and shooting me right off my horse, so I quickly perished that thought.

After all, this was the 1860's and men were men, sore asses or not.

I took my time that day, enjoyed the warmth of the bright sunshine on my young bones. It was a time for soul searching and I reflected on my plan thus far. It wasn't pretty—not by a long shot—nonetheless I had gotten myself into the inner circle of the conspirators. My goal was to help kidnap President Lincoln, then disable his captors so I could steal him away and dispatch him back to Washington, thus clearing my family name. Afterwards I'd hustle back to my point of origin in Richmond and hopefully return to my life in 2014. Funny thing was, I didn't remember asking Rabbi Endras for a round-trip ticket. Like I said before, I was terrible on details, and realized that flaw may come back to haunt me.

***

I arrived about six in the evening, as the sun set. I tied off "Trigger"— or whatever his name was—to a hitching post and walked the quarter mile or so to McGhee's boat shop. Walking by I heard three too many voices and figured he talked to his crew, so I walked back to the tavern aptly named "**TAVERN**". Sitting at the south end by a window I ate pork, mashed potatoes, with only one lump per spoonful, and had a beer and two, double shots of bourbon for dessert. Until then, I shook like a leaf.

It was dark when the men left, so I paid my tab and made the "High Noon" walk to a place I didn't want to go. I had one clear choice in this; to convince Amos somehow to leave here and go to Maine or someplace where the Golden Circle couldn't find him. If I did this, then I saved two lives; mine and his. I called upon all the television and movie slick-talking heroes of my past to help me with my presentation. I didn't knock, I just walked in.

"What the *HELL* do you want now, Wood?" He yelled as he looked up and sprayed some of his dinner my way.

When I called the man a gluten before, I pegged him right. Before him was a Thanksgiving-size plate of beef, at least one whole chicken, a few greens and a mug of something steaming on the side. I was glad I was ten feet back or I would've needed a dry cleaner to sanitize my best suit, but realized that was fifty years in the future.

"I came to talk, Amos, because I heard you were a reasonable man. I have a favor to ask."

"Favor my ass! It's like this, rebel. You ain't getting' shit outa me from now one. In case you ain't heard the war's almost over and your side got its ass kicked. Get outta my town."

I walked over, grabbed a chair and sat on his left side. I did it calmly, nonchalantly as if he didn't scare me, which he didn't. I wasn't leaving until I got something concrete from this pig.

"Now, now, Mr. McGhee, let's not get your panties in a wad. My proposition is simple. I will pay you fifty dollars now and fifty per month if you leave here and go north. All I will need is an address so I can send you your due on time. The South may have lost this war, but there are a group of very selective and *wealthy* men who are bound by their honor to continue this in a different direction. Eventually these men will come looking for you and it would be unwise of you to discount their reach. Think about it for a moment."

For a few seconds, I thought I had him. He continued to chow down on a huge chicken breast, holding it with his filthy bare hands. As he filled both jowls he seemed to yield to my advice but then his forehead grew red and the veins bulged from his neck.

"Now hear this, *Mr. Wood.* The only person leaving this town tonight is you. Now git your fancy-lookin' smooth-talkin' ass outa my shop before I open this drawer."

Brushing small McNuggets off my shoulder, my whole personality changed in a flash. I no longer disliked the man, I hated him.

"Wrong answer, my friend, but open that drawer anyway," I said as cold as I could, hoping to bluff him out.

My best Raylan Givens didn't work, and he pulled the drawer open quickly. Faster than he, I slammed the door shut with the calf of my leg, then stood there and stared him down, almost daring him to make a move. Feeling like he had no recourse, he took a wild right cross which came almost in slow motion. I ducked it and swiftly came back with my own haymaker, knocking him off his chair. He slid into a tall cabinet with a thud, a grunt and an eerie groan.

As I walked over to kick him in the shins—not hard, just enough to get his undivided attention—he looked up at me with this frantic stare. Then a chunk of something white flew out of his mouth like he tried to spit it free. His chest heaved up and down and he grabbed his throat and tried to ask me for help. The man choked on his chicken and if I didn't help he would die. I rushed over and put my arms around him to do the Heimlich and then I let go, retreated to a corner out of his sight.

And I let him die. God help me. I watched the man die.

Panting like a winded hound, I knew in the back of mind it might come to this. All he had to do was telegraph the whole story to John Surratt and all my efforts would've been for naught, and my life wouldn't have been worth spit. History would continue and my family name would still be soiled and I would be stuck in 1865 and maybe on the run the rest of my life. *No*, I knew, *this was a gift*. Yet, I couldn't let the word get back he choked to death on food; that wouldn't do for my reputation with the Knights.

As I calmed down I resigned myself to the cold hard facts. Directly across from me was a red, metal can with the words LAMP OIL stenciled on the front. I rose, straightened my coat and put my hat back on. I took the liquid and poured a circle around Amos, then gently closed his eyes with a thumb and forefinger. I walked backwards to the front door, leaving a trail of the thick liquid in my wake. With all the will I could muster I lit a match and dropped it. I walked back up town, mounted my horse and left like I didn't have a care in the world. At its edge, I turned and looked back. The flames grew and there was a mad rush of men manning the fire buckets, but as the inferno came through the roof I knew it was a total loss. I knew then these truths were evident. I was a murderer, an arsonist as well as depraved and indifferent to the gasps of a dying human being. All the way back to Washington the same emotion gripped my soul.

I just wanted to go home. Home to my simple life in Richmond, Virginia 2014.

-2-

About midnight I stopped at another boarding house and paid the man two dollars for a bath and breakfast. After seeing to my ride's meal, I mounted and rode to Surratt's house. Grabbing my bag, I hoped for a quick exit, but John Surratt met me as I came down the steps. I froze, not knowing what to expect and then he flashed a huge smile.

"Lewis, I have a message from Booth," he said.

"What does he want?"

"He wants me to shake your hand for him, and congratulate you on a superb job. Well done, brother, well done."

"News travels faster than I thought," I said as I accepted the greeting. "Does he have any more instructions for me?"

"Not at the moment. He wants you to go back to Baltimore and someone will contact you through the Branson's. You deserve a rest."

Next stop, Baltimore and the waiting arms of my Maggie.

-3-
Wednesday February 8th, 1865. Evening

I received a warm welcome when I arrived at Branson's Boarding House, with Rebecca cordially greeting me and instructing the young, black maid—who I heard called Beulah—to carry my luggage to my new room. It was twice the size of my old one-room accommodation with a little parlor in front of a large bedroom. Speaking of large, the bed looked king size and I couldn't wait to chase her daughter around it from end to end.

I was thinking that, of course, not saying it out loud. I'm a little dense at times, but never that stupid.

What shook me for a second was the way Beulah glared at me.

This was the first time I'd met the young lady, yet her large, brown eyes did their best to stare a hole in me. She didn't set my bag down; she let it drop to the floor, then turned in a huff and walked swiftly away. I didn't give the incident a second thought, and spruced up a bit before I made my next social call.

***

Miss Maggie served two couples their dinner and I quietly sat in a far corner where I watched the front and kitchen doors. For some strange—or paranoid—reason, I felt the need to see everyone's entrance and my quickest exit now. As much as I hated it, I'd become a highwayman and would have the nagging feeling that someone would always be gunning for me. It was an unfortunate side effect of the path my life had taken, and I told myself to get used to it.

As Maggie turned to take some dirty dishes to the kitchen my eyes were upon her. She was a lovely woman no matter what the dress or the lack thereof. She smiled as she noticed me surveying her every curve and instinctively knew where my mind was, and I hoped hers was in the gutter too. I needed to feel her warmth against mine and to experience the normality that her essence brought to my twisted and unsure world. Just as I was about to approach her my view was blocked by a dark figure clothed in black.

"Well, Mr. Karr, please sit down," I said.

"As you wish, Lewis, but I can't stay long," he said as he sat on the edge of a chair. "I have a message for you from Mr. Booth. He has instructed me to tell you to rest the remainder of the week and be ready to travel Sunday morning. He said for you to dress in the warmest of attire."

"Why? Where are we going?"

"To Toronto."

"Toronto where?" I asked, not even thinking about the obvious.

"Why, Canada, of course. We have many friends there. Good luck."

And with that he was on his way, and I thought, *Friends of the Confederacy that far north?*

Chapter 12
My Midnight Special

After spending five great days and as many luscious nights with Maggie, I realized something was happening. As hard as I fought it, I was falling in love with her and this was the worst possible scenario for her. If things went my way I would be gone from this era in less than two months and would leave her here. I didn't even know *if* I could go back, but then I had a thought,

Maybe if I do all this and save the day Maggie and I could get married; settle down and have children; live a normal life in this timeframe. Yet, I have my murderous past and it will come back to haunt me. Maggie may be involved due to guilt by association. They hanged one woman when Lincoln was killed. Who's to say they won't harm Maggie? Shut up and enjoy the happiness you have today, and take it for what it's worth.

I dismissed those thoughts and continued to savor my time with her. If memory of this stage in United States history served me right, I was about to be in the company of some very powerful and rich men. I decided to splurge, take Maggie to an opera Saturday night and then depart at Booth's command. Young Beulah came with us, uninvited, and stayed behind us all the way there and home. She gave me an uneasy feeling because it seemed she watched every move I made, especially with Maggie. *Maybe,* I thought, *she was here at the behest of Rebecca.* If that was the case then there was nothing I could do but act like a southern gentleman during daylight hours.

-2-

Sunday February 12ᵗʰ, 1865

"Lewis, are you ready for our informative journey?" Booth asked as we sat down for morning coffee.

"As ready as I'll ever be. Can you fill me in on the details?"

"The particulars of our excursion are better left to the privacy of our train ride to New York. The ambience of the traveling noise is more conducive to private affairs, away from prying eyes and ears," Booth said as he looked at Beulah.

"I have a bad feeling about that young lady, John. She watches me—and now you—way too closely for my comfort."

"As I said before, never judge a person by the color of their uniform or even the color of their skin. The negro has become more brazen since the President emancipated them, but that shan't last much longer, if we have our way."

He phrased the statement as "matter-of-fact" and with a cold and convinced look. I knew then that John Wilkes Booth was not looking for fame or fortune in what he'd planned. He was committed to his Cause and I knew I'd be introduced to men who were as adamant as he, only they were much more dangerous because they had the money to see their whims through.

"One more thing before we go, Lewis. I will try to phrase this as delicately as I can … but is that the best outfit you own?"

"Yes, it is. I am but a poor man and have always been that way. Does this pose a problem?"

"Not entirely, because it can be fixed when we arrive today. Bring only your grooming materials, tobacco and any personal items you need. The rest will be supplied. Now, drink up and let us check out."

I rose, went to my room and packed a few things. Before I left I caught Maggie alone in her mother's office. I kissed and hugged her tightly goodbye, telling her I'd be gone but a few days.

-3-

During the trip, we stayed in a two-occupant cabin with John immediately pulling the blinds down as we left the station. We lit our cigars and John offered me a hit from his silver flask. After we gulped down a big swig of good bourbon, he began.

"Lewis, I take it you have a lot of questions. What are your concerns?" he asked.

"They are not concerns, per see, but bewilderment that we had operatives in another country. I thought our movement was purely regional."

"We have sympathizers all over the western world, but our real brothers are in the North Country. There are men of great means and vision who have found refuge in Toronto and Montreal, unencumbered by our Federalists. When we meet the man I have contacted, you will be surprised at his planning, for the South *will* rise again, only this time in new lands, far from the clutches of our dictator and his so-called righteous culture."

"I look forward to meeting him," I said.

"I am sure he will reciprocate. Your reputation precedes you."

I sat quietly the rest of the trip, contemplating not having the notoriety I'd earned at all.

RUNNING WILD NOVELLA ANTHOLOGY

-4-

John hailed a horse-drawn cab and we checked into the Revere Hotel, and revered it was. Situated on the corner of West Fork Avenue and Second Street, it was a five-story brownstone of exquisite wood trimmed in white on the outside and all-natural cherry inside. The doorman let us in and after John paid for two rooms, side-by-side, we unpacked. We met at their spacious in-house restaurant, had a delicious late lunch and topped it off with large cups of aromatic coffee. That's when we got down to business.

"Lewis," John said in a serious tone. "When it comes to the people we will meet, presentation is everything. Today we will meet another brother who is a specialist in fine men's clothing. He runs a haberdashery a few short blocks from here."

"Isn't his shop closed on the Sabbath?" I asked.

"Yes, it is, but not to us. Observe and learn."

***

1177A, New Amsterdam Street was a tall, brick building with arched windows front and back. The frontage was closed but Booth and I walked up the fire escape to a door on the second floor. Booth slowly tapped ten times on the window with his knuckles and quickly it opened.

"John Wilkes, it is indeed a pleasure to see you again. Come in, come in," the occupant said.

We walked in and stood a few feet from the door, presumably waiting further invites. The man was short, a little plump with grey hair circling the sides of a bald and shiny head. His glasses were of the style Ben Franklin wore, half-moons and hanging low on his nose. What caught my eye was a cloth measuring tape wrapped behind his neck and trailing off both shoulders. It was Sunday and, with no business allowed to be conducted on that day, I assumed he slept with it on.

"Lewis Powell, meet Clovis Bingington. Mr. Powell will be accompanying me to the North." Booth said.

He and I exchanged handshakes with a quick and polite man bow. Clovis stood back, looked me up and down, then laid a thumb and forefinger under his chin.

"John Wilkes, this gentleman needs a new look. Follow me."

Booth cocked his head towards the fleeting tailor and pointed the way. I followed Clovis to an inner room, stood on a one-step up platform and stretched, bent down, stood straight up and assumed all the accepted measuring profiles.

"Mr. Powell, I will start you out with the standard suit of the day on this side of the Mason Dixon. You are almost a perfect fit for that, as styles up here are quite plain and tasteless, if you ask me. The other outfits will be of the Southern style. You should wait until you cross the border before you wear them. They will need minor alterations. You and John can wait in my sitting room and enjoy my latest shipment—banned up here, of course—of fine Louisiana coffee or Tennessee whiskey."

"Is there any reason why we cannot have both?" I asked, trying to break the ice.

"No, no, not at all," Clovis said with a chuckle. "Try any combination you desire, but as for me, I have work to do. Gentlemen, at your leisure," he said as he pointed towards the other rooms.

John and I retired to the parlor with cups in hand. We talked about our upcoming trip, when I should speak and when to listen, and I asked if he was still serious about the kidnaping aspect of the plan.

"As serious as a Lincoln impeachment, but that is not likely to happen. I know this is the best course of action and I am hoping I

can count on you to persuade a few of our—how should I say? —
more squeamish partners."

"Exactly how many partners do we have?" I slipped two fingers of
whiskey in my cup.

"A minimum of four, a maximum of six; that number the
preferred."

"How many are wary of your plan?" I asked.

"Two men are hesitant and want to go straight for a kill. The other
is a sheep and will do what he is told. Yet, we are still in the planning
stage. Many of the minute details still need to be explored. This will not
happen overnight. Lewis, I believe Clovis wants your presence."

The tailor stood in the doorway holding a pair of black pants and
a "Frock" coat to match. It resembled a tuxedo with a long tail that
hung almost to a man's knees to be worn with a white, long sleeve
shirt and a pale, blue vest. As I tried it on Clovis and John nodded
their approval. When I asked about a tie Clovis took a regular bow
tie but tucked the ends up inside a very stiff collar. I think today it's
called an Ascot and I looked and felt quite the dandy.

"Perfect, Lewis, just perfect," Clovis said. "Now, what time do
you depart tomorrow?"

"Nine o'clock in the morning," Booth answered.

"Good. I will have his other two suits altered, pressed and
delivered to him by eight sharp. Have a safe and, I pray, a successful
trip."

-5-
Tuesday February 14th. Late morning.

Twenty-four hours later we arrived in Toronto; a pleasurable
experience nonetheless. Booth and I shared a two-berth cabin,
enjoyed fine dining, the best of cigars and wine. Once I wondered

where Booth got the financing for these excursions because actors didn't make kind of money then and, seeing as how he paid for this, I enjoyed the simple and slower lifestyle of this era.

After several stops in Elmira, Buffalo and Erie, Pennsylvania we departed for Toronto city. It was a beautiful town complete with Gothic-style cathedrals, lavish parks and wide streets. We checked into the Queensbury Hotel which made the Revere look like a Motel 6. After settling into our "suites" we went downstairs for coffee mixed with Canadian Club whiskey.

"Lewis, you are about to meet the number one operative in Canada. His name is Jacob Thompson and he is a very prosperous man. Turn to your right."

I did as Booth said and without thinking I immediately stood, as if at attention. I knew by his stature and the sureness of his eye contact that he was a very serious individual.

Chapter 13
The Grand Plan

"Lewis Powell, meet Mr. Jacob Thompson," Booth said.

I extended a hand and Jacob graciously accepted it. He was tall, over six foot, with black hair and with a small growth of beard under his chin. His dark, brown eyes relayed a man convinced, sure of himself and his hands were the soft texture of one who'd always been rich.

"Gentlemen, let us rest," Booth said.

We sat at a table for four and there was one conspicuous seat empty. Booth looked at it, and then at Jacob.

"Where is Clement?" Booth asked.

"Mr. Clay has been called to Montreal on important business. The first part of our prisoner program starts this week. You will undoubtedly see him soon, if all goes as planned," Jacob said as he lit a huge cigar.

My look of being in a complete fog must've been obvious. I was clueless about any of their programs and, judging by the way my two compadres smiled at me, they noticed it immediately.

"Jacob, I will now vouch for my friend. Lewis rode with General Mosby for two years and has the intelligence and tenacity to help see our plan through. I must also credit him with taking care of our Port

Tobacco problem," Booth said.

"Lewis, I am impressed. Your handling of the fisherman was just what we need to deter others who refuse to take us seriously, on our side and the enemies'. My compliments." Jacob raised his glass and tipped it my way. "Now that you are a Knight of our Golden Circle I feel I can tell you our plans. My partner, one Clement Claiborne Clay, and I have combined our resources to raise an army that we will need to back our stratagem. There are thousands of our troops detained at Union prisoner camps in Michigan and Ohio. We plan to liberate them as security there has loosened somewhat in anticipation an early end of this wretched war. We will see to their transport back to the South, their re-arming and training for our move against Mexico and Central America. What say you so far?"

My first instinct was to tell this man he was absolutely and positively batshit crazy, but that seemed a bit harsh. I knew this would cost a lot of green, so I formed my reply with that in mind.

"Sir, it has been my experience with General Mosby that plans are made in the mind but completed through the purse. Clothes, food, armaments and the convincing of Union camp guards to look the other way will be expensive. Mosby was never afraid to *grease* the wheels of progress and, as you well know, his wagon ran smoothly. That would be my only concern."

"Would it ease your mind if I was to tell you that at the end of business today we will have six hundred thousand dollars to our credit?" Jacob said.

If my eyes had gotten any bigger they would've popped right out of my head. $600,000 was, in 1865, like millions in twenty-first century money. My Pap always told a braggart to never let his mouth write a check his ass couldn't cash, but that didn't apply here.

"That surely does amaze me, Mr. Thompson," I said with a tone of respect. "A lot of mountains can be moved with that kind of push.

Exactly what prison camp are you planning to liberate, if I may be so bold as to ask?"

Thompson looked over at Booth with the wide-eyed expression that I took meant, "Can I trust this man totally?"

"Jacob, I believe in Lewis. I have seen him at work and been told tales of his exploits. You can speak your mind."

Jacob re-lit his cigar, took a long drink from his bourbon cup, and addressed me.

"Lewis, have you ever heard of Camp Chase?"

Think quickly, RJ, I thought. *Its Civil war history, you know this, it's in Ohio. That's it, a POW camp.*

"Yes, sir, I have heard of it, the caliber of the detainees and its top-notch security. Why do you ask?"

"Because that will be our primary target. Of the five thousand men around three hundred are officers. They must come out first and quickly, for we have transportation for them down the Ohio River and then the Mississippi all the way to Alabama. What we desperately need is an operative inside the camp. Someone who can be convinced to look the other way while fifty of our finest and brightest warriors flee unencumbered."

"Judging by your presentation, sir, I assume you have someone in mind." I said.

"We do." Jacob slid a letter-size, leather folder my way. "This is his dossier. Examine it and share your thoughts."

Right now, I thought, *is the time for you to think like a highwayman, even if you detest it. Look it over once ... no, twice, and make a believable response.*

His name was Ashael Fleetwood. His picture showed a man of forty to forty-five years of age, with dark hair and a full beard. Dressed in a Union officer's best blues, he had the aura of a tough and no-nonsense man. Yet, I knew all men have a weakness they can't control.

"Mr. Thompson, for appearances sake I'd say this man would be a tough nut to crack unless, of course, he has a need that requires fulfillment."

John and Jacob looked at each other and smiled. I assumed I'd past the first test, but I knew there'd be more.

"Very astute of you, young man," Jacob said. "Read on."

Down close to the bottom of page one I saw Mr. Fleetwood's "financial report". He, his wife, and three children lived in a two-room log cabin about a mile from the camp. Being head of security, I knew he made good money plus whatever he could extort from the POW's. Something was amiss. At the beginning of page two I saw he frequented a tavern called the Lighthouse. If beer and spirits were served then so was poker and blackjack.

"Mr. Thompson," I asked as I close the folder. "How far is this man in debt to a loan shark?"

"Last count was six hundred and fifty dollars, which is a sizeable sum for his class. He may or may not ever be able to pay it off."

"Oh, I think he will. If the price is right," I said.

"You are surmising that he will come close to treason for sheer monetary gain. How can you be so sure?" Jacob asked.

RJ, use a line from the Godfather. It won't become the standard for over a hundred years.

"I will make him an offer he cannot refuse. Just give me a voucher for no more than a thousand dollars, and I will reason with the man. Trust me, I know his kind."

Booth nodded in approval and Jacob took out his wallet. He counted the money in small bills, put it in an envelope, and slid it across the table. I put it in my inner coat pocket and took a large gulp of coffee.

"Rest assured I will accomplish this. Is there a timeline?" I asked.

"The arrangement can be confirmed any day you wish. Mr. Booth will then coordinate a day of reckoning for the sinful three who are responsible for this whole abomination. We should begin our strike to coincide with that. Now, if there is nothing else I have business to attend to in town. I bid you a good day."

Jacob rose, gave a small but curt bow to both of us and disappeared into the fray. We sat there silent, finishing our coffee and then filling our glasses with bourbon. Booth seemed quite at ease with this man but he *was* an actor and they're hard to read. I knew then, after my second swig of what I wished was good, old-fashioned Jim Beam, I'd met a bonafide mad man. I'd do his and Booth's bidding because I knew the war would be over before their plan could materialize.

-2-

Thursday, February 16th, 1865

The trip from Toronto to Columbus, Ohio took the better part of a day, with stops in Detroit Michigan, into Ohio's Toledo, Findlay, Delaware and then the National Road Station in Columbus. We acquired rooms at the Rail Way hotel and made ourselves comfortable. As we ate a scrumptious supper, I watched our waiter at work. He was a young man in his early twenties, tall and as clean-shaven as me. He walked with a noticeable limp and struck me as the informative type who could use the extra money. As he figured our tab, I laid a ten-dollar bill on the table.

"What on earth are you doing?" Booth asked me.

"Accurate information comes at a price, my friend. Observe."

As he laid our tab on the table, he eyeballed the ten spot. I asked him his name.

"Homer, sir. Homer van Dorn."

"Now Homer," I began. "You look like an enterprising young

man. I was wondering where, in this neck of the woods, a man could find a decent brand of spirits, a good poker game and maybe some sportin' ladies."

"Well now, I'll tell ya'. There are several places where a man could whet his whistle—and anything else for that matter—right down the road from here. The locals know it as the Lighthouse, and ifin' you caint find what you desire there, then it ain't invented yet."

"A man could play five card stud all night?"

"Absolutely. I play a hand or two myself now and again. Done all right most of the time."

Then I went with the pitch.

"My friend and I have heard—through the grapevine, of course— that there is a man who plays there quite often and he is one to watch. They say he's hard to beat."

"What be his name?" Homer asked.

"Ashael Fleetwood."

I believe poor Homer had to bite a whole in his lip to keep from laughing. "Well, sir, I do not know who sold you that load of horseshit, but he should be hung for tellin' a whopper that big. The poor man keeps getting cleaned out every Friday and Saturday night, and it is a damn shame too."

"Why is that?" I asked.

"'Cause he has got a loving wife—a good Christian woman to boot—and three youngin's who are half starved and shoeless most of the time. Ifin it wasn't for the ladies at our Baptist Church, they would all be passed on or put in a pauper's home. Now, if you are wantin' to make a lot of money—and your conscience ain't an issue—then he is the man you want. Good 'nuff?"

"That will do fine, Homer. When we leave here do I go left or right?" I asked as I slid two singles his way.

"Hang a right and just follow the smell."

And to think I paid twelve dollars to hear that.

Aw … horseshit!

-3-

Dark of night

In my younger days, I frequented an out-of-the-way biker's bar where the bad boys would hang, and they nick-named the place "Ptomaine Tommie's". The Lighthouse was a step or two below that, and my dinner told me to keep this as brief as possible. Ashael wasn't hard to find. He nursed a beer in the corner looking forlorn. I took it he'd just lost all his money and I was about to make his day. I strolled slowly over to him.

"Why the sad face, pardner?" I asked.

"Who is asking?" he answered in a smartass manner.

"Someone who may solve all your problems." I sat down.

"Now, stranger, how the hell are you gonna solve my problems? Who are you anyway?"

"Well, sir, I can tell you I am a terrible poker player. Let's go a few hands and I will show you."

I pulled a deck off an unused table, shuffled them clumsily and offered him a cut. He smiled as if he'd found a sucker and split it three times. I laid a twenty-dollar bill in the middle, dealt five apiece and awaited his reply.

"I caint play you mister. I am broke."

"Not to worry, Ashael, not to worry. You will not be penniless for long. Check your cards."

He looked them over and gave the appearance of a man with only a pair of twos.

"How do you know my name?"

"I know a lot about you, *Captain* Fleetwood. Enough to know you need a change of luck. I fold."

His look of astonishment told me I had his attention. He showed me his winning hand; a pair of threes. He dragged the money over.

"Let us play one more hand. You deal," I said as I leaned back and folded my arms.

He shuffled them like a Las Vegas pro, offered me a cut and I tapped the table (a pass). He dealt quickly and I put forty dollars in the pot. He looked at me funny for a second, and then put his only Jackson in with mine. As soon as he checked his cards I laid mine down.

"I give up."

He now had sixty bucks. The hardened soldier leaned back and thought for a moment, then spoke his mind.

"What are you up to? This ain't making any sense," he said quietly.

"It will if you follow me outside. I have a proposition for you."

To my surprise, the desperate man walked out with me, not knowing if I was a serial killer or a Methodist minister.

Chapter 14
The Uncommon Clay

We moved from the front of the bar to an alley. Ashael followed me, but at a slight distance. As a military man, he sensed a possible trap and was ready to react. I turned to him slowly, withdrew my pistol and handed it to him with the barrel down, grip first.

"What is this?" he asked, a little dumbfounded.

"It is a sign that I mean you no immediate harm. Maybe now we can talk as one man to another."

"I'm listening." He flipped the business end of the firearm towards me.

"I will make this as brief as possible, sir. You have a debt that needs paid. I am prepared to relinquish you of that obligation, and then some. All I—and the powerful people that I represent—need from you is your cooperation at a later date."

"What kind of cooperation?"

"On a night to be determined in late March or early April we will require a gate to be opened at Camp Chase. We feel that you are the man best suited for this, and are prepared to pay you handsomely for your effort."

His looked astonished. His posture loosened so much I thought he might pass out, and his hand shook so badly I was ready to duck if he accidentally fired the gun. Yet, he didn't say no.

"Let me get this straight. You want me to allow some or all of those slimy rebels just to walk right out to freedom. Is this what you are telling me?" he said as he raised a hand behind one ear.

"Not all, just fifty selected officers. These men are trained in expert night maneuvers and will be out and long gone before they are missed. All you have to do is look the other way and see to it that your men do the same."

"How much are you prepared to pay for this act of treason?"

"One thousand Union dollars," I said, nonchalantly.

As my gun shook I gently removed it from his loosened grip and put it back in my holster. I awaited his reply, but could see by his REM that his wheels turned.

"I—by the way, what is your name?"

"Mr. Wood will suffice."

"I might entertain this proposal, but I will surely get caught. My Commander is no fool, and will smell this rat immediately. I need reassured that I will not be held accountable, for what good is all this money if I end up at the gallows. I have a wife and children to consider."

And I thought, *Yeah, right dickhead. If you were thinking just about them you wouldn't be in a mess like this. Try to be diplomatic with this doucebag, even if it hurts.*

"Then, sir, let us reason together. Our people will cause a diversion; a fire, or a fight. It will start at the end farthest from the escape way. Our side will be blamed for it all, and your superiors will be none the wiser. Will this suffice?"

"That would surely work, but I have not seen any money yet," he said.

I reached inside my coat pocket and gave him the barter. He looked the money roll over, shook his head but put it in his pocket.

We shook hands, I turned and started to walk away.

"Mr. Wood," "Judas" Fleetwood said. "I sense you are a trusting man, but maybe too much. What makes you think I won't pocket this and then not keep up my end of the bargain?"

I turned to him slowly—remembering my past mistake with McGhee—with the best black-eyed look I could muster, told him why I knew he wouldn't renege. Instantly, something biodegradable in him chilled.

And it wasn't his beer.

-2-

On the long ride back to Washington, D.C., a good hour passed before Booth and I spoke of my encounter with Fleetwood. Finally, he broke the ice.

"Tell me, Lewis. How can you be so certain this man will do our bidding?" he asked.

"You remember me saying I would make him an offer he could not refuse?"

"Yes, and I can't wait to hear it."

"I told him that if he did not do what we paid him to do, then I would kill his wife, his children, his dog and burn his house to the ground. I would spare his life though, and he could forever remember why such a calamity befell him. I trust he will do what is planned."

For the first time since I met John Wilkes Booth, I saw a momentary sign of genuine fear. I had him right where I wanted him, so I propped my feet on the seat across from me, pulled my hat over my eyes and took a nice, long nap.

-3-
March 10th, 1865

I spent the next two weeks traveling between Washington and Baltimore frequently, meeting the other financier of this charade. Clement Claiborne Clay was as tall as Thompson and dressed better as he wore a black, three-piece suit, wide black tie tucked under a white shirt collar. His topcoat looked wool, ample for this season, and his hair and beard were long but trimmed. As we entered his room at Surratt's House he stood pompously with his top hat in one hand and the other leaning on a cane. Oh, how I wanted to kick this arrogant piece of shit right square in the ass, but I belayed that because it wasn't enough to break a foot over.

I shook his ice-cold hand as Booth introduced us and I sensed he was as impressed with me as I was with him. We exchanged some small talk and then Clement got right down to business.

"John, I wish for you to assemble your whole team tonight. There is a restaurant not far from the White House that is friendly to us. I have told Mr. Gautier to expect a party of eight at eight o'clock. Can you arrange this?"

"... Eight? I have only five men currently enrolled, including myself," Booth said.

"Yes, but I am sending you three more trusted men. Jacob and I feel that eight total will be what you will need to be successful. John Wilkes, you do see the wisdom in our choice, do you not?"

Clay looked Booth square in the eyes, not blinking nor moving off target. Clay was the real top dog in this insanity and would replace the assumed leader in a heartbeat. I was impressed, for some strange reason.

With that, the meeting abruptly ended.

As we walked quietly back to Booth's room I pondered what was going through his mind. *Was he having second thoughts,* I wondered. *He was blind-sided by this change in plans. What would he do now? Would he cross a high-ranking member of the Circle?*

"Lewis, I want you to go to David Parr and have him inform the others of our meeting. He knows Mr. Gautier personally, and will set this up properly."

"Do you want me to tell him about our newcomers?" I asked.

"Absolutely not. That is my cross to bear."

In 2014-speak, my gang would call that a "no-shitter", because I knew I wasn't going to do it.

-4-

The ride to 252 Pennsylvania Avenue was a short one as Booth and I took a horse-drawn cab to the front door. It was a classy-looking brownstone with huge windows in the front and a canopied entrance. The doorman helped us out of the coach and cheap-ass Booth paid the man, adding a fifty-cent tip. I didn't know if that was ample, so I gave the driver another four bits and he rolled away smiling like a teenage boy in a French village during WWII.

I mean all the men were gone off to war, if you get my drift.

***

We assembled in a spacious back room, illuminated by candle-laden wall mounts, chandeliers and several silver holders on the long, dining table. Present were I, Booth, Surratt, Weichmann, Arnold and the three newbies. We milled around with them and Arnold the chattiest. Our little "bourbon social" was quickly interrupted by the sound of slow-moving and deliberately loud boot heels.

In Clay came, as proud as a horny peacock with a two by four stuck up its ass. He looked the room over and said, "Let us be seated."

Clay sat at the head of the table with the rest of us, four on each side. We pulled our chairs up and awaited Caesar's instructions. He lit his fine cigar and looked at each one of us, eye-to-eye. The others seemed to be intimidated by him, but I had a reputation to keep, so I stared at him as long as he stared at me. Truth be known, I found Thompson a likeable type—as crazy as that sounds—but I detested this conceited prick and his ilk because, when the shit hit the fan, men like him were rich enough to flee prosecution in other lands and continue their Illuminati-type Utopia plans in safety.

"Honored gentlemen of the South," Clay stated, "I bid you all my warmest greetings. Tonight, we will plan a military coup and in that we will render inoperative the President, the Vice President, Secretary of State and General Grant. The latter is an option we will explore if things go our way, yet I have no doubt you will complete these tasks as any son of the Confederacy would do. Are we all in agreement?"

I heard eight "ayes", zero "nays".

"Mr. Booth. Have you assigned teams?" Clay asked.

"No, Clement. I was waiting until you present our new members. Then we can assess where best their talents lie and appoint them appropriately."

"Forgive me, I moved too quickly. Mr. Atzerodt, Mr. Herold, Mr. O'Laughlen, please stand."

George Atzerodt was a mean-looking bastard who reeked of whiskey. David Herold seemed to be but a boy amongst a brood of vipers with a strange, wild look about him and Michael O'Laughlen looked as much an assassin as Pee Wee Herman would. They stood in line next to Clay and we shook hands with them, yet I wasn't a bit impressed with these three stooges.

No wonder, I thought, *this plan would fail. Two of these men look scared of their own shadow. The only thing they'll be good for is to rat the rest of us out.*

"Now that we have been properly introduced," Booth said, "Let us regain our seats."

We sat obediently, and I intently studied all of them, trying to figure out who would be the most likely to shed blood. Atzerodt reached for his flask, took a two second swig and I knew then he was out. You can never trust an alcoholic to do anything right. O'Laughlen would follow his partner like a sheep in heat but would fold when the going got tough. Herold ... David Herold was another matter. He sat with a blank stare in his dark, blue eyes that I'd seen many times on the television show "Investigative ID". He had the cold look of the average serial killer, and itched to get this going. Before anyone else grabbed him, I made my move.

"John, I request to be paired with Mr. Herold. I believe we will make a great team."

Booth looked at me and Herold, and smiled.

"Of course, Lewis. I could not have done it better myself. If it is agreeable to Mr. Herold then so be it."

"I could care less who I work with, Mr. Booth. As long as I get to kill at least one of these nigger-lovin' Yankees, I'll be satisfied. You okay with that there Lewis Powell or Paine or Wood or whoever the hell you are?" Herold said like the punk he was.

This was going to be fun, especially when I called him the name his mammy used to.

Chapter 15
Hooray for Belarus

"Well, let me tell you something, *Davey* boy, it is *Mr.* whoever to you! I rode with Mosby for two years and castrated a few piss-ant hooligans like yourself, so if you want to sire any kids as dumb as you then the smart thing for you to do is shut the fuck up and listen," I stated as harshly as I could.

The boy's eyes grew blacker and more threatening as he tried to stare me down, but I was a bit more intense. He caved as Booth leaned over and put his hand on Herold's arm. A gentleman, in this era, never used the "F" word, yet it does have its shock value in all time frames. Just the fact I used it startled everyone. Finally, Clay stomped his cane on the floor and brought the meeting to attention.

"Gentleman! Gentlemen! We will have order. Mr. Powell, I will caution you on your language and presume I will never have to do it again. Mr. Herold, you are new to this affair and I suggest you listen before you speak. And the plan thus far is kidnaping, not outright murder. For this meeting Mr. Booth will fill you in on the details."

I can't speak for Herold, but as for me, I couldn't remember a time when someone told me to shut the hell up so politely. I took notes on that aspect of proper diplomacy. Booth stood with the authority of the average school principle and set the itinerary.

"Tonight, we are gathered to plan, dissect and examine a most perilous mission. After I reveal the operation to you the floor will be open to discussion, and your thoughts will be appreciated. After all, we are not Yankees."

That brought a round of laughter from everyone. Any chance to chastise and make light of anyone north of the Mason-Dixon always brought a round of applause from this crowd. Booth continued.

"I have learned, from my sources at the White House, that on the morning of March 17th Lincoln plans to attend a play at the Soldier's Home on Florida Avenue. The traitor has always visited *his* troops unescorted by police or bodyguards. I, along with one of you, will kidnap him there. At that time, the rest will accost the Vice President and Secretary of State. Those teams will be assigned within the next week. Any questions?"

From the look on Samuel Arnold's face, he itched to provide input and he didn't look a bit happy.

"With all due respect, Mr. Booth, do you actually think we can pull off a plan as dastardly as this? And in broad daylight? Why don't we just run all three of them through and be done with it?"

John Wilkes Booth was not only an accomplished actor, but a great motivator too. His reply showed why he would be the assured Captain of this brood of killers.

"A very good question, Mr. Arnold. If this can be done, and God is with us, then this gang of three will be immensely more valuable to us alive than in their graves. For if it is our intention to slay them, run and hide the rest of our lives then yes, three bullets are all we need. Nonetheless, I do not wish to live like that. My vision—or better I would say my passion—is to stand as their judge before a Confederate Court and show the rest of the world what real free men do to despots. What a glorious day it will be for one—or all of us— when we can pull the lever on the gallows trap door and revel in their last gasps of liberty, just like they have so ruthlessly done to our brothers in arms. My only wish is that all of you will weigh this plan and see the wisdom in it. I rest my case."

And I was thinking, *Now who can argue with that?* For a split second Booth almost had *me* won over, and I knew what a madman he was. Sam Arnold hung his head a little like he mulled the presentation over.

"Mr. Booth," Sam said. "I now see your mind in your plan, and while I cannot speak for these other men, I will yield to your leadership in this, our sacred duty."

From across the table two mighty hands pressed the flesh, a nod was given each, we sat and poured ourselves a drink. I knew then these were men of conviction—however misguided it was—who saw a distinct difference between political assignation and murder. And then I wondered, *If someone had taken a 9 and popped a cap in Hitler's ass after the Munich Conference in 1938, would the world be better off today?*

I pawned that momentary lapse of sanity off to too much bourbon. I drank one more round anyway and drifted off in the amorous thoughts of Baltimore and my sweet Maggie's charms.

-2-
March 12th, 1865 Baltimore

I arrived quietly at the Branson Boarding House around five in the morning. I napped on the train ride up from D.C. and was ready and rearing—if you men know what I mean—to go as I stealthed my way to Maggie's boudoir. She lay, on her right side facing the wall, the vision of loveliness and femininity that I'd left. I quietly disrobed, took my boots and socks off, and crawled under the covers, caressing her form until we were the appearance of two, human spoons. I rested my cold feet against her toasty ones, and then all hell broke loose.

"*Lewis Thornton Powell!*" she yelled. "What in blue blazes is wrong with you? Did you walk across a frozen pond in your bare feet before you came to my bed? I almost peed my crinolines. Git your artic-feeling butt over there by the stove and take care of those icicles before you return. And do not take all day about it. I really missed you."

So, I did what any horny man worth his salt would do in a situation like this. I stuck my feets in the coal stove.

***

Before taking another chance at getting lost in the throes of passion, I tested the waters; I mean my toes next to hers. That brought a comforting "hmmm" from Maggie. I snuggled my nose against the soft nape of her neck and held it there for maybe three or four seconds and then my love asked a very sincere but untimely question.

"Lewis," she said softly. "Have you any idea what time it is?"

"Ahh … what does my minute hand say?" I replied as I pushed my manhood against her crinoline-clad buttocks.

"*That thing* says you are late. Shall we catch up?" she said, oh so erotically.

"Absolutely."

***

As we lay there basking in the moment I lit a cigar, and to my surprise, Maggie took a hit. Then she said a cup of coffee would really taste good, so I got dressed. When I put my boots on I noticed the crooked angle of a shadow coming in under the front door.

"Who is there?" I yelled.

"What is wrong? Be quiet or you will wake the guests." Maggie said.

"Baby, there was someone outside the door."

"Oh, not to worry. It was probably Beulah. I think she has a crush on you. Whenever you are around she watches you constantly," Maggie said, giggling a little.

"No, no, I doubt it is that. You take cream in your coffee?"

"Cream and two sugars."

"I will not tarry."

***

As soon as I turned the corner, I felt like someone bored a hole in my back. I swung around to find Beulah hiding in a doorway. I knew she'd been eavesdropping on Maggie and me and my temper started to get the best of me.

"Beulah, what the hell do you think you're doing? You ain't supposed to hang around like that. What have you got to say for yourself?"

"I got nothing to say to you Lewis Powell. That is right—I know your name, and I know what you is. You is one of them filthy Johnny Reb spies. I knows you is up to no good and I aim to tell somebody about it. I might even tell the preacher man who stays in 204 that you and that *whore* Maggie have been making indecent and fornacatin' every chance yous get. Just you try and stop me."

All the rearing my parents gave me about violence against a woman went right out the window. How dare she call my Maggie a whore? Without forethought, I raised my hand to her and smacked her hard right across her mouth. She fell against the wall, slinking slowly down to the floor.

"Little girl, don't you *EVER* call Maggie that name again. Do you understand me?"

With a look of terror, she nodded an affirmation. I went down to the kitchen, fixed two cups and returned. I no sooner finished my first cup when there came a hellacious banging on our door. I almost ran to the door thinking the place must be on fire, only to be greeted by a stone-faced Union officer with sergeant's stripes and the look of a hangman.

"Is your name Powell?" he yelled.

If there was ever a time for you to play deaf or dumb or both, it's now RJ. Act like you don't understand English.

"Nada. I understand not much English. I am ...how you say ...a sojourner in your great land. I mean no harm to any citizen."

That act, plus the totally dumbfounded and dumbassed look on my face chilled his approach a bit. Truth is, I'd seen a skit like this on SNL once, so it wasn't an original idea, although this dude had a real gun and I was armed only with my best bullshit. The Sergeant looked over at the two Privates with him.

"I cain't understand a word this shit kicker is saying. Boy," he said as he looked back at me. "What foreign country are you from, or you just from Alabama?"

"I am Belarus. I am here for work on your railroads."

"Is that right? Then why did you just whip the shit outta this young lady?"

"Because, it is a custom in my country. This lady ... how do you say? ... she defamed the voman I love. She called her a 'painted voman' and I must avenge that. I vould not be a man in my country if I did not. In your country, is it not said 'a man must do vhat a man must do'?"

"Yeah, we do. Only we speak the Queen's English here, not that Rousky shit you utter. Lemme see your papers. You do know what paper looks like, Vladimir?"

I handed them over and he looked at it, front and back. "Boy, it says here your name is Lewis Paine. That does *not* sound like anything I have ever heard coming out of your vampire land. How do you explain this?"

"It vas not spelled correctly. My last name is Painezsky," I said, doing my best to keep a straight face.

"Well horseshit. Come on boys, this crackerhead is too damn dumb to spy on anybody." Then he turned to me and got right in my face. "Let me give you some advice, shit-for-brains. You watch your ass."

As they turned to leave I almost told him that'd be hard to do seeing as how I didn't have eyes in the back of my head, but I figured to leave well enough alone. I grabbed two cups of fresh coffee and headed back to warmer greetings.

Chapter 16
Disappointments and Deserters

That perilous day came and went, and only five days remained until our mission formally began. I knew what Booth had schemed would fail but planned on looking shocked and then offer my heartfelt advice that the kidnapping plan would work. On March 17th Booth called us together at the tavern next to Surratt's House for a briefing.

"Gentlemen," Booth said, "I will go to the Soldier's Home and await Lincoln. As soon as he enters the house I will come back and get you. Today is our day. Lewis, you and the others stay here till I return, then we will assign teams."

With that he stomped out and mounted his horse. I ordered a round for everyone and I even spotted Herold one, to gain his confidence and so I could keep an eye on him. After a two-hour wait—and we were all pretty much shit-faced—Booth came back in looking lower than I'd ever seen him. We waited for him to speak.

"Well boys, the no-good sonbitch did not show. He changed his mind and went and talked to a bunch of Indiana soldiers. He slipped through this time, but his luck cannot last forever. Somebody pour me a double."

-2-
March 18th to April 8th

For the next three weeks we planned, we schemed and we got frustrated because Booth's "inside contacts" were about as reliable as an ashtray on a Harley. Every time Booth thought he had it in the bag one or all the marked men weren't where they were supposed to be, which got me to thinking. Maybe sincere people around Lincoln took evasive moves to throw *any* assassin off the track. The fateful shot at Ford's Theatre always struck me as too easy, but maybe it was as Lincoln had more enemies than Booth & Co. One night Samuel Bland approached me.

"Lewis, can we talk privately?" he asked.

"Sure. Outside?"

We stepped into an alley, with drinks in hand. "Lewis, you seem like a level-headed sort at times. Can I share something with you?"

"I am all ears."

"There is this rumor going 'round that the South is close to surrendering. Any man worth his salt can see the fallacy of fighting further. Grant has Lee surrounded at Appomattox, and I've been told—by different sources than Booth's—that Lincoln will pardon everyone after this is over. Have you heard of this?"

Drawing on my knowledge of the future I told him I had.

"If that be the case, one wonders if we should abandon our current course of action and quietly blend into the mix, would it not?"

I pegged Sam as the most cautious in the group and I saw I was right. I couldn't say anything to test my loyalty to Booth, so I tried to sow the seed of futility without getting directly involved. I carefully chose my next words.

"Samuel, I cannot speak to that because I will never surrender. It is my code of living that would prevent me from doing that, but every man has to make his own path in life and reap the rewards of his decisions. If you—and some of the others—are having second thoughts, then by all means vacate this town with all due haste, for your very neck and soul may depend upon it. As for myself, I will stand with Booth to the bloody end, if need be. I hope I have eased your mind, for mine is shut."

Samuel looked at me, then down at the ground. He finished his bourbon and gave me his cup.

"Lewis, please give this back to the bartender. I need some time alone right now. May God have mercy on our souls."

I took the cup and offered him a handshake. He accepted it, turned and walked away. His recompense in this would-be prison time and even though he wasn't in on any of the attacks, his guilt was association with Booth and the failure to report it. I almost felt sorry for the man because he'd gotten caught up in what he thought was a noble cause, but chose to abandon it too late.

-3-

April 11th, 1865

Two days after Lee surrendered to Grant at Appomattox Courthouse, John Wilkes Booth was in a solemn and dark mood. He had but a handful of followers left but he insisted that kidnapping President Lincoln was the best course of action. I knew this wouldn't happen, but there had to be a catalyst in moving Booth to killing him. On this evening Booth and I went to see the President address a crowd from the balcony on the north side of the White House. In this speech, Lincoln discussed his plans for accepting the rebellious states back into the Union. Lincoln also announced that he wanted to see African-Americans given citizenship. Booth seethed at the idea of giving blacks political power, and said what I knew then to be the game changer.

"Lewis, do you know what this means? It means the niggers will have the right to vote. Now, by God, I will run him through. That will be the last speech he will ever make! We must move to Herndon House and finalize our plans."

"Why a new place?" I asked.

"Mary's house is being watched. She need not have anything to do with this. Follow me and I will take you there."

I was closing in on my time to act.

-4-

14 April 1865

On this fateful day, I was surprised by the hard knocks on my hotel door. I ran towards it, pistol in hand concealed under my night clothes and asked who was there.

"It is me, Lewis, David Herold. I have good news that I would rather talk about inside."

I let him in and told him to sit. He was almost out of breath and I thought he'd pass out. I got him a glass of water, told him to drink it and settle down. He did and then composed himself.

"Lewis, John just told me that Lincoln will be at a play tonight at Ford's Theatre. There ain't but four of us left and Booth said the first plan is off as of now, and he ain't changing his mind."

"So ...we are to kill all three tonight?" I asked.

"Yup. We will be rid of those black bastard luvin' Yankees all at once."

Herold expressions were reminiscent of a teenage boy's look at his first car. He really was a sick pup and if anybody deserved the Big Swing it was him. I showed no emotion one way or another and I think that impressed the kid.

"What now, David?"

"John said we all would meet here in your room at eight o'clock tonight."

"Who now is 'all we'?"

"Just you, me, Booth and Atzerodt. We are going down in Confederate history as heroes, Lewis."

"Yeah. It will probably be the longest walk we ever took."

The Afternoon

Seeing as how I'd rather milk king cobras than stay in a room all day with that idiot, I cleaned up and suggested we take a walk down by the White House. On Pennsylvania Avenue was a small theatre by the name of Canterbury Music Hall. What struck my eye was the beautiful woman plastered on the marquee by the name of Mary Gardner. I bought tickets and we sat in the center, front row. When Mary came on the stage my hormones got the best of me and I started some serious flirting with her. Occasionally she looked my way, winked and when her set was over I excused myself, and headed for the dressing rooms.

I don't know how to tell you delicately what happened next. In plain and simple terms, after a few minutes of small talk we became locked in some ferocious fornicatin', as it was called back then. All I can say in my defense is that I left there questioning my purpose in life, my own sanity and whether I was morally up to what I once thought was my noble mission.

Was I any better of a person than my uncle Lewis? He had the morals of a snake and it was all I could do to stop myself from hopping a train back to Richmond, find the rubble of the house where I first stayed and plead for Rabbi Endras to take me back to 2014. As Herold and I walked back to our hotel I decided to try one more time to do what I came here to do.

Eight o'clock p.m.

Right on the hour Booth and George Atzerodt knocked. They came in with blood in Booth's eyes and bourbon on George's breath. Booth got right with the program.

"Lewis, you and David go to Seward's home. Take this little package with you and tell anyone guarding him that it is his new medicine as ordered by his doctor. Whatever happens after that *do not* leave him alive. George, you must sneak into the White House and kill Johnson by any means necessary. Do all this as close to ten tonight as you can, and then make your way separately as deeply into Virginia as you dare. There will be an intense manhunt, but if my plan goes accordingly then it will be split three ways. Do we have an understanding?"

We nodded in agreement and everyone knew Booth was going to kill the President, but I wanted him to say it out loud.

"What are your plans, John Wilkes, and why ten o'clock?" I asked.

"I know the play he and his wife will watch. Sometime between ten and quarter past that hour the band will perform a crescendo with symbols being struck several times. At that moment, I will shoot Lincoln and then escape to the horse I will have tied up behind the theater. By the time this tribulation hits home they will be so slow to organize we can make a clean escape. Are we together in this?"

We gave him the "all for one and one for all" head nods and he and Atzerodt left. It was just me and Herold again and the way he paced got on my nerves; because I only had one left.

"David," I said forcefully. "Sit down and relax. We have a little time to plan first."

"I gotta go take a shit—do you mind?"

"No, not at all. Better for you to do it here than in your pants later."

He looked like he was going to strike me but I pinned his skinny little ass against the wall and put my right kneecap against his balls. "You listen to me you little shit. I call the shots on this job and you obey. *You understand me?*"

"Yeah, yeah," he squeaked out in a high-pitched tone. "I really do need to relieve myself. I'll be right back."

I let the turd go and went about my business. Ten minutes went by, then fifteen and I got a bad feeling about this situation. I grabbed my coat, hat, the box Booth gave me and ran down to the outside privys. I checked each door with gun in hand, which caused one man to really shit his pants. The little bastard was nowhere to be found and I ran to the Hotel's front hitching post and found his horse gone. I didn't hesitate, but mounted my steed and flew to Seward's house.

If I was to set my families' legacy straight, I had to beat Herold there before he drew blood.

Chapter 17
Overreaching

Washington D.C., at this time, was a very well-lit city with tall, coal gas fired lanterns on each corner. I needed the help because I was low-riding towards Layette Square where Seward lived. A few weeks before he 'd been badly hurt in a carriage accident, was bed ridden at his home and the newspapers reported it; the dummies. Seward's house was a large, two-story Victorian with a hitching post outside for people's horses. Herold's steed wasn't there, but I thought maybe he parked in back so I slinked around but found nothing.

Good, I thought. *I beat him here. Maybe I can make this right after all.*

I announced myself by tapping the large, lion-headed door knocker in the middle of the huge, oak door. A well-dressed black man in a butler's suit met me and asked me my business.

"I have some extra medicine for the Secretary, sir, as per his doctor's orders," I said.

"Medicine? Well, Doctor Verdi just left here 'bout an hour ago. He failed to tell me 'bout any new alchemys," he said with a hint of doubt.

"What be your Christian name, friend?" I asked.

"Well, sir, they call me William Isaiah Bell, plain and simple."

"It is like this, Mr. Bell. I am a delivery boy, just a cog in the sternwheel of life. If I do not get this to Mr. Seward I could lose my position. You do not wish that upon me, do you sir?"

"I suppose not. C'mon in and go up those stairs right there. Be quick about it. Mr. Seward is a fairly troubled man."

"I shan't tarry, and thank you."

I walked up the thirteen steps—and I have no idea why I counted them—to find a tall man standing on the landing in his night clothes.

"Halt! Who goes there?" he stated.

"I have some pain-relieving medicine from Doctor Verdi. He said to give it to Mr. Seward personally."

"Sir, you do not look like a man of medicine to me. I am Frederick, Mr. Seward's son. I will give it to him."

"If you give him too much it may kill him. Doctor Verdi said specifically for me to do—"

That sneaky little weasel Herold tried to slip behind us by crouching low against the wall. He had a long, bowie knife. I pulled my pistol and aimed over Freddy's shoulder to cap the punk before he got to Seward's room and *damn!* ... it misfired again. Immediately Freddy took it personal and thought I shot at him. He grabbed the gun and tried to wrestle it away while throwing wild lefts at my jaw that didn't connect but made me angry. I was trying to save his old man's life. Finally, I got ahold of my gun and with the barrel in my hand I pistol whipped him until he collapsed on the floor. Shocked, and breathing hard, I ran into the open bedroom to see Herold raise the knife to this wretched-looking old man who appeared to be on his death bed. A woman was up against a corner hiding her face and sobbing unmercifully while another man lay bleeding from a severe arm wound. Neither one of them looked up and as Herold was about to deliver his first downward stroke. I jumped on his back and tried to get the knife off him, but he was insane with adrenaline. He stabbed Seward below the rig cage. Blood squirted from the wound and sprayed both of us. This excited the madman even more. He got two more in before I could stop him. He was so much smaller than me that I covered his whole worthless body. His thrusts took my arm down with him. As hard as I tried I couldn't get him to release the man. This was my first time at trying to disarm anybody and I had no idea how hard it would be. Maybe that's why I might have done more damage than good. The weight of my body on top of his had to add to the ferociousness of the attack. I didn't know what else to do and oh God why did you let me try to set this right when I'm just making it worse. I felt like I could throw up … and then Herold collapsed.

As I looked down at the man my anger gave me a surge that I never knew I had. I grabbed the knife from this ruthless little prick and grabbed him by the hair and ass and *threw* him into the hallway. He slowly got up on all fours, gave me a psychotic grin and pulled out another knife and then ran down the steps. I heard him stop and a man scream. I knew he'd struck again. I turned around to see the other people in the room staring a hole in me. The young lady still sobbed and looked at me like I was Satan himself. The man had the look of revenge directed at me. Seeing as how I was so much bigger than Herold they may not have even saw him. Oh Lord in Heaven I couldn't have screwed this up any better if I had trained for it. I dropped my arms and yelled the only thing I could think of.

"I'm going mad! I'm stark raving mad!"

I ran down the steps to see another man with blood gushing from his back. He saw me standing there still with the bloody knife, and tried to mouth the word "Why?" He thought I'd stabbed him in a cowardly fashion. I ran to my horse and dropped the knife in the gutter.

I had to get to the theatre. Maybe, just maybe, I could stop Booth in time.

-2-

Galloping along at high speed I had a revelation. I had no idea where Lincoln took his last breath. I stopped a man and asked.

"Sir," I yelled. "Where is Ford's Theatre?"

"Over on the northwest side of Tenth Street," he answered.

"Please, point to me the way."

He did, and I took off again. I had no idea what time it was but my heart told me it was close to the end for our President. As I came to the Play House that looked like an old church, I dismounted and tied my horse to a post. By the front door were three heavily-armed Union troops. As soon as I walked up they went on the defensive.

"*Halt*" they yelled. "Stop your advance, stranger, and state your business."

I rushed up to the one who looked in charge only to be met by his bayonet. Another soldier pointed a revolver at me and cocked the trigger.

"Sir ... *Sirs*, I must get in to see the President, for he is in dire straits at this moment."

"What does that mean? We do not recognize you. Be still and be gone."

"You do not understand. There is a man who is making his way up the back steps to shoot the President. You must follow me and stop this travesty."

"No one can get to Mr. Lincoln. One of my best men is outside his door. Sargent McCoy is—McCoy, what are you doing down here? Who is guarding the President?"

"I came down to take a piss, Captain. I am gonna go right back ... what the hell was that?"

We heard the muffled but unmistakable sound of gunfire and then screams. I knew what had happened and I hung my head and let my tears slide to the ground. All this planning and scheming and lying had been for naught, and it's a helluva thing on a man when he sees he is a failure, and a total one to boot. I walked away wiping my eyes with my dirty hanky, slowly mounted my horse and headed back to Herndon House.

Knowing I hadn't changed a thing, and knowing my uncle had disappeared for three days after this, I slowly walked up the hotel's service entrance to my room and grabbed the only thing left important to me. If my mission was indeed over, I needed to fill out my journal for whatever reason. I knew I wouldn't erase a thing. My sexploits, my con man act, my misjudgment of Herold and every other seamy detail that showed my misgivings in this era were to stay intact. *Why hide it?* I thought. *Maybe you can find a way so that your family can read it someday. I know Pap would be proud of me just for trying to set things right.* I put on my long, ankle length winter coat to cover my bloody clothes.

I felt the irresistible urge to go back where I started. I needed to go to Richmond.

-3-

I left D.C. train station sometime after midnight and tried to sleep. That was a waste of time and I think I relived the last four months at least three times total, trying to pinpoint where I went wrong. Then I remembered the one thing Rabbi Endras told me.

"The 'Powers That Be' will allow your success if your cause is righteous in nature."

Righteous? I'd been far from that. Hell, I'd outright murdered one man; might as well have killed another. I committed sexual immorality three times and never felt a bit shy about it. As my coach eased to its final stop I knew I had to make my ending acceptable or explainable to someone. I rented a horse and headed for the outhouse where it all began.

***

Long before I got to Uncle Lewis' cabin I smelled it. The stale stench of burnt wood, roasted metal and faint scent of burnt flesh in the damp, morning air. Slowly I rounded the turn to see the cabin's chimney, piles of ashes and trees stripped of bark and leaf. I rode up close enough to see the bleached skeleton of the man I dispatched. Then I had an epiphany.

I dismounted, took two broken branches and fashioned a cross by tying them together with my left bootlace. I took a rock and pounded it into the ground about two paces in back of my smelly ex-time machine, cut my other bootlace in half, strapped up and decided to become a horse thief too. "Sugar" and I meandered back to Washington, sleeping and eating whenever we felt like it. I had one more chance to do the right thing for someone.

Chapter 18
Rope Therapy
April 17th, 1865

Around midnight I crept up to Mrs. Surratt's front door. I knew the
D.C. Police would be there as they suspected her son John from the
onslaught. What a cowardly scumbag John was; to leave town and
stick his mother with this mess. She was automatically deemed guilty
by owning the home where this serpentine cabal had met. I walked
in my bloody clothes, only to meet the same Captain that refused my
attempt to save the President.

"What the hell are you doing here?" he demanded. "Did I not see
you at the theatre entrance? Officers, arrest that man."

I offered no resistance as they turned me and put the cuffs on.
Before I went I had something to say.

"Officers, please hear my plea. This fine woman is of no interest
to you. *I* am guilty of many a crime, but she is blameless in this affair.
I can tell you who the demons are, but we must go outside."

We walked swiftly and silently to a small alley. After a few steps
inside it—and out of sight of any passersby—we stopped abruptly
and I found myself surrounded by angry and impatient men.

"Traitor, what is your name?" the Captain demanded.

"Lewis Paine, sir. My papers are in my inside pocket."

Roughly, one of his men jerked it out and showed it to him. He looked it over.

"Tell me now, Lewis Paine and before God tell me the truth."

"I can only tell you what I know. John Surratt, Mary's son, and an actor named John Wilkes Booth were the ring leaders. The coward Surratt is on his way out of the country; I think Italy. I heard Booth limped off the stage. Is that true?"

"It is."

"Then he travels to Virginia—southern Virginia—probably with a broken leg. He will undoubtedly seek a doctor to have it set, for his pace is greatly diminished," I said.

"Tell me stranger. How do you know these things? Why should I believe you?"

"Because, I have been with them since the onset. I know their minds and what they have discussed in private."

"How did you become privy to their privacy?" he asked.

"Captain," I said with a smile. "Surely you must know that all boarding houses have maintenance hallways behind each outer wall. It is not hard to find a cracked board and bend one's ear to it. I'm sure your own detectives have done as much."

"Is there anymore that you can tell me now?"

"No, other than Mrs. Surratt had nothing at all to do with this."

"That will be for a judge to decide. Off to jail with you and step lively or we shall drag you there."

I kept up their cadence stride for stride, knowing full well that I was only giving up one more person. Herold had his fifteen minutes of fame, and I planned to make him pay dearly for it.

I was taken to jail and then within the hour transported to the Monitor (warship) Saugus. They put me in a four by eight-foot cell complete with a wooden bed—no comforts—and a "slop jar" in lieu of a toilet. It was indeed Spartan, but I didn't need much. All I wanted was privacy and a chance to think about Herold's fate. History—which I found I could not change—had David swinging right alongside me. I wanted him to feel pain before that day. It was then I met a man who would become my best friend.

"Laddie, is there anythin' I can get ye?" he asked in a thick, Scottish accent.

The man was tall, stout with the standard wrap-around beard and moustache of the day. His Yankee-blue uniform complimented his grey hair and beard but his bushy eyebrows were dark brown. His demeanor screamed "no bullshit" but I could see a little heart in his brilliant blue eyes.

"Let us start with the keys to my cell," I answered with a grin, trying to add a little humor to this gloomy day. He didn't get it.

"Anything other than that, rebel?" he stated.

"No, sir, nothing other than that. Can I ask you your name?"

"Me mother christened me one Robert MacMillan, and a fine Christian lass she was. I shall be with you to your very end so let me tell you upfront. You are a guilty man, a man of homicide and anything you say will not carry any weight with I. Do we understand one another?"

"Yes, we do. My Christian name is Lewis Thornton Powell. It is a pleasure to meet you."

"Do not count ye blessings yet, laddie, for you have shed blood and I canit abide that. Save ye energies for the barrister who has the misfortune of representing ye."

"Then when will I be able to talk to him?" I asked.

"He comes up the stairs even as we speak. Look lively ... for as long as that lasts."

-3-

William E. Doster was a short, middle age man of slim build and ever-searching brown eyes. MacMillan usher him in and my military court-appointed lawyer stared at me for the longest time. My jailor brought in a chair and a small desk and proceeded to make himself scarce. Doster laid his briefcase on the table and unsnapped its locks, all the while never releasing his gaze from me. He didn't want to be there and he didn't like me; that was obvious. I stayed silent, not wanting to play his game or back off either. He took his hat off, pulled a familiar-looking book out and dropped it on the table.

"Mr. Payne or Powell or whoever the hell you are, tell me something. What in God's name is this?" he asked as he pointed to my journal.

"Just my thoughts on different things, that's all."

"I've been reading some of this bullshit and I need an answer, and I need it before we go any further."

"Shoot, or is that a poor choice of words?" I replied in a smart-ass manner because I didn't like this uppity prick anyway.

"It will be in a few weeks. Is this your handwriting?"

"It is."

"And I assume it's a first-person narrative?"

"You are smarter than you look, counselor. Why you ask?"

"Then you want the court to believe you are some sort of traveler from the future? Is that what you are telling me?"

"That is the plan," I said confidently.

He closed the lid on his case, snapped it shut and got ready to leave. He tapped on the cell bars and put his hat back on.

"Mr. Powell, the only way I can save your worthless hide is to plead you not guilty by reason of insanity which I can testify to without a shadow of a doubt, for you are the craziest one sonbitch I have ever met. I will be in touch, but do not hold your breath—or is that a poor choice of words?"

"Nah, it fits. One more thing before you go."

"And that is?"

"David Herold. He helped me attack Seward, but he will never own up to it. He is a tough little shit so maybe one of your interrogators can beat it out of him. Maybe make him feel the pain that he has afflicted on others and more than once, I 'magine. Just throwing that out there."

He nodded his head affirmatively, and Mac let him out. I don't know why, but he left my journal there complete with pen and ink. I wasted no time filling in everything to date.

-4-
July 7th, 1865. Five minutes past midnight.

The trials were a sham, the verdicts a foregone conclusion. Mr. Doster—to his credit—did everything possible to save my skin, but to no avail. Our guilty verdicts and punishment—Mary Surratt, David Herold, George Atzerodt and myself—came down on July 6th with our "hanged by the neck until dead" decree to be carried out swiftly the next day.

With but a few hours to write to the people I loved the most, I penned my innermost thoughts to the two ladies of this era who'd shown me the most kindness and understanding. I thanked Adele for her loving and gracious ways and to Maggie I pledged my undying love and passion for the experience of her charms, telling her I would love her always and apologized for bringing her into my wretched and derailed life.

Then, I ran out of ink.

"Mr. MacMillan, might I have a moment?" I asked.

He rose slowly from his wooden chair and walked over with the standard "What the hell do you want?" look on his face.

"Make it simple, laddie," he gruffly said.

"Could you grant a dying man three wishes?"

"Maybe. What may they be?"

"I have one more letter to write and I have run out of ink. Is there any way possible that you could bring me a typewriter and a few sheets of fine paper?"

"And whilst I am at that commission, would you like for me to fetch ye wheel barrel too?"

"What wheel barrel?"

"The one ye carry your balls around in. Ye have a lot of nerve."

It must have been God's will to assign me a jailor with a sense of humor, because I did get a chuckle out of that one.

"No, I will not be needing that but I thank you just the same. I want to write one more letter to my lawyer and I want it to be as legible as possible. My penmanship leaves a lot to be desired," I said, humbly.

"I will see what I can do fer ya. Stay right where you are," he said, with a smile.

At that time, they paid comedians upwards to two dollars an hour in the Big Apple, and I wondered why he wasted his time here.

***

The Collins and Travis contraption he brought me was the weirdest looking thing I'd ever seen. It was shaped like a huge telephone of the 1930's and must have weighed upwards of a hundred pounds.

The paper was thick, cream colored and the edges crisp. He handed it to me quickly and I almost dropped it. I sat down at the table and put in the first sheet carefully and thought how I'd phrase my last testament.

Who do I blame? I thought. *I've got to blame myself and no one else. It was an ill-prepared, half-assed plan and I thought nothing through. Or maybe ... maybe it was not meant to be. Rabbi Endras gave me no guarantees and I stupidly asked for none. I'll address this epilogue to my lawyer in the hopes he'll pass it on as directed. Now I must convince MacMillan to deliver these in secret and pray he'll grant my dying wish.*

***

I carefully folded my last three letters in thirds and walked up to my cell door. Mr. MacMillan sat with his head down and arms crossed. I cleared my throat to get his attention. He looked up but straight ahead and not at me. As the hot, morning sun broke the horizon he spoke.

"Ya' know, laddie, I jest had the strangest dream. I dreamt a small man, dressed in black and wearing some sort of cap on his head, asked me kindly to do what ye are going to ask of me. He said you have two last requests and the Man Above wants me to grant them. You *are* a strange one, Lewis Powell, yet ye have someone special lookin' out for ye. Name your wishes."

"I have three letters here. Two are to the ladies I have loved and I ask you to put them in the next post but please keep this to yourself. There are innocent of any crime but their brief association with me will surely haunt them."

"Aye. I kin do that handily. And the other one?"

"On the outside are directions to a burnt out cabin a mile south of Richmond. One hundred and twenty paces east of that you will find the remains of an outhouse. By it is a cross. I ask that you bury my journal three feet deep in a lead box wrapped in at least three sheets of strong canvas. It will weather many years before it is found."

"How many years?" he asked.

"One hundred and forty-eight."

The look on his face was priceless. If he had any doubts about my insanity, they were long gone.

"I will do this for ye, laddie, but for now ye must get your mind and soul ready. They are coming up the steps, but before they arrive I just wanna shake your hand and tell ye that it has been a pleasure knowing ye. May the Almighty show mercy to you this day."

With that, we shook hands and I saw a tear flow from his strong eyes. As they led the four of us I had a few last thoughts. One was I'd become afraid of time and the misery it can bestow on men, families and nations. And the other was the realization it was time to quit this quest for as fragile and fruitless as it was, my time had run out. Please pray for me. Petition the Good Lord for justice for me and my cause. I did the best I could.

I bid you farewell.

Bio
Tom Rinkes

Tom is a sixty-four-year old, retired truck driver who caught the writing bug in 2010. He's married to the same pretty lady for forty-six years now. Their union has produced two special children and two very special grand-children. He enjoys writing science fiction and especially anything time travel, which he thinks is entirely possible. When not writing, Tom is an avid wood worker who has built everything from end stands to entertainment centers in his basement shop. He lives in a small, farming community in East Central Ohio, where all the neighbor's dogs and cats, when they venture onto the road, have the right of way.

Newly Minted Wings & Salty French Fries
Morgan Cruise Takes Flight

By Lisa Diane Kastner

Morgan spread her feathers and relaxed. The evening breeze cooled her sweaty skin as she balanced on the rustic metal balcony. Pinks and oranges framed Mulholland Drive, which wound downward to the twinkling lights of The Valley. She had hoped her off-peak maiden voyage would be less visible, but she had forgotten about In-N-Out's Two Ton Tuesday Special with half-priced half-pound burgers before 3 PM. She licked the ends of her fingers and noted the distinct taste of sea salt and freshly fried potatoes. She figured if she crashed then she may as well grab a bite on the way down.

For her first attempt, she hadn't flown as badly as she had anticipated. If you don't count losing velocity and clipping impatient bystanders. Her surgeon Dr. Snolten had warned her to wait until the early morning hours, a time in which few Angeleans would be awake. Earlier this same day, after the doctor confirmed the incisions had healed, she bounced off of the examination table eager to try them out.

Dr. Snolten originally came up with the idea for flying humans during his residency days in a Las Vegas hospital. A teenage boy had taken his sister's butterfly Halloween costume and, while high on LSD, jumped off the roof of his parent's rancher and launched toward the Strip ten miles away. Although the patient's pursuit of flight yielded only a broken ankle and bruises, the med student's interest was sparked. Snolten's inspiration was further synergized by his minor studies in ancient histories and mythology. Fravahr the Persian guardian angel, representing a king's divine mandate, sparked the intern's interest. The next day, he refocused his energies from neurosurgery to plastic and reconstructive surgery.

Fast forward to today and after much research, testing, and studies, his vision materialized with Morgan and her quest for differentiation. When she stepped off the examination table during the final stages of recovery, her vocalizations of joy caused concern.

Proud of his work and a tad paranoid as to how the world would perceive his genius, he requested her to be cautious in leveraging her new appendages. She had shushed him the way she quieted other, she smiled and thanked him for his work. She redressed in the specially crafted clothing to accommodate her new appendages and made her way up The Drive to her home.

Morgan practiced yoga to test her new body. Her wingspan reached from one side of the living room to the other, the seafoam blue feather tips just brushing the walls. Using her weakened muscles felt wonderful. She perched atop a table on the balcony. In mid-contemplation she spread her wings, leaned forward, and took flight.

Her heartbeat increased with each second of risk until she fell forward, eyes closed. Only when she didn't hit cement did she open her eyes. The fear in her heart reflected in the discombobulated flapping of her wings. Acknowledging her terror, she used the relaxation techniques the doctor had shown her. She told herself everything was wondrous and wonderful. She slowed her breathing while she reminded herself of life's beauty. She visualized soaring through the sundrenched sky. With those thoughts she opened her eyes and realized the visualizations were true. She found the affirmations in The Valley's panoramic view and mountains. She flapped her right wing more than her left and steered. She tested this method and then tried to increase speed, not much but enough for her primal fear to return. She breathed in deeply and refocused to enter the central place that held serenity. Just as she said, "This is the shit," Dr. Snolten's voice resonated within her, "You shouldn't try this yet. You need more time." She recalled his cautionary words: "Morgan, you won't know how to use them. You could find yourself in predicaments." Predicaments? He had no idea.

Eager to feel her way around town, she launched toward the Hollywood Bowl. Her blue, white and silver tinged wings instinctively followed her mind's guidance. Left here, right there, a little upward. What she hadn't understood was that to save energy, she needed to glide rather than flap. The cramping in her back and shoulders reminded her of this. The muscle spasms began as she climbed higher in the hopes of reaching The Phoenix Bar in West Hollywood in time for the happy hour specials. If she estimated correctly then she had burned more calories in these few minutes than she had burned in three sessions of hot yoga. Her growling stomach and instantaneous decrease in energy meant she better hurry. Her upward mobility ended abruptly as her lackadaisicalness gave way to exhaustion. She tried to flap her wings harder to regain momentum, only resulting in the muscle cramps worsening worsened as she dove downward. In search of a safe place to land, she witnessed the fattened line of burger buyers and headed toward them.

Focused on survival, Morgan forgot that the crowd had never seen a winged woman. The angry outbursts, especially from the gentleman who had purchased the scammed fries, came as a little shock. She caught a burst of wind, swiped the extra-large fries, regained speed and returned to her Hollywood Hills home. Spent from the clunky trip, she collapsed on the balcony and shoved fries into her mouth. Morgan's sheer hunger was greater than she had anticipated. She scoured her kitchen for more, finding low fat Greek yogurt, cleansing drinks, and celery. Morgan gorged herself on the meager dietary findings and then passed out in her living room, to be awakened hours later by messages from the Doc. The room had darkened; the only light provided by her answering machine's flash and the face of her smartphone. She missed the days when her maid would have the house cleaned and organic meals waiting for her. Now she relied on infrequent trips to The Discount Store and Trader Joe's as a treat. She skipped through phone message after message, not ready to discuss her indiscretion (his words, not hers). Peppered in between his messages were others from people trying to confirm if "it" was "her." The one message she returned, albeit via text, was Paul's. His note had been brief.

"In-N-Out - well done. Let's use this."

Her note back:

"Def. Forwarding now."

She reset her answering machine and smartphone to forward all calls to Paul. She massaged her sore muscles and checked the evening news. She eyed her phone and noted the messages popping up from the doc. She swiped left and continued resting.

When she'd first met Dr. Snolten at his office, she thought he was odd. She had returned from an audition in which the casting director implied that the age on her resume didn't match her skin's resiliency. Perhaps trying to pass for twenty-five had been a stretch since her own daughter neared twenty, but her family genes had always been youthful AND the cashier at Trader Joe's requested photo ID whenever she bought Crane Lake red blend wine. Years had passed without winning a role. She needed this.

After the audition, Morgan had immediately called her agent, Paul Gould (his real name was Paul Patchinsky but he changed it to Gould thinking a less Polish, more Jewish-relatable name would give him an edge in entertainment). The two agreed that they needed to come up with something... Something so different, so unique that casting agents couldn't toss her aside. "We need something... you know... Kardashian-esque," Paul said.

He had been with Morgan since her USC days when she sang on downtown Burbank street corners to make enough money to buy ramen. USC's tuition, even with her scholarship, had been a bit much. Morgan waited to finish college after a short run on *Joanie Loves Chachi*. The brief success enabled her to pay off tuition, finish her undergraduate, and give her the visibility to be considered for bigger roles. At the time her success felt like it would never end, especially when she landed her own medical drama *CUT!*, and was featured on the cover of PEOPLE and interviewed by *The TODAY Show*. Before her decline Morgan had been invited to Morgan Freeman's house (unheard of) and even to Brangelina festivities. She had been whisked to award ceremonies and movie premieres. Sultans, kings, and the world's elite invited her to their celebrity filled revelries. Her performance on *CUT!* gained her an Emmy nod. Paul arranged for her to date one of the hottest rockstars, secretly a transsexual who had gone through the transformation from Jane Elite (aka Esfrastic) to Joe Elite, which explained his ability to hit the high range of soprano notes. Joe and Morgan looked amazing together, even if he had no inclination toward her. But no Emmy win and the viciousness of tabloids (in Morgan's case, no attention from the press—a total black out) revealed her public's fickleness. Next thing she knew the only callback Paul managed was from a Lake Tahoe murder mystery dinner theater. Even her personal calls to dear friends resulted in nada. Without the success vote of an Emmy, Joe swiftly found a new love interest.

You'd think she was the only person seen in public with a transsexual. Hell, half of Hollywood were transsexuals, wish they were, or dated/married/was related to a transsexual. Hence the reason she concluded that the lack of an Emmy win was what brought her down. Either that or the stint at the Omni-Mani-Patti (OMP) Chanting and Self-Realization Center. A retreat in the middle of California's less explored hills, Morgan visited for a month after the Emmys. She needed something to ease her aching ego and a month sweating, chanting, and cleansing seemed ideal, especially since the Founder Ompi-man had personally invited her. Unfortunately, not too shortly after Morgan's stay, *60 Minutes* revealed OMP to be a cult with plans for a mass spiked Kool-Aid suicide at the first full moon of 2020. OF COURSE, Morgan adamantly denied being a part of that section of OMP. Heck, when she heard of the plot from one of the OMP leaders, she hightailed it off of the grounds and switched from meditating four times a day to the OMP gods to renewing her interests in hiking, juicing, and mornings filled with Starbucks java shots. No matter the reason for her downward spiral, she had been screwed.

She was amazed how Paul represented her throughout the harder times. Friends disappeared once the public's adoration turned to disillusionment, or rather dispassion. Hate she could stand. Hate meant buzz. But dispassion? That was a death knell. Paul and Morgan spent the subsequent years trying to figure out how to turn that dis into fire.

As luck would have it, her appointment after the less than flattering audition had been with a plastic surgeon from Las Vegas. Morgan's best friend's best friend's acquaintance had suggested Dr. Snolten when Morgan mentioned wanting a little freshening up. Dr. Snolten's address on the fringe of Silver Lake emblazoned "green for go" signs in Morgan's psyche. If she wanted to be up on the latest trends, then a Silver Lake surgeon was the way to go. Plus he took her insurance, and his website said he only worked with organic and non-GMO materials. She parked her vintage Bentley (she'd paid it off and owned it for over a decade) in his office's back lot behind Sunset and straightened her ripped jeans.

Once Morgan expressed her displeasure over her audition and desire for change, Dr. Snolten said, "I hope you don't mind but I want to propose something truly groundbreaking." She assumed he would suggest a modern day Barbie makeover, the antithesis of groundbreaking. More like flat lining. As he dug through his filing cabinet she searched for her car keys. "Ah, this is it." She glanced at his file that outlined the transformational process. Before he could say augmentation surgery or transmogrification, Morgan glanced at the drawings and said, "You're fucking with me."

"Not any wings," he said. "These are functional."

"Functional?" She stared at the pencil drawings with cryptic descriptions and medical terms. Thankfully she had done well in biology and chemistry, plus those years on the medical drama came in handy. "Functional."

He handed her the pages. She skimmed them and looked warily between the file and her new doctor. "Functional?"

"Yes," he said. Maybe this wasn't the best idea. The last patient with whom he shared his secret project (without full screening) called him a nut and reported him to the medical bureau. When the investigators found no evidence, the patient insisted the Doc was crazy. The investigator informed her that the Doc dreaming big didn't make him crazy. Dr. Snolten kept his license, but the former patient went on a rather elaborate social media spree to defame him. That's when he decided to ditch Vegas and start over in the only other city that would value his skills.

The moment Morgan walked into his office, he saw her desperation, smelled her need. If he pitched this to anyone, she was the one. He had been in town for two years and quickly amassed a sizeable clientele due to his uncanny knack for keeping secrets, his preciseness and expediency, and his willingness to provide house calls. Still, Morgan's hesitancy made him wonder if he should move to New Mexico.

"What would they look like?" she asked. She really wanted a cigarette. Heck, even an e-cigarette would be welcomed.

"However you want them to look," he said. "There are some limits. I doubt you want wings three times the size of your body. Your core needs to be able to support the weight of the additional appendages and their affiliated plumage."

"That makes sense," she said. She closed the file and put it on the examining table. She hadn't even changed her clothes for the initial consultation. She figured she'd walk in and ask him how he could make her more youthful. Instead the words, "standout, rejuvenate, and revive" came spewing from her lips. "Can I pick the colors?"

Before committing to the surgery, she dialed Paul and gave him the rundown. "Seriously? He can do this?" Paul asked.

"Trinity Spalling aka Jessica T. Pann recommended him." Morgan replied. Trinity was a world famous actress who had transformed her physical self so dramatically that she went by a new name. Morgan reveled at the possibilities—experience, knowledge, skills, youth. That's why Morgan had gone to the Doc. But this, this was better than decades of eradicated age. When she named Trinity and her alter ego, Jessica T. Pann, Paul's initial response was disbelief until Morgan told him to "Compare Trinity's Oscar-nominated performance in *Heartbreak Island* to Jessica's role in *Less Than Destiny.*"

Upon which he responded, "Holy shit. This is real."

"I'm thinking big, I'm thinking, high-viz, I'm thinking…"

"Taylor Swift," Paul interjected.

They planned out her comeback. She would fly over Taylor Swift's concert at the Hollywood Bowl. She would gracefully float over Taylor singing "Wonderland," hover beside the songstress, then elegantly glide over the audience and back to the safety of her home. The wings a critical component. Morgan anticipated that if her newly minted wings didn't garner the needed career momentum, they would be a great way to make side cash with deliveries, appearances, and the occasional marriage officiant gig. Once the media got hold of the real life angel story then sponsorship offers would roll in. Top on her list: Victoria's Secret and Virgin America. Only apropos since Victoria's Secret had shot her down for their catalog five years ago.

No way they could say no now.

Since the maiden voyage, Morgan's phone hadn't stopped ringing. Paul texted her with "*E!*, *The Today Show*, *LA Times*, *Deadline*. Buzz baby BUZZ. 🐝 🐝 🐝 🔥 ☺ 🔥" Snaps and Instagram posts of the out-of-control woman-bird spread. One clever observer zoomed in on her face and made the connection: The Silver Angel was Morgan Cruise from *Joanie Loves Chachi* and *CUT!*. One person unearthed her lone solo album, "Love ME Now," which hit the *American Top 400* pop charts in the 90s. Morgan didn't think anyone would unearth her past quickly and was flattered that Americans held her close to their hearts. Paul reminded her of the miracles of Google and smartphones, but she preferred to believe in humanity's generosity.

Morgan's mom—the mastermind behind Morgan's original bouts with fame—didn't know about her daughter's latest attempt at rediscovery, so the dozens of emails and calls were a shock. Morgan gently folded her wings behind her and relaxed on her couch, in preparation for the inevitable mother/daughter conversation.

"What did you do?" she Skyped Morgan. Before Morgan could finish the three-minute voicemail, she was interrupted by an incoming video call. Her mom's image appeared. Morgan Cruise the First, also called Ani, was vacationing in Atlantic City. Morgan Junior had done well for the family, while her mother had done well spending from the family accounts.

Ani's black thick straight hair haloed her head. Once suntanned skin now draped darkened and crispy. Her luminous, green and grey flecked eyes bloodshot from too many lemonade vodka martinis. Morgan figured her mother began the morning ritual with Bloody Marys and then graduated to martinis.

"Have you seen the news?" her mother asked.

"I haven't had the chance."

"Is it true?" The question mark punctuated with high-proof spirits.

"Depends on what you mean by true."

"Don't get fresh with me, Morgan Margaret Cruise. You know what I'm talking about." Her mother pointed at the screen as if they were in the same room.

"I needed a change."

"Does Brian know?" Ani said this in a whisper like the way Morgan's grandmother said "masturbation."

"Brian has decided that artistically he needs space so we're on a 'pause.'" Brian Ferdinand had been Morgan's on again off again boyfriend since early 2005. Ani conveniently forgot Brian came out as bi to close friends and family in 1997 and hadn't gone back. Morgan gave her mom a little bit of a break since Brian, true to his nature, came out on national television the morning of 9/11, which ever so slightly overshadowed his major life announcement. Purely to help Morgan through the agonizing conversations with Ani, who to this day swears the pair were meant to be together like Tim McGraw and Faith Hill, Brian agreed to be Morgan's moustache or whatever they called it. Not that Morgan needed a moustache. She needed someone to help field her mother's fantasies about Morgan's life and how she should live it.

"He says that and then he comes to his senses." Ani sipped. "Hopefully this fiasco won't ruin things with you two. I've been getting calls all day trying to confirm it's you."

"Yeah." Morgan looked at her fingernails and noted that she needed a mani-pedi before another sighting. Not that anyone focused on her hands and feet, but she needed to feel polished. "Ani, do me a favor and don't confirm anything yet."

"Why would I do that?"

Because that's what you always do, Morgan thought. Like the

time Morgan was on vacation in Bora Bora to escape the media and masses when Ani showed up with a crew to film the *Morgan Cruise LIVE* documentary. Of course, Ani hosted the special. Or the time Morgan had a 103 fever and her mom insisted she go to the Grammys, as she'd arranged for Morgan and Brian to sit beside The Backstreet Boys. Ani was right behind her within camera shot. Morgan was pretty sure Brian got lucky with one of The Boys, meanwhile she ended up in the emergency room for exhaustion and dehydration.

"I'm serious. I need you to keep your promise."

"Of course." Ani looked to the right of the screen. "Sorry, I gotta go. Robert is calling."

Before Morgan could respond, her mother dropped the call. Ever since Morgan's father had died, Ani had gone wild. Dividing her time between high-profile men and her daughter's career, Ani would always be Ani. This reality hinged on one truth: the world revolved around Ani.

Morgan knew that if she told her mother the truth, and warned her not to share it, Ani would call every single person in the media to spread the news. Ani conveniently forgot how Morgan had dumped her as an agent as soon as she hit legal age. Even after giving her mother official notice, Ani somehow stayed on the scene. Resentment reigned.

Morgan dialed Paul. They had tentatively made arrangements for interviews the following day and Morgan wanted to confirm the plans. She paced her living room, awkwardly bumping into furniture, her feathers caught on corners. Her frustration erupted at Paul, "Are you kidding me? You want me to go where?" with feathers flying.

"Stay with me, Morgan. You know how much people love angels. You'll be great!"

"We're not talking Macy's Thanksgiving Day Parade. We're talking Christmas Village in La Cienaga. Have you watched the news? Have you seen the coverage? I'm everywhere."

"Which is why you need to start making appearances. Nicole said…"

Morgan's new publicist Nicole Newman had worked with her for a month, and had the reputation of finding clients on Craigslist.

"Are you kidding me? You're listening to that snot-nosed wannabe."

"She got Karine a guest on *Ellen*."

"For less than a minute. She brought in pizzas for the audience."

"Still. Consider it, okay?"

Morgan hung up the phone. In the darkness of the 8,000 square foot modern Mexican rancho style home, scattered feathers glowed in the evening light. She needed to call her assistant to clean this up. But first, time to call La Familia grocery around the corner and order Ben & Jerry's Peanut Buttah Cookie Core. During the seminal flight, her jeans nearly fell off. She needed to (happily) rethink her grocery shopping strategy.

The last of the peanut butter smudged on the sides of her mouth, Morgan slept deeper and with greater happiness than she could remember.

The Angel and the Journalist

The abrasive sound became overshadowed by the pain of Morgan's attempt to reach over and click the alarm clock's snooze button. She cried out as she draped her arm over the antiquated hardware and slammed her palm down. Now was the time to switch to using her smartphone's alarm. Less effort to turn it off and more sound options. Morgan lay on her stomach and slowly tested each muscle to find the least painful way to get out of bed. She decided to roll onto the floor, that way she didn't need to use her arms and legs.

With a thud and a gasp, she looked around the room for her smartphone. Sadly, she'd left it in the bathroom next to her toothbrush. She took a deep breath and got up on her knees and then shimmied to the tiles and made it to the toilet. Thankfully, she kept Percocet from the last time she had gone to a doctor for a recharge. She downed two and dialed Paul.

"Reschedule."

"Have you lost your mind? We can't reschedule."

"Paul, I can't go out like this. We need to reschedule."

"What? You molting or something? I'll come get you. We'll go to Joan's on Third for old times' sake."

"You're not listening." Morgan stretched, which provided relief and proof that muscles don't like being used in such an aggressive manner as flying without preparation. "I can't even walk."

"Is this permanent?"

"No. At least I don't think so. I overdid it yesterday. I'll be fine. Just not today."

"I'll be right there."

Morgan protested as he ended the call. She wanted a day to recoup—alone. Dr. Snolten had warned her that the initial flights may be challenging, but she never imagined that her entire body would hurt. This pain reminded her of training for *CUT!* when she had a fight scene and the producers sent her to this hyper-aggressive kickboxing coach. Four hours a day this coach had her punch, kick, run, and use muscles she never knew she had. The next morning she had a very similar reaction. A little surprising considering this time she only flew for a half hour max. Crap, what would a full flight be like?

She heard the jingling of keys in the front door. Paul knew where the spare set had been hidden.

"If you keep showing up like this, people will start talking."

He found Morgan in the bathroom, her back bruised, hunched over. The look of it made him wince. But he had to give this doctor credit, those wings looked like she had been born with them.

"Isn't that the point?" He put one arm underneath her and supported her back to the bed. At least she could walk over with support, albeit her feet dragged. "This is a bit wackier of an idea than most of your ideas, but I never thought I'd find you like this."

"Ha. Ha." She leaned against the headrest and Paul covered her with a lavender down comforter. "I'll be fine by tomorrow."

"Are you sure about that?" He went into the bathroom and got her a glass of water. "Maybe you should call this Doc?"

Morgan was still avoiding Dr. Snolten. He had been exact in his physical therapy recommendation. Days one through three: no flight, only light lifting (less than five pounds) and stretches. Day four: she could hover over the flooring. He gave her recommended exercises for her wings and arms to grow strength. After the fourth day, she was supposed to do the appendage exercises every day, gradually increasing in time and complexity.

Morgan picked up the phone and dialed the familiar number.

"How do you feel?" Dr. Snolten asked. No "hello." No "what were you thinking?"

She described her escapades and the resulting challenges.

"Take a hot bath to relax your muscles. I'll call in a prescription for muscle relaxers and painkillers. Morgan—I need you to listen to me this time. Do not fly at least until I have a chance to do a thorough examination."

"I'm a little sore—"

"I need to see the extent of the damage. I'll be over this afternoon." The call ended.

"Is he serious?" Paul asked.

"You said to call him."

"We agreed to an exclusive with the LA Times and they specified today. TODAY, Morgan. Not tomorrow. Not next week. Not next month. TODAY."

"You are seriously overreacting. We can do the interview."

Paul plopped at the end of the bed. "Let me put it this way—if they want an interview, then that means they'll want proof and the only proof is a sample flight."

"Right."

"Right." Paul eyeballed her bruises. "We could still pull this off. A little body make up."

"Paul. You heard him. No flying."

"You yourself said that you needed to glide. So, take a glide down Mulholland, meet the Times interviewer and then I'll drive you back. No fuss. No muss."

The tiredness in her body increased just thinking about it. The Percocet hadn't kicked in, at least not fully.

"I'll do the interview. I'll even show the wings but I'm not flying. I'm not gliding. None of that."

Morgan knew this was a long shot. She feared ending up in the hospital and trying to explain what was wrong. Plus, who knew if the emergency room doctors would know how to treat her? Most likely the answer was no.

"Fine. Interview. No fly in. Show wings. Fine." He swiped on his phone and started talking. By the time he finished, he had reconfirmed the interview for 1 PM at the Nancy Hoover Pohl Overlook. "I gotta tell you, they sounded eager to see you in action."

"That can be interview number two." She didn't tell him that she doubted she could fly if she wanted. She felt the weight of the Percocet hit her, her muscles relaxed while the room became calm and dark.

She awoke to an achy bod. Paul lounged in the living room. "Didn't know if you'd wake up."

She eased into the room and took a seat next to him. "Thanks for staying."

"I took the liberty of grocery shopping. Nothing much, but something." In the kitchen she found Jiffy peanut butter, white bread, and jam. Freezer: store brand ice cream.

"What about organic? I can't eat this." Her stomach reminded her that *yes, she could.*

"After we land that first deal, then I'll gladly fill your entire kitchen with organic, non-GMO, Superstar fare. Until then, I'm happy to make you a peanut butter sandwich."

"It's okay I've got it covered." The white bread smelled sugary sweet. She spread a piece with peanut butter and shoved it in her mouth.

"You better hurry. We only have an hour before your interview." Paul clicked on the television to find grainy clips of Morgan in flight, Morgan crashing through a crowd, Morgan nabbing a handful of fries, and Paul's favorite—Morgan regaining stability and flying into The Hills.

"Holy crap." Morgan said through a mouthful of sandwich. "I'm lucky that guy didn't sue me."

"Yeah, well. We can talk about that later. First, let's get you in the shower."

Morgan stepped out to find a blushing Paul in the entryway of her bedroom. The strong sent of patchouli clung to the air.

"What? This isn't the first time you've seen me in a towel. Hell you've seen me—"

"They're here." Paul said this in a near whisper. Morgan swore she heard him incorrectly.

"What do you mean?"

With greater vocal projection, Paul said, "I knew you'd be eager to talk to Belinda."

"Belinda? You've got to be kidding me. Why did you set up the interview with her?" Morgan and Belinda McDonald had been on *The Happy Time Children's Show* together. They played best friends, which was true until Belinda stole THE role in a Steven Spielberg film that had been created for Morgan. "I'm not feeling well." Morgan stormed into the kitchen (as best she could), grabbed the vodka from the freezer, went into her bathroom and slammed the door. She sure as hell wasn't going to give that stinking hippie bitch the interview of a lifetime. Hell to the no.

Paul banged on her door. "Morgan. You wanted buzz this will get you even more buzz. Think about it! Two childhood enemies meet for the first time since their falling out? One an angel and the other a reporter. Come on. This could be huge."

She sat on the toilet lid and gnawed on her fingernails. She swallowed two more Percocet, as a precaution, and a shot of vodka. This news called for two shots.

Morgan came out of the bathroom with full make up and wearing a lightly shimmering, flesh toned shift dress that had been altered so she could fit it over her wings. She even tossed on a slightly heeled pair of sandals, finishing the long-legged look. "I'm only talking to her because this is the LA Times. And she only has fifteen minutes."

Paul raced to prep Belinda and her crew. Morgan was doing Belinda a favor. After the Spielberg film bombed—the only Spielberg film that truly bombed—Belinda couldn't attract a speeding ticket. On television Belinda came across as a quirky, bright kid. On film, she became a bratty, know-it-all, awkward child. And not in an 80s nerd kind of way. More in a "Who-the-hell-picked-this-kid?" way. She disappeared from the film industry and popped back up a few years ago as a beat reporter for the Orange County Register, and then graduated to the LA Times. Admittedly, she has a knack for unearthing great stories.

Morgan entered her living room to find Belinda overlooking the balcony and no one else in sight. You've got to be kidding, Morgan thought. The least she could have done was bring a photographer. That's fine, Morgan would send her own shots to accompany the article.

"Belinda." Morgan stood in the doorframe, sure to pose in such a way that the lighting hit her just right. Her childhood friend and former confidant turned, and for a split second Morgan noted the sourness behind Belinda's faux smile. She hadn't changed much in thirty years. No more braces and glasses but her dour face, awkward stance, and air of precaution preempted any other physical statement.

"You look great for someone who scared the hell out of half of LA yesterday. Is this where you took off?" Belinda looked over the balcony to the tree tops and houses below. "Pretty convenient."

"I hear you are with the LA Times now."

"Yeah. They seem to enjoy my work. You?"

"Well, you know."

"Right. Shall we?"

Morgan motioned toward the couch and readied to sit opposite Belinda.

"Before we begin, do you mind if I take a gander? Always good to confirm before we start."

Morgan slowly twirled so Belinda got the full view. Morgan even lightly spread the tips, to give the hint of her true wingspan.

"Impressive. Do you mind if I touch?"

"Maybe later," Morgan blurted. She didn't want to be in the same room with this woman let alone be touched. "Would you like a glass of water?"

"Paul is handling that but thank you." Belinda pressed a button on her phone and sat down. "I hope you don't mind me taping this. I figured you're used to it by now."

"Of course."

"I have to ask the questions everyone is asking—why and how."

Morgan had rehearsed with Dr. Snolten a story about going away to Eastern Asia and finding a medical practitioner specializing in spiritual reawakening through physical augmentation. A little heavy for Morgan's tastes, but the public would lap it up.

"How'd you get back here so fast?" Belinda in her natural state was a cynic. Not surprising she'd make this harder.

"I signed an NDA with the doctor to not discuss the operation. I can tell you that when he and I met, I knew this was my true path."

"Right." Belinda got up and paced the room then stopped,

leaning close in front of Morgan's face. "Cut the bullshit. You haven't had a decent gig in ten years and I'm being generous. This is a ploy isn't it? You didn't fly. You had some wires or device that made it look like you flew." Belinda yanked on Morgan's wings. "Obvious fakes."

Morgan did everything she could not to scream. "Get off of me." She shoved Belinda away. "You call molesting your interviewee professional? Have you lost your mind?"

Paul ran into the living room, spilling red wine and ice water on the carpet. "What happened?"

"I knew you were desperate, but this? You thought people would believe this crap?" Belinda ripped out a handful of feathers leaving trails of blood. Morgan's kickboxing defense training kicked in and she punched Belinda squarely in the jaw.

"Look who's talking about desperate? You can't even get a staff job. When's the last time anyone called you? Never?"

Knocked on the floor and holding her jaw, Belinda responded, "at least Steven had the sense to pick me." (Belinda later realized that this wasn't the best response considering the situation.)

"You stole that from me and you know it." Morgan flew, full wingspan forward and hands arched like talons. Adrenaline and booze fueled, Morgan wildly punched her nemesis. "How dare you come into my house!"

Belinda fought back as best she could. Her real weapons the smartphone and pen. Paul raced to the fighting duo and with difficulty pulled Morgan off of Belinda. He hadn't anticipated Morgan's strength nor the power of her new wings. With the tips she pushed him away like a mere playtoy. He eventually went under her wings and grabbed Morgan by her torso causing her to lose balance and topple to the side. "Morgan, stop this."

At first Morgan fought to return to the battle. How dare this traitor come into her home and make such accusations. This bitch would see the true power of her enemy. She clawed at Belinda and then made the error of glimpsing at Paul as he tried to calm her. She had never felt such fright and concern from him. Maybe she had taken things too far. She looked over to see a terrified Belinda with a banged up face, covered in blood, and fists full of feathers. Morgan tossed Belinda aside and shook off Paul.

"Interview over."

Morgan's House Call

"Come over now," Paul gasped into the phone. "I don't know what happened. She passed out."

Paul dragged Morgan into her bedroom and covered her with a faux shearling blanket. He feared tucking her because he couldn't tell how much damage she had taken. He called 911 and requested an ambulance. "There's been a violent domestic fight and the perpetrator needs to be taken away immediately," he told the 911 operator. From the living room, he heard Belinda grumbling. Time for damage control.

He flew open the bedroom door and found her limping through the front door, clutching her backpack. Bloody feathers scattered like petals in her wake, a few stuck to her ironically new vintage jeans.

"Belinda. Wait! You can't leave. I called for an ambulance. You need to be looked at." Paul raced behind her and tried to get her to stop. "Please, wait."

Belinda turned on him. "Are you kidding me? She's fucking insane!" Belinda's face bright red, covered in scratches and blotted with blood, her clothes in shreds, her response wasn't surprising.

"She had a rough day that's all. Give her a few days to recuperate and we can do this again."

Determined to get out before anything else happened, Belinda pushed forward and made it to her Prius. She didn't care what Paul wanted. He's the one who insisted the interview happen at Morgan's home. Instinctively she knew this was a bad idea. She should have listened to her intuition. She fumbled for her keys. "I'm not going anywhere near her. She's worse than before."

As Paul reached Belinda, he confirmed she was running on adrenaline. If his assumptions were correct, and oftentimes they were, she'd better rest before she crashed. The peaked look that glossed across her eyes meant it could happen any moment.

"You should sit down. You don't look too well."

She pulled on her car door. Aware of her panicked state, Paul opened it for her. In that moment, the glossed look had spread throughout her body and she nearly dropped to the pavement. He grabbed her by the arm and helped her sit down. "You've been through a lot. You should take a breath."

Belinda hadn't realized her breathing had turned shallow. She clutched her hand to her chest, never letting go of the backpack, and slowed her breathing. From the winding road, the sound of the ambulance's siren came closer along with the LAPD. She eyed Paul with distrust. Why would he want her to be okay other than another ploy to save his beloved Morgan? This said, Belinda felt like shit. Woozy even. Maybe this whole sitting down and waiting a second was a good idea.

Paul waved the ambulance down and guided them to Belinda. Like a crumpled doll, she leaned her head against the cushions, her limbs akimbo except for the one hand that gripped the backpack. Paul knew he needed to get ahold of her smartphone and whatever else may be in that bag, but he also knew that if he went for it she would scream like hell. And that was the last thing he needed. He needed to contain this and get back to Morgan. Seconds later, the LAPD arrived. He greeted them in the driveway.

The officer got out of the car and asked what had happened.

"Domestic fight. Longstanding argument. She came to do an interview with Morgan Cruise and well... You see what happened." Paul motioned to Belinda who was being treated by the medics.

"Where's the other one?"

"She's inside. I want this documented. That one's been after Morgan for years. She was supposed to do a story about Morgan's comeback and started a brawl. You should see the mess inside."

"Yes, we should." The officer walked into Morgan's home to find flung and overturned furniture, shattered glass, blood spatter. "Feathers?"

"This," Paul showed him one of the YouTube videos on his phone. "Remember, comeback."

"Oh yeah. My daughter showed me that. Can we see Ms. Cruise?"

"She's unconscious. I've already called her personal physician."

"And you are?"

"I'm Paul Gould, Morgan's manager and fiancé." He couldn't resist the last part. All the more to feed the headlines. "You're welcomed to look in on her."

He guided the officers into the bedroom and then within seconds they came back out. "You said you called her doctor?"

"He's on his way now."

Paul filled out the paperwork and came outside to find Belinda being loaded into the ambulance. She glared at Paul with pure fury.

"Officers, I want to be sure Morgan is safe and do what's best for Belinda. I'll file for a restraining order in the morning."

The medic tried to take away the backpack but she refused and clutched it closer. "Please take good care of her," he said to the medics. "She's been through a lot today." Paul figured they must have given her some good meds because by now he thought she would have jumped him. Can't say he didn't blame her.

The police rode off behind the ambulance. Paul imagined they would get Belinda's side of the story, which was perfect. More fuel for the media machine.

As soon as the ambulance and LAPD were out of sight, Paul hurried back inside to check on Morgan. Within moments the doorbell rang. Relieved, Paul opened the door to find Dr. Snolten and his assistant Felicity Gorge.

"Your timing is amazing." Paul guided them to the bedroom where Morgan remained passed out.

"I'll need you to wait in the living room," Nurse Gorge said to Paul. Dr. Snolten focused on Morgan while Nurse Gorge kept her gaze on Paul. Her voice full of love, compassion, and caring. The kind of sounds that caused muscles to relax and tension to dissipate. His first reaction was to tell her that he wouldn't leave but that sound, that calming symphonic tone gave him the relief he needed. Without additional fight, he allowed her to guide him out of the bedroom, onto the sofa. She closed the bedroom door behind her.

Felicity had warned Dr. Snolten that Morgan wasn't the best candidate, especially not for such a key role. He had seen an opportunity and decided to take the chance. In part because Trinity's judgment for past recommendations had been sound. But from the moment Morgan had walked into the doctor's office, Felicity knew she couldn't be easily controlled. Morgan had her own goals and she was certain to complete them.

Felicity pulled out the IV bag and syringe, preparing them for the patient. She hooked it up to Morgan while the doctor checked on her. "Not too significant. She's going to be in pain for a while though."

"This won't work." Felicity checked Morgan's pulse and temperature. "She isn't a believer."

"She will be." The doctor lovingly patted off pearls of sweat and washed Morgan's face, arms, neck, and body. He had under-exaggerated when he said the damage wasn't significant. The revival solution had worked wonders on others and would do the same for Morgan. Felicity assisted in cleaning the patient. Even though she didn't believe that Morgan was the right choice, she was still a human being... well... almost human... and deserved to be cared for. "She will get stronger. She needs time."

"She won't get stronger if she keeps acting like a fool."

"Would you consider bringing in Tess?"

He continued caring for Morgan. He didn't respond to Felicity's question. Tess was an extreme; a last resort. He rinsed out the washcloth and then covered Morgan with clean sheets. "It's not time."

"We can't have another Ascentia."

"She's not and she can't be. It's not in her."

"But—"

Without fire, without venom, without anger he stated, "The decision has been made."

Paul was enjoying the view from Morgan's overlook. He hadn't watched the sun set in ages and nearly forgot the beauty of the oranges, pinks, yellows as they dove into a deep jade night sky. Eucalyptus and plumeria wafted on the warm air. The doctor and his assistant came out of the bedroom. Their calm seemed contrived, with no overt signs of concern. Paul wanted to be sure that Morgan was okay. He had done what he set out to do, push forward the cogs of the media machine.

"You'll need to give her these two times a day and these three times a day. She's on an IV right now. This will help her heal."

"All right." Paul took the pills and reviewed the instructions. This seemed simple enough.

"She cannot, I mean CANNOT, fly for any reason." The doctor said this with force. He needed to be sure that this man understood. "If she flies or exerts herself in any way then she could irrevocably harm herself."

"Got it."

Dr. Snolten looked Paul in the eye, with a seriousness and intensity he had not seen in years. Not since Paul's mother was diagnosed with diabetes mellitus when he was in his thirties. "Irrevocably."

The sound in Dr. Snolten's voice made Paul uncomfortable. He felt the guilt of forcing Morgan to meet with Belinda creep into his stomach and up his chest. His throat tightened. "Irrevocably."

"I will send people to check on her a few times a day. I want to see if an old friend, Don, is available. He's used to protecting the injured. I'm a little worried about Morgan's welfare considering this media storm."

"I wouldn't worry," Paul said, offhanded. Although he did, much more than he wanted to admit.

"I would. She needs to be protected at least until she heals," Felicity said. "I'll check on her tomorrow, doctor. If that's okay."

Dr. Snolten nodded. Felicity lightly touched Paul on the arm and that wonderful calm warmed through him.

In the background, Paul heard the phone ring and ring and ring some more. Someone adamantly wanted to reach Morgan. After what seemed like the one hundredth ring, at which point, Paul readied to rip the phone out of the wall, the ringing stopped. Lightly from Morgan's room, he heard her say, "Of course. I'd be happy to."

The Journalist, The Angel, and The Seer

"Thank you for agreeing to be interviewed." William Traft from The New York Times, Los Angeles Division, looked over the rustic metal railing to The Hills below. "I'm assuming this is where—"

"Well, yes." Morgan hesitantly came forward. Wrapped in an oversized robe, she nursed a lemon infused ice water. "I decided to try them out." The last words came out in drabs. Nurse Felicity had stopped by earlier and cared for Morgan's wings. The appendages newly covered in salve and wrapped against Morgan's torso, she felt better but not great. Felicity said they were healing, which put Morgan at ease. She still felt like someone had tried to rip her back off. Felicity recommended (and Morgan agreed) to continue taking her medication to help with the healing and pain.

Woozy, Morgan regained her composure by holding onto the side of the couch. She was exhausted, but this felt more drug-induced like an opiate. William, surprised by her instability, had assumed from the media hype that Morgan had come out of the altercation with minimal damage. In person, she seemed frail. He came forward, concerned, and helped her to the couch. Although he had never met her before, he empathized. He had researched in preparation for the interview and was surprised at her likeability. He anticipated dealing with an aging starlet, fearful of a public demise. Yes, those elements were there, and so was one attempt after another to genuinely change her path. Including her time at The Center. Maybe that's what caused his greatest empathy. He too had sought more from Ompi so many years prior and found it to be a sham. He never thought he'd find himself doing Ompi's bidding again.

The way she walked, her look of a deep bone ache, reminded him of past interviews with broken souls. But those people had broken. That deep bone ache had seeped through their pores, into their marrow, and rested in their inner beings. Morgan's hadn't reached her core yet and that made him root for her.

"I'm fine." Great, Morgan thought. She sounded more Bette Davis than Superwoman. She needed to check back with the Doc to see if he could put her on something less potent. She was more than thankful for the help of Felicity and for Don, her new body guard. A bodyguard recommended by the Doc and, so it turns out, previously worked for Trinity Spalling. Couldn't ask for better credentials. Don conveniently showed up earlier in the day, scoped out the area, and then immediately took his place near the door and ensured Morgan was within view. At William's insistence, Don patiently waited outside. William's stipulation for the exclusive was that the interview be one-on-one, even if it meant that Don strip-searched the journalist. As far as Morgan could tell, neither Don nor William seemed unhappy about performing the search.

Centering herself, Morgan refocused. They sat on the bench and admired the city. William didn't strike her as a typical reporter. She reveled in the shared moment of silence and reflection. The warmth of William next to her eased her anxiety in a way the painkillers could not. William's hand touched Morgan's unintentionally, but neither complained. His thoughts floated away from the purpose of his visit and trailed to the comfort and ease of the moment.

Don opened the door and asked if she was okay, his tall surfer build strong but not menacing. This interruption snapped William back to refocus on the interview.

"The In-N-Out is over here?" He got up and pointed at a shopping center in the distance.

William didn't know what to expect when he agreed to talk to Morgan. He didn't think his editor would go for it but her enthusiasm surprised him. "Are you kidding? This is all over the place," she said. "That crappy interview by what's-her-face-"

"Belinda."

"Yeah, Belinda. Good for the LAT to get such a viral interview. Hot damn if you can get Morgan's point of view then we've got something with legs."

Journalism had changed its focus from news to gossip. If this meant he could get a front page spread and get Ompi off his back AND put him up for a full-fledged staff writer, then this odd interview was well worth it.

Ompi had shared the official documents proving William was clear of charges related to the Omni-Mani-Pati fiasco, and eagerly signed the statement that "after completion of the interview and upon Ompi's receipt of the recordings," William owed him nothing. William ensured the contract was as specific as possible.

Morgan pointed and confirmed her fateful flight path. She wondered when he would ask more about Belinda. She knew it was coming.

He stood behind her, trying to get a feel for the wings. She hadn't shown them and he was afraid to ask. Paul had made it clear that she wouldn't fly. "Too much strain in the last few days. She needs rest." From the way Morgan moved, William understood. Curiosity started to get the best of him. He was a reporter.

"You want to see them?" she asked. Wary and childlike, she

turned her back to him and wiggled.

"It would help the story." He reached out and hovered his hand over her robe. As if the act of a physical interaction would make this real.

Morgan disappeared into her bathroom and then returned. This time with the same shift dress she had worn for Belinda. No heels, only bare feet and a vulnerability that ate at him. Years ago William had scoffed at Ompi's ridiculous words foretelling an angel's return, but now he experienced some strange magnetic faith. Something he never believed he could feel.

The wings had been taped against her torso, this much he could tell. Damp with gel, the feathers looked like they had been lovingly matted down. As if, were one single feather to fall, so would Morgan.

"I can't fly right now. Doctor's orders. You can touch if you want."

He came closer and brushed the softness of the feathers with the back of his hand. The wonder of their feel and that... Dear God... They were real. He noticed the fading gray, black, blue, and magenta bruising along her back. The scratches and fresh scarring looked like tears. Some scars taped shut and others stitched. "All of this from Belinda?"

The severity made William wonder if Morgan should have gotten into that ambulance instead. Belinda had described the fight in the article but never went into detail about the damage she caused. Heck, that hack Belinda was well enough to go home and knock out a multipage spread about the desperate, downtrodden actress, Morgan's life leading up to the fight, and the supporting evidence that Morgan was a fake. The last part in question. "Another failure frantically trying to make a name for herself with the abuse of media," Belinda had written. In ultra-fine print was the disclaimer that Belinda and Morgan had previously known each other. The article went viral. Comments crashed the site. William hadn't been surprised when Paul told him a background check and strip-search were required before coming near Morgan.

"Not all of this was Belinda," Morgan said. She shifted away as if the question had caused her pain.

He had read some of the comments. Folks baulking at the claims. Others angrily stating that Morgan was an abomination, unnatural, and a sign.

TMZ mocked Morgan and Belinda. They had followed Belinda and tried to follow Morgan. Belinda encouraged them. She had covered her face in makeup to hide the bruises and her arm was in a sling. The damage wasn't as bad as Belinda had described. Which of course, TMZ duly noted. They also noted that until a year ago Belinda had been covering dog shows and county fairs, but suddenly she landed primo articles that made the front page. The implication was that she illicitly moved her way up, which didn't sound right to William. He knew David Mahal, the senior editor at the LA Times. David may be a lot of things but he wouldn't risk his paper for an affair. TMZ couldn't find anything more than Belinda's ability to write high profile articles.

When TMZ staked out Morgan, they found that she hadn't left her home in forty-eight hours. They also found the miracle of a six-foot-four bodyguard with unnaturally wavy blonde hair, sea eyes hidden behind massive Ray-Bans, and a professional surfer body. More pictures floated of Don (who remained stoic throughout the paparazzi onslaught) than of Morgan. Hashtags guessed at the mystery man's identity.

William wondered what it was like for Morgan to find herself in a self-made prison. He figured more paparazzi waited in hiding for a Morgan Cruise sighting.

"Should I take you to a doctor?" he asked.

Morgan smirked. "It's okay. I have a specialist caring for me." William felt foolish asking the question. Of course she had a specialist.

"May I take pictures?" He held up his iPhone. "I promise not to publish them without your consent."

Morgan hunched deeper into herself. She agreed to this interview because Paul said it was a good move. She needed as many interviews as she could get. Nevermind that she had agreed to it from a drug induced stupor, or that Paul nearly jumped out of his skin when he found her on the phone with William. Of course when Paul realized that William was with The New York Times, he saw the potential and quietly encouraged her to go ahead with it ("No flying though," he kept saying, "no flying.") Morgan researched William and found him above board. She definitely didn't know him, so there was no history to avoid. When he walked in he seemed genuine. And Paul looked calmer after shaking his hand.

The aftermath of Belinda's article had surprised Morgan. She had encountered the public's anger before but not like this. Who wouldn't love an angel? It's not like she made end-of-the-world prophecies or ate babies.

"Morgan? Just a couple snaps?"

"It's fine." The words soft and slow and tired. "You haven't asked me about Belinda." She looked at him. "You can if you want."

After dedicating her life to making others happy—to provide entertainment to the world—she realized at the tender age of forty-eight that the world didn't like aged women. Even worse, the world didn't see them. She was tired of being hidden. She had wanted to be more than the words on a page or the images on a screen. Morgan now acknowledged that she was quickly becoming an icon. She wondered if becoming this icon was a smart move. She didn't know if it would last a day or a week or eternity.

Morgan looked at William and saw truth. She didn't know how else to explain it. He seemed like a man who represented truth and sought it. Whatever "truth" meant. She dismissed her worries. May as well go full throttle.

William photographed the wrapped wings, the scratches, the bruises, the stitches, the fresh pink scars. She shared tidbits about her fight with Belinda. Things she hadn't intended to tell. She unwrapped and carefully lifted the wings so he could take pictures of their span. He was sure to get close up shots of where the wings met her upper back so the world could see they were holy-shit-mother-of-God real. Morgan excused herself and then returned in the comfort of her robe.

"Thank you. May I ask, why? I know why Belinda said you got them. But really, why?"

She paused.

"To learn how to fly."

As they spoke, William witnessed the sunset that Morgan enjoyed every evening. "That's why I bought the place," she said. "I saw the house a few times and couldn't quite decide. I didn't want to be one of those foo foo, chichi television stars who bought the biggest most expensive place because I could. I wanted to find someplace that refueled me. The last time I came here before purchasing it was right at sunset. I drank in the view for an hour. I simply couldn't move. Breathtaking."

William and Morgan stood side-by-side as the bright yellows turned to burnt oranges and vibrant reds only to rest into the blue and purple jewel tones of a Los Angeles night sky.

He wrote the article and submitted it. Begrudgingly, he sent the notes and pictures to Ompi. Did William regret his decision? Did he wish he didn't make such a deal with a man like Ompi? He chose not to think about it. Instead he admired the pictures of that evening sky off of Morgan's balcony and remembered that feeling of completeness. Disturbed by the flashing neon that bled through the side of his blackout curtains, he took the call from his editor. "This is perfection," she said. Glee barely hidden in her voice. "You have this on tape?"

"All on tape."

"And the research. You have it double-checked."

William closed the picture file. "Triple."

"I'm going to send it to fact check. If Belinda wants to challenge this she can."

"She will. I have no doubt. She won't get very far other than a social media spree." William opened a fresh email and attached a text file and several additional photographs. In the "To" line he entered his favorite editor's email address and clicked send.

For a moment, silence on the line. He heard her clicking through page after page. "This, my friend. If this all checks out, then this is absolutely page one."

"Check your email again. I sent you more files. Might be good as a quick follow up on the site."

More clicking. "You are brilliant." William was sure he could hear her salivating over the phone.

"Thanks."

She quickly hung up, which William knew to be good news. He locked his computer and put his notes away in a cubby that had been closed up and sealed. William hid the spot with a velvet neon painting of The King. One that made him laugh. He pocketed his keys and returned to his favorite dim sum joint. William smiled, knowing his dear friend would arrive any minute and they would pleasantly recreate the first time they met.

The Angel, The Journalists, The Aftermath

She hadn't anticipated the crash. Thankfully Don did.

William's article landed on The New York Times front page, with an elaborate and detailed follow up piece on The Times' website. Morgan called William to thank him for his kind spread. After the interview with Belinda, she expected this would make page ninety-nine of the Sunday edition. Even Huffington Post, The Wall Street Journal, Variety, and a dozen other rags published tag-on stories. This isn't to say she was unaware of the media engine called Craigslist Nikky (CLN) and the fantastic Paul. To help her sanity, Paul shielded Morgan from the hype. She was still fragile, less physically and more emotionally. He recommended she stay away from the TV and stay offline as much as possible.

Her phone hadn't stopped ringing, which as Paul pointed out was the purpose of the article. "To keep you in the public eye. To set the record straight." With the last word, a series of bricks shattered through her front window and sailed into her living room. Don grabbed Morgan and put her into her bedroom. As the coverage swelled, Don and his team had adapted the home to be a lockdown spot, equipped with a triple lock and triple-pane secured windows. To Morgan it was the safest and most claustrophobic place in Los

Angeles. After moving Morgan to her room, Don called for backup and the local police. The backup appeared in record time while the police took a little longer.

The road leading to Morgan's was so heavily congested with onlookers that her neighbors had moved to temporary housing. Morgan's lawn was littered with protestors and admirers, which made getting to her front door a bit more challenging for the emergency crew. It was as if everyone on the planet had called their friends to come and have a look at the winged woman. She didn't get this kind of attention during her days on *CUT!*. At the time she thought she had hit the epicenter of stardom, but she realized those days were minute compared to now.

Within moments of the threat, Don's team had all spots within a fifty-foot radius cleared. They put up barricades along with guards every twenty feet. Before the bricks, the phone calls, the emails, the threats, the pounding at her windows, she would have thought the guards, the barricades were extreme. Now she understood the necessity.

Paul never left after the Belinda fiasco. He camped out in a guest room across the ranch house to give Morgan her privacy. His workload had quadrupled and the thought of leaving her alone with Don and purely under the care of the Doc made him nervous. Amazed at how quickly Morgan healed, he still worried about her being weak and out of it. When he talked to her, Morgan's sentences came out in fragments as if she became sicker instead of better. While physical evidence pointed to the contrary.

When the bricks crashed through the window, Paul was in his room fielding request after request to meet with the newly minted angel. He had brought on an assistant to purely work with other clients so he could focus on Morgan. Paul agreed with CLN that they would only go after paid gigs, or ones that had a tie in for Morgan to start her own lines—perfume, makeup, even a clothing and brassiere line to rival Victoria's Secret. He limited what he divulged to her, concerned with her frailty and how she would react to the percentage deal he'd cut with Nikky. Even he had to admit the socialite earned every cent. She just needed to keep producing. The latest call, which came right when he heard the crash, was from a person he never wanted to hear from again—Ompi.

Before he could finish telling Ompi that Morgan was booked through the next five years, Paul heard crashing glass and hung up. All Ompi heard was a faint declaration and then silence. No matter. He would go on with his announcement without Morgan at his side.

Once Don declared the area clear, Paul asked to visit Morgan. With permission, he found her resting in a lounge chair in her bedroom. Albeit he had to convince Don it was okay to go in. Across from Morgan the flat screen remained off, as if she wanted to hear the silence.

"Good news, good news. We have you booked on all the majors—*TODAY, Tonight, Late Night*, you name it." He stood underneath the television. "We arranged for a private car to take you to and from each location. Don't worry, we'll be sure that Don is there."

Morgan got up and peeked through the closed curtains. After a moment, her eyes adjusted to the abrupt sunlight. The gorgeous view no longer interrupted by crowds. She had remembered fame like this, but not like this. Not this kind of hate. Not this kind of adoration. "You know there are sites dedicated to me," Morgan whispered. "Well, not me but what they think I am."

"Morgan, I need you to focus. Tonight we have an arrangement to secretly meet with Jimmy."

"They're calling me a demon. Me? Unnatural."

"You've heard worse. Remember when People magazine named

you one of the fastest falling stars in 2002? Or when Cosmo called you the ugliest woman alive? This is nothing."

"That was press. These people actually believe it. What about the bricks? You think someone 'adored' me so much they figured they'd show me love?"

"Morgan that's why we have guards. You have a ton of people looking out for you."

"This isn't what I signed up for, Paul. I figured we'd get the wings, do a few stunts, get back in the public. Maybe have the damn things removed once I got my savings back. No harm, no foul. Just another pop culture icon. Whatevs. But not this."

"You are all those things. You will be all those things. Remember Alice Cooper? Ozzy? Hell, name a band from the 90s and 2000s. They were all demonized. So what? We ride this. We use this. We move on."

Morgan knew he was right. The bricks affected her more than she had known. The crowds, fine. The death threats, no problem. The love letters, the fan letters, all of that... All of that she had anticipated and loved. What she hadn't anticipated was her home being invaded on the day of the biggest article of her life. If she got this big of an emotional reaction then what would happen tomorrow? Could she handle it?

She went into her bathroom and washed her face and neck with a cool damp cloth. "You were saying? *Tonight.* Jimmy. What time?"

City Hall off of Spring Street seemed like the appropriate place to make the announcement. Unfortunately Ompi couldn't get a permit, and when he showed up with the podium and his own camera crew, the police summarily kicked them off the property.

Not quite according to plan.

No worries, he had a better idea.

Ompi found a little known outlook along The Hills that had a pretty good shot of the now infamous In-N-Out. The lines quadrupled with customers eyeing the skies for a Morgan Cruise sighting. Perfect, perfect, perfect.

Ompi cued his cameraman. Dressed in a charcoal suit with a yellow tie, Ompi motioned toward the fast food restaurant below.

Morgan reached out to turn on the television.

"What are you doing?" Paul asked.

"I'm bored. What's a little daytime TV going to hurt?"

"You don't watch daytime TV."

"Come on, Paul. Why can't I see a little bit?"

"You can't handle this right now."

"Fine." Morgan picked up her smartphone and surfed. Paul grabbed it from her.

"This is how you know about the forums. Morgan, I thought we agreed that you would stay offline. No radio, no TV, and no internet."

"This isn't really the internet," Morgan said.

"If you can see what's going on in the media, then it counts." Paul pocketed her phone.

"You're confiscating my phone?"

"Until this dies down."

"I am not a child, Paul." Morgan said this and heard the juvenile tone before Paul could comment. "It got to me a little but I'm over it." She put her hand out with the expectation that he'd give her the phone.

"I never said you were a child." He slapped her palm. "I acknowledge you are a human being and this is a tense situation. I don't want you to get upset again."

"I like reading the fan mail." She tried to skip through the nastiness and get right to the welcoming letters. Those letters reminded her why she went through this in the first place. Only a few short months ago, she was unable to be cast on TV. She was lucky if she could get a commercial.

"You can read the fan mail later. Let's stay focused on tonight."

They reviewed the plans for her first big appearance since the original flight debacle. Then Paul left her to prepare. Morgan's preparation meant setting out clothes and reviewing what she would and would not talk about. The "not talk about" list was rather long. On paper Jimmy and other interviewers were informed not to ask about her relationship with Belinda, the flight, and her transformation. In private Paul gave them the nod to, if they wanted, inquire more deeply. And that maybe, just maybe, Morgan would divulge. He wanted them to ask and ask and ask so that when Morgan got to her dream interview—either with Oprah or Diane Sawyer—then all the refuting and hesitancy would melt away. The world would find out the "truth" behind the controversies. Very old skool and very effective. He sketched out another meeting. This one could have a big payoff. Morgan had gotten an email from an ex who worked for one of the biggest Hollywood producers. Thankfully, Paul had access to Morgan's email and filtered through the crap to gold.

Morgan finished rehearsing her responses and prepped a few more potential questions and answers. Always good to have backups. And then found herself alone in her overcast room. She couldn't remember the last time she was so bored. She had no interest in reading from the myriad of books on her shelf. She had read most of them two or three times. Morgan turned on the television.

Now this, this was not what she expected.

Maybe a TMZ briefing.

Maybe she expected more discussions about her on *The View* or

The TODAY Show or interviews with those who saw the original flight. Maybe even an interview with Belinda, who had surprisingly decided to go dark after she had blabbed to the world her incredibly biased and slanderous views. Belinda going dark made a lot of sense since William's reports came out. Great move to set up a counter interview with the rival paper. The pictures alone represented a huge black eye on Belinda's reputation.

But maybe what she saw in that moment… Maybe part of her always expected it.

Ompi behind a podium at the secret overlook along Mulholland Drive. She'd never wanted to see that man again. The last she had heard he was the object of a manhunt. How the hell did he get on television?

In the corner of the screen a shot of Morgan's healing back and wings. She turned up the volume.

"In 2005 I had predicted that Morgan Cruise would return from a fallen life."

He held up a weathered leather bound journal and turned to a page with scrawling.

"In 2006 I predicted that someone would return from a fallen life and this would represent the coming of a new world. A new identity for all of us." He put the journal down. "These predictions have come to pass."

"In 2006 I was falsely accused of many acts and I have since been exonerated. These foretellings, which I will publish over the upcoming days, will prove that I am the giver of truth and of light."

Ompi continued talking as the camera changed to a wide shot and a pair of police officers stepped into frame. She watched as they led Ompi from the podium and into a police car. He didn't struggle or fight. Instead, he put his hands behind his back as if he anticipated arrest. The camera panned away from Ompi and tightened to the valley below. A closer shot of the In-N-Out with a long winding line of customers. Some with binoculars scanning the sky.

The shot returned to Ompi and the officers. Someone Morgan didn't recognize came into view and handed the officers a folder. He must be Ompi's lawyer.

Meanwhile, the camera returned to the TMZ newsroom. The reporters mocked the broadcast. "Just another nut," one reporter said. "How did he get away with this?" One reporter who seemed a little faster in researching, read from her screen. "Looks like all charges against him were dismissed six months ago."

"Who would do that?"

"Doesn't say who," she responded. "Looks like he's legit."

The reporters continued to banter while Morgan tried to absorb what she saw. Ompi. He probably saw the press and couldn't wait to tag his name to her.

As she moved to turn the television off, she heard one of the reporters ask, "What if he's right?"

How could this man roam free? He had nearly killed hundreds to simply prove a point. To prove his own righteousness. Somehow he was at it again, but this time using his relationship with her to drive the point home. His own renewal. Morgan paced her room trying to remember what he predicted while she was at The Center. Too many late nights and too many conversations after hours of chanting. She barely remembered the details.

Maybe she wrote them down somewhere? She kept journals here and there throughout her life, but she couldn't quite remember journaling at The Center. Honestly, most of the journal entries consisted of two or three sentences about being tired or annoyed or happy. Nothing of significance, hence why she didn't keep at it. Might be time to dig into her storage space to see what she could find.

The police uncuffed Ompi, sadly off camera. "That would have made a great closing shot," Ompi told his lawyer.

"You're lucky we had this on hand," the lawyer retorted.

"Yea. Luck." Ompi checked in with his camera crew. As he anticipated, TMZ picked up the broadcast. His cameramen picked up the rest of it. He directed them to release the remaining shots— Ompi being detained, Ompi's lawyer handing the proof of Ompi's innocence, Ompi being released and pleasantly shaking the officers' hands as they bid him farewell. Ompi straightened his tie and looked out over the cliff. Soon the crowd of followers would be for him.

She had hours before the interview with Jimmy. The bedroom became smaller and smaller with each passing minute. Morgan decided to skip her meds until the undercurrent of nausea dissipated. Feeling a little refreshed, she went into her bathroom and unlocked the window. She crawled out onto the veranda and spread her wings. The stretch felt amazing. Now this was what she had imagined her life would be like. A light cool breeze played with her hair and feathers. She stretched her arms, legs, and spread her full wingspan. It was as if someone breathed life back into her being. The ink night sky had won the battle with the day's light. Morgan sat on a cement bench and wished for a cigarette. She hadn't had one in years but for some reason in that moment, she craved one.

The Fallon interview didn't intimidate her. In fact, it felt like coming home. She felt out of place off-screen. She peered down along the porch wall. In the neighboring room, she saw security at the window and further down she saw Paul on the phone. He was probably planning out the rest of her week. The more to do, the better. Morgan scanned the view, taking in the trees, rolling hills, and twinkling lights of the city below. She curled her wings back and sighed when she smelled sour sweat. She heard a knock, and then felt the full body weight of someone shoving her over.

"What the he—" Morgan went face down on the cement veranda. Dazed, she thrust her full body against whatever or whomever had jammed against her. A sharp pain hit her side.

"That's fucking it. I've fucking had it!" She threw open her wings and heard the attacker roll off the veranda and hit the lawn. She looked over to find a man in black holding nunchucks. He hopped up and lunged at her again. Furious, Morgan kicked the nunchucks out of his hand and punched at his face. He tossed backward like something out of a Jackie Chan film. Morgan fired curse after curse. Pinned against the side of the house, he punched at her kidneys, which normally would have taken her out. She fell for a moment, long enough for him to get on top of her and try to tie her down. "What is wrong with you?" Morgan yelled. Before he could hog tie her, she flipped him over and ran for it. "Don!" Just as she yelled for him, the attacker tackled her and tied her wings and hands back. Morgan swore at that moment that her advantage was gone. The man stood over her with a hood. As he (where the hell he got that, she'll never know) reached over to cover her, a rush of adrenaline struck. Her hands and wings burst free. She returned the same kidney courtesy. Then, instead of politely punching him in the face, she chopped him in the throat. He lost breath, then consciousness. Morgan leaned over the attacker, ready to strike again.

Paul came racing over with Don not even a step behind. "What are you doing out here?"

"Shouldn't your question be 'who is this maniac who attacked you?'" Morgan caught her breath and got up from the ground.

"Well, that too."

"I don't know, thank you for asking."

Don called over two security guards who tied up the intruder. "We'll call the police and have him arrested for breaking and entering."

"And assaulting me."

"Yeah." Don looked at the intruder and looked at Morgan.

"Where were you five minutes ago when that maniac came barreling after me?" Morgan's words more pointed than she intended. She was shocked at the attack, but proud of how she'd handled herself.

"Doesn't look like you needed my help."

Paul put away his phone. "You did that all by yourself?"

"What am I, five?"

"I'm just saying that you looked rather peaked this afternoon. Surprising you would be able to take that guy on."

"Maybe he's not as strong as you think."

Morgan and Paul followed Don to flashing lights at the front of the house.

Don had removed the guy's hood. Morgan definitely didn't recognize him, but Don looked like he did. "You know him?" Morgan asked.

"No." Don handed the guy over to the police. Before she lost a clear shot of his face, Morgan took a few pictures.

"He looks pretty tough to me," Paul said.

Morgan, feeling surprisingly energetic, ignored Paul's comment. Paul was right, compared to this afternoon, she was kicking ass and she didn't need to take names because she took photos instead. Ones she would check with an online face search as soon as she got back from the taping.

"I better get ready," Morgan whispered to Paul.

"You want me to field this one?" Paul motioned to the police. Just as Morgan headed into the house, her mother pulled up in a Ferrari.

"Where did she get that?" Morgan asked.

"Do you want to know?"

No, Morgan didn't want to know. Because inevitably if it

involved her mother and something expensive this meant some kind of exchange occurred, and typically that exchange involved Morgan—without her knowledge.

"Sweetie!" Ani cooed. She got out of the Ferrari as if she were walking into a 1950s photoshoot. She hugged her daughter. Morgan, aware of the repercussions of not reciprocating, embraced her.

"What are you doing here?" Morgan pasted on a smile and mirrored her mother's tone. She didn't have time for this, but knew she needed to make time otherwise she would never get rid of Ani.

"I needed to see how my baby-kins was doing. You look fantastic." Ani twirled Morgan. "Oh. My. God. They are real." She petted the tips of Morgan's wings as if she were a domesticated bird.

"Absolutely. One-hundred-percent."

"I'm going to head back inside. I have a few more arrangements to make." Paul escaped the reunion.

"Now darling, you need to tell me all about this."

"What's to tell?"

"Oh come on now. You are everywhere. Every television station, every broadcast, every Twitter feed, every meme, every—where. I've never seen anything like it. You may have surpassed the Kardashians."

That comment sent a surge of excitement up Morgan's spine.

"I am sure you are exaggerating. How are you?" Morgan guided her mother into the living room and away from the scene of the fight. She didn't need her mother to ask more questions and the faster Ani was out of the way the better.

"Oh dear. I'm fantastic. Had a lovely flight although I only got business class which is so subpar compared to first but I needed to get here as fast as possible to see my baby girl."

"Did you and Thomas break up?"

"Tom? Oh no. No, no. He's finalizing a deal." Ani's obvious twinkle told Morgan this was the real reason for the visit.

"A deal? With whom?"

"No one special. Do you happen to have any lemonade? Maybe a little vodka?"

Morgan plopped onto her couch. "No mother. I do not have any vodka."

"Right." Ani fiddled with her purse, clearly unsure what to do.

"I can send one of the guys to get you some."

Ani looked around the room and realized the doors were guarded. "Who are these men?"

"Just protection. It's not a big deal."

"Morgan. What aren't you telling me?"

"Nothing."

"I am your mother."

"You remind me of that regularly." Morgan went into the kitchen and got her mother a glass of ice water. "I love you, Mom. But you're not known for visiting without a reason."

"What's your name?" Ani approached one of the guards who summarily ignored her. "Aren't they allowed to talk?"

"Yes, mother, they are. I think you're making this awkward for them."

"Oh. I see. Well." Ani floated back to the coach.

"The reason?"

She looked at her daughter vacantly.

"The reason you are here?"

"Oh. Right."

"You said something about a business deal."

"Did I?"

"Mom, I don't have time for this. Why are you here?"

"You don't need to get short."

Morgan took a deep breath. She knew this was her mother's M.O. Delay, stall, and try everything she could to seem innocent. Then lay on whatever it was she wanted to guilt Morgan into doing it.

"I'm sorry, mother."

"Morgan, you know that everything I do is because of my deep love for you."

"Okay."

"You know that, right?" Ani actually looked worried. As if the center of the universe was Morgan.

"Sure mama. I know."

"Good. Well, Thomas and I were given an amazing opportunity. One that I think you would be thrilled about."

"What does this have to do with my well-being?"

"You see, Thomas was in a bit of a bind to pay his half of the latest hotel and casino so he asked a friend for a favor."

"No. Mom, no."

"It isn't a big deal. They asked that I come out here and verify that you're real and then ask if you could do something for them."

"Mom, you promised. No more underhanded. No more Mob."

"Who said anything about the Mob? I was referencing Thomas's business partner, Tonald Drump."

"That's even worse."

"Well, he wasn't..."

"You have got to be kidding me. You flew all the way out here to get me to do a job for Drump? Have you lost your mind!" Morgan said this with such affirmation and anxiety that the guards stepped forward. "It's okay. She's crazy but she's my mother."

"Who says that about their dearest mom?" Ani sounded wounded. Good thing Morgan knew about her mother's stint at acting. She could have won an Oscar.

"Get out."

"I haven't even told you what they want."

"I said, get out."

The guards stepped closer.

"It's for you to make an appearance at the casino opening. They have some stunt thingie planned and said you'd make the perfect addition. It's right along the lines of your normal repertoire."

"I need you to leave." Morgan opened the front door and waited.

Ani reluctantly followed her daughter. "But dear. It would take so little and truly save us."

"Don't be melodramatic."

"I'm not." Ani said flatly and honestly. Morgan had never heard such sincerity in her mother's voice. What the hell had she gotten into? "Think about it, Morgan. I'm staying at the Beverly. Normal room. Let me know in the next twenty-four hours." Ani kissed Morgan's cheek and then drove off.

"What was that?" Paul entered the living room. "I could hear you two from China."

"If I told you, you wouldn't believe me."

"Try me."

The Angel and Two Jimmies

Of course, Morgan nailed it. She was born for film. Fallon fawned all over her. She gloried in showing off her wings (and of course she was sure to have an assistant sprinkle glitter on the feathers so they sparkled under the bright lighting). Ani being Ani called several times before the taping, during the taping, and after the taping to check on her beloved child. Thankfully Paul had Morgan's phone, anticipating the motherly disturbance. Fallon promised (on the air) to have Morgan back. Her charm amped well beyond more recent interviews. As expected, he dug and dug and dug regarding how she got the physical augmentation and could he have her surgeon's number, and why didn't she and that journalist (Belinda) get along and what was it like having a certified SEAL (Navy that is) acting as her bodyguard. (This wonderful revelation about Don provided quite a pleasant surprise for Morgan. She needed to do a bit more homework on him.) The classic questions arose - did she have other superpowers and could she loan them to him?

Her favorite part was being asked to participate impromptu Celebrity Tweets. With the request, Paul looked nervous, but Morgan being a professional coolly accepted. She acted shocked in all the right moments, feigned embarrassment when needed, and oozed humility. By the time the taping was done, Paul had several numbers for other shows, producers, and the like, all wanting a bit of the Morgan Cruise wing-ed bliss.

Paul whisked her away in the rental limo (which he ensured Fallon's producers paid for) and directed the driver to a location unfamiliar to Morgan. Don a few car lengths behind, Morgan's own ever present angel.

"It's good that I didn't see those tweets before. Added greater realism, don't you think?" Morgan peered out the tinted windows. The blur of street lights spotted the freeway.

"Now this is my old Morgan. Change of heart?"

Morgan wanted to ignore his snippiness. "No. I still believe everything I said before. This isn't what I signed up for." She took out her makeup mirror and powdered her face. Refreshed her lipstick. "It was nice being on live TV again. Nice of Jimmy to come out here for the interview."

"He was already in town." Paul smirked.

"Still. Nice of him." Replacing her mirror and lipstick, she clicked her bag shut.

"I need you to read this." Paul handed Morgan a script. "Apologies for the non sequitur but you need to look at this before we get to Carmel."

Morgan thumbed through the pages, then dug through her bag for her spectacles. "What's in Carmel?"

Paul ensured the separator between them and the driver was up. He even asked the driver a question to make sure they couldn't be heard. With the lack of response, and Morgan looking at him like he was a certified lunatic, he answered. "Remember Brian Ferdinand?"

"You mean the man my mother, to this day, swears I am meant to marry and he will soon realize he's not gay? That Brian Ferdinand?"

"He sent you a lovely note. Did you know he's now engaged to Rob Barker, head of Charisma Studios?"

"Get out. Why don't I know that? I thought his partner was that guy from New Kids On The Block. The ugly one…"

"I guess they broke up. Who knows? What I do know, is he sent you a lovely note at the behest of Rob."

"Really?" She knew Brian well enough from their moustache days to see that the only reason Brian would contact her—or even mention that he's with such a high-powered, high-profile studio exec—was if something significant happened.

"They have a new project in the works." Paul reached into the side door and pulled out a small bottle of champagne. "Rob wants to talk to you about it." He popped the cork and poured them each a glass. "We earned this after Fallon."

Morgan waved it off. She wanted to be sharp for the upcoming discussion. "What's the catch?" Morgan knew that if this meeting happened in the wee hours of the night and no mention of Brian being there, there had to be a catch.

"Fine. I'll imbibe for both of us." He sipped from the flute. "Seems as though a little convincing may be needed for Rob to pick you up. He's stuck on the whole 'back in the day' thing."

Morgan put on her glasses and started reading the script. "What? About me and Brian? It wasn't even real."

"No. Something about you ignoring him or saying no to him or something…" Paul's words trailed off. He took a bigger gulp of the bubbly.

"Paul, I have no idea what you're talking about."

"Do me a favor, if it comes up, then just apologize profusely."

"Seriously? I don't even—"

"I love you. Now shut up. Read the script. And put on your Morgan Cruise charm."

"You're not going to tell me."

"Morgan. Love. I know you. If you don't remember the reason

for him being pissed at you, then it wasn't a big moment in your life. It's best to leave it alone unless he brings it up. And if he does, just apologize."

Morgan eyed Paul. Rarely did he speak to her in this cryptic manner. She decided to move on, and continue studying the script. It wasn't bad. Actually it was damn good. The kind of script that actresses fight over. Lots of cameos too. This had the potential to become a fantastic franchise. The script was based on a combination of Swift and Dove, comic book heroines. She understood why she was being considered for the role, yet truly had no idea why Rob needed to meet her in secret.

They flashed past town after town until they reached the edge of Carmel. The limo rolled up to a cliffside house that overlooked the ocean. The blue-black view lit by a silver moon was breathtaking. She could hear waves kiss the sand below. The house, a two-story Spanish style home with a wraparound porch glowed by a single light inside. She straightened her outfit, puffed her hair, and headed toward the light. Paul had told her to turn on the Morgan charm and she did so with pleasure.

"Hello," a faint voice said. From the house's shadows came a figure familiar. Whiskey breath mingled with ocean air. Oddly she knew she had met this man, yet couldn't quite place him. He stepped into the moonlight and reached out his hand. "Morgan. Fantastic to see you. May I show you inside?"

She followed Rob into a spacious room with Mexican and Spanish décor. The walls that overlooked the ocean had been converted to floor-to-ceiling triple-paned glass. She approached, enchanted by the view.

"Matchless," she said.

"I'm glad you enjoy it," Rob said. "May I offer you a glass of wine?"

Morgan reminded herself of her purpose. "Oh no. I'm fine." She turned. "My apologies for being so rude." She reached out to her host and hugged him. "Thank you so much for seeing me at such a late hour."

Rob looked Morgan over derisively. "Yes, of course. Please sit."

Morgan hovered near the couch. Something in his mannerisms rang familiar. "I read the script. It's truly fantastic. I'm honored to be considered for such a complex role."

Rob lounged on a faux distressed leather couch. His soft black shirt and matching pants contrasted against the red, yellow, and white furniture. He stared at Morgan for a moment, just long enough for her to shift uncomfortably. "Cut the shit," he said. "You want a job."

Now that was unexpected. Morgan held back her automatic defensiveness and anger. She maintained her composure. This wasn't the first time someone tried to psyche her out at an audition. She kept eye contact and slid onto the couch, just a touch away from him. "Of course. It would be an wonderful to work for such a superb studio as Charisma. We could be good for each other." Her voice calm with a touch of sweetness. Even she was impressed.

Rob's rigid fury softened with her words. He wanted her to beg for this role. He wanted her to plead. Especially considering his fiancée still talked about her. He couldn't pinpoint if Brian's longing was for a lost friendship or a broken love. Either way, he was sick of it. And then there was the other thing. The reason Rob and Brian had fought over Morgan even being considered. Brian left briefly before Morgan's limo arrived. "If you're not going to take my feelings seriously, I'm not going to be here for this," Brian said. Brian looked so hurt that Rob began to wonder if maybe he'd misjudged. Maybe he should trust his fiancé's faith in Morgan.

Charisma studios had a lot riding on this film. He had the bigger names fighting for the role. He didn't need to gamble on a has-been. But Brian had countered that right now, THE name on everyone's lips was Morgan. Plus they'd save a ton on special effects if she did her own stunts. And who didn't like to save money? Plus— REALISM. Rob got up and poured himself three fingers of Macallan. "What is your favorite Charisma production?"

Thank God for Google. "By far *The Heinous Hotel*. Truly a masterpiece." Morgan folded her hands in her lap, sure to keep her gestures small and refined. The longer they were in the same room the more her subconscious searched for how she knew him.

"That's one of my favorites too." He strode to the overlook and peered out. "I am considering several actresses for this role. Brian suggested you." He sipped from his tumbler. "I will admit, it took a bit of convincing. The others are willing to back the film in exchange for a percentage of the box office."

Morgan tried to hide her unease. She knew she couldn't put millions of dollars behind a film. She was lucky that her home and car were paid off, otherwise she'd be homeless.

"Before you feign an offer, I know you can't do the same. This is why we're here." Rob pulled out his iPhone. "I need you to read for me. Recorded obviously."

Morgan randomly selected a scene from the script. Rob blankly listened as he recorded her. At one point he raised his hand for her to stop. "Let's head outside."

He took her to the cliff's edge. In the distance, Paul leaned against the limo. Morgan checked her phone for a text. No signal.

Rob held up his phone and commanded. "Fly."

"Excuse me?"

"Fly. This is part of your audition. If you fly over the cliff and then back, you'll get the part. If not then we're done here."

Morgan peered over Rob's shoulder in search of Paul or Don. The

Doc had insisted no flying at least for another day. But Morgan felt fine. She felt better than fine, she felt euphoric. Even healthier than her days of cleansing and hours of yoga. Yet something in Rob's tone bothered her. This was more than an audition. This was a threat. She observed their surroundings to see if she was missing something. The night too dark to see much farther than the house. The moonlight illuminated the ocean, Rob's glass, and the house well, but nothing else.

Rob pulled from his drink. The whiskey half gone. He sneered. "I didn't think so." He pocketed the phone and began back to the house. "Goodnight. I'll tell Brian you said hello."

Morgan stripped off her dress. Much easier to fly with full range of motion. A second and then she jumped. She prayed the wings would work. Her mind commanded them to spread and glide through the evening sea air. Eyes closed she envisioned herself soaring over the ocean and toward the silver moon. The cool salt air brought her skin to life. Her hair flowed behind her. She opened her eyes to see a never-ending ocean like the promise of a new beginning. She steered back toward the house, hoping that he had stayed to watch her take off. As she neared, she realized he had continued his retreat inside the house. She glided around the home, enjoying the freeness of flying. In her first flight, she didn't have a moment to really enjoy it. She had been too surprised that the wings worked, and then there was the collision. But this—the early morning hours, light of the full moon, sky studded with stars and the sea's mist cooling her skin—in this she reveled. She glided around the area and realized they were quite isolated. The nearest home acres away. Well beyond easy walking distance. Rob had selected this home so he could be away from it all. She hadn't paid much attention when they drove in, but now she calculated that the closest neighbors had to be at least a ten minute drive. She spotted an open beachside and empty public rest areas. She flew back to the home reinvigorated by the beauty of the sand, the sea, and the evening.

She looked within the house and saw that Rob had turned on the wall-sized screen and was watching a pre-recorded show. The granularity of the picture meant it had been made before digital tapings. Morgan made out the familiar shapes of the classic Nickelodeon game show, *Double Dare*. She hovered nearby watching the screen when on came a mini-Morgan, and beside her a mini-Rob. Although his name wasn't Rob at the time.

The kids were asked a question and the person who got it right won and moved on to another round. For Morgan, this is how she had been selected for the subsequent shows that began her career. She watched on, anticipating what came next. Her stomach tightened.

On the screen the little boy answered the question. Although she couldn't hear what he said, she knew that his answer was incorrect. Then child-Morgan answered. Her stance filled with pride bordering on arrogance. She smugly turned to the boy and stepped out of the way as he was slimed. The little boy screamed and cried. Mini-Morgan taunted him. She laughed and pointed. In her memory, Morgan remembered the names others called him, and how more kids joined in the taunting. She remembered the look on his face change from embarrassment to anger. He looked off camera to his parents. The camera turned to show them nodding in disapproval; his father headed to the edge of the set, motioning for Jimmy to get off. That was his name, Jimmy. Not Rob. The mini-Jimmy's expression changed again in a way that had scared Morgan. As if the fury of the moment had been painted on his soul. She stopped goading him and started to move away when the production coordinator spurred her to continue jeering the upset boy. "All in good fun," the coordinator would later say. "It was all meant in good fun." Clearly the mini-Jimmy didn't see this as good fun at all. He picked up the nearest prop and threw it at Morgan, then found the next closest item and lunged it at host Marc Summers. He pounced on anything that wasn't held down and destroyed it. He chased kids around the set to gales of laughter, all the while his face contorted in fury. Mini-Jimmy ran toward the camera, it shook and the taping abruptly ended.

Rob got up and began to refill his tumbler when he saw Morgan aloft outside his home. His face reddened in fury, he rushed to her.

"Fuck you!" He yelled. "Fuck you and your goddamn holier than thou shit."

"Is that you? Jimmy?" The name of the boy on *Double Dare* was Jim Reynolds. Jim came from a long line of Hollywood performers. Expectations of his success were huge. His agent had arranged for Jimmy to win and thereby jumpstart his young career. He lined up a cereal commercial and several auditions. But the adorable blue-eyed, dark-haired boy with rosy cheeks and an effervescent grin turned demonic on camera. He forgot the answer to a simple question, and he got slimed. His grand public loss meant that he didn't get the cereal commercial, and his mass fit meant he couldn't get cast anywhere else. Jimmy disappeared from the theatrical scene.

Jim threw his glass at her. Morgan caught it and placed it on the deck.

"You fucking ruined me!"

"You should calm down."

"You should stay the fuck out of my life."

Morgan hovered nearby. "You called me here."

"Because BRIAN insisted. I ONLY did this for Brian. ONLY. You fucking ruined me. You have no IDEA what that was like." Morgan knew well what that was like, but this was neither the time nor the place to discuss the pros and cons of showbiz and the crappiness of kids. She searched the horizon to see if she could find Don or Paul or someone.

No one stirred near the limo. Where had they gone? She checked her cell phone one more time and reconfirmed no signal.

"I am sorry, Jimmy. I really am. I had no idea." He ignored her and retreated. He disappeared into a back room. Morgan flew to the deck, hoping he had gone inside to calm down. She figured they could have a civil conversation. Have a cup of tea.

He returned with a shotgun.

There goes civility.

She quickly rerouted her approach and flew away from the deck. "What are you doing?" Morgan, now aware of her mortality, readied to take off as fast as possible.

"You bitch." He cocked the gun.

Holy shit, this was really happening. She looked beyond the house for someone. Anyone.

"I'm sorry," she said. "I'm so, so sorry. But look, you have such a wonderful life. Look at you. A high-powered executive. You make careers. You are the master of fates."

"Damn straight."

Jim aimed.

Morgan found a speed she didn't know she had. She heard the blast and anticipated the impact. She flew as far as possible over land. If she was going to get shot, better to be over land than water. She heard another shot and quickly switched direction, this time heading into a cluster of pines and cypress.

She clutched at the canopy and looked behind her. The house only a block away. Maybe she would be lucky and he'd pass out from the drinking. She saw car lights coming toward her. It looked like the limo. Thank God. Finally, Paul. How could he not realize what was happening? After gunshots? And where the hell was Don?

As the limo approached, something inside her said the limo wasn't hers. Shit.

She spotted an old oak and sailed behind it. The limo's front door flew open and out came Jim. He pumped the forestock. Morgan searched for her next move.

No point in talking this psycho out of killing her. Morgan sped toward another cluster of trees behind him. She shot downward, picking up stones and tossing them in different directions. Jim aimed wildly from tree to tree. Behind him came the Fallon limo at full speed. Jim turned to see it barreling toward him. He aimed at the vehicle and pumped again. Morgan took that opportunity to race down at him, putting both fists forward and knocking him over. She grabbed his gun and threw it as far away as possible. Shocked, he wildly punched at her. Morgan, full of adrenaline and a power she had never experienced before, countered his punches. Each point of Jim's impact felt like a light slap instead of the full force of a drunken, jealous, revenge-filled man. Even though he wanted to kill her, she didn't want to hurt him.

Paul and Don ran up. Paul pulled Morgan back while Don picked up the movie exec and wrapped his arms behind his back. Jim unsuccessfully fought the grip. Don pulled back on Jim's arm so the threat of a broken arm felt real. Jim held back a cry of pain and stopped struggling.

"Are you okay?" Paul asked Morgan.

She realized she was shaking. More from adrenaline than fear.

"Yeah, I'm fine." She looked over at Jim. His clothes clung to him from sweat, his face haunted. She released herself from Paul's embrace and walked over to Jim.

"That's not a good idea," Paul said. "Morgan, are you listening to me?"

Morgan ignored Paul. Jim was in pain. Not just physical, but an emotional torment that few could understand. "Are you okay?" Morgan asked Jim. She wanted to hug him and apologize for the last thirty years. She had not kept track of the Jimmy that lost on *Double Dare*. He had been just another kid on another game show. Even when she heard of him anecdotally, she was apathetic. He was right. She was a pompous, self-righteous kid. He deserved to be angry at her. But she didn't deserve death.

He looked at her like he had never seen her before.

"I am so, so sorry. I never meant to hurt you." She reached out to hug him and Don motioned for her to stay put.

A third car came down the path. Morgan wondered if someone had called the cops. In the street light, Morgan saw that it was a red Fiat. "Brian?" She hadn't seen him in ages but who else would show up at this hour in a red Fiat?

Brian came out of the car and ran to Jim. "What are you doing to him?" Brian questioned Don. "Let go of him!"

"We need to have a chat." Paul came over and tried to pull Brian aside. Brian slipped out of Paul's grip and continued toward Morgan.

"What the hell is going on here?" Brian asked. "Why are you half-naked?" Everyone turned to look. Morgan remembered she only wore panties. Thank goodness they were the clean plain ones and not the FireStorm briefs she normally wore for television interviews.

Paul went into the limo and retrieved a blanket to cover Morgan.

Morgan looked at Brian. "I think we have a lot to talk about."

"I gave him a sedative." Brian exited Jim's bedroom.

"Is he going to be okay?" Morgan asked.

"I guess," Brian said. "He should be a little better in the morning. Can you tell me what happened?"

Morgan explained the wild night to Brian while Don guarded the bedroom door. Paul poured a scotch.

"I had no idea," Brian said. "He talked about that moment and how he felt it was pivotal, but I didn't know he meant you."

"I heard about the deals his parents and agent had made. The grapevine said his parents punished him pretty severely after that. He could not get a gig, his agent fired him, and his parents rejected him," Morgan said.

"He went to boarding school," Brian said. "I thought it was 'the thing to do' but I guess they sent him away."

Morgan wrapped herself more tightly into the blanket. "I feel so bad. I mean, I had no idea all of that would happen."

"I'll take care of him," Brian said. "We'll just take a vacation for a little bit. He's probably over stressed."

"Not before we press charges," Paul sat down beside Morgan.

"No." Morgan said.

"What do you mean, 'no'?"

Morgan rose and walked over to the overlook. "I mean no. He's been through enough. He doesn't need the press or a law suit. He needs to rest."

"Have you lost your mind?" Paul shrieked. "This man tried to kill you—"

"I was part of a moment in his life that he will never get back."

"I don't know you—" Paul threw the glass down. "If you need me, I'll be at the car." He slammed the door behind him.

Morgan looked to Don, who glanced at the door and then back to Morgan, unfazed.

"I better go."

"Are you pressing charges?" Brian hugged her. "What happened tonight was crazy. Jim's a good guy."

"Do me a favor?" Morgan asked. "Take care of him. Right now he really needs you."

Morgan got into the limo. Paul texted furiously.

"Do you want to explain to me that insanity?" Paul asked.

"I thought I did."

"I don't mean what drove Rob or Jim or whatever the hell his name is. I mean why the fuck aren't you doing something about this?"

"Because I get it."

"You make no sense."

"I'm not saying he was right to shoot at me. I'm saying that I've been there. I've been face-to-face with someone who seemingly was the undoing of everything I cared about. The desire to get even. I totally get it."

"And?"

"If I retaliate then we get bad press. If I call the cops then I ruin Jim's life again."

"As it should."

"No. He already has enough going on. I have no reason to crush his career. He was so destroyed from *Double Dare* he changed his name. Can you imagine that? Being so ashamed of something that you completely alter your persona, your identity? If Brian is with him, then Jim is a good man. Brian will help Jim back from whatever darkness he's facing."

Paul put his phone down. He didn't make eye contact with Morgan. Instead he searched for words. A laundry list of reasons why Morgan's compassion was wrong. Yet he felt in his core that she was right, and that disturbed him. He wanted to protect her, but she seemed damn good at protecting herself. "Are you sure about this?"

Morgan paused. She looked at the ocean and the Spanish style house. At the lone light that shone from within. A figure went into the bedroom and closed the door.

"Yes, I'm sure." She turned to Paul. "By the way, where were you two?"

"Part of the agreement with Rob-Jim was that we would leave you two alone. Only when we heard the gunshots did we realize things had gone bad. By then, you were somewhere over the trees and Rob-Jim was nowhere to be found."

"I'm glad you came along." She held Paul's hand and smiled.

Don motioned that everything was fine to leave, he got into his car and led the way home.

"I could kiss Nikki." Paul munched on a piece of wheat toast. No butter.

"What'd she do now?" Morgan chomped on avocado toast. Lots of avocado. The adventures of the night before had drained her energy. She woke up five pounds lighter.

"Did you see your Twitter feed? It's insane."

"No. Remember? 'Someone' commandeered my phone."

"Oh right." Paul went into the living room and pulled the phone out from behind a picture of Ani.

"Seriously?" Morgan said.

"I figured you'd never look there." He tossed it back to her. "Here. Nikki's well worth every penny."

Paul had fed Craigslist Nikki images of Morgan's midnight flight, sans gunshots. The Twittersphere was ablaze with the Fallon appearance, memes created from Morgan and Belinda's fight (they were hilarious), the stalky ninja attacker, and most recently a fellow starlet's failed attempt to be the European Morgan (more on that in a bit). Not to mention Belinda's inability to keep her mouth shut whenever someone had a positive comment about Morgan. At first Morgan responded to the jibes and then, at Paul's behest, decided Nikki could take care of it for her. Morgan realized watching the show was a lot more fun than being a part of it. Everywhere Morgan went, news, rumors, and snapping cameras followed. Well aware that some of the world truly hated her for reasons that were real, false, or whatever, Morgan refocused on her own goals and what she needed to accomplish them. She took a quick selfie biting from her avocado toast and posted on Snapchat, which fed Twitter and Instagram. Thank goodness for Nikki, again.

"What's up for today?" Morgan asked Paul. The house unusually quiet compared to the last few days. Morgan enjoyed the semblance of solitude.

"Well, your old pal is up to it again." Paul flipped through the news on his phone. He showed Morgan a recent article with The New York Times. Front and center on the page: Ompi.

"Oh right. I forgot about that." In all Ompi's previous "foretellings," none mentioned Morgan gaining the gift of flight. He barely acknowledged her. Instead he focused on other star studded or up-and-coming clients.

The article reviewed a follow-up news conference that Ompi had conducted. This time pre-recorded from an undisclosed location. Very meta of him. She read the article with Paul looking on. The story recapped her time at the ranch, Ompi's recent pronouncement of Morgan's revelation of gifts as a true sign, his premonitions of a turning point in humanity, and his claims that only he could guide humanity's fate. She laughed out loud. Where did Ompi get this stuff? She saddened when she saw the byline: William Traft. She never thought he would lower himself to this type of story.

At least the article ran with a companion piece about the suicide pact at the Omni Mani Patti ranch, in which Ompi came out unscathed while his followers lost their material possessions, or lost their lives. She looked up at Paul. "Is this something to be concerned about?"

Paul took back his phone and skimmed the news again. "Well... I'm not sure."

"What does that mean, Paul?" Morgan poured herself a glass of cucumber water and drank the cooling concoction.

"As you know, the articles are great press. At least the guy had enough balls to publish the pact story."

"Right…"

"I'm just wondering… We may need to increase your security."

"How did we get from loony Ompi to more guards?"

Paul went into the other room. "I'll be right back. I want to confer with Don."

What the hell? Since when did Paul not answer her questions? While waiting for him to finish the conversation he had started, Morgan checked her email. She had messages from people she had never heard of before. She quickly learned to delete them or move them to a folder for Paul to deal with later. She wasn't willing to risk her mental health over a few crazed fans. One email from William stuck out to her. She hadn't heard from him since their interview, and missed their interaction. With all of the activity she didn't have a chance to circle back with him. His email a simple one—please call. He gave her a heads up on the Ompi article. The email had been sent last evening while she interviewed with Fallon. Her gut reaction was "too late," but this was a chance for her to talk to him. She emailed him a few pictures of Don, of the attacking ninja, and of the Doc, and asked William to look into them.

Morgan heard commotion outside and peeked out the window. She swore she saw Trinity leaving from the side door. Morgan walked out front to catch up with her, but only found a Big Red tour bus, clumps of onlookers, and the usual guards. She searched the gathered crowds for the one who had recommended her to Dr. Snolten, the one who had been the catalyst for this renewal. She didn't find her. Morgan waved at the fans and posed for photo ops. (Morgan's wings spread, Morgan sexy à la Jane Mansfield, Morgan waving à la Jackie Kennedy, Morgan blowing a Marilyn Monroe kiss. Audrey Hepburn innocence. Lasso of Truth. She hit all the classics.) Satisfied, Morgan returned to her living room.

She quickly shot off an email thanking Trinity for all that she had done, suggesting they get together to catch up—Morgan's treat. Which reminded Morgan that she had a follow-up appointment with Dr. Snolten and needed to get prepped. She showered and checked out her body for any signs of damage from the last few nights. Shockingly she found none. The feeling of reinvigoration and overall energy had only strengthened. Dare she think herself invincible? Not a cocaine-induced invincible, but some spirit renewal that blazed from within. She dressed, put on light makeup and her favorite sunglasses, and entered the living room. Paul had returned.

"You clean up nice. I talked to Don and he agreed. We're going to increase security. Just to be safe."

"What has you so spooked?" Morgan asked.

"Every time Ompi appears, shit happens. I just want to be cautious, that's all."

"Fine." Morgan picked up her bag and headed to the side entrance. "We have a date with a doc."

"It better be quick because Vicky's Secret convo is right afterward. Then we have a meeting with Variety, Hollywood Reporter, and a half dozen other mags."

Morgan tied her hair into a ponytail. "Fine. By the way, did you see Trinity?"

"Yeah, why?" Paul got into the driver's side of her Bentley.

"Why was she here?"

"She and Don are old friends. They wanted to catch up on something. Sorry, did you want to say hi to her?"

"No. It's fine. Just curious. I can catch up with her later."

A Doc, A SEAL, And A Bill
Walk into a Room …

"You look fine." Dr. Snolten put down his stethoscope. Nurse Felicity wiped it down and proceeded to clean up the equipment.

"I feel great." Morgan closed her robe. The doc had completed the standard exam, even threw in a few coughing tests for good measure.

"You haven't been over exerting yourself?"

Morgan couldn't look at him. She hadn't followed his rules but didn't know of a way around it. She needed to prove her value to the film. How could she know the demo flight would really be a fight for her life?

"Well, maybe a little…"

"Don mentioned you've had additional activities that were outside the norm." Dr. Snolten wrote notes in his chart. His comment made Morgan perk up. She looked between Felicity and the doctor.

"Really?"

"You don't honestly believe that I'd send one of my top men to look after you and not request that he report back when something out of the ordinary occurs."

Well, that's fair. "I guess not."

"Don is fantastic." Felicity said. "He has helped many of our patients."

"He was a little late to the game, this time," Morgan murmured.

"Sounds like you handled yourself very well," Felicity replied. She placed a hand on Morgan's shoulder, easing Morgan's anxiety.

"You look very well for suffering such a traumatic event," Dr. Snolten said.

"He didn't mean harm," Morgan said.

"If I understood events correctly, I'd say he most certainly did," Felicity said.

"What I mean is. He's had a hard time. Sounds like his studio is at risk and then there's all the other stuff..."

"Why didn't you hurt him?" Felicity asked. Her voice calm, but she looked perplexed. "You could have done anything to him."

"He didn't deserve it." Morgan felt like she was in a dream state. The words flowed through her without thought.

"How so?" the doctor asked.

"He has a good soul. Just tortured. He needs time to recenter. Brian is good for him. Will help him heal." When had she started talking in fragments?

"Good." The doctor made a few more notes then closed the file. "Excellent." He looked to Felicity and exited the room.

"You're doing superbly," Felicity said. "You can dress now. We'll see you in a few weeks."

Want to know what happens with Ompi? Who sent the ninja? Why is the doctor having Morgan followed? And what happens with Jim-Rob? Does Morgan get the movie deal or is that dead? What happens with her and William? What kind of mess does Ani have in store for her daughter?

To find all of this out, and more, read the novella series, *Newly Minted Wings*. Sign up for updates at www.runningwildpress.com

Lisa Diane Kastner, Co-Founder and Executive Editor, Running Wild Press
Lisa's been published in numerous journals, newspapers, and magazines. She's run a few as well. For fun she speaks at conferences and teaches creative writing. For more fun, she finds little known authors and works with them to make their stories and prose sing. Originally from Camden, NJ, she lives in Los Angeles California with her briliant husband and maniacal twin kittens, The Master and Margarita. www.lisadianekastner.com

Jade Leone Blackwater, Co-Founder and Executive Editor, Running Wild Press
Jade Leone Blackwater lives and writes in the forests of Western Washington. She is the co-founder of Running Wild Press, where she gets to spotlight new authors and be among the first people to read fresh stories. She's the owner of the Brainripples studio, specializing in marketing for small businesses and entrepreneurs. Jade's writing appears in *Wild River Review, Line Zero, The Monongahela Review*, as well as technical, trade, and scientific resources for popular audiences. Her favorite projects support healthy people, neighborhoods, and wildlands. When Jade isn't writing she's out getting dirty in the garden, or hiking the local forests.

Past Titles

Running Wild Short Stories Collection, Volume 1
Jersey Diner by Lisa Diane Kastner
Magic Forgotten, Jack Hillman

Running Wild Press publishes stories that cross genres with great stories and writing. Our team consists of:

Lisa Diane Kastner, Co-Founder and Executive Editor
Jade Blackwater, Co-Founder and Executive Editor
Jenna Faccenda, Production Manager
Rachael Angelo, Business Relationship Developer
Eric Mayrhofer, Social Media Guru
Lizz McCullum-Nazario, Blog Afficionada
Jodie Longshaw, Blog Afficionada

Learn more about us and our stories at www.runningwildpress.com

Loved this story and want more? Follow us at
www.runningwildpress.com, www.facebook/runningwildpress, on
Twitter @lisadkastner @JadeBlackwater @RunWildBooks